Caroline Evans and Andrea Malone have little memory
of their pasts...and it might be best to keep it that way.

But in order to find a future with the men they love,
they each must return to darker times and discover...

Where Memories Lie

Relive the romance...
Two complete novels
by two of your favorite authors!

Four-time RITA® Award finalist **Gayle Wilson** never dreamed of becoming a romance novelist. She was too busy being a teacher for gifted children, a wife and a mother. However, she was always a compulsive romance reader who loved to escape the stresses of modern life by retreating into a good book. With a master's degree in English and history, it was probably inevitable that she try her hand at writing a historical romance in her "spare" time. That first book sold to Harlequin Historicals and was a RITA® Award finalist in 1995. Gayle has since written over twenty romance novels for Harlequin Historicals and Harlequin Intrigue. She has won numerous awards, including the Dorothy Parker Award for Category Romance, given by Reviewers International Organization. Gayle is a lifelong resident of Alabama, where she lives with her husband of thirty-two years, a stubborn English shepherd and five cats. She has one son, who also teaches gifted children, and a warm and loving extended Southern family.

Born and raised in a small Southern town, **Amanda Stevens** frequently draws on memories of her birthplace to create atmospheric settings and casts of eccentric characters. She is the author of over twenty-five novels, the recipient of a *Romantic Times* Career Achievement Award for Romantic Mystery, and a 1999 RITA® Award finalist in the Gothic/Romantic Suspense category. She now resides in Texas with her husband, teenage twins and her cat, Jesse, who also makes frequent appearances in her books.

GAYLE WILSON

AMANDA STEVENS

Where Memories Lie

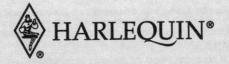

HARLEQUIN®

TORONTO • NEW YORK • LONDON
AMSTERDAM • PARIS • SYDNEY • HAMBURG
STOCKHOLM • ATHENS • TOKYO • MILAN • MADRID
PRAGUE • WARSAW • BUDAPEST • AUCKLAND

HARLEQUIN BOOKS

by Request—WHERE MEMORIES LIE

Copyright © 2002 by Harlequin Books S.A.

ISBN 0-373-21732-3

The publisher acknowledges the copyright holders of the original works as follows:
ECHOES IN THE DARK
Copyright © 1995 by Mona Gay Thomas
THE SECOND MRS. MALONE
Copyright © 1997 by Marilyn Medlock Amann

This edition published by arrangement with Harlequin Books S.A.

Visit us at www.eHarlequin.com

Printed in U.S.A.

CONTENTS

ECHOES IN THE DARK

Gayle Wilson

Prologue

"Give me the keys," he said, the patient humor evident in the deep voice. The faint accent ran like an echo through his English.

When she ignored his command, he caught her wrist, and the sight of dark, tanned fingers against the paleness of her arm caused a reactive tightening of her stomach muscles. She watched, mesmerized, as he slid his fingers up her inner wrist. She could tell by his eyes that, as always, he knew exactly the effect his touch had. She resisted the memory of the pleasant roughness of those fingertips moving over her breasts earlier tonight when he had coaxed her to dress and join him at the reception she had just disrupted.

She took a deep breath, fighting the hunger that his hard body could always evoke. It was so easy for him to manipulate her. She was so ready to do whatever he asked because she loved him and she wanted him. God, how she wanted him. She shook her head to destroy the images produced by the remembrance of his familiar possession. If she allowed him to touch her, she would lose the anger, and he would win.

"Let me go," she ordered, punctuating her command

with a sudden jerk against the strong hand that held her prisoner.

Perhaps the element of surprise made her successful or perhaps his desire not to hurt her made him loosen his hold. Suddenly she was free, running again toward the Mercedes convertible he had given her. She opened the door and, slipping into the driver's seat, tried to insert the key into the ignition.

Her trembling fingers failed in the first attempts, and by the time the engine finally roared to life, he had moved into the passenger seat beside her.

She glanced at his face and saw he was still amused. Her temper, never under any reliable control, especially lately, reacted predictably. No one had ever angered her as he could, with only a look or a word. The blow she ineptly directed at his face fell harmlessly against the hard forearm he raised between them.

''Kerri,'' he protested, laughing, and again caught her wrist. His reflexes were so much faster than hers, honed by years of activities that demanded speed and dexterity to escape the constant threat of injury.

''Why are you so angry? What have I done this time?'' he asked, still smiling.

''Don't pretend you don't know. 'What have I done?' I can't believe you can ask that. You couldn't take your eyes off her.''

''Is that what this is all about?'' he asked, laughing, relieved. ''Of course, I couldn't take my eyes off her. She was practically nude. A palace reception and the ambassador's wife shows up in something most women wouldn't wear to bed.''

''She seemed to think you liked it well enough. She certainly wanted you to get a good look. A very good look. A close-up.''

His only answer to that accusation was the quick upward slant of his beautifully molded lips, but this time he controlled his laughter. He reached to run his knuckles gently down the slim column of her throat, knowing it was futile to argue with her in this mood. She slapped at his hand and moved as far away from him as the confines of the car would allow.

"Have you slept with her? Have you slept with every woman in the country? Every damn woman in the whole damn world?"

She hated the hysteria she could hear building in her voice, wished she could control the ridiculous accusations, the same accusations that she had made too many times in the past weeks. One minute she wanted to cry and rage at him, and then, perversely, she wanted to bury her head against the elegant dark dinner jacket and vent all those frustrations. Even she didn't know what she was crying about or why she couldn't seem to stop these bitter scenes.

Eventually he would tire of the ranting denunciations. Just as he would tire of having to explain to her his world of art and music and literature. She knew so little of those things, and he knew so much, she thought with despair. The gap between their backgrounds seemed too wide to bridge, no matter how hard she tried. Deep in her heart she knew that their time together was flashing by in an ever-increasing spiral, fueled by her jealousy and her endless insecurities. She knew it, but she didn't seem to be able to do anything about slowing that inevitable destruction.

He tried to pull her into his arms, and she wondered why she resisted what she wanted so desperately. He brushed tendrils of sun-streaked blond hair out of the tracks of her tears. She turned her face to rest against those caressing fingers and saw pain in the lucid blue depths of his eyes. Then he masked what was reflected there with the downward sweep of thick, coal black lashes, so that when he looked up at her again there was only concern and, as always, the reassurance of his love.

"No, I haven't slept with her," he said resignedly. He lightened his voice deliberately. "But you're right. This is my fault. Everything is my fault. The fact that you are only nineteen and very pregnant and very far from home. All of those things are my fault."

His voice softened seductively, and his thumb teased slowly along her bottom lip. "And I am delighted to take full responsibility for them. We should be at the villa, watching old movies. I could massage your back and show you how much I love you. I shouldn't have brought you tonight—"

"Because you're ashamed of me. Ashamed to be seen with a cow in a tent while everyone else—"

"Kerri, for God's sake, stop this. You're not a cow." He laughed suddenly at the ridiculous comparison to her graceful body, and at the sound, she raised her eyes to focus on his, to launch another round of vitriolic bitterness, but the look of tenderness on the spare planes of his face arrested the impulse. "You are so beautiful it's all I can do not to make love to you in public," he whispered. "All night I've wanted to run my hands over you, to touch our son. To hold your breasts. So full. God, so sensitive…"

He stopped, the impact of those memories blocking his throat. He couldn't believe she didn't know how he felt. How could she not know after all this time?

"Why don't you know how I feel?" he asked, pain darkening the timbre of his voice. "I don't know what else to do. Nothing I do or say seems to be enough. Tell me what you want from me, Kerri. What do I have to do to convince you?''

For the first time she heard despair in the voice that always before had been gently patient, tenderly amused at her tantrums, loving, caressing. With her fears, she was destroying what they had, and she knew it.

She looked up to reassure him, to tell him how much she loved him, adored him, thought she couldn't live if she lost him.

Perhaps the answering tenderness in her eyes made him think that it was over, a display of fireworks like all the other scenes, bright and intense, but fleeting when confronted with his concern. Perhaps he regretted letting her see what these emotional outbursts did to his control. Whatever the impulse that produced his next words, it was a mistake.

''And a tent?'' he repeated, smiling at her. ''Believe me, my darling, if that's a tent, it is the most beautiful, and probably the most expensive, one in the world. Not that it wasn't worth every franc. You look—''

''You bastard,'' she hissed at him, suddenly and unreasonably furious again. ''You told me to buy something special for tonight. I didn't want to come. They all hate me, and it doesn't matter what I put on. I'm still going to look like a cow. And then you tell me I'm too extravagant.''

''I don't give a damn what the dress cost. I don't care what you spend, and you know it.''

She could hear anger beginning to thread through the rich darkness of his voice, the accent thickening as it did when he became emotional. As it always did when he made love to her.

''This is insane,'' he said, bitterly. ''Everything I say you pounce on. You *wait* for me to say something you can use against me. There's no way I can win," he finished, turning away from her to look out the windshield.

"And God knows you have to win," she mocked, another familiar battleground. "God knows your whole damn life revolves around winning. All the little games. You have to be the best. You always have to win. Well, you certainly won the prize this time. And you're stuck with it. Is that what's wrong? You've begun regretting this particular trophy, haven't you?"

"Only at times like these," he said quietly, a contrast to her fury, and he didn't look at her.

It was what she had dreaded. And expected. Finally he'd said it. She didn't acknowledge how long it had taken her to goad him into it. Another self-fulfilling prophecy.

She slewed the Mercedes out of the parking place, leaving a trail of smoking black, and pushed the accelerator to the floor. The car fishtailed in response, and as she corrected the movement, she felt him reach across to find and buckle her seat belt. It took him several attempts, but he was successful, despite her fist beating ineffectually against his hands.

He leaned back in the seat and closed his eyes. He trusted her driving. He had taught her how to drive on these mountain roads himself. Repeating the lesson, instructing, demanding, until he was sure enough of her competence to present her with the car that was now speeding toward the first series of hairpin turns that led away from the palace terraces.

She touched the brake, anticipating, as he had instructed her. She felt the difference in the response, the sponginess of the pedal, but then the car was into the curve, and she concentrated on guiding it smoothly through the series of switchbacks. As soon as she reached a relatively straight stretch of road, she touched the brake again, more strongly this time, recognizing that the speed of the car was approaching a level beyond her competence.

He would have been able to handle the rocketing vehicle, smoothly and nonchalantly, she thought bitterly. Nothing ever challenged his sure control, his hard certainty. She had never seen him at a loss. Years of privilege, blue blood and too much money insulated him from the fears people like herself faced every day.

In the midst of that familiar litany came the realization that the brake was having no effect on the downward plunge of the Mercedes. There had been no perceptible slowing in spite of the fact that she was practically standing on the pedal.

"Julien," she said, and the panic in her voice made him open his eyes, pulled him from the contemplation of how he had mishandled tonight, from the regret he felt over the pain he had caused her.

"Julien!" This time she screamed, begging for his competence against the rush of the wind, and as her eyes sought his face, she lost control of the car. The right front tire touched off the pavement and the steering wheel jerked from her hands. It spiraled against the frantic reach of his fingers, but by then it was too late.

The Mercedes plunged off the sheer drop of the curve and almost to the bend below, its downward hurtle stopped only as it caught between two of the trees that lined the twisting mountain roads. Caught and held. She was strapped inside by the seat belt that he had fastened only moments before, but the wrenching deceleration threw him from the convertible to the road below.

HE NEVER KNEW how long he was unconscious. He awoke to the smell of gasoline and absolute silence. He wiped ineffectually at the blood obscuring his vision, and then his only thought was to find her.

The brutal journey was agonizing in the darkness. He was never sure that he was crawling in the right direction, guided only by the smell and then by the soft crackling that he had thought at first was the metal of the car expanding against the forces that had left it a twisted ruin.

It was not until he was close enough to feel the heat that he knew he was wrong. What he had heard was the fire that had begun to lick around the shattered Mercedes.

He had been calling her name for a long time, willing her to answer him. Finally his long fingers found the handle of the door, and he used it and his desperation to pull himself up in spite of his shattered leg. As he reached for the seat, hands groping to find her in the pitiless blackness, the explosion rocked the night, throwing him to lie once more against the gravel of the road below.

This time he didn't awaken even as careful hands loaded him into the ambulance. It would be a very long time before he was again aware of anything at all.

Chapter One

"I'm sorry, but she's extremely insistent. She has something she wants to show you, something she's sure you'll want to see."

The secretary watched the ironic smile of his employer, but he knew better than to apologize. That was the unforgivable sin—to apologize for the references one made quite naturally, and so he hurried on with his story.

"We've all tried, but she'll speak to no one but you. She says it's personal. She's clutching some sort of package wrapped in brown paper, and she won't budge. Short of having her thrown out bodily, I don't know what else to do."

The man seated behind the massive desk could hear the frustration. His secretary didn't deal well with unexpected interruptions to his schedule. He sometimes wondered who was really in charge here, but because he cared so little, he let his staff's efficiency carry him effortlessly through the long days. There was no longer any challenge in running the businesses he had pulled from bankruptcy only three years ago. Everything in his life was too well-ordered, the wheels all turning smoothly, oiled by his efficient employees, his softspoken servants and, most of all, by his money. At least the old woman offered a break from the routine. That, of course, was why Charles was so annoyed.

"There's nothing that can't be put off the few minutes it will take to listen to whatever she has to say. Ask Rachelle to bring in a tea tray. And if it's private, there's no need for you to remain. Show her in when the tea arrives."

"But—"

"That will be all, Charles. Thank you for attempting to handle this. I'm sure it's nothing."

He waited until the door had closed behind the retreating secretary. Only then did he remove his glasses, rubbing the bridge of his nose and then briefly massaging his temples. He could feel the beginnings of a headache. He hoped that Rachelle would include his afternoon coffee with the tea. He closed his eyes and rested his head on his hands, elbows propped against the gleaming mahogany desk.

When he heard the door, he opened his eyes and put the glasses back on, standing up to turn toward his visitor. Her hesitation was obvious, but Rachelle's friendly voice urged her forward, and finally they advanced across the parquet floor, their footsteps echoing hollowly in the quiet elegance of the room. When Rachelle had seated her in the chair before his desk, he, too, sat down and waited. It was not until she had been provided with a cup of tea, his own coffee poured and placed, fragrantly steaming, on his desk, and the door closed behind Rachelle that he spoke.

"They tell me that you have something to show me," he said softly, working to keep the amusement out of his voice.

She rustled the package in her lap, until, with trembling hands, she succeeded in freeing whatever it contained from the wrappings. As he waited for her to speak, the silence stretched too long between them. Finally her voice quavered into the sunlight of his expensive office.

"Then you don't recognize it? The jeweler assured me it belonged to you. I tried to sell it, but he wouldn't buy it. He said it belonged to the Duc d'Aumont and that you would perhaps pay me more than its value to recover it," she suggested hesitantly. "He said it's very old."

"They didn't tell you," he said softly, and she sensed somehow that it was a question.

"I don't understand. Tell me what?"

"If you are showing me something I'm expected to recognize, we're both doomed to failure," he said gently. "You see, I'm blind." He could say it quite naturally now, after all these years. He could even smile to reassure her.

"Of course." Her voice was relieved. His lack of response was not a lack of recognition. "I should have known from the glasses, but they didn't tell me. It's so bright in here, I didn't think. I suppose I envied you their protection against the glare."

He laughed easily and stood to adjust the shade behind him, dimming the painful brightness. There was no fumbling in his movements, so that she found herself watching those sure fingers in amazement.

"They won't complain. They think that would remind me that I can't see," he said, smiling at her. He could hear the answering laughter from across the desk and, judging his movements carefully by that sound, he reached across its expanse and held his palm open before her. She laid the locket she had guarded these years

against the outstretched hand, and the long, dark fingers
closed around the delicate golden chain.

He sat down, carefully examining the object she had
placed in his hand. As his fingers traced the shape of the
entwined hearts and then the roughness of the faceted
emeralds that outlined them, she could almost read his
emotions by the play of the muscles in his jaw, by the
involuntary tightening of his lips and the effort to swallow against the sudden constriction of his throat.

She wished she could see his eyes. She needed so
desperately to know if he would be willing to pay what
she intended to ask, but the dark glasses were a barrier
she couldn't penetrate.

"Where did you get this? My God, how did you—"
he asked finally, his hands no longer deftly examining
the locket, but one locked hard around it. She could see
only a small fragment of the gleaming links between
those clenched fingers.

"I intended to tell you that she gave it to me, but
that's not the truth. I stole it. I didn't think there was
any reason... She didn't need it. I thought someone
should have some good of it, and we had nothing. But
then I was frightened. I was afraid that if I tried to sell
it, someone would know I'd stolen it. She was dying.
Stealing from a dying woman—that's something God
won't forgive me for, although I've prayed for her soul
every day. And for the baby. I thought that might make
up for the wrong I did," she said piously, hoping to
convince him of her remorse.

She looked up to read his reaction, and at the look on
those handsome features, she was really frightened for
the first time. She had decided years ago that she was
going to hell for what she had done, but this man looked
as if he might already have been there, might already

have tasted that punishment. She wondered if he would have her arrested, imprisoned, and all this long journey would have been for nothing.

"It's my grandson. Maybe that's a punishment for what I did, but it's too hard. He's just a little boy, a baby." She knew she was making no sense, but his stillness was confusing her. She had expected anger, was ready to deal with that, but not this terrifying stillness.

"Where was she when you took this?" he asked, calmly enough, but she was somehow aware of the effort it took him to achieve that control.

"With the nuns, the Sisters of the Sacred Heart," she said. She had thought he might have known that, but she could see its impact on his face and knew the information was a surprise. "I helped deliver the baby. It was too early and she was— I don't know what she was. She never said anything, not even during the labor. Most women cry or scream, but she…there was nothing there, behind her eyes. The baby was too small, so fragile. The nuns and I did what we could, but when I left, I knew he wouldn't live.

"They left me alone with her while they went to get the doctor and while they worked with the baby, but she just lay there. They couldn't stop the bleeding. I knew she was going to die. I've seen too many like that. The doctor couldn't have gotten there in time to stop it. I took the locket. I'm not a thief, but she was dying. I thought…"

Her voice whispered into silence. She waited for him to speak and finally he did.

"Your grandson?"

"Cancer—and the doctor bills are so high. Perhaps if there's money, they'll do something for him. He's only a baby."

"How much?" he asked. She watched his hand reach for the button that would summon his secretary.

"The jeweler said it was very old. I thought—" But the opening door and the secretary interrupted whatever she intended to ask for.

"Get her out of here," he said softly from across the desk. "Give her whatever she wants, but get her the hell out of here and find my brother. I don't give a damn where he is or what he's doing. You tell him I want him here now. Tell him he has some questions to answer. Some questions about my wife. And my son."

The old woman was as frightened by the cold voice as she had been when she thought he might call the police. She realized suddenly that the olive complexion of the hovering secretary had blanched to a sickly gray. She knew he would be obeyed, and in spite of her fear, she began to recalculate what she would ask. Whatever she wants, he had said. She was already going to hell. What did it matter? Her mind was busily reconsidering her request as the secretary hurried her from the office, wiping his brow with the handkerchief he had pulled from his pocket. She hardly noticed how much his hands shook. She was too elated by the success of her morning's work. It had all been so easy.

"I DON'T WANT another lie. I want to know why you told me she died in that car. Why you've let me think all these years that if I had only reached her sooner, if I had been a little quicker— You've let me live with that. *Now* I find she didn't die there. She died at the convent. She died, giving birth to my son, *alone*. She bled to death, *alone*."

His cold voice paused to bank the emotions that were clearly threatening the icy control. "Why was she carried to the convent? My God, one of the finest medical facilities in the region was only a few miles away. I was carried there and lived, despite…'' He stopped because they both knew what his condition had been.

"I want an explanation for this entire pack of lies you've fed me all this time, and damn you, Andre, it had better be a good one. I swear, I could kill you for letting me believe I let them die.''

"I thought that would be easier than the truth,'' his brother's voice spoke quietly. Julien could hear the bitter resignation behind the calm answer. "I knew how much it would hurt you to know the truth.''

"Hurt more than the belief that I let my wife and son burn to death? What truth could have twisted my guts all these years more than that?''

"No one blamed you for her death. No one could believe you'd even reached the car in your condition. The idea that you'd failed her was only in your head. She was the one driving, too fast, as she always did. Everyone at the reception had seen the beginnings of that tantrum, and, of course, she'd been drinking.''

"She didn't drink. She was pregnant.''

"Maybe that's what she told you, but she had. Too many people saw her. Several came forward at the inquiry. She was drunk and angry and she killed her child and almost killed you. The only fault is hers. I never knew you blamed yourself. If I had known, I would have told you a long time ago, but I thought it would be kinder to have you believe—''

"Kinder to believe that she burned to death? My God, Andre, what could have been worse than that?''

"That she killed her son, blinded you and then walked away. She chose to leave. At least—''

"Are you telling me she wasn't injured?'' he interrupted. "Are you trying to tell me she just walked away from the wreck?"

"She tried to get help," his brother's voice said, attempting, he thought, to be fair. "She tried to flag down a car, but they thought she was drunk. Someone found her wandering down the road. She had a head injury. She was disoriented. She thought you were dead. They brought her to the hospital, but when she found out you were alive and so badly hurt, and that she'd left you there... She was so frantic that they thought, for the baby's sake, she should be taken somewhere where she could be cared for. I don't know who thought of the convent, but it seemed the best solution. She didn't want to leave you, and she was in no condition to wait through the hours of surgery. She needed to be under observation, but when they tried to make her leave you, she got hysterical. Finally they gave her a shot, a sedative, and she was taken to the convent. Perhaps that was a mistake—"

Andre paused, took a deep breath and then admitted, "As it turned out, it was, of course, a terrible mistake, but everything was so confused, and she'd shown no signs of going into labor. It was far too early. Moving her seemed to make sense at the time."

Andre stopped. Julien could hear the sigh, but he had to know it all.

"Go on," he said bitterly into the silence. "Tell me about my son's death. Explain that lie."

"The baby was born prematurely. There at the convent. By the time the doctor arrived... He said it wouldn't have mattered. Even if they had been in hospital, they couldn't have saved the baby. It was too early. The baby was stillborn. I swear to you that's the truth."

"And then? Did my wife bleed to death there where

you'd sent her? Is that what you've been afraid to tell me all these years. That she died because she wasn't where she could get medical attention? Was that your decision, Andre?''

There was no answer for a long time and he waited, impassive now. Was it less painful to believe that the fault had not been his? Less painful to picture her gradually sinking deeper into a bloodless lethargy from which not even the doctor, when he arrived, could save her? Better than the images of the fire and the smell of the gasoline?

Even now he couldn't stand the smell. It was like the smell of a hospital. He couldn't enter one. It brought it all back again: the agony of the burn tank, the struggle to walk again, to cope with the blackness of his world that had threatened so often to drown him in its dark depression.

''She didn't die.''

The words interrupted his return to the hell of those memories, and he felt his heart take a great leap as he realized what Andre had just said. He forced himself into stillness and waited, and finally his brother continued.

''She recovered. I don't know where the old woman got the idea that she was dying. She recovered more rapidly than anyone believed possible, but she was very young and strong. She came to the hospital to see you as soon as she was able. I'll give her that. She had good intentions, but…I suppose the shock was too great. You were so terribly hurt, and there was no response for so long. When the doctors told us the full extent of the injuries, she blamed herself, of course. She damn well should have,'' Andre said harshly. ''That stupid bitch and her everlasting tantrums. She put you there, and as soon as the doctors told us the truth about your condition…that you were blind and probably would never walk again. That you—''

''I know what the doctors said,'' Julien interrupted. He allowed himself to ask only when the angry voice had been silent a long time, ''And when she knew?''

''She left. She left the note on your bed, in an envelope with my name on it. She couldn't live with what she'd done. She couldn't live with you as you were going to be. As soon as you came out of the coma, she realized that you were going to live, to know what she'd done. I could have killed her, Julien. I swear if I'd found her, I would have. The damned coward did what she did and then left you to—''

''So you let me believe she died?'' the passionless voice interrupted again.

''You woke up convinced she was dead. All your questions were about her death, about whether she'd suffered. The doctors were so concerned about you, not just the physical injuries, but— I didn't know what to do, what would be kinder to do, so I just said nothing. I'm guilty of that, and I admit it. I chose to let you believe that she died, rather than to know that she blinded you, killed your son and then walked away. All those months I watched you struggle through the pain, I hated her. I never tried to find her because I knew I'd kill her. I could kill her now.''

He could hear the conviction in the quiet voice.

''Do you *swear* to me that this is, at last, the truth? Do you swear it, Andre?''

''It's the truth. Why would I lie to you after all this time? Perhaps I made the wrong decisions, but at least I tried. At least, *I* didn't run away.'' Seeing the pain in his brother's dark face, Andre whispered, ''I'm so sorry.''

Julien took a deep breath, forcing himself to calmness. "I think it's best that we don't talk about this again. It's very painful for me, Andre. I hope that what's been revealed today won't be mentioned again. Will you agree to that?"

"Of course. I'll do whatever you want. I never intended to hurt you more. You were already—"

"I know. Let it go. There's nothing you can do after all these years. Let me learn to deal with this. It's simply a different ending to an old story. Now if you'll forgive me..." The words were polite dismissal, and in spite of so many things he wanted to say, Andre was forced to recognize that what had been said was enough for the moment, all that the man who sat so calmly in his prison of darkness could deal with, and so he left.

When the door closed, Julien rose and went to stand by the window. He removed the dark glasses and raised his face into the warmth of the sun, trying to think about what he needed to do, and none of the possibilities were pleasant.

THE INTERVIEW HAD GONE more easily than she had anticipated. The elegant and expensive office had intimidated her at the beginning, but the lawyer had been very kind. He had gone over her résumé with polite interest, not even glancing at the letters of reference she'd handed him. She had been sure that she wouldn't be called in when she had seen the mob in the outer room. The women waiting there had looked as formidable as the suite of offices they all had been asked to come to for the interviews.

She had dressed carefully, but her suit was not of the same quality that several of the applicants who had entered his inner sanctum before her had worn. However, he had never even glanced at her suit or the carefully polished shoes, her only pair of real leather ones. He had been far more interested in her background, in whom she had worked for and her education. Her limited schooling was another weak point she had attempted to present in as strong a light as was possible. Then he had asked the question she had dreaded from the beginning.

"There's a time period here that is unaccounted for professionally, Ms. Evans. If there's a problem, then it is far better to let us know now than to have it turn up in our later investigations. The truth is always better coming from your own lips," he said gently, like her grandfather.

She smiled at the sudden mental comparison to the old man who had instilled in her his values. He had tried so hard to make her whole, to repair the ravages of her parents' failures. He had given her the only home she had ever known, a sanctuary from that pain in the small, peaceful village he had taken her to. Simply thinking about him gave her courage, so she was able to answer calmly, "A problem? As if I were dismissed for failing in some way to satisfy my employer? That sort of problem? Then, no, I assure you that's not the explanation."

"And?" he said, waiting.

She should have known she wouldn't be able to fob him off. The gray eyes were also, like her grandfather's, far too shrewd. She had never been able to hide from the old man's keen insight. He had seen into the depths of her soul. If only he had been there when she finally came out of the long darkness, she thought again with regret.

"I was ill. For a long time. An illness caused by depression."

The lawyer spoke only when it was evident she had

nothing else to add. "I'm sorry. I didn't intend to bring back unpleasant memories. I apologize for forcing you to talk about that time."

"It's all right. There are no unpleasant memories of 'that time.' No memories at all—" She stopped, and then tried to explain the unexplainable. "Whatever caused the depression, whatever trauma, I've forgotten. Blocked or repressed it, the doctors said."

"You've never remembered?" he asked softly, wondering if this was the key to what he had been ordered to do.

"My childhood. Growing up." She paused, the bleakness of the memories that *had* returned affirming that the ones her mind still denied must be much worse. She continued finally, telling him a truth she never talked about. "Then…" she whispered, "there's just a void. Whatever happened to cause that blackness, I've never remembered, and now they believe I won't. My mind doesn't want me to." She didn't tell him about the punishing headaches that were the price she paid for trying to delve into that emptiness, to find those lost memories.

Instead, she forced herself to speak more strongly, with a confidence she was far from feeling. "As you can see, that was a long time ago. All my references are since that period. My amnesia doesn't affect my work. It's better, perhaps, that I can't remember whatever happened."

"I'm sorry," he said again, and she thought that he did regret forcing the painful admission.

"I've learned to expect the question. Some interviewers assume…all sorts of things. Being fired and wishing to hide it is only one of the scenarios they imagine."

"Have you had so many interviews? Your skills seem more than adequate."

"No one seems to need a *permanent* bilingual secretary whose skills are, by today's standards, as we both know, merely adequate. The larger corporations are looking for someone whose training covers a broader range of computer knowledge. My training was of a different sort."

"Yet it seems very suited to the position we have in mind. Not one of the other applicants I've seen today has a Swiss finishing school in her background."

"I spent five years there. Not that it's done me much good," she admitted, smiling. "Most people think that only means I'm qualified to be some minor diplomat's wife and not much else."

"Or someone's social secretary," he suggested, and she knew then he was seriously considering her for the position. She dared, for the first time, to hope.

"I haven't done that before, but I'm sure I can." She was pleased that she could hear the conviction in her own voice.

"There are, however, several conditions that you'd have to consider if we decide to offer you the position."

"What kind of conditions?" she asked carefully. She had known there was a catch to this. It had smelled too good to be true, had smelled from the beginning of fine leather and old money.

"For one thing, it would mean a relocation. My client lives on an island in the Îles des Saintes. It's a rather isolated situation for someone as young and attractive as you."

"Excuse me," she said, smiling at him again. "I told you my education had been lacking in all but the social skills. The Îles des Saintes?"

"They are part of the Lesser Antilles. You would be working on one of the smaller islands, privately owned

by Madame Rochette's family. She's living there to recover from the recent death of her husband, after a pro-
longed illness. You would be not only her secretary but,
I suppose, a companion. She's not so many years older
than you, I should imagine." He glanced at her résumé
and then at her face, and she saw the swiftly hidden
surprise.

"I'm twenty-five," she said quietly, knowing that she
looked older. Something in her eyes, people often told
her, not intending to be unkind.

"Then more than I believed, but still the difference
between thirtysomething and twentysomething isn't so
great," he said. "Would you be willing to relocate for
an unspecified time? Or do you have commitments here
in Paris that would make that impossible?"

"I have no commitments, no ties of any kind. I am
literally the most uncommitted person you are ever likely
to meet."

She laughed softly at the reality of that, and when she
saw he didn't understand, she shook her head to reassure
him.

"I'm sorry. That's not really funny." She realized she
was about to blow it, to miss this opportunity, so she
tried again. "I'm very interested in the position. I would
have no problem in relocating, and I think your client
will find I have the skills to handle her social correspondence and her companionship. I hope I'll have the
opportunity to meet her and convince her of my qualifications."

"I'm sorry. I thought you understood that *I'm* to make
the decision. Madame Rochette prefers not to return
from the Caribbean. I'll be in touch, whatever the out-
come of the other interviews. Thank you for your time."

"Thank you. I hope…" She paused, trying to keep

the desperation hidden. "How long before you'll have reached your decision?"

"We'll decide within the next few days. I have your number."

She could think of nothing else that she might tell him to convince him of her qualifications, so she rose, walking from his office with the grace taught at that expensive finishing school her grandfather had finally rescued her from.

The solicitor tented his fingers, appearing to study the file before him, but his mind was on what the woman had told him. He knew she was perfect. It all fit. However, the one who would have the final say on that had not yet been consulted, so he pushed himself to his feet like an old man and moved to the open door that she had apparently never noticed in the deliberate dimness of the office.

His client was seated in a high-backed chair just beyond the open doorway. The solicitor walked around the chair and stood for a long time facing the tall, dark figure. The smile that played around those lips was not a display of pleasure or amusement. He wondered again about the purpose of this search that had involved his staff now for more than a year.

"Well?" he asked finally and watched the smile broaden.

"You've done very well, Beaulieu, very well, indeed."

"She fits every qualification you gave me. Will she do? Is she what you wanted?"

"She is *exactly* what I wanted." The man in the chair controlled the triumph in his voice with an effort. "You understand the necessity of complete confidence."

"That's always our policy. You've depended on us in

the past. Have we ever given you cause to question our integrity?''

The listener could hear the stifled anger in the lawyer's voice, but he was paying him enough to put up with a few insulting questions. It was vital that no one should be able to trace her here or to him.

''Does she look like the picture I gave you?'' he asked suddenly, surprising himself by his curiosity. He wasn't sure he wanted to hear the answer, but when it came, it was only what he had expected.

''Their mothers couldn't tell them apart,'' the solicitor said. There was no pleasure over the success of the search in his voice, only regret for the woman. He had found himself liking her quiet, self-effacing humor. He didn't, however, ask any of the questions that stirred darkly in his mind. That wasn't part of his job. He had done what he had been paid to do, and any misgivings he had he would keep to himself, but he didn't envy the woman he had found. He already knew far more about all this than he wanted to, far too much for his own peace of mind.

Chapter Two

The flight to Guadeloupe had been restful. There was something to be said for flying first class and being waited on. It was an experience she thought she could grow accustomed to. All she needed were a few more opportunities to try it, she thought in amusement.

The call had been unexpected in spite of the approval she had sensed in the lawyer's attitude. She had learned in the past few years not to expect anything good. She would have rejected that thought as self-pitying, would never have consciously allowed it to form, but it was true, and it colored her view of the world. The offer of this job had been, to her, truly a miracle.

She watched the islands unfold below the plane in a seemingly endless chain of green dots rimmed with the white pearl of surf against an iridescent shimmer of blues. The scene looked like something out of a travel film, except she was here. She was to be the social secretary to a wealthy widow whose family owned an island. She smiled at the image of herself in that setting, but the reflection in the plane's window mocked her doubts. She certainly looked as if she belonged.

She had put her long, sun blond hair up today and had worn more makeup, in hopes, she supposed, of making a good impression. She had even bought a new dress—an emerald linen, very businesslike, except for what it did to the green of her eyes. There would never be anything businesslike about her eyes.

She had followed to the letter the lawyer's instructions about what to pack. She had also read the friendly note from her future employer so many times the paper threatened to come apart at the folds. It had been reassuring, warm and inviting. Of course, Madame Rochette had been under no obligation to write at all, so the gesture seemed to indicate that she would probably enjoy their relationship as much as she hoped. She tried not to, but she found that she was, indeed, hoping that this all would work out to be as pleasant as it seemed.

The lawyer had given explicit instructions about arrangements for reaching the island, including travel from the airport, ferry times, an endless list of minutiae that she also intended to carry out to the letter. She was surprised to find, however, that when she came through customs and presented her passport, there was an immediate flurry of officialdom that led her eventually to the door of a private office while her escorts went rushing off to find her bags. She followed their instructions, entering the office to find it occupied by someone quite different from the officials she had encountered so far.

"Ms. Evans?" he asked, unfolding his long body from the leather chair. He had been reading a newspaper, comfortably invading someone else's office with a tall, cool-looking drink within arm's reach. A tropical-weight tan jacket draped broad shoulders and fell loosely to his narrow hips. The lean length of the legs below was emphasized by the skintight and well-worn jeans he wore. His hair was darkly curling and long by current standards. It fell below the collar of the jacket, but on him it looked right, finished the picture of a man who was perfectly at ease with the persona he had chosen, perfectly suited for the tropics. He was, of course, deeply tanned, the contrast as sharp between the crystal blue of his eyes and the dark gold of his skin as it was between the flash of white, even teeth in the smile he gave her.

"You *are* Caroline Evans?" he said. "My reputation won't stand an attempt to pick up some strange woman at the airport."

I'll just bet it won't, she thought, but she smiled, extending her hand to reassure him. "I'm Caroline Evans."

"Andre Gerrard," he said. His handshake was pleasantly firm and brief. "My sister asked me to meet you. Our transportation arrangements can be a little confusing for someone not born to boating everywhere. She asked me to take you to the island. I have my boat and can have you there, resting from your journey, much quicker than if you wait for the ferry. I hope that's all right. I have identification," he said, perhaps seeing the hesitation in her face.

"Since Madame Rochette didn't mention her brother's name, I don't suppose that would help. Besides, it seems that everyone here knows who you are. The cooperation of the airport staff should be recommendation enough of your credentials. I don't think they'd contrive to *help* you kidnap 'some strange woman.'"

The laugh that broke from him was rich and full, and its ease touched a chord somewhere deep inside. She liked men who were unselfconscious enough to laugh like that. She found herself studying the laugh lines around the blue eyes and realized that he was now simply smiling at her scrutiny.

He's probably used to having that effect on women, she thought. *He certainly has the right equipment. And knows it. And knows how to use it. And I am a cynic,* she chided herself, smiling, but he took the smile caused by that admission as an answer to his own. By that time, her bags had arrived, and there was no more time for conversation.

When he handed her into a Porsche, she wasn't surprised. It wasn't new, but classic, lovingly cared for, and he drove it well. They didn't talk against the force of the wind. Eventually she took the pins from her hair and let it whip in tangling strands around her face. Not very businesslike, but what the hell. He'd been sent to pick her up, and she'd had no choice in her means of transportation. She'd attempt repairs once they reached the island.

The boat, too, fitted her image of the man at her side. It was sleek and fast, not new, but again classically styled, wood with brass fittings. She knew nothing of boats, but recognized the money and time it would take to care for something like this.

He controlled the boat with the same unthinking competence he had used to handle the convertible while the salt air finished the disorder of her careful hairdo. He had handed her in and out with that strong brown hand, and as she walked up the steep steps from the landing, she could still feel the strength in those steadying fingers tingling against her palm.

He had held her hand a fraction of a second too long, and she tried to ignore the long-forgotten messages such a gesture evoked, but she was attracted. She was honest enough, with herself at least, to admit it. She couldn't remember when she had been so attracted to a man, and the irony of that thought wasn't lost on her.

She took a deep breath as they neared the top of the stairs and the beginnings of the flagstones of the patio that stretched behind the modern house that commanded the summit of the island. It was nothing like the ancient family estate she had imagined. Instead it was sleek glass and cypress, but it was as imposing in its size as her imaginary mansion.

She shivered involuntarily, wondering where the sudden chill had come from in the warmth of the tropic sun. She must have paused because she felt his hand in the small of her back, a gentle movement of its thumb against her spine.

"It's all right. Don't be nervous. We're very informal around here. It's the ambience of the tropics, I suppose. All this lushness," he reassured. When he laughed, she glanced up into that beautifully masculine face to find a look of real compassion for her nervousness. "No one's going to eat you. I promise. No big bad wolf."

She smiled at her foolishness and, unconsciously straightening her shoulders, started across the wide expanse of the patio. He followed, easily carrying both her bags, which he set down just inside the room they entered through the French doors. They waited a moment for their eyes to adjust to the pleasant dimness, so she missed the rise of the figure from the long coral couch across the room. The woman was halfway across the gleaming quarry tile, her hands extended, before she was clearly visible.

"Caroline? Of course. I was quite specific in my instructions. I wanted someone young and attractive and fun. I really do need help with those endless letters. God knows, I'm weeks behind, but that wasn't my prime motivation. I just wanted someone to be friends with. I hope we will be. I'm Suzanne Rochette."

By that time she was there, but instead of taking Caroline's outstretched hand, she pulled her into a quick hug and then held both her shoulders to study her features.

Caroline's first impressions were jumbled by the unexpectedness of the greeting. Nothing was as she had anticipated. The figure before her wore jeans as aged as her brother's, a faded T-shirt and was barefoot.

Even given the ambience of the tropics her brother had talked about, the attire seemed strange for such wealth. Of course, she knew nothing about that. Who was she to judge? She realized that something was expected of her, so she smiled into the friendly blue eyes and was rewarded with a quick squeeze of those small, almost tomboyish hands on her shoulders.

"I'm so glad you're finally here," Suzanne said, smiling.

"I'm very glad to be here and very grateful that you chose me. I'm looking forward to helping you."

"Well, I didn't really choose. Paul did that, but I already feel that he made the perfect selection. Has Andre treated you nicely? I have to warn you. He is much sought after and far too sure of his attractions. He's really a nice boy, but take everything he says with a grain of salt. It's all too practiced. That's not his fault, of course, but regrettably true."

During the monologue on her brother's character, she was guiding Caroline to the couch she'd been occupying when they arrived. Caroline glimpsed the genuine amusement on her brother's face and was relieved that this, apparently, was an old joke between them, not something directed at her attraction to him, which she hoped hadn't been that obvious.

"I'll remember that," she said, smiling. She glanced

at Andre who winked at her and gently swatted his sister's bottom.

"How am I going to succeed in luring young lovelies if you persist in warning them off? You're supposed to be on my side." He dropped a swift kiss on the blue-veined temple exposed by the dark gamin cut of his sister's hair. "Why don't you let me show Caroline upstairs for a rest. She's had a long journey and would probably like to change and lie down before dinner. You can finish destroying my character later tonight."

Suzanne released her hand and nodded. "You're right, of course. I'll finish my book, and we'll talk after dinner. Slacks are fine. We only dress if there are guests. I'm very glad you're here," she finished, reaching to touch her lips gently to Caroline's cheek.

"I'm very glad to be here." Caroline's answer was sincere, and she felt the prick of tears behind her eyes. She couldn't have imagined a warmer greeting than she had been given. It was balm to the tension that had held her since the plane had touched down. "Thank you. I'll see you at dinner, then."

"Somebody will come for you so you won't get lost. We eat around eight. If you're hungry now, I can have something sent up. I didn't think to ask if you'd had lunch."

"I'm fine. I ate on the flight. I'll be ready by eight."

She smiled again into the friendly blue eyes and followed Andre up the stairs. He had retrieved her bags, and she found something reassuring about that, as well— about his carrying them himself instead of summoning some hovering servant. All her preconceptions and fears were dissolving in the ease of their welcome.

"I think you'll like your room. Suzanne spent days deciding where you should be. You're close to her, of course, and it looks down on the garden pool. The surf here is dangerously strong, so I wouldn't advise swimming in the sea, but the pool is available at any time. There are light switches for the atrium in every doorway. I thought you might prefer looking out on the sea, but those rooms are too far from Suzanne to satisfy any urge for a quick nighttime conference, so she decided on this one.''

The suite was beautifully appointed, but not at all formal. The colors were the muted greens of the waters closest to the shore and the creams of the surf. The decorator had used a shell motif sparingly in the border and spread. Andre opened the floor-to-ceiling louvered windows, and the garden that the house surrounded was just below, lushly planted around the pool. The tiles of the pool were navy, the richness of its dark depths contrasting the sparkle of the sun on its surface and the colors of the flowers that surrounded it.

''It's so beautiful,'' she said, breathing in the fragrance of the blooms that were wide and drooping in the afternoon heat.

''I'm glad you like it,'' he said, apparently assuming her comment to refer to the room rather than the tropical paradise she supposed he was too accustomed to even notice anymore.

''I like it very much. Thank you for everything, especially for taking time to meet me personally. I was a little concerned, despite all Monsieur Dupre's careful instructions.''

''You'd have managed. Everyone's very friendly. I *wanted* to meet you. It was my pleasure.'' He smiled, the blue eyes warm.

The silence grew between them. She wondered if his words had been intended to convey the attraction she was attributing to them or if, as his sister had said, he was simply so practiced at flirtation that he did this intimate smile and meeting of the eyes automatically.

"Well," he said finally, "I'll let you rest. I'll see you at dinner. I'm looking forward to seeing you at dinner."

There could be no mistake about the intent of the fingers that closed gently around her hand and raised it to his lips. They barely touched the skin, but the warmth of his mouth and the gentle breath he took before he released her hand was electric. The current flared briefly in his eyes before he turned and retreated across the thick, foam green carpet.

When he had closed the door behind him, she looked out into the richness of the garden again. She shook her head in a slow, deliberate, negative movement and then closed the doors against the reflected glare of the pool.

She slipped out of the linen dress that had already begun to wilt in the heat and humidity. She hung it carefully in the cedar-lined closet and removed her heels and hose. Turning back the thick spread, she lay down against the cool, lavender-scented sheets that seemed vaguely comforting and, because she had slept so little the night before, she drifted easily into sleep.

"I TAKE IT our guest has arrived?" The quiet voice was carefully emotionless, but Suzanne knew Julien well enough to read a lot that he intended to hide.

"She's here, all right. I just don't understand *why* she's here. What possible purpose do you believe allowing her to come here will serve?"

She ran her small hands across the broad shoulders and massaged the tension she could feel in the strong column of his neck. He rolled his head in response to the release that her fingers were kneading into the tight muscles, but he didn't answer her question, just as he had refused to explain his reasons from the beginning.

"Why? Why? Why are you putting yourself through this?" she asked, her small fist pounding an emphasis to each question against the corded muscles of his upper arm until he caught her hand and held it still with the tensile strength of his. His thumb massaged her knuckles, and he laughed.

"Expiation," he said, and his voice was rich with the laughter that still lurked behind the word.

"Expiation?" she repeated, pulling her hand free. "Expiation." This time it wasn't a question. "Are you sure that's the right word? Are you sure that's what you mean?"

"What word do you think I mean?" he asked, still amused by her anger.

"Retribution," she whispered, wondering as she had from the beginning if it were possible he had not told her the truth.

"Like some Old Testament injunction? An eye for an eye? Is that what you expect?"

"I don't know what to expect. I thought I understood you. I thought I knew you, and then..." She shook her head in frustration.

"I need to understand why...after all these years..." The deep voice faded, unable to put into words what he felt.

"You *always* tried to understand. God, Julien, sometimes..."

The taut mouth relaxed at her anger for his sake, and he smiled. "Because there's *always* a reason. I just have to determine what it is."

"I don't want her here," she said, knowing the other

was an argument she couldn't win. "I don't like this. I don't want any part of it."

"But it's too late for that. She's here. We're here, and I think we need to find out what this is all about. Don't you? Don't you really believe that it's time to finally finish whatever this is?"

"Is that what you intend? To put an end to it?"

She ran her hand through the dark hair that curled against her fingers. She rested her palm against his temple and finally bent to lay her cheek against the ebony curls. His lips curved again into a smile in response, and he raised his hand to touch the small, comforting fingers.

"Expiation," he repeated. "I told you."

"I just don't want you hurt again," she said.

"She can't cause me pain. I promise you that. I don't think—" he began and then paused.

"What?" She raised her head, moving so she could see his face. "What don't you think?" she asked again and he smiled at her.

"I don't think I want to talk about this any longer," he answered truthfully, "but I don't want you to worry. Let me worry about what's going on. It's not your concern."

"You know that's ridiculous. I don't understand what you're thinking. Talk to me. Who is she?"

"I don't know who she is, but I damn well know who she's not," he said harshly, bitterly, and then deliberately modified his voice to hide the anger. "I promise you, that's all I know. What Paul told us. Nothing else."

"And in spite of that, you're still…"

But she watched as his eyes moved away from her face to the sound of the surf that pounded against the volcanic rocks below the deck on which he was sitting. When he shook his head against her questions, she knew he had told her all he intended. She moved her hand down the back of his head, touching his neck again, and then silently, on bare feet, she left him to contemplate alone whatever it was he was planning.

She had never been able to change his mind, not once he'd decided on a course of action, and obviously he'd decided what to do about the woman who had just arrived.

"Expiation," she whispered, and went to look up the word, to verify that it meant what she thought. In spite of her accusation, he would never use the wrong word. He was far too careful. When she found it, it meant *exactly* what she had thought, so she was left to wonder still what he planned.

CAROLINE WAS ASLEEP when the maid tapped lightly on the door. She awoke instantly in the tropical darkness, disoriented for a few seconds.

"Mademoiselle," the maid spoke from beyond the doorway, *"Madame* asks that you join the family for dinner if you've rested enough."

"Of course. I overslept. Please tell them I won't be long, and then, if you would, come back for me?"

"Of course, *mademoiselle.*"

She felt drugged, too deeply asleep, but she knew that she had to rise and dress. She ran her fingers tiredly through the tangled strands of her hair, realizing with dismay that she hadn't even unpacked.

She pulled one of the suitcases onto the bed, rummaging until she found a pair of white slacks and their matching top. They were slightly wrinkled, but surely everyone would expect that. She slipped them on with a pair of white sandals and pulled out her makeup bag to repair the ravages.

She wished she had time to remove her old makeup and start over, but she hated making everyone wait. She brushed her hair to untangle it and could feel the effects of the salt air. She left it loose, worrying that it might be too casual, but at least it was quick.

She was ready when the maid returned. She followed her down the long hall and the wide, freestanding central stairs into the room she had entered today, a room whose long windows looked out now only on dark sky and sea and moon.

Suzanne rose gracefully and took her hand. "You look rested. Did you manage to sleep?"

"I probably have sleep creases. I was still asleep when the maid knocked. I'm so sorry I made you wait."

"It doesn't matter," Suzanne reassured. "That's one art you learn in this climate. It's fatal to hurry. No one does. We're one drink ahead of you. What would you like?"

"Juice, soda, whatever you have. Nothing alcoholic," Caroline requested, following the small figure to the bar.

Suzanne had changed into a turquoise silk jumpsuit that fit every curve of her perfectly shaped body. She made Caroline feel as tall and gawky as she had always felt as a teenager.

"A teetotaler," Andre said, laughing. "We make our living here making rum, and you've invited a teetotaler."

"Andre," his sister chided, handing her a glass full of ice and some sort of mixed juices. It was very refreshing, its cold tartness chasing away the last of the grogginess.

She knew they were wondering if she had a problem with alcohol. Most people who didn't drink at all were either alcoholics or had strong feelings about the use of spirits. She fell into neither category, but she couldn't think how to phrase any explanation of her situation that would fit into this casual atmosphere.

She simply sipped her drink, watching Andre fix two Scotch-and-waters. He carried one to the fourth occupant of the room who had been sitting so quietly that she hadn't noticed him in the low lighting. He had chosen the most shadowed corner, and she wondered suddenly if that might have been deliberate. It had certainly afforded him the opportunity to study her without her being aware of his scrutiny.

Suzanne spoke at her elbow, "You haven't met my older brother. He's the patriarch, the one who keeps us all in line. Come and meet Julien."

Their footsteps sounded unnaturally loud against the stone tiles of the floor. She wondered suddenly if that's why Suzanne had been barefoot this afternoon, to avoid this echoing parade across the room.

"Caroline, I'd like you to meet my *favorite* brother."

They both heard Andre's soft laugh behind them, but Suzanne ignored his response to her provocation and continued her introduction. "Julien, this is Caroline Evans. I've invited her to be my secretary and companion while I'm here."

Caroline's thoughts that night after she had gone to bed all concerned her stupidity in not putting it together sooner. The dark, aviator-style sunglasses in the dimness of the room. Andre's solicitude with the drink. She hadn't yet realized the reason those things were necessary. She had simply extended her hand and waited.

Suzanne reached out and took her hand quite naturally and, holding it gently in her own, lowered their joined hands between them as if they were such close friends they couldn't bear to be apart. She smiled into Caroline's eyes to banish the embarrassment, but they both knew that somehow the man who sat so quietly in that shadowed corner was perfectly aware of what had just happened.

He was very like his brother, as deeply tanned, with the same strong, squared chin and darkly curling hair. He was, perhaps, even better looking, his features more classically shaped. It was difficult to tell behind the dark glasses.

His tone was completely neutral when he spoke, his voice deep and rich, his English only slightly accented. Since she had expected him to address her in French, as the others had naturally done, his decision to greet her in her native language seemed a nice gesture.

"Ms. Evans, I'm delighted you've consented to join us here. I hope you'll enjoy your stay. I doubt that even Suzanne's social correspondence will totally occupy your time. Please feel free to enjoy the islands. If you need anything, I hope you'll ask. Andre will make an excellent guide, and if I know my brother, he'll be more than willing."

"Thank you," she said quietly, still embarrassed by her faux pas, "but I'm here to work, to help your sister. I don't think I'll have time to play tourist."

"Andre will probably insist you find time. He's already been extolling your beauty," he said. Realizing that comment demanded some explanation, he continued softly, "I hope you'll forgive my curiosity which, I admit, prompted his comments. We don't usually discuss our guests, but a brief description helps me to visualize someone I'm meeting for the first time." The dark glasses were focused somewhere beyond her left shoulder.

"I don't mind. Especially since your brother chose to

be very flattering. I'm looking forward to staying here. Your home is very beautiful.''

''And not at all what you expected,'' he suggested. His lips lifted into a slight smile, and something about that movement caused a flutter inside her already nervous stomach.

''No,'' she managed. ''To be truthful, I'd expected a much older house.''

''The original house was destroyed by Hurricane David. Not a very romantic name for a storm, and that house was very romantic, steeped in history and haunted, I'm sure, by several well-authenticated ghosts. I built this house to replace it. It's about ten years old.''

''You don't miss the other at all.'' Suzanne laughed. ''He hated it. He couldn't wait to design and build this one. He talked for months about what the site demanded and stresses and forces and who knows what else. I don't know how the workmen ever got anything done with him adjusting every beam and pillar.''

''You're an architect?'' Caroline asked unthinkingly and knew by the tension, by the sudden movement of the small hand that finally released hers, the error she had made.

''Not anymore,'' he said into the uncomfortable silence that fell in spite of their well-bred politeness. ''I finance houses. I invest in companies that build them, but I don't design. Not anymore, Ms. Evans.''

His voice had softened on the last, and she could almost hear the effort he made to speak naturally when he continued, a change of the awkward subject her remark had forced. ''Suzanne, if you'll take me in to dinner?''

He rose too suddenly, unaware perhaps of how close they stood to his chair or still bothered by the insensitivity of her comment. He moved so quickly that her instinctive step backward unbalanced her, and she grasped the nearest object to keep from falling. The solidness of the muscle under the navy silk shirt was reassuringly steady. She quickly regained her balance, releasing his arm as if she'd been scalded.

"I'm sorry," he began, his words conflicting with her own agonized apology, so that they both stopped and waited.

"It was my fault," she said finally, knowing she was blushing.

"I don't think so, Ms. Evans. I hope you'll forgive my clumsiness. Suzanne?"

He fitted his hand around his sister's upper arm, and she led the way to the small table that had been set on the patio.

The meal was long and the atmosphere relaxed. The food was simple and delicious, a mixture of French and Creole dishes that reminded Caroline of New Orleans. The conversation flowed easily with Andre and Suzanne bearing the burden, seemingly without any conscious effort.

The man at the head of the table said little, and Caroline wondered if that were because his full attention was required for the process of eating. She was fascinated by the movement of his long brown fingers against the array of crystal and china. He never made a mistake. There was no clink of misplaced glass or fork, no need for the use of the napkin. She would never have known he was blind, she thought, not from this.

She wondered how long since he'd lost his vision. Less than ten years. She thought of those long years of darkness and wondered if he had ever been as laughingly sensuous as Andre, as confident of his power to attract.

He was still, in spite of the dark glasses that hid the sightless eyes, a very attractive man.

At the realization that she had been watching those lean, tanned hands, she dropped her gaze to her plate and tried to concentrate on the story Andre and Suzanne were telling together, running over each other's best lines. Something about a visitor to the original house who had been a sleepwalker. It was an old routine they had obviously used often in the past to entertain, but, although she laughed when they finished, she had lost the thread. Eventually, a relaxed silence fell over the group.

"Why don't you take Ms. Evans to the deck and show her the surf," her host suggested to his brother. The glasses moved toward her face when he explained, "You can hear it even from this side of the house. It's a sound that will become as familiar as your own heartbeat, but the first sight is awe inspiring."

Suddenly, she knew she didn't want him pushing Andre to entertain her. It wasn't necessary, and it was somehow insulting.

"Tomorrow," she said, rising. She hoped she wasn't being rude, but she was tired, and she wanted to sort out the impressions of the crowded day. "If you don't mind, I think I'm going to turn in. I was up very early this morning, and in spite of the nap, I still feel the effects. Forgive me, please, and good night."

Both men had risen automatically, but it was the older who again commanded.

"Of course. Andre, would you show Ms. Evans to her room? I hope you sleep well."

"Good night, Caroline," Suzanne spoke, still curled comfortably in her chair. "I'll see you tomorrow. We'll get started on the endless grind. I'm really very glad you're here.''

Caroline followed Andre through the French doors and across the tile to the stairs. Neither was aware of the angry voice that spoke behind them on the patio.

''What the hell are you playing at? Blindman's buff? *Take you in to dinner.*'' Suzanne's voice was rich with ridicule. ''I almost threw up. My God, Julien, what kind of act was that?''

He laughed in the darkness and stood, holding out his hand for her. She finally took his fingers, and he pulled her up. They walked arm in arm to the edge of the patio, but she wasn't the guide this time.

''I thought it was wonderfully affecting. A moment full of poignancy. Personally, I was deeply touched,'' he said, smiling, but the mockery was all self-directed.

''Damn it, Julien, you explain what you're doing, or I swear I quit. I swear I'm on the next flight to Paris. You almost knocked the poor girl down.''

''The poor girl?'' he questioned softly. ''I thought you didn't want her here. I thought your sympathies were all for me, your concern.''

''When I think you need it. Not when you're putting on some helpless blind-man routine for the tourists.''

''And how did the tourists respond?'' he said softly. She knew suddenly from something in that carefully emotionless voice she was used to reading how much he wanted to know about their guest's reaction to his blindness, and to know that, he needed her help.

''She did all right. I'd say she even…''

''Even what?'' he asked finally when she refused to go on.

''She watched your hands. At dinner.''

''And?''

She could feel the tension in the hard body beside her, leaning lazily against the stone railings of the patio.

"She was all right. It didn't make her nervous. As a matter of fact, I'd give her an eight, maybe even a nine." They had devised the code years before, rating reactions to his blindness.

They didn't speak for a long time, and in the silence she could hear the surf booming against the rocks. Like a heartbeat.

"Take me up to bed, Suzanne," he said softly, hugging her small body close.

"You go to hell, you bastard. You always get your way. You go to hell," she said.

She could hear his laughter following her inside and up the stairs to her room. She didn't know why she was so angry with him, but thinking about that dark laughter, it was a long time before she slept.

Chapter Three

Caroline awoke suddenly in the cloying darkness and sat upright in the tangled sheets. A nightmare. It had been so long. The stresses of the day, she supposed. She took a deep breath and found she could smell, almost taste, the salt, the flowers from the garden below, the heat of the sun leaving the tiles beneath her windows.

It had been a mistake to leave them open. She was gathering the energy to climb out of the clinging sheets and close them when she heard it again. The sound that had dragged her, panting and shivering, from a too-sound sleep. The faint mewling cry of a newborn. She had heard babies cry through the years, and none of them ever sounded like this. So lost. So sick. As the last echo died, she buried her face in her hands. *Not again,* she prayed. *Not again, dear God. Please, not now.*

She waited, hoping, and after so many long dark minutes that she had begun once more to breathe, deep shuddering breaths of relief, the wail whispered again. Not through the open windows, but from the hall outside her room.

She had the door open before the sound had stopped, but in the darkness of the long hall she had no idea of its direction. Here there was no echo to guide her. It had stopped as soon as she opened the door, not fading into the blackness, but cut off.

She cried out against the unfairness of it. Realizing where she was, she pressed both hands against her mouth, attempting to suppress the racking sobs that always left her exhausted, incapable of any rational thought. *Not again,* she begged, feeling the blackness of her fear close around her.

"Caroline," the voice spoke softly beside her, "what's wrong? Why are you crying? What's happened?"

She tried to regain control, to answer his concern, but she was too far into the panic the dream always caused.

Finally hard masculine arms enclosed her, offering the timeless comfort of human closeness that penetrates even the deepest hysteria, and she leaned into the warmth, the alive solidness of his chest. She let him rock her gently until the sobbing eased. Until the blackness retreated again to a manageable distance. She could smell the cologne he used and, underlying that, the scent of his body, warm and hard against her cheek. That evidence of life and sanity overwhelmed her with gratitude, so that she rubbed her face against the smoothness of his chest, turned her head to savor the reality of muscle and skin.

She was aware of the deep breath he took, and then he turned her face up to his and touched her trembling lips with his own. She wanted that touch. Her mouth opened automatically under the invasion of his tongue. She was surprised at the depth of her desire. She of the frozen emotions, the frigid indifference, wanted the lips that were moving over hers so skillfully, evoking memories that made her knees weaken and her hands clutch his shoulders.

He broke the contact, lifting his head, trying to see her face in the moon-touched darkness of the hallway. "What's wrong?" he asked again, gathering her close.

She swallowed against the dryness. "A nightmare," she whispered.

"That must have been one hell of a nightmare," he said, smiling. "Not that I'm not grateful. Do you have these often?"

She was aware of the sexual teasing, the gentle invitation cloaked in the question, but she shook her head, still held safely against his body. "Not in such a long time. I thought they were gone. It's been so long."

They both were aware of the trembling despair of the last phrase, and his arms tightened comfortingly.

"You're just tired—a long flight and then a bunch of strangers, maybe some of us stranger than others," he teased gently. "Just tired."

She began to breathe against the rhythmic caress of his hands moving soothingly over her back. Perhaps he was right. Perhaps she had been asleep, still dazed from her exhaustion.

There was no sound now in the hallway. No sound from her open door but the boom of the surf against the rocks. His brother had been right. It was becoming a familiar background, as comforting as the hands against her spine. She was enfolded in its sound as Andre was enfolding her in his arms, arms that felt hard enough to protect her from any nightmare.

Embarrassed, she moved finally out of their circle, and he let her go. There was enough light now to see the smile he directed at her. She touched his face, unable to express the gratitude she felt.

"I'm all right. I promise. It was just a bad dream."

"It's almost dawn. Do you want me to stay with you?"

"Why were you up?" she whispered.

"I'm going to Marie Galante. To the distilleries. I told you we make our living here producing rum. That's my domain in the many provinces of the family businesses. Julien runs everything else, but this is mine. I usually leave at daybreak and come home midafternoon. Suzanne told you how we operate in the tropics. The heat makes everything else impossible. But if you want me to stay—"

"Of course not," she denied, pushing the tangled waves of her hair back from her face. "I'm fine. Really. And you're probably right. Just too much happening at one time, too much excitement. My life is usually very dull. I hope you won't tell Suzanne. I'd hate for her to think she's employed some kind of neurotic."

She regretted the word as soon as she'd uttered it. She didn't know why she'd used it, hated the sound of it between them, but he only laughed.

"Everybody's neurotic about something. Comparatively, I think nightmares rank fairly low. Stop worrying. Why don't you try to sleep? There's still a half hour or so of darkness. You'll feel better if you lie down and relax."

She smiled and nodded, although in the dimness of the hall she doubted he saw the gesture. "I think you're right. And thank you."

"My pleasure," he said softly. Finally he turned and walked away.

She stood a moment longer until the silence drove her back to the open doorway of her room. The windows were still open, and the lightening gloom of the tropical false dawn drew her to stand beside them and look out.

She knew she couldn't go back to sleep. She knew that instead she would lie listening for the sounds that would signal the past had once again overtaken her, so she stood, blocking all thought, simply watching the gathering light.

She saw someone enter the garden and thought at first it was Andre, but the body was wrong, the chest too deep, the shoulders too broad for Andre's tall leanness.

As he moved toward the pool, she saw that he wore only a pair of black bathing trunks that fitted his narrow waist and hips like a second skin. She had always hated the European styling, but somehow it was right for him, outlining the tight muscles of his buttocks and emphasizing his masculinity, the almost concave stomach, the strong thighs. She felt like a voyeur, but she watched, unable to move from the windows as he walked without hesitation to the edge of the pool and dived into the dark depths. There was none of the uncertainty he had shown in his movements last night.

He swam a long time, until the sun touched the sky into real dawn, and she wondered how he could know that. He pulled himself from the edge of the pool and used the towel he had flung down beside it to dry his hair and his face. She realized suddenly that he wasn't wearing the dark glasses. She wanted desperately to see the color of his eyes, but the light was too faint and the distance too great.

He looped the towel around his neck, moving again with the quick, sure stride back across the tile of the garden and into the open doors. She swallowed, wondering about the emotion that churned her stomach and tightened painfully against her temples. She rested her head against the louvers of the windows and felt, but didn't understand, hot tears gather and begin to trace down her cheeks.

SHE AND SUZANNE WORKED a long time from the seemingly endless list of names and addresses. The dictation was rapid and spotty, her employer trusting Caroline to fill in suitable expressions of gratitude for kindnesses that Suzanne enumerated in the beginning of each letter. They worked until lunch, which they ate alone. She hadn't expected Andre to return, but she wondered about Julien and found herself listening for him, looking at the doorway throughout the meal.

They ate this time in the small breakfast room because of the midday heat. She didn't ask, and Suzanne offered no explanation for her brother's failure to join them, chatting instead about the tourist attractions that she insisted Caroline wouldn't want to miss, the dinner party for a few old friends on Monday night and the fact that tonight was the servants' night out.

"They go back to attend Mass in the morning. I've tried to get Julien to build a chapel and get a priest. I swear it would be worth it not to have to worry about Saturday night supper and Sunday's meals. I'm afraid they're never much. The cook leaves salads, and we snack. Julien cooks sometimes if the mood strikes him, but not me. I hate to cook.''

Suzanne was curled again in the comfortable chair that, like those around the patio table, was more armchair than dining chair. No wonder meals stretched pleasantly long after everyone had finished eating. They were sipping iced coffee, and because of the afternoon sunlight and Suzanne's laughing voice, she had lost most of the tension of the dawn, relaxing again in the undemanding companionship her employer offered.

"Julien?" She questioned the last comment in surprise and watched the telltale realization break across the heart-shaped face before her.

"He does it very well," his sister said finally, with a decidedly Gallic shrug.

"I'm sure he does. He seems to do everything well. I saw him swimming this morning." She thought that perhaps Suzanne's open nature would lead her to give some background about her brother, but for once, Suzanne didn't answer. She drank her coffee instead, and when she looked up, it was to find the green eyes waiting.

"You haven't asked. It's all right. Everyone does. Some people even have nerve enough to ask him, and he tells them."

The silence stretched for the first time into discomfort between them. Finally Suzanne broke it, resignation and something else Caroline couldn't identify coloring her voice.

"Julien lost his sight six years ago in an automobile accident in Monaco. He was very badly hurt, besides the blindness. His recovery took almost two years of rehabilitation. There are still lingering effects, although he makes sure that no one is aware of them. Whatever my brother suffers, he covers very well. He's open about his blindness because that's not something he can hide, but not the other. He's a very private man, very closed. He wasn't. He was…"

"Like Andre?" Caroline asked into the brittle pause.

"Andre?" She could hear the surprise in Suzanne's voice at that thought. "I suppose he was in a lot of ways. He was athletic, really a daredevil. His leisure activities were all dangerous: racing—cars and boats, polo, flying, even skydiving. He was never hurt, never injured. He was too good, too quick. It's so ironic that after all the years of those things, he was instead…destroyed in the way he was.''

''Destroyed?'' Caroline questioned, rejecting the finality of that choice of words. ''Surely not.''

''What he was,'' Suzanne amended. ''How he was. Funny. Clever. Passionate. Relaxed. Like Andre, but stronger. You always knew you could depend on Julien to have control. He was so sure of everything.'' She took a deep breath, raising blue eyes to study Caroline's face before she continued.

''He's *so* different now. Contained and careful. I know he has to be because…'' Her voice faded, and then she continued, almost thinking aloud now. ''He hates to grope, to stumble, hates to *look* blind. He hates his blindness, but he never says that. He won't express his anger and resentment. I always thought that if he would express it, say how he feels, it might ease. If he did, however, he'd have to blame her, and he's not ready to deal with that.''

''I don't understand. Blame who?'' Caroline asked. She became aware of a growing tightness at her temples. She even put her hand up to rub against the beginning pain as she waited.

''Julien's wife was driving. Drunk and angry at some imagined slight. I never met her. I was too occupied here with my own marriage, with Edouard's illness, and Julien never brought her to the island. Andre says she was like a child, a spoiled brat when she didn't get her way. God knows how Julien put up with her. Love is blind, I suppose.''

Suzanne stopped suddenly, raising stricken eyes. ''I can't believe I said that, but he was. Blind to her faults. She wrecked the car and walked away without a scratch and then walked away from him. She just left him to deal with all she'd done to him.''

When the words finally stopped beating inside her head, Caroline lowered her face against the coolness of her glass to fight the rising nausea. She didn't understand why the story had upset her so. The images formed in her head by Suzanne's words had pierced her, like the nightmares always did, and she was glad when Suzanne stood and dropped her napkin beside her plate.

''I can't write another one of those damn notes. Let's give it a rest. We'll start again in the morning. I think I'll ride in with Andre when he takes the staff back to Terre-de-Bas. Until then, I'm going to sleep. We should take lessons from the Spanish. They know how to deal with long, hot afternoons. Think you can entertain your-self for a few hours?''

''Of course. I'll be fine. I may get some sun by the pool if that's all right.''

''Be careful. You'll burn before you know it.''

''I'll use screen. I just feel so city white.''

''I know,'' Suzanne said, smiling, ''but I fight the urge. Sun hats and beach umbrellas for me. Don't tell anyone, but I've discovered an age spot or two. Why don't men get those? God, it's so unfair.''

They laughed together, the tension suddenly evapo-rating, and then Suzanne climbed the long staircase to the upstairs rooms.

With Suzanne's departure, the quietness of the house closed around her. She found herself wondering where he was. She shook off the thought and climbed the stairs herself to change into the pale pink swimsuit she had brought with her, another item on the lawyer's precise list.

She looked down on the pool when she was dressed,

feeling the inviting pull of the waters. Everything was going to be all right. She just needed to relax and fit in. Forget this morning. The nightmares would fade as they had before. She had simply been too tired, overstimulated.

She touched her lips, remembering the feel of Andre's mouth against hers and, instead of the pleasure she had felt this morning, she remembered the familiar emptiness. The long years' emptiness.

IN THE COOL SHADOWS of his office Julien heard the sounds from the pool. He knew it wasn't Suzanne, so he walked to the window and listened to the movement of the waters. He knew by the sounds when she had stopped swimming, had walked up the steps at the shallow end and found one of the loungers. He even heard and identified the ritual of opening the lotion, the replacement of the bottle on the tile beside the chair.

He found himself imagining her fingers moving against her arms and legs, against her neck, her breasts. "She can't hurt me," he had told Suzanne, and in those images he knew that for the lie it was. He leaned, as she had, against the window and for the first time allowed himself, almost against his will, to remember.

"ARE YOU SURE you don't mind if I leave you?" Suzanne questioned as she slipped her feet into her sandals. "Julien's here, and we'll be home before dinnertime, I promise. Knock on his office door if you need anything. He's really a very nice man, doesn't bite or anything."

"I'll be fine," Caroline reassured. "I'm going to address the letters we got through this morning, so Andre can take them to mail tomorrow. Don't worry."

"I just need to pick up a few things and get out of the house. Unless you want to come with us?"

Caroline shook her head, knowing the invitation was only a polite afterthought. She had been hired to do a job, not to join in family outings.

SHE WORKED A COUPLE of hours in Suzanne's small office and didn't realize until she heard the rain how dark the sky had become. The coming storm was clearly visible from the long windows that looked out on to the patio. She was surprised to notice that all the furniture had been removed.

The flagstones stretched gray as the roiling clouds, and the wind pressed strongly enough against the long glass of the windows to rock them in the wooden frames. She thought briefly about the open boat and wondered if they would return now in time for dinner. She walked back to the office to finish sealing the last of the envelopes, wondering where she should leave them so Andre wouldn't miss them. She wished she'd asked Suzanne.

By the time she reentered the living room, she had to turn on one of the lamps against the growing darkness of twilight and the storm. The wind and rain beat against the glass, and she watched a moment. She wasn't afraid of storms. They were elemental and always made her feel strangely alive, turned on to the power they created.

She decided on a quick shower before dinner to wash the pool's chlorine out of her hair. When she entered her bedroom, she opened one of the long windows, but the wind was too strong, blowing the rain in a fine mist over the carpet. She stood a moment, raising her face into the force of the storm, and then she closed the window and turned on the low light beside her bed.

JULIEN WAS STANDING by the sink in the kitchen when he heard the upstairs shower begin. He lowered his head and listened to the pounding of the wind and rain against the glass. He touched his watch to feel the time, and finally he walked to the box against the outside wall. His hand moved unerringly to open it and find the handle he sought. He pulled it, waiting before he walked back to the sink.

He concentrated against the growing noise of the gale, and he could still hear the water from upstairs rushing down through the pipes. He walked then to the clock above the doorway to touch the face. The slight vibration of the electric motor that drove the hands was still, and in spite of his determination, he found himself hurrying to the stairs, climbing too quickly to lean against her door.

He wondered again at his own motives, but since he had listened to Paul Dupre's description, he had known that this moment would come. Finally he would confront her. There had been no doubt in his mind from the beginning that what would happen tonight was inevitable. He breathed deeply to calm his trembling fingers before he knocked.

She had stood a long time with her eyes closed under the hot spray of the shower, feeling it relax a tension she hadn't even been aware of.

Enough, she urged herself mentally. *This is something you've conquered. Enough.*

The soft knock was an interruption, and she opened her eyes to blackness. She fumbled briefly for the controls of the shower and, in the sudden silence when the water stopped, she heard him call her name.

"Ms. Evans? Are you all right?"

She groped for her towel and dried her face and hair

before she wrapped it sarong fashion to answer the repeated knock.

"I'm all right. I was in the shower. What happened to the lights?" she asked, adding unnecessarily, "The lights are out."

"I know," he said, his amusement at her explanation clear even through the barrier of the door. "I have a computer that talks. Suddenly it stopped talking to me, and I realized you must be in the dark. It's the storm. We have our own generator, but this happens too often. I thought you might like to come downstairs." He waited, and then he said into the silence, "If you're afraid."

The door opened suddenly, moving away from his fingers, and he could smell her. The same soap, the same shampoo, Kerri had always used. God, how could she know that? He closed his eyes behind the lenses of the dark glasses, but that didn't stop the tightening of his groin, the painful engorging that even her smell, after all these years, could cause.

"I'm not afraid," she said. "I like storms, but I would like to come downstairs. If you'll wait while I get dressed."

"Of course," he said. He wondered if she could hear the tightness in his voice. "Do you need any help?" he asked seriously, and heard her laugh.

"I've been dressing myself a long time. I think I can manage."

"So had I," he said softly, a rebuke against her amusement. When he spoke again, he had lightened the darkness. "But if you get it wrong, I certainly won't notice."

This time he smiled when she laughed. She closed the

door, and he smiled again in satisfaction and leaned against the wall to wait.

It wasn't long before the door reopened. He could hear the movement of whatever she wore against her body, could smell her fragrance. For the first time, he was uncertain about what he had planned to do, so she was forced to stand in the open doorway waiting. He could hear her breathing, and finally he spoke.

"There's a proverb for situations like this," he said.

"But you're not, surely, going to say it," she answered, her voice calm and unembarrassed. He was surprised to feel her fingers close around his upper arm. He pressed them against his side and wondered if he could do this, if he still wanted to. He guided her, without speaking, to the stairs and loosened her fingers from around his arm to place her left hand on the railing. He was surprised when she touched him once more, gripping his sleeve.

"Don't," she said into the darkness. He could hear, for the first time, unease in her voice. "Don't leave me."

"I'm right here. I just thought the railing might be easier. I have you."

She moved down the stairs beside him, but he felt the deep breath she took when they reached the bottom.

"I don't think I could do that," she said softly. He didn't respond, didn't want to form an answer, because he understood. He hadn't thought he could, either. He had—out of necessity and because he had had no choice.

"Are you hungry?" he asked instead.

"Shouldn't we wait for the others? Suzanne said they'd be back."

"I don't think that now, with the storm, they'll try it. Maybe later if it clears, but not with that going on."

They listened to the force pushing against the house,

the movement of the long panes of glass between them and the wind.

"Then, yes," she said, "I'm hungry."

He led her to the kitchen. With each step she relaxed into his guidance, surer now with following his movements. He didn't hesitate, and she felt again a kind of admiration for his cleverness in conquering the dark world he'd been forced into.

She was gently deposited on a tall stool near the island that she knew dominated the center of the modern kitchen.

"Let's see what's here."

She heard him open the refrigerator and begin removing lids and placing containers on the counter.

"I just thought," he said suddenly. She heard him open a drawer and the brush of his fingers over the contents. She couldn't tell what he was doing, until the flare of the match allowed her to watch him light by touch the wick of the candle he'd found. The soft glow moved out against the darkness. She took a deep breath when he turned to bring the candle and its holder to the island.

"That's better," he said, as if the light were for him also. She smiled at the satisfaction in his voice.

"Much better," she agreed. "Dinner by candlelight."

When he moved back to the counter to fix whatever he'd found for their supper, she carried the candle and her stool across the narrow space that separated them. He stopped what he was doing when he became aware of her nearness.

"I want to watch," she said, "or help, if you like."

He carefully cut the long loaf he'd found in the pantry into two halves with a knife that moved easily against the bread.

"I think it's safer if you watch. I like doing this, but

I'd hate to miss and ruin our dinner. Your fingers are safer in your lap, Ms. Evans,'' he said, and she could see the quick slant of his smile in the candlelight. His rejection of her offer didn't slow the preparations his hands were making.

''Caroline,'' she corrected and watched the sudden stillness of his fingers.

''Caroline,'' he repeated before he went back to the sandwich. She lapsed into silence, enjoying the swift dexterity of his hands against the items he'd placed on the counter.

When it was finished, he used the knife to cut the sandwich into two equal parts, which he lifted onto the plates. She carried them to the island and sat on one of the stools.

His fingers found the neck of one of the bottles that rested in the wine rack above her head, and she watched as he carried it to the counter and poured two glasses. When he held hers out to her, she took it. He found the stool with one hand and pulled it to the island, and she moved one of the plates in front of him. She watched him sip the burgundy, but she sat hers down untouched beside her plate. Even the smell would nauseate her.

''I forgot. Would you like something else to drink?'' he asked. He put his own wine down, standing up to find whatever else was available.

She touched his hand then, and he stopped to turn toward her. The candlelight moved across the metal rims of the glasses, briefly reflected in their dark lenses.

''Nothing. It's all right.''

''Why don't you drink?'' he asked suddenly. The invasion was so out of character with the politeness they had all shown her, she was surprised.

"I just don't. I can't," she said, knowing that she couldn't explain any further than that.

Before she understood what he intended, he poured the glass of wine he held down the sink. He found the neck of the bottle that was still standing on the counter and replaced the cork. She turned away, embarrassed by what he was doing.

"You'll have to hand me your glass," he said quietly, but she didn't react. He waited and then reached carefully across the island. His hand moved gropingly, searching for the glass he had asked her for.

"Don't," she whispered, unable to watch the movements of those suddenly uncertain fingers.

"Then hand me the damn glass."

Hearing the bitterness in the command, she forced herself to obey. She placed the glass in his waiting fingers, and he poured her wine down the sink, this time turning on the water to follow. When she finally raised her head again, he was facing her, leaning against the counter.

"I'm sorry," he said softly.

"It's all right. It's not what you think. I'm not an alcoholic. I just can't…" Her voice stopped, and she shook her head.

When she didn't explain further, he found the stool again and sat before her. For something to do in the awkward silence, she tasted the sandwich and was surprised to find that she was still hungry and that it was delicious.

"This is very good," she said, watching the slow smile that was his response. "You do everything so well."

It wasn't what she had meant to say, far too personal, but she wanted him to know that she thought he managed beautifully. She didn't know why telling him that was so important, but it was.

"As long as everything is exactly where it should be. As long as everyone cooperates. You can't imagine how many servants don't understand that or can't tolerate the exactness. Suzanne can do it only because she cares if I fall flat on my face. Neatness is against her nature," he said, smiling again.

"I can't imagine you falling."

"I have, I assure you, and I will again. I manage here because my family and servants are part of the conspiracy."

"Conspiracy?" she repeated, questioning what seemed a strange choice of words.

"The conspiracy to pretend that I do everything 'so well,'" he mocked. "As long as I know where every item is. As long as they are exactly in the same place to the exact centimeter. It's a very demanding conspiracy, but the choice for me is chaos, falls and groping, and that makes everyone uncomfortable. You were uncomfortable watching me fumble for your glass. You see, everyone enjoys the illusion that I deal well with my blindness."

His voice stopped, harshly cut off, and he looked down as if at his untouched sandwich. Then he deliberately took the plate in his long fingers and threw the whole high against the wall behind her. She gasped with the unexpectedness of the gesture. As if in response to that sound, he caught her chin in the hand that was still raised.

His fingers fitted on either side of her jaw, and he controlled her with the pressure. He lifted, and she rose, drawn steadily across the wooden island, his grip not painful, but not to be denied. She watched the glasses glint in the candlelight as his head lowered toward hers.

"Don't," she whispered. "Oh, God, don't. Please don't."

The pull of his fingers was arrested, and he released her slowly. Her knees tremblingly gave way as she sank against the stool. She put her head down on the striped wood of the island top.

He stood a moment, listening to the harsh sound of her breathing, and then he found the candle by its heat and blew it out. He left her there, alone in the darkness he had caused.

Chapter Four

There were no nightmares that night, no crying infants to trouble her sleep. There were dreams, images that floated through the darkness like scenes from a silent movie, flickering against her consciousness, but she remembered almost nothing of them when she woke.

She had slept on the longest of the coral couches. She didn't know where Julien was in the darkness, so she chose the coward's way and slept downstairs. The first rays of the dawn sun pouring light into the long windows woke her. She listened and knew that the storm was over. She heard no one else moving in the silent house. She could smell the coffee from the kitchen and, unable to resist, even if he were there, she rose. She intended to clean up the mess against the kitchen wall. She couldn't explain to Suzanne and Andre what had happened, and she knew he wouldn't explain.

The kitchen looked ordinary in the morning light. No echoes of whatever anger and pain had come between them. The island and the counter were clean, all evidence removed of their interrupted meal. He had also apparently cleaned the wall and the floor below. She walked across the room to make sure and saw him outside on the deck that looked down on the pounding surf.

He was dressed in jeans and a knit shirt, and he was barefoot. He was standing with one hip propped against the railing, and his absolute stillness was a little frightening to her. For some reason she wanted him to move, but the only movement was the soft lift of black hair in the strong wind off the ocean.

She watched him a few minutes and then, seeing a remnant of the sandwich that had apparently eluded his searching fingers, she bent to pick it up. She wondered how long it had taken him to clean up the scattered pieces. Finally she ran water on the kitchen sponge and wiped the wall carefully, removing completely all physical evidence of his anger.

She poured coffee, pulled out a stool from the center island and sat, watching the still figure outside. He raised his face finally into the sun and then turned. Her heart jumped as he moved to the doorway and came inside. His face focused on hers, perhaps helped by the sudden involuntary movement of her fingers that slid the mug a millimeter against the wood.

"Did you get it all?" he said politely.

He hadn't shaved and the dark shadow below the glasses made him more sinister, a stranger.

"Yes." She didn't bother denying what she had been doing.

"And without light," he said gently.

She knew he was aware of the brightness of the sun, had felt it on his face.

"How clever," he complimented, turning to the box by the door. He opened it, his fingers moving with that same unhesitating accuracy that had fascinated her last night, and pushed the handle inside. The lights in the kitchen came on. She could hear the hum of the refrigerator begin.

"Close your mouth, Ms. Evans," he mocked. She realized that the shock of what he had done, the revelation that he had controlled the darkness last night, had caused exactly the reaction he had anticipated. She closed her lips against the sudden sickness, watching him move with unhesitating certainty past the island to pour his own coffee. His hand went unerringly to the mug and the carafe, and the liquid filled exactly the level anyone would pour.

He turned to face her, leaning the long length of his body against the counter. She didn't like him behind her, so she picked up her cup and walked to the kitchen doorway that would lead to the front of the house.

"Running away?" he suggested softly. The tone this time was obviously hostile.

"Why did you do that? With the lights?" she asked, fighting her building fear.

The slow smile that answered her was as menacing as his question. "I thought it would be more romantic," he said softly. "Moon glow and candlelight. And the storm. She always liked storms. God, how she liked—"

The abrupt ending to whatever he was about to tell her sent a sharp, familiar stab of tension against her temples, so that she fought both the pain and the urge to turn and run.

"Or didn't he tell you about her reaction to storms?" he asked.

This time she left, driven by emotions released in the bright room that she didn't understand, but knew she couldn't face. She heard the bang of the stool she had left pulled away from the island, and then his colorful profanities. She even heard the shatter of the stool against whatever it hit and knew he had thrown it, too. She ran from the sound, and the blackness and the pain receded finally only with the comfort of the tranquil view of the ocean through the tall, clear windows.

She sat on the coral couch and watched all morning, but there was no boat, no laughing couple climbing the stairs from the pier, no reprieve. Her head began to throb slightly, so that before noon the band that the pain wove was corded around her temples. She found aspirin in the kitchen and poured another cup of the now too-strong coffee and realized the slight nausea was probably caused as much by hunger as anything else.

"Feed the body first," her grandfather had always said, "and then you can worry about the soul." His French practicality and old-world wisdom had truly fed the lost soul she had been when he'd found her. After her childhood, she had been so hungry for someone to care about her. Again there was a deep sense of warmth and love in remembering him, unlike the agony that was the inevitable result of trying to capture the elusive images that sometimes moved just outside her consciousness. She didn't understand so many things that were happening here. She closed her eyes against the sudden vertigo. *Feed the body,* her grandfather's memory spoke from the darkness, and in its warmth, she was again in control.

She found fruit salad in the refrigerator and, in the pantry, more of the crusty bread Julien had used last night. She fixed a bowl of salad and ate it standing, realizing only then how hungry she really was. The luncheon she and Suzanne had shared twenty-four hours ago was the last meal she'd eaten.

She didn't question her motivations when she fixed the tray. Her only hesitation was whether to include a spoon or a fork for the salad, and finally she put both beside the plate. She buttered the bread, wondering if he would resent that.

What the hell, she thought. Whatever he disliked so much about her to cause the stunt he had pulled last night wasn't going to be helped or hurt by buttering his bread. She didn't understand the compulsion to take him the tray. Except she knew he'd be hungry too.

Good, she thought viciously, the anger catching her unaware. *I hope the bastard's starving to death. It would serve him right.*

She threw the serving spoon into the sink and watched the juices from the salad splatter against the porcelain, and she took a deep breath against the unaccustomed anger. And then another. She never got angry. It wasn't allowed within the careful limits of her existence. This time, however, in spite of her fury with him, the pain remained at bay.

She rinsed the fruit stains from the sink and turned to see the tray sitting on the counter, her concern about his hunger mocking her anger with him.

She closed her eyes and caught her lip with her teeth. She stood there a moment, steeling herself for a mission she didn't understand, and then carried the tray across the echoing quarry tile, announcing her arrival before his office door as she now knew was the intent of that expanse of bare flooring. It was uncarpeted by design, so that, even in his blindness, he would know where everyone was.

The computer voice had been playing softly against her consciousness for a long time, and she could hear it clearly now through the door. Something in its mechanical quality grated, so that she wondered how he could listen to it all day. She knew suddenly that he had rather

do that than be dependent on someone else, some human
voice in his darkness.

She didn't knock, but opened the door and, without
speaking to the suddenly upturned face, she put the tray
on his desk.

"There's fruit salad and bread and coffee."

She wondered if there were other instructions she
should give, but somehow she couldn't imagine herself
telling him fruit at six o'clock and bread at three. There
was something so ludicrous at that thought she almost
laughed.

"What made you think I wanted you to—"

"The nearest wall's behind you," she interrupted.
"About three feet. There are a couple of paintings, but
nothing that appears too valuable. If you don't want it,
just heave away," she said and turned and walked out
and, without thinking, slammed the door. She thought
she heard him laugh, but she couldn't be sure over the
noise of the door and the annoying voice of the computer.

SHE WAITED all afternoon in the bright room where Suzanne had greeted her. As the sun began to lower in the
sky and long shadows fell over the gray of the flagstones, turning their silver to charcoal, she moved to the
windows, knowing now they weren't coming.

She was still standing there in the deepening twilight
when he came into the room. He'd shaved; she'd heard
the whine of the electric razor earlier this afternoon, but
he was still dressed the same and still barefoot.

She didn't need sound to know he was there. There
was something kinetic about his presence. But of course,
she found herself thinking, there always had been. At

that unexpected thought, the pain that had been gone since lunch began to beat again at her head.

"They're not coming back, are they?" she asked, not really a question.

He crossed the room to stand beside her, close enough that she could smell him. She suddenly knew exactly how his skin would taste against her tongue, warm with the sun and yet dark, slightly salty and so sweet. So clean.

As if in reaction to that knowledge, the pain tightened again, and she almost gasped with its viciousness.

"I don't know," he said, softly. "You tell me. You tell me what's supposed to happen next."

"I don't understand," she whispered.

"Of course you do," he answered, smiling, "and you're doing very well."

She watched him breathe against her hair, not touching his face to the waves that brushed her shoulders and below, but very close.

"You even smell right," he said quietly.

The sensuousness of that whisper loosened something inside her body, something tight and hard, so she had to fight the urge to rest against his strength.

Instead she leaned back against the glass. Its coolness in the shadow was refreshing against the hot skin of her back, exposed by the low neckline of the lime silk shell she had put on last night. His movements followed hers until she could feel his breath against her neck. Her head fell back, sliding against the glass, exposing her throat and the top of her breasts for his touch, wanting his touch.

When it came, it was fingertips, delicately tracing the outline of her jaw, the softness of the skin below, the ridged column of her throat and its hollow, and she swallowed against their exploration.

She put her hand over his to hold it, to stop what he was doing to her, and he waited. She could feel the slight tremble in those long fingers. Incredibly, she found that she wanted to tighten her hold to reassure him.

"What do you want from me? Why are you all doing this?" she asked instead.

She heard the soft laugh before his lips began to move where his fingers had left off. And then his tongue. He was so gentle, touching her skin, tasting it. The softness of his hair was against her throat as his mouth followed the valley formed by her breasts.

She pulled her hand from his and pushed against his chest. He stumbled slightly, allowing her enough space to move away from the windows, away from the entrapment of his hard body.

"Why are you doing this? Who told you what to do?"

She had begun to cry, and the sound of tears in her whisper held him still for a moment. He listened to the pain and suddenly doubted her motives, doubted what he had been so sure of.

"I thought this was what you wanted," he said softly, forcing himself to smile at her. "I'm trying to be the accommodating host. I'm trying to give you what you came for. This *is* what you came for, you know."

"I don't know what you're talking about. I can't stand this. Don't you understand? I can't stand this."

"No, I don't understand." The hostility was sudden and terrifying against the memory of his gentleness. "I could never in a million years understand someone doing what you're doing. Why don't you explain to me how you can be here?"

"But I haven't done anything," she whispered, watching the cold anger build in his face.

She edged away from him, trying to put more distance between them, but his hand was like a snake, striking and holding her wrist.

"Don't you even know what you've done. Didn't he tell you what you're doing? Don't you even know?"

"Was my baby part of this? Did you plan that, too? Sound effects and then your stupid light show? How could you do that?"

Suddenly he was very still, very quiet, not even breathing into the gathering darkness.

"What are you talking about?" he asked. The tone of his question was different somehow, even more frightening.

"The baby. The crying baby. How could you do that to another human being? How could you *do* that?" she accused and saw something in his face that was recognition, realization, admission, she thought, so she hit him. Not with the flat of her hand, but as hard as she was capable, awkwardly, with the side of her fist against that dark jaw.

In his blindness he had no way to avoid the blow, and it rocked him. She saw the blood from his lip that had cut against his teeth, and she was glad.

"You bastard," she screamed, the anger erupting too suddenly, and with the onslaught of her fury, the pain that had been building behind her temples released its grip. She pounded at his face again with both hands.

Then he was holding her wrists, easily controlling her. She knew she had been able to hit him only because she had taken him by surprise, but she didn't understand why her accusation had surprised him even when he spoke.

"Don't you talk about crying babies to me," he grated, holding her wrists with viselike tightness that she knew would leave bruises. "Don't you *ever* mention my son. Anything else you want to play, I will play. But not *that*. Not ever *that*."

His anger that she would use even the death of his son wiped out the careful control. He pulled her hands up suddenly and pushed the hardness of his body against hers. She fell against the glass, the force banging it in the frame as the wind had last night. She thought they might go through, break the glass and fall out on the stones below, but it held, shivering in its framework.

He ground his body against hers, and the sensation of those hard muscles against her softness gave her a panicked desperation, so she twisted and writhed against his hold. He laughed and began to pull her up by her wrists, to raise her body so that it would rest captured between the glass and his, breast to chest, with the strength of his thighs holding hers captive. His fingers loosened slightly, seeking a better grip for the lift, and suddenly she was away from him, running across the room and to the stairs.

She knew he was following the sound of her sobbing. She tried to stop crying, to control even her breathing, but her fear overwhelmed rational thought, so by sound alone he found her. His hand gripped her bare ankle and pulled her back down the two or three steps she had managed before he came.

He fell over her, and they lay, stunned by the fall, against the unyielding hardness of the wood. He recovered first, his fury still apparent in his features and in the snarl of his lips when he lowered his head to find her mouth.

He knew somehow this was the way to punish her,

knew she was afraid of, or disgusted by, the hard masculinity of his body. Maybe because he was blind.
Maybe that was what repulsed her, and with that
thought, his desire to punish her raged even more
fiercely.

She twisted her head, and his teeth collided with her
jaw, hurting, matching the pain of the steps against her
back. She felt his fingers find the neck of the shell she
wore and tear. The strength of the silk was no match for
the fury of his hands, but tearing the shell had required
a loosening of his hold, and she used her free hands
desperately to pull up one step and then another, climbing backward and away from his body.

He stopped her by finding her long hair, and as his
groping fingers tangled in the shimmering strands, the
sudden pain brought tears. He lunged over her, his legs
locking around hers, so she was again caught and held
by the rigid muscles of his thighs.

She panicked then, hitting him again and again. One
blow knocked the dark glasses crooked and, seeing them
glint, her anger was bizarrely directed against them. She
deliberately grabbed for them. With the movement of
his head to avoid her blows, she missed her grip, and
the glasses flew off, over the edge of the riser.

She saw his face completely for the first time. The
network of scars around his eyes. And the blueness—
the same blue as his brother's—crystalline around the
blackness of unmoving pupils.

She felt her breath stop, and then her body responded
to the familiarity of that crystal blue gaze looking down
on her. She hadn't wanted a man's touch on her body
in years, and she didn't need to understand the rush of
knowledge that assured that his touch was right and necessary and hers.

He had felt, and thought he understood, the shuddering breath she took under his body. He lowered his head to find her mouth, to punish her revulsion at the scars. Instead, her lips opened, like a flower responding to the sun. The heat of her tongue moved against his.

She moaned softly once when his chest lowered to touch the hard peaks of her breasts. He deepened the kiss into her response, and she was vaguely aware of the relaxation of his muscles that had held her prisoner.

She lifted her hand to cup his head, to move her nails first through the close-cut hair at his temples and then to slide her fingers opened wide through the softness of its length, to feel the alive warmth against her palm.

She moved again up the stairs and let her hands draw his head to lower now over her breast. She didn't understand the force that guided her, but she trusted the instinct and knew again, when he touched her, that this was right.

His tongue circled her nipple, and he used his hard palm to cup and hold the softness of the aching globe. He rubbed his face against her skin. The slight roughness of his beard caused the noise she had made before to sigh again through her throat. He felt her catch her breath against the pleasure of the sensation.

"Please," she begged softly.

The throbbing pounded through his body now, no longer localized, but controlling. He hadn't intended this. Making love to her would be playing into their hands, helping them succeed with whatever they had planned, whatever stupid game Andre was playing. He had only, in his anger, wanted to frighten her. But it was different now. And it had gone too far.

She felt his tongue trace lightly down the hollow between her breasts, as gently now as when he had first touched her downstairs. His thumbs found each rib in the delicate cage and his fingers moved, following, flowing like silk against her sides. He felt the sudden concavity of her stomach beneath his trailing lips and the shiver when they found and pushed against the barrier of her waistband.

''Please,'' she whispered as before, moving her body upward again, pushing down the silk shorts, kicking them away from her feet and legs. Her hands guided his mouth against her need and, at the first movement of his tongue, she arched and cried out. His hands found her hips and held them against the involuntary motion that shook her body as the glass had shivered under the force of the storm. Finally, after a long time, she was still again. She took his wrist and pulled him with her until his body was over hers, and somehow they were at the top of the stairs.

Her fingers ripped at his shirt until he helped her remove it. She struggled with the buttons of the jeans, sobbing a little with her frustration, until finally they, too, were loose. She pushed them with her bare feet down over his thighs. Reaching, he stripped them over his feet and turned back to find her hands waiting for him.

She guided him again by touch, but it wasn't because of the blindness of the blue eyes that she watched open and then close tight against the warmth and wetness of their joining. She moved under him, and his mouth found the softness beneath her ear and trailed through the dampness of the curling strands that tangled against his face and tongue and tasted of light. She lifted her hips, responding automatically to his need, and when he felt her bare feet lock around his waist, he surged deeper, hearing the roughness of the breath that sawed through her throat at the movement.

He was afraid then that he was hurting her, but he couldn't stop. He needed to push and possess and claim. To hold against the darkness. When she whispered his name, the power came in a great rush of sensation, emotion, that rolled him against her body and caught him as the surf could, so that he was powerless against its force, drowning, beaten against its motion. He thought he cried out, and he felt her stillness at what he had said, and then she was moving again beneath him until he wasn't sure of anything but the intensity of what she was doing to him.

They lay a long time at the top of the stairs. The shadows were solid now, broken only by the afterglow of the sun reflected from below the horizon.

He thought he would never find the strength to move away from her warmth, back into the cold darkness where he had been so alone. He raised his body away from hers, lifted his chest, unconsciously, a remembered habit. He wanted to see her face so badly he felt the force of tears behind his lids. He blinked before she could see.

Her fingers touched his cheek, and she said softly, "It's all right. Everything's all right."

"There are beds," he said, smiling down at the passion-caressed voice.

"Old man," she teased, laughing, and at her tone, so sweetly familiar in the darkness, his groin tightened again. How could they know? All his memories...

When she had felt that sudden fullness, her hands had caressed over his shoulders and down the narrow waist and between their stomachs to find where the joining began. In response to what she was doing, his brief anger dissolved like mist. He moved against her, driving, pushing, until again, so strongly it shocked him, he exploded into the welcoming warmth of her response.

And at last she agreed, "There are beds. Help me find one."

He was still reluctant to move, afraid that if he let her up, he would lose her somehow. She took his hand, and he knew she was waiting for something, waiting for him to lead. Finally he pulled her to his room, deeply shadowed with the growing night.

She dropped the hand that had guided her here, and he waited, listening to the soft rustle of whatever she was doing. She moved unconsciously, as in a dream, to open the louvers and let in the night air to stir the long curtains that brushed against her bare body. Then she pulled the silk comforter off the bed.

She smiled when she felt its smoothness against her legs. She carried the silk to where he stood so still, listening, she knew, to follow her movements.

She moved the material to glide against the front of his body and watched his hardness grow with the sensation. He heard her soft laugh and reached out to find her, but she playfully eluded him. And then her fingers caught and held the groping hand.

"I'm sorry," she said, melting against him, her body as soft as the silk and, in contrast to its coolness, warm, coiling over him. She touched his shoulders, lifting for his kiss. He pulled her close and held her too hard.

"It's all right," he said, forgiving. He could hear the hoarseness of his desire in the rough whisper.

"No, it's not. I won't do that again. Ever. I promise."

He swallowed against the pain of that promise, against its necessity, and she saw and understood.

"I want to turn on the light beside the bed. I want to look at you. Please."

He took a deep breath, knowing that if he refused, she would obey, would perhaps even understand and forgive, but it would destroy something, some fragile, unexpected trust. So he nodded and felt her move away from him and heard the switch.

As the soft glow broke the twilight, her eyes sought his body, wanting to see clearly what had been hidden by the shadows on the stairs. He thought he could feel her gaze, tracing over the scars, studying each mark and burn. His stomach tightened against the dread of having her examine him.

He was unaware that she had moved, so her hands against his were a surprise. She pulled, and he followed, powerless to resist what she offered.

The sheets were cool under his overheated skin and lavender scented. He held her next to him a long time. Her body was relaxed and still, limp with the storm of what they had done to each other. She was exhausted and perhaps in pain. That thought was distasteful, and his hand caressed the clean line of shoulder and spine, the soft fullness of her hip and the silk of her thigh. She flinched once against his touch.

"I hurt you," he said, waiting.

"Yes." Her fingers found his broken lip and felt his smile under her fingertips when he understood her forgiveness.

She pushed him down, lowering her head to lick gently at the blood that had dried in the corner. Her nipple touched the smooth contour of his chest. The muscle lifted with his sudden breath, and she smiled at his response. Her lips touched his mouth, and when it opened, her tongue pushed inside, caressing the cut and then moving for a different reason.

When his eyes closed, she was glad, reassured by the naturalness of that movement, by its familiarity. She closed her own as his hands found her breasts and touched them, the delicate roughness of his fingers playing against her skin. He turned her under his body and moved over her, his weight on one elbow, his hand tracing downward from her breast to outline each rib and across the slight rise of her belly and then into the soft curls.

Her legs opened for his fingers, tenderly invading against the soreness, and they found the moisture, hers and his. He used it to touch her, gently caressing, and she trembled suddenly against the sensation. His mouth lowered to hers, open and gasping slightly with what he was doing. When he touched her lips with his tongue, she raised her head to pull against that invasion. His chest lowered into the softness of her breasts, but she was powerless to respond to what he was making her feel.

She lay still and let him touch her, brand her everywhere until he felt the distinctive movements start under his fingers. He was so tactually sensitive that he knew exactly when to replace that touch with another, exchanging softness for strength, moving with sureness against the sudden pain of his entry and using his lips against her throat and breast to reassure that pleasure would follow.

And it did. Deep, blinding waves of sensation lifted her hips to meet his and moved down nerve pathways that suddenly seemed joined to the dark, hard body that strained and drove above her. His body arched and gasped with her response until finally they lay again like flotsam on some sea, drifting against the current that had peaked and then passed, resting dreamlike together in the shallows.

He laid his palm against her face when he could move, and she lay very still, waiting for his fingers to trace her features. She thought he would want to see her in his way perhaps, but he didn't move again, resting his hand gently against her cheek.

"It's all right," she reassured. "I don't mind."

"Mind what?" he asked.

Because she could tell his thoughts had been somewhere else, not on her face at all, she was silent.

"Mind what?" he repeated, lowering his mouth to nuzzle her lips. His kiss was very soft, touching but not invading.

"I thought—" she said and stopped, knowing she was wrong and feeling foolish now with his questions.

He raised his body away from hers, propped again on his elbow and waited.

"What did you think?" he asked and felt her take a deep breath before she whispered.

"I thought you wanted to touch my face. To see what I look like."

His stillness was as humiliating as she could have imagined. He said nothing for a long time, wondering again at last, finally capable of thought again, about the motives behind the unexpected invitation, and then his fingers trailed over her nose and eyelids and finally down the ridge of her cheek where they stopped with heart-breaking suddenness.

"I don't do that very well," he said finally, the bitterness carefully hidden. "Maybe everybody else can, but I can't tell anything."

They lay a long time, still touching. Finally he lowered his body and, against all his careful logic, he gathered her to lie close along his length. Because he wanted her there.

She left on the light that she knew he had forgotten and watched him until finally they both slept.

the frenchy and Lizard ... way well be at the trey to be! ... forth, already sel outbox. The print as there.

try to hear and hear lying in the coth, be had brought or well in bold, half it stood the bearing

Chapter Five

She awoke to his body moving over hers, and she shifted automatically to welcome the weight, the roughness of the hair on his legs, the passage of his hands, at once familiar and strange, against her body. Her mouth sought his and clung as he pushed against her, deeper than before, harder, feeding on her response and his own long denial.

She held him through the shuddering climax, sated herself, satisfied by his design before his own release, but she had wanted the movement of his body beneath her hands, the panting effort. Finally he kissed her again and lay beside her, and she smiled.

"They thought I'd been raped. Obviously they were wrong." He heard the low whisper, feeling the chill of its wrongness.

"Who thought you'd been raped?" he said, wishing again he could watch her face when she talked to him. He put his hand instead on her breast and felt the heartbeat slow under his fingers.

"The doctors. They thought it explained everything."

She let what she had said lie between them, but he waited. There were enough raw places in his own soul. He didn't want to probe anyone else's, even someone...

He buried that thought and slid his hand slowly down her body and his lips found the pulse in her temple instead. She moved back away from his mouth to watch the faint furrow form between his brows. When she smoothed it with her fingers, he turned his head slightly, moving away from her hand.

"Why do you wear the glasses?" she asked. "You have beautiful eyes."

He laughed, but she could hear the surprise. "Habit, I suppose. The scars. To hide behind. I don't know."

"There are no scars," she lied. "Or perhaps a few, so faded they're invisible."

"There are scars, and you can see them. They wanted me to have them removed. Plastic surgery. It seemed unnecessary. No one sees them."

"I don't mind them," she said, raising her head to touch his eyes with her lips, and he closed his lids beneath their soft caress. "You close your eyes when you kiss me. Did you know that?"

"No," he said, and she again saw his smile.

"Do you do that when you make love to other women? Do you close your eyes when you kiss them?"

"I don't make love to anyone. I don't want to make love to anyone else," he said softly.

"I don't want you to," she whispered.

"I know." Because he found he had to know, he asked into the silence, "Why did they think you'd been raped?"

"I was sick a long time. I told your sister's lawyer about it. I didn't hide it."

"Go on. It's all right."

"Our grandmothers would have called it a nervous breakdown. The doctors said an episodic depression. I couldn't remember. It was a long time ago."

"And you'd been hurt?"

"Not like that. Not what you're thinking. I couldn't remember anything. Not even how to talk. But they all talked to me in French," she said, laughing. "I wondered, afterward, if I would have responded sooner if I had understood anything they said."

"But—"

"If I knew French then, I'd forgotten it. All I remembered was English. So what they said meant nothing. For a long time. Finally I guess they said things often enough, or I recovered from whatever had happened enough...then they tried to make me remember what had happened."

"And you didn't? You never did?"

"No. So they took what they knew and decided that I'd been raped. They even tried to work with me, therapy, against that fear, but I wasn't afraid of that. I didn't know how to tell them what I *was* afraid of. I didn't *know*."

"Why did they think you'd been raped?"

She was quiet a long time, but he waited, moving his hand gently over her breasts again.

"I'd had a baby. Only a short time before. I couldn't stand the smell of spirits. Couldn't stand the sound of raised voices, of anger," she said.

He felt and then denied the response of his heart to that whisper. She continued even more softly, "I wouldn't let anyone touch me, not even the doctors, so they decided that someone had raped me. Someone drunk and cruel and angry," she finished calmly, their story, and not hers. "I knew it wasn't rape, but I didn't know what had happened. I couldn't tell them what I thought."

"What did you think?" he asked, knowing what she

would say, dreading the confirmation of her part in this, but he was wrong and confused again.

"I thought I must have let my baby die. That maybe I was drunk and had left the baby to die. I could hear him crying, but I couldn't find him. I tried, but I couldn't find him. And finally, after a long time, he didn't cry anymore," her voice faded. He was surprised when she spoke again, thinking the explanation was ended. "Except sometimes in a nightmare I hear him crying."

"Is that what you meant downstairs?"

"I had a nightmare the first night here. I hadn't heard him in a long time."

He was so still that she was afraid. She shouldn't have told him. She had lived with the horror of what she must have done so long that she thought he could perhaps accept, as she had, the knowledge that it was her responsibility and that she must simply bear, somehow, the awfulness of that responsibility.

"Whatever I did," she said, telling him what she had finally decided after the long darkness she had condemned herself to, "I didn't mean to do. I didn't *want* to do. I was afraid of that for a long time, but that's not what happened. I know now I didn't kill my baby deliberately. I can't prove that to you, but it's true."

He knew suddenly that he had to leave, to get away from the whispering pain in her voice. To get away from the desire to believe her. Just get away and think. He moved over her body and out of the bed. He opened the door to the room and left. He found their clothes on the stairs and dressed there in the growing light of dawn, carefully sweeping the stairs, hunting a long time to make certain nothing remained. He couldn't be sure what she'd had on. He couldn't remember anything but tearing the blouse, and he found only it and the shorts.

No underwear. And he couldn't find his glasses. He took her clothes with him into the kitchen and then into the laundry room, hiding them finally at the bottom of the half-full hamper.

He came back into the kitchen, but when he heard a door close, he thought that she had gone to the patio. He knew he'd been cruel to leave her. He could imagine what she was thinking. He hurried to catch her while he could still hear her feet against the stones. He would never find her if she reached the beach.

The cook greeted him happily as he came through the kitchen door, commenting about the storm, and then he heard Andre's voice from the steps below cheerfully yelling instructions to the boy who had begun moving the furniture back onto the patio. Andre was inside before he could decide what to do.

"You weren't worried, were you? I told Suzanne you wouldn't be. She had a telegram, something about the estate. She had to fly to Paris, but she said not to forget about the guests tonight. She gave the cook a long list of instructions, so I don't know what you're supposed to do. She suggested you ask Caroline to play hostess."

"Where were you yesterday?" he asked.

"I decided to go to Guadeloupe. Some of us aren't ready for the monastery yet. What happened to your face?" Andre asked, touching the bruise beside his mouth.

He flinched away from his brother's fingers, wondering if Andre could know.

"I fell," he said.

"I didn't do it," Andre denied, laughing. "I've been especially careful lately. We can't do without you. Suzanne and I have already proven that. I didn't warn our houseguest. I thought Suzanne would. Do I need to—"

"No, I just fell. I was careless. It wasn't anyone's fault." He didn't want Andre to say anything to her. He wondered suddenly if she would hear their voices. If she would know Andre was back.

"I'm going up to change for work. I'll be back in plenty of time for dinner. Leave it to Suzanne to invite a crew and then disappear."

He could hear Andre moving to the stair and then his steps stopped.

"I found your glasses. They're broken. Did you fall on the stairs? Julien, are you all right? I saw you were limping, but—"

"I'm all right."

"Do you want these?" Andre asked. Julien could hear the concern in his brother's voice.

"No," he forced himself to answer, "I have a pair somewhere. You could buy another spare today for me."

"Of course," Andre said. "Do you want me to get the other glasses? Are they in your office?"

"It's all right. I'll find them later."

"But Caroline's up. I hear her now upstairs. You better let me find them before she comes down."

"It doesn't matter," he said, listening for her, his face turned to the stairs, and hearing nothing, in spite of his brother's words.

"Look, we're all used to your eyes, and to the scars, but I think that you better... I just don't know how she's going to deal with all that. You look so normal with the glasses. She won't be expecting the rest. Let me find them for you," Andre said, putting his arm on his brother's shoulder.

"Andre?" Caroline said from the top of the stairs. "I thought I heard your voice. Is Suzanne there?"

Julien pulled his shoulder from Andre's grip and

walked across the cool tile to his office. He heard behind him his brother's laughing explanation of the storm and the telegram and Suzanne's request for the dinner. He closed the door and sat in the chair behind his desk and carefully felt the ridges of scar tissue that surrounded his eyes.

DINNER PARTIES were his own personal form of purgatory. He knew that he should refuse when Suzanne planned them. To hell with whatever position she thought they had to maintain. These people couldn't care less if they never saw him again. The old days of that kind of responsibility were gone. His father perhaps, and certainly his grandfather, had needed to do this. But not him.

Dinner was almost over, and he had done his share of conversation, at being the perfect host. These were all old acquaintances, so there was no strain to overcome. The conversation eddied around him. He could hear Andre's voice, slightly relaxed with the wine, and occasionally her voice from the other end of the table.

"...a crying baby..."

The words came laughing at him out of some jumble of conversation. His hand moved suddenly, upsetting a glass. His concentration was so broken from trying to hear what she might be saying that he didn't even know *which* glass, and then Andre's fingers were there, moving them all away from his hand, which he had stilled immediately.

"It's only water," Andre said beside him. "Nothing's hurt. No harm done." And he could breathe again.

He heard the flutterings of the conversations start, and then her voice, clearly, through the stirrings.

"It's wine. Red wine. No one else is affected. The

table is slightly damp, but your shirt was splashed, stained.'' In the returning silence, he heard a gasp from the subprefecture's wife.

He stood, looking down the table, and spoke directly to her, "Thank you." And to his guests, "If you'll excuse me, I'll change and meet you on the patio. Andre, would you tell them to serve the dessert, please."

He touched the table and then the back of his chair to be sure. He could feel the hot flush growing under his skin, so he moved quickly away from the embarrassed silence and across to the stairs. He put his hand on the rail and hurried, as he had done to her room, away from the murmur behind him. He thought he could hear Andre's voice, but he found he didn't want to know what he might be saying.

He reached his suite and closed his door, leaning against it. He waited a long time for the humiliation to fade and wondered that he could still feel it, could still care after all this time. What could it possibly matter?

Finally he removed his jacket and tie and then the shirt. He ran his fingers over the dampness as if he could determine through his fingertips the truth of what she had said. He closed his eyes and dropped the shirt. He found another in the closet, carefully marked, but he checked it twice to be sure of the color and style. He shrugged it on, feeling the soreness. His back and leg had hurt like hell all day. Finally, before the guests arrived, he had taken some of the pain medication he tried to avoid.

"Old man," Kerri had always called him, mocking the difference in their ages. It was true now. An old man at thirty-six, put together with pins and screws. *Too old to take a woman on the stairs.* He thought about the phrase he'd just used, and knew he avoided what they had called it this morning. Making love. He had forgotten a lot this morning and last night.

Now he had had long hours to think about what she had told him. He had been so sure yesterday. Then he had lost that surety in her body, in her responses. He didn't understand why the lovemaking had confused him. He had known what she was supposed to do. He had expected exactly what had happened between them. What he didn't understand was how she could make him feel like he did, want her like he did. How she could feel so right under his body. Familiar. That was what frightened him. *God, she was so familiar.*

He closed his eyes, forcing his fingers to button the shirt and then, to be safe, he chose another tie of the same color. He found the coat and made himself open the door to his room before he could think about having to face the guests. He walked to the stairs, pulling his cuffs down, and her hand touched his arm. He wondered that he hadn't been aware of the scent of her hair before she touched him.

"I'm sorry," she said. He felt her hand move, caressing, against the material of his sleeve.

"I'm very grateful, actually, for what you did."

"I was wrong. Andre told me they're old friends. No one would have minded. I didn't understand."

"*I* would have minded," he said. "I would have minded a great deal, and Andre should have known that."

"He was only trying to do the kindest thing. The easiest for you," she said, hating the tightness of his face. "And I ruined it. They were all angry. They really are friends."

"They don't understand."

"They try. They care."

"Would you want to stand around all night facing people, not knowing..." He had felt the tension in her fingers at his growing anger. When he spoke again, his voice was calm and indifferent. "It doesn't matter. Let it go. Forget it. It's not worth all this angst. It goes with the territory."

He pulled his sleeve away from her hand and moved to the stairs, but she never came down again.

FINALLY, THE GUESTS were gone. He was drinking a Scotch, free to relax the rigid care he exercised in public. It was his second drink, taken against the pain that grew because he hadn't stretched out the old injuries. He had sat instead in his office, pretending to work, and had sat again tonight with his guests, and he ached in all the old, familiar places.

"Did you enjoy yourself?" Andre asked as he took his glass to freshen the drink. He listened to the pleasant sounds of ice moving and felt the alcohol begin, finally, to relax the tension.

"God, no. Are you serious? That's something to get through. No more. Remind me to tell Suzanne."

The glass was replaced in his hand, and Andre stood beside his chair. "I don't mean tonight," he corrected, laughing. "Last night. That must have been a hell of a storm. You're moving like an old man and, my God, the bruises on her back. Where did you take her? On the rocks? In the lightning and the rain?" The laugh was brotherly, but the touch on his shoulder was from some club room, men talking about the tennis tart. His eyes closed behind the dark lenses.

"I don't know what you mean," he said, working at keeping his voice neutral. "What's wrong with her back?"

"Nothing that wouldn't have been less obvious in a dress cut higher. I don't think anybody else noticed. I saw her when she first came down, and I had seen you, so I put things together."

"And you were wrong."

Andre's disbelieving laugh grated. "You were always like that," he said. "Even with the ones we eventually shared, you never would compare notes. Personally I think she's a little obvious. I prefer the chase. She seems too easy, *too* available. However, since you don't have to worry about any consequences from taking what's offered..." Andre's mocking voice continued, still jarring against his memories of last night. "I'm only sorry I didn't stick around for the storm. Some women..."

Julien stood suddenly and walked across the echoing tile. He heard Andre calling his name, but he ignored him and moved up the stairs, away from the words, leaving his brother alone.

THE SOUND TRAILED away before she was sure again. She had not been dreaming about the baby. Her hands had not been reaching, searching in the dark rooms for the child. The suddenness of her awakening left, for once, the dream clearly etched on her conscious mind. She had been touching Julien's face as he smiled down at her. She had felt the hard pressure of his body inside, moving within her. In her dream she had seen his eyes, and they weren't scarred as they were now. She closed her own to block the images, moving her cold hands to caress her own shoulders, and she waited for what she knew would come again. As the sound trembled out of the blackness, she gasped with the pain, although she had been expecting it, thought she was prepared. She had been right. This was no nightmare.

She willed her body to wait. It had been a mistake to leave her room before, to cry in the hallway. To scream against this assault there where they could hear. She waited a long time, but there was no sound now. She rose and went to the window and finally she was rewarded. Julien moved in the darkness across the tiles and into the pool, visible only as a blur of lighter motion. She watched the rhythmic lift and descent of his arms, pale against the darkness of the water. Finally when she could stand it no longer, she moved down the silent hall and across the cool tiles.

She slipped off her gown and slid nude into the warm water. She was surprised by its depth. She struggled a moment and then began to swim to the shape that was gliding swiftly back and forth against the gently moving warmth. He stopped, warned perhaps by her motion against the familiar pressure of the water's passage on his body. She touched his shoulder, exposed above the darkness that lapped against his chest. She wondered why she had come, and then his arms closed around her and pulled her tightly against him. She could feel the accelerated heartbeat from his exertions.

"What are you doing here?" he said, but his mouth found hers, so she couldn't answer.

She finally drew away and touched his face. "I don't know. I wanted to make it right between us. I needed it to be right. I thought—"

"That you'd let me take you again? Here in the garden? And then it would be all right? I wouldn't be able to think—just like before. The garden's a good choice. Very romantic. The smells are especially nice for a blind man. The tiles, however, may be a little difficult for your back. Andre's very observant. I wonder how many of the others were. Is that part of the plan?"

"I don't understand."

"Or maybe here in the water. That's good. Easier for me actually. The water will help with your weight and its warmth eases the pain. Here," he said. He took her hand and pressed it against his hip and then ran it down the long bone of his thigh. "Maybe a massage when we're through. You can tell me how you'd like to care for me, to begin to make up for all…" The harsh voice stopped and she waited. When he spoke again, he had regained some control.

"Only I don't think with that part of my body, so keeping me occupied that way isn't going to work again. In spite of your many talents," he said bitterly. "You tell Andre that I suddenly find I'm tired of all this. Let's get on with the rest. Whatever the hell the rest is. Will you tell him that for me?"

He jerked his shoulders from her grip, and she floundered in the too-deep water, and then, pulling himself out of the pool with a single motion of those hard arms, he was gone. She could still see the dark marks left by the water from his feet on the tiles that led away from the pool.

SHE WAS PACKED, her bags waiting beside the door when Andre came whistling up the stairs that afternoon. She saw the surprise on his face and spoke before he could express whatever other emotions began to play there.

"Suzanne's gone, so I have nothing to do. There's no use in my staying. I need to leave."

He frowned a little as if trying to understand. Then his fingers touched her hand that was clenched whitely around the handle of her purse.

"Suzanne will be back in a few days. Relax. No one expects you to work now. Rest by the pool. Do whatever

you want. Enjoy the quiet. If I know my sister, she'll
have a thousand things for you to do when she gets back.
Until then, it's the tropics. Remember what I told you.''
He smiled at her, the flash of white teeth beautiful
against the brown of his lean cheeks, the laughing blue
eyes.

"Your brother said to tell you he's tired of this." She
let the words fall into his laughter and was satisfied to
watch the effect on his face. She didn't understand why
she needed to gauge his reaction to those words. She
had known, but the reason had faded back into the mist
again before she could understand its importance. All
she was sure of now was his shock. He hid it quickly,
but the surprise had briefly been very evident.

"I'm sorry he said that to you. He's a very difficult
man to understand. He was hurt in so many ways. I'd
like to explain if you'll let me."

She waited, wondering what he would say. She found
that she wanted to hear whatever explanation he intended to offer, and so she nodded. He took her arm,
leading her, not to the couch as she expected, but to the
kitchen with its bright whiteness. It seemed somehow
incongruous for what she expected. He waited until they
were seated, facing each other over the wooden top of
the island.

"My brother..." he began. Then he smiled, shaking
his head. "My brother was perfect. I loved him so much.
Our father died when I was still a teenager. We're only
half brothers, really." He looked up suddenly. "Did you
know that?" he asked, and she shook her head.

"No one remembers that now. Suzanne and Julien's
mother died very tragically, slowly and painfully from
bone cancer. Father married my mother too quickly.
They should have resented it, and I think Suzanne did.

She was old enough to be jealous of another woman in her father's life. It was natural, and my mother accepted that. Julien, however, was kind, concerned that she feel welcomed. Even as a child he tried to include her in everything, to go to her with his achievements and successes, even the failures. She said he made up a few of those to allow her to comfort him. She adored him, loved him like her own son.

"When I was born, she was afraid he'd feel threatened. Instead, he adopted me. He was more a father than my father, who was always busy running the businesses. Julien was never too busy. He taught me to walk, she said, endlessly patient. To ride, to drive, to fly—everything he did so effortlessly. When Mother died, he also taught me how to deal with that. He'd been through it all already, more painfully perhaps than my experience. When my father died, it wasn't as bad because, I suppose..."

She waited, but he left that thought and moved to what she had expected, what she'd heard from Suzanne.

"He married a girl, an American." Even now the negative movement of his head expressed disbelief that his brother could do that. "She was so unsuited to him. Volatile and childish. Intimidated, maybe, by his wealth, his position. She embarrassed him a thousand times, and they said he would simply smile at her, touch her hand or shoulder and explain. I heard she once struck him in public. Another time she threw a glass of wine in his face. That was at home, a small dinner party for close friends, but still, they couldn't stop talking about it, about her. They said he danced with her after he'd changed clothes. He held her against him and protected her from everyone's outrage. He always protected her. Endlessly patient."

"As he had been with you?" she suggested softly. The swift anger flashed in his eyes and was carefully masked.

"It wasn't the same. I was a child, his brother, and I didn't do to him what she did."

"No," she said, "of course not. I'm sorry." She cleared the darkness from her voice and mind. "I don't understand why you're telling me this."

"She blinded him, crippled him—"

"He's not crippled," she denied, unthinkingly.

"Crippled in so many ways." The defiance of what she had said was deliberate. "You wouldn't know, but he's so changed, so different. He laughed then. Women adored him, and he could have had any of them. I don't know why he wanted her. She was beneath him, so worthless compared to him. He could have had anyone. We didn't need her. He didn't." She heard the anger and the bitterness build and, fearing that, tried to move him past it with her question.

"How did she blind him?" she said. She wasn't sure why she needed to hear this again, to compare Andre's version to what Suzanne had told her, but she knew she did.

"They were at a palace reception in Monaco. The roads are notorious."

As he said that, images flickered in her mind. A white convertible. A woman with long blond hair was behind the wheel, but she couldn't visualize the face of the man beside her. She tried to think. A movie. Something about a thief, she thought, but she couldn't remember what happened in the story. Her head began to ache with the effort, so she pushed the scene away and concentrated instead on what Andre was saying.

"She'd come alone because she couldn't get ready in

time. Julien had to be there, so he went on. She drank too much and thought he was paying attention to some woman at the party. She left, in a temper, another tantrum. He followed and got into her car with her. She wrecked only a few miles down. She wasn't hurt, but Julien was thrown from the car. He shouldn't have been in the car at all. He didn't have to follow her. If only he had stayed at the reception—"

"Then no one would have been hurt," she interrupted softly.

"Not Julien," he said, looking up in surprise.

"You said she wasn't injured. If he hadn't been in the car, then no one would have been hurt in the wreck." She watched the import of that thought move through his brain, and then she smiled at him.

"But he loved her. And so he followed," she finished quietly.

"When it was over, when we knew what he was going to be like, what he faced to ever again lead any kind of normal life, she walked away. I tried to protect him. I didn't want him to know that she couldn't live with him like he was. God, if you'd only watched him those months. So much pain. I'm the one who held him while he struggled to make those shattered bones move again—crutches and then canes. And finally, after more than a year, he could walk. So they gave him a different kind of cane."

She swallowed, sickened at what was in his voice, in his eyes.

"He hates it. He hates it all, and yet he just goes on. He works, runs the businesses. They're so complex, but he still does that well. He lives like a hermit in Paris. He doesn't go out. He never entertains. He'll never marry again." The dark conviction echoed through Andre's voice. He controlled himself and said again, "It's all her fault. I'm sorry he's treated you badly. Everything's so hard for him. Just stay away from him. He'll leave you alone, I think. I'll speak to him if you want me to."

She smiled again, shaking her head, "Don't you think I should leave? Don't you think that's best?"

"No, I don't," he said. His eyes were serious when he touched her face with gentle fingertips. "I'm sorry this happened. Stay until Suzanne gets back. Be patient and try to understand. I know he hurt you, but surely you can understand. I shouldn't have left you alone here. I never dreamed that he would… It's so out of character. Really. He won't bother you. Just wait for Suzanne."

He caressed her cheek gently. She closed her eyes, and turned her face away from the comfort of those long fingers. Her eyes were still closed when his lips touched hers, and she moved back and simply nodded. Maybe he was right. If she waited and stayed out of Julien's way, perhaps it would be all right.

"Would you like to go out in the boat this afternoon?" he asked, suddenly smiling again.

"It looks like it might rain," she said, "and it's rough."

"Not really. It will calm just before sunset and the water will be very beautiful. Let me show you. You've not seen anything of the islands. We could have dinner somewhere and then come back in the moonlight. I'd like to take you. You deserve to enjoy your time here."

She wondered briefly at the wisdom of accepting his invitation, and then decided he was right. She deserved this, so she smiled and nodded.

Chapter Six

She dressed carefully, choosing a long, flowing cotton skirt, the material so fine she could see the shadow of her legs through the greens and blues that bled together like the colors of the sea. Her top was low necked and white, tight at the waist and ruffled over her breasts and shoulders. She studied the woman reflected in the mirror a long time, and then she walked to the window and looked down at the garden pool. Everything was bright in the afternoon heat. There was no mystery as there had been this morning. She didn't really understand why she was going with Andre, except for what Julien had said.

If this is what he wants, then this is what I'll give him, she thought. In her anger with him, she pulled the louvers together too hard, the echoing noise pounding against her skull. She closed her eyes, fighting the pain, a reminder that anger wasn't allowed. She wondered why her head hadn't hurt before, when she'd hit him. It was all so strange. Whatever was happening here. Sometimes she thought she knew what things meant, and then they just slipped away, drifted out of her head like smoke.

She had told Andre she'd meet him downstairs, and all at once she was in a hurry to get away. She knew now how Suzanne had felt on Saturday: the need to get out of this house.

It wasn't Andre at the foot of the stairs. Julien waited there, and she stopped before she reached the bottom. She hated the way the sunlight glinted off the dark glasses when he raised his face to her, as if he could see her.

"Where are you going?" he asked.

"With Andre. On the boat and out to eat. He invited me. And since you said—" She stopped because she didn't want to think about what he'd said.

"Since I said what?"

"That you were tired of me. That it was time for whatever came next, we decided that he'd take me sight-seeing."

"And I'm supposed to be jealous. Is that it? You have to help me with this. I'm not sure exactly what's expected of me. Sometimes I miss things that anyone else would see. You go with Andre and I stay here, seething with jealousy, perhaps?"

"Stop it," she said fiercely, not understanding his mockery.

"Then he makes love to you. Or is it enough for me just to think that? Am I supposed to be imagining every bump and grind of your body under his? And the sound effects? You *do* have very nice sound effects. I will give you that." His voice was very low and seductive, but she had to control the urge to strike again at his face, at the slow, sardonic smile that was directed at her.

"And then what?" he continued sarcastically. "What will we play next? You have to help the blind man follow all the cues. 'Take me with you, wife,'" he quoted lightly. "That's *Romeo and Juliet*, I think. Isn't it?"

"I don't know. You *know* I don't know any of that.

You're the one..." She lowered her head against the onslaught of pain, gasped and held the rail. Whatever thought had produced those words faded and was lost in its agony.

When the tension around her skull finally began to ease, the vice grip over her temples relaxing, the fragment of memory was gone. She remembered only what he'd said.

"Wife?" she repeated it softly, head still lowered. "Andre said...he told me it was your *wife* who blinded you." She forced herself to raise her eyes, forced herself to look at him. There was no laughter now in his face. It was absolutely clear of mockery, of any emotion she could read.

Compelled by some impetus she didn't understand, she moved down the steps that separated them. She stood before him and, reaching up, pulled off the hated glasses before he knew what she was doing. He flinched and then was still, locking those blind eyes on her face. She closed her lids to block the tears and had to force herself to reopen them.

"If that's true, maybe it's *Lear* you mean," she said very softly. She saw him flinch again, saw the impact of her words move across the dark muscles and scars of his face, but not into his eyes. Never again to see emotion in his eyes.

"'Dark and comfortless,'" he quoted softly, and she watched him gather control. Finally he smiled. "But she would never watch *Lear*."

"They were all so stupid," she said softly, remembering. She had gone to a performance last year in Paris, seeing the playbill and slipping into the darkened theater without any idea of why she was there. Despite what she had felt, she had stayed to the end, hating it. "So stupid and so proud."

He stood absolutely motionless, and then he said, just as quietly, "Maybe pride was all they had left."

She thought about that. Finally she took his hand and put the glasses, folded, into it. "I told you that you don't need these."

She moved past him, close enough for him to feel her skirt against his legs, like the silk comforter. He wanted her so suddenly that he hurt, ached against the confines of the tight jeans. He caught at her hand and missed. He cursed his stupid blindness that was going to allow her to go with his brother.

He deliberately groped in the air, reaching for her, willing her to come to him. He heard her breathe, but before he could react to that sound, she had caught his hand. He held her fingers, feeling the bones, longer than Suzanne's, trying desperately to remember if they were right. Was it possible? He closed his heart to that sudden hope, but dear God, how could she know so much? Even her response to his mocking question had been a familiar refrain, echoing Kerri's insecurities.

He heard Andre's door close upstairs, and he knew, no matter what, he didn't want her to go with his brother. He pulled her to him and felt her melt against him, touch him briefly where he ached for her. He pushed into her hand, and her mouth was under his, just as before. He could hear Andre above them moving toward the stairs.

He lifted his mouth away and whispered, "Don't go. God, please don't go. Don't go with him."

She touched his face, caressing. They both heard Andre begin to run lightly down the wooden steps. She broke away from Julien, and he missed where she had moved with the sound of Andre's feet coming nearer on the risers.

"The line is, I believe, 'Am I interrupting something?'" Andre said into the heavy atmosphere. "Have our plans changed?" he asked her lightly.

"I don't know," his brother answered, the anger shimmering beneath the politeness. "I was just trying to figure out what this particular phase of the plan involved. What my role is supposed to be. But I wasn't getting any answers."

"No," she said, defeated by his switch from seduction and tenderness to accusation. She cleared the huskiness from her throat. "Nothing's changed, Andre. Not unless you want it to," she spoke more strongly.

"*I* don't want it to," Andre said. He sounded surprised that she would think so. "I'm looking forward to showing you something of the islands."

He turned to look at his brother who was rigid as stone, the glasses still in his hand. They watched as he unfolded them and put them over his eyes. She turned away then and heard Andre speak to him, "I thought we'd eat at Tatie Babette's. Do you want to go? We'll get better service if big brother goes," he explained to her and laughed. He touched Julien's shoulder with brotherly affection, but he shook his head.

"Not tonight. Another trip perhaps. Have a good time. And be careful. There's a storm brewing."

"Julien's better than the weather service. He feels storms before you can see any evidence. It saves wear and tear on the patio furniture."

She remembered it had been moved before and asked, "Did you know the storm was coming Saturday night?"

Andre thought she was still talking to him. "Of course, but Suzanne wanted to go, anyway. I thought we could get back. Julien said we'd have time, but it hit too quickly. You missed that one, big brother,'' Andre said laughing, but she knew he hadn't. He had wanted them away so he could play his trick with the lights. So he could seduce her. She had made that remarkably easy, and she still didn't understand why.

"You'd better get started,'' Julien said, turning to walk across to his office.

"Are you sure—'' Andre began again.

"I don't want to go with you. Show her the scenery. All the scenery.'' She could hear the bitterness and the anger.

When he was gone and the door closed behind him, Andre comforted softly, "It's all right.''

She shivered when he touched her spine, the thumb moving seductively as before. This time, however, she stepped away. He asked, the frown marring the handsome planes of his face, "You're not afraid of him, are you? He won't hurt you. I won't let him hurt you. He just gets angry sometimes at his limitations. At what was done to him. Surely you can understand that anger.''

She turned to him and wanted to scream that *he* didn't understand. None of them seemed to know what he felt. They all did it wrong. So wrong.

And you're going to do it right, she mocked herself. *You, who have never done anything right in your life, are going to make it all right for him.*

She shook her head at the ridiculousness of that intent, but Andre misinterpreted her movement and, smiling, he gathered her close. As he hugged her, she relaxed and let his arms comfort as they had once before. They weren't the right arms, but she had nothing else.

THEY WENT to the restaurant first to place their order, and then Andre took her on a tour of the main attractions of the island while the meal was prepared. Even the food for their dinner would be purchased in the market *after* they'd ordered.

They drove to the distilleries and saw cane fields in the afternoon haze. He took her to the Galeries and they listened to the surf pound there as it did at his brother's house. And then to caves that frightened her with their darkness. She didn't like them, and Andre laughed at her anxiety to get back to the sunlight. There were caves on Julien's island, he told her, but no one ever went there. The tide filled them, so it was too dangerous. In the sun nothing could seem threatening. She relaxed under the beauty of the island and Andre's undemanding companionship. There were no sexual overtures, no undertones. She enjoyed the afternoon. Later they ate the delicious food as he drank the wine he had chosen, not, it seemed, as sensitive as his brother had been to her refusal to join him.

In the late afternoon they walked on the beach, and he insisted on holding her sandals and his shoes in his hand, leaving her free and unencumbered, like a child. As she ran against the wind, she realized that she had forgotten what it felt like to be free, to let someone else carry the burdens. She had forfeited that privilege so long ago. And now, for the first time in years, in the heat and beauty of these islands, she was free to remember how it had felt.

The wind was the first reminder of Julien's prediction, and by the time they had driven back down the coast to the boat, even she could smell the hint of rain and electricity in the air. She was still too relaxed to worry as she watched Andre's hands on the lines. It was very beautiful in the fading light, so she sat where he told her to in the boat and didn't think about the approaching storm.

The water moved beneath her trailing fingers. The noise the wind made in the sail was something that she knew she had heard before, the sound pushing at her mind, moving through the mist of her dreams. She didn't try to remember, not wanting the brutality of the pain. Instead, she relaxed against the hiss and snap of the cloth. Andre smiled at her when she took off her sandals again and dropped her feet into the warmth of the blue-green water. She leaned back and locked her hands on either side of the seat, allowing the wind to carry the long strands away from her face. The fragrance of her hair drifted across the deck even against the smell of salt.

The rain began suddenly, meeting the thrust of the skating boat, pelting them with the size of the drops, but she laughed as he hurried to adjust the sail. The cloud was black, and they were into the darkness before she was ready. She held on to the suddenly plunging boat that shook like a hard-ridden horse in the gale. Only then was she frightened. As she moved to take her feet back inside, Andre made some adjustment to the sail. Somehow the swinging boom caught her body as she turned, and suddenly she was in the water.

Choking against the waves breaking over her head before she could get a breath, she gasped, taking in more of the burning salt, streaming into her nose and throat, aching, so that she could think of nothing but fighting against its sting.

She finally managed to get her head up between the waves to breathe and cough up the agony. She knew she was going to die in this warm water, and she wondered why she was fighting against something that she had thought so often about, would have welcomed not so long ago.

Giving up life was against all she had been taught. It profaned everything her grandfather had held sacred, so she had rejected that easy escape then as she rejected it now, fighting desperately to breathe.

Her eyes were still blinded by the water, but she was aware enough to hold her breath this time as the wave washed over. Then she was again in the gentle slough between them. *Breathe,* she commanded her lungs, and they obeyed and held through the next. She got the rhythm and finally had time to search for the boat. There was only blackness, but she couldn't see very far because of the rain and the coming of the next wave. When it broke over her this time, she lifted her body, not fighting it, but riding.

It was very dark now in the heart of the storm. She knew it would be hard for him to see her in the veil of the driving rain. She was in control enough now to be aware of the long skirt tangling about her legs, hindering her movements. She fumbled with the band, but without the lift of her arms, the next wave choked her again. She pushed up, panicked once more, and waited until she could breathe. In her effort to remove the skirt, she was more careful this time to fit her movements to the lift of the waves. Even with the force of the storm there was a rhythm to them. Moving over her body. When she realized what that movement reminded her of, she knew that she didn't want it to end here in the warmth of the ocean. For the first time in so long, she wanted something. Wanted it enough to fight, to push against the constraints that locked her mind and her memories, banding her very soul with pain.

The skirt came free suddenly, and she kicked against

its sodden weight until it was loose, gone into the waters it had matched. Although its weight had not been much, she felt freer. She began to swim, not fighting against the waves, but moving with them. She thought they had been a very long way from the shore, but if she didn't tire and if nothing attacked her in the dark waters, perhaps she could reach the islands, could survive. She wondered if Andre were still looking for her. If she were swimming away from the circling boat. But she couldn't think about that now.

She swam for what seemed an eternity, but whenever she tried to stop and look, there was only the swell of the next wave. There were no lights to head for. At least none visible in her dark world of salt burn and pitch of water. And she was tiring. She could feel it in her shoulders first and then in her arms. They were heavy, and, in spite of her exertions, the water was chilling now, or perhaps it was the rain that beat against her, tiring her, too. She tried to think about anything she had read that might help. When she remembered, she turned to float, but the slap of the waves against her face made her feel the way she had at first. She knew at last that she was probably, even after all she had done, going to die. She regretted it bitterly, wanting to weep for her dying and because no one would care.

She almost missed her chance in her self-pity. Her grandfather, gently chiding, would have made a lecture out of that. She had thought it was a piece of driftwood or a fish, but the pain of the salt in the scrape jolted her numb mind enough to realize that it was a rock, jutting out of the darkness of the water and she was being carried past. She turned and used all her remaining strength to go back. The next wave broke against it, a line of white in the black sea to guide her. Her hands caught

and held, and she pulled herself across it, in spite of the
cutting edges. As her blouse and the skin beneath it
ripped, she thought about the blood that would seep into
the water. She didn't even know if there were sharks in
these waters. What could it matter to someone who had
only shortly before decided she was going to drown?
She was safe for now.

She lay across her little island, panting with tiredness.
She didn't know how long she lay there, and when they
came, she was only dimly aware of the shouting voices
and the lights. And finally someone's hands pulling her
off the rock. It hurt a lot, and she cried with the pain,
but no one seemed to think that was strange, so she cried
a long time, wrapped in a blanket. They said Andre had
gone for help. Someone went back to Terre de Haut to
tell the other fishermen that she had been found, but they
were going to take her home, to *monsieur le duc*. She
nodded her agreement, knowing that was right.

She was still crying when they brought her up the long
steps to the front of the house. The lights were bright
against the dark of the flagstones. She heard them explaining to the servants, and then his voice, questioning.
Everything was quiet while only one voice explained to
him. He took her in his arms, and she could feel his
uneven stride as he walked. She tried to protest, but he
ignored her, carrying her easily to her room. When he
laid her on the bed, she could see the red on his white
shirt in the low light of the lamp, but she didn't understand why it was there. She had told him. At the party.
They had all been angry. Andre had been angry.

"You didn't change your shirt," she tried to say, but
her lips were too cold.

He was rubbing her feet with a rough towel and with

his hands, trying to warm them, but he raised his head at her words and moved over her to hear the whisper.

"What did you say?"

Although she knew he would hate it before all those people, she didn't think she had the strength to say it again. These were different people, she remembered, a different night, so she made her mouth form the words.

"Your shirt. Did you spill the wine again? It's all right. Everyone does."

The crease was back between his brows. She reached to smooth it away, but her hand fell as soon as she touched his face, too tired to complete the gesture.

"I'm glad you took off the glasses. I can't tell what you're thinking with them on."

His hands gripped hers to warm the coldness he had felt against his face. They were slick under his fingers, and she cried out when he touched them.

"My God," she heard him whisper. He said something else she didn't know, didn't recognize, although she had thought her grasp of French profanities was very idiomatic.

He called the women, and she heard them exclaim and then reassure. Cuts, scratches, they told him, but he demanded, questioning, until they convinced him. They cleaned her with warm water and salve and then wrapped a part of a sheet they tore around her. They thought that was clever, but by that time she didn't care what they did. She was just so tired. She knew she could sleep now if only he would come back. She must have said it, for they told her over and over. Monsieur Gerrard was back, very relieved she was all right. He was safe and back at the house. They said it many times until finally she stopped them.

"Not Andre," she said. "*Monsieur le duc.* Tell him." She closed her eyes and waited.

She had sent for him, and he had come. She could feel him beside her, but she didn't know when he had lain down. It didn't matter. All that mattered was that he was there. His skin was warm, and she turned into the warmth. She was still so cold. Still moving with the lift and fall of the waves, but his body was solid and still against hers. She felt his arm come around her carefully.

"It's all right," she said. "It's just the front."

"I didn't know you were hurt," he whispered. She felt his lips over her temple.

"It wasn't much. I found a rock and held on. I don't know how they found me."

"The white blouse. One of the lights caught the white against the darkness. You had come a long way. You were very near the islands." She could hear something in his voice, incredulity, disbelief. "Do you have any idea, in all those miles of ocean, how lucky you were that they saw you?"

They were quiet a long time, content simply to hold.

"What happened?" he asked finally. "How did you fall in?"

"I was trailing my feet in the water. When we hit the storm, I turned to bring them back into the boat. Andre was adjusting the sail. He had told me to sit still and just where. I suppose I moved to the wrong place. I was off-balance. The boom hit me, and I fell in."

"Andre still had the sail up?" he said sharply. "In the storm?" She could hear the disbelief.

"You don't ever believe anything I tell you. Why should I try to talk to you? You think I lie about everything."

"I don't think you lie. It's just— Are you sure he had the sail up? And the storm had begun?"

"Maybe he was taking it down. I don't know what he was doing. We had just sailed into the storm. Do you think I'm making this up, too?"

" 'Making this up, *too*?' " he repeated.

"You always ask me what's going to happen next and to let you know what to do. What game we're playing. I never know what you're talking about. I don't *know* what Andre was doing with the sail." She was too tired to argue, and so, in her exhaustion, the words seemed to whisper into the darkness without conscious effort, "You think you're so damn clever. And I'm so stupid."

He laughed suddenly at the familiarity of that response and leaned to kiss her. She was surprised by his reaction to her anger.

"I don't think you're stupid," he said, remembering how many times he'd been forced to deny that same accusation. "Maybe I am. If, dear God, this can possibly be…"

"What are you doing?" she asked as his hands began to move over her stomach.

"I'm trying to see where you're hurt."

"Not there," she gasped suddenly.

"Good," he whispered. She could hear the quiet satisfaction in his voice. When he turned her gently on her side, she understood why he had asked.

SHE LAY AWAKE a long time, thinking about being glad to be alive for a change, afraid to close her eyes in case it was a mistake. Sooner than she thought possible, dawn began to touch the edges of the louvers, so that the fine cracks between them glowed eerily in the darkness. Eventually she could see his profile, outlined against the growing light. Finally she saw that his eyes were still open, and she knew that he hadn't slept.

"I didn't know how late it was," she whispered, touching his chest, moving her fingers down the breast-bone between the ridges of rib and muscle. "It must have been very late when they brought me home." She hadn't meant to use the word, but the fishermen had, so she left it between them.

"Yes."

"Were you worried? You weren't even undressed?"

He didn't answer, but she watched his eyes close, so she waited.

"I was listening," he said finally.

"For the boat? For us to come back?"

"In my head."

"To what?" she asked. Her fingers discovered that some time in the short night he had undressed completely.

"To the sound effects."

"There *were* no sound effects," she said fiercely, turning his face to hers. "There is no reason for someone like you to be jealous of someone like Andre."

"Maybe a couple," he suggested. His short laugh was not successful.

They were quiet again, listening unconsciously to the sounds begin in the rest of the house.

She leaned over him, in spite of the pain across her breasts and stomach, speaking only when she was very close, so close he could feel her breath against his lashes.

"Close your eyes," she whispered, waiting until he had obeyed. She kissed each lid gently, and then she moved away so she could see his full face.

"Open them," she commanded softly and waited. "Well?" she said finally.

"Well what?"

"Are they better?" she asked seriously and saw him struggle with the disbelief that she would say that to him.

"No," he said harshly. He turned away from her watching eyes.

"We'll work on it. I'll get it right eventually. I haven't had that much experience kissing things better."

The tension relaxed in the clenched muscles of his beautiful mouth, outlined against the light from the windows. She watched the slow smile, followed by the slight negative movement of his head, and she knew that she had succeeded. He was amused.

"*You* could try," she suggested, putting her wrist gently against his lips. They found the raw ache, perhaps by the salve or the subtle difference in the smoothness of the skin inside her wrist. He kissed her there. She saw him swallow whatever emotion he was feeling, and then he turned to her, his hands moving the salt-stiffened hair from around her throat. Tracing over her shoulders and the fragile collarbone, his lips sought out and found the soreness, the scrapes, even the burns from the rock's pressure as the waves had pushed her body against its roughness again and again. She tried to sit up to remove the sheet they had wrapped around her breasts and stomach, but his fingers stopped her when he realized that intent.

"Later," he whispered, laughing. "I'll do those later, after the doctor has seen them."

"No," she gasped, and the tightness banded her head. "No doctors. I don't need a doctor."

"You're hurt and exhausted. Of course, you need to be seen by a doctor."

"Don't," she begged, desperate. "Don't do that to me. No doctors. Promise me, Julien. Promise me. I'm all right. I swear to you. You can examine every inch of me, or the women if you want. But no doctors.''

"That's ridiculous. You don't even have to go there. Andre will bring him here. You don't even have to move.''

"You don't understand," she said and began to cry. Her tears defeated him. He had no defense for the sounds she made, like a child. So he held her and eventually gave her the promise she wanted. Finally, comforted against the strength of his hard chest, she slept.

Chapter Seven

When she woke again, the sun was flooding the room. Someone had opened the windows and the scent of the flowers from the garden below, open in the heat, pervaded the air. She stretched and then wished that she hadn't. Everything hurt. Every overextended muscle, bruise, scrape and salt-burned inch protested.

She closed her eyes, wondering when he had left. She had not been aware of it. Only that he held her when the dreams came, soothing her back into the safe world created by the knowledge that his arms surrounded her.

"Am I forgiven?" She opened her eyes to find Andre loosely spread in a chair across from the bed. His long legs were stretched against the carpet, the blue eyes very concerned.

"Before you answer that, please note that for every inch of skin that rock took off you, my brother has removed two strips from my hide. I am very much in his disfavor for dumping a guest in the ocean and losing her. Put in a good word for me if you have a chance. It was a very dark night." His voice was teasing, but she knew that he spoke the truth about the disfavor. She could imagine.

"It was," she agreed, "a very dark night."

"I did tell you not to move," he said, returning her smile.

"Yes, you did. I told him. I'm sorry you were chastised. Part of the tribulations of being the youngest, I suppose."

"Only a part." He laughed, sounding relieved that she, at least, didn't seem to blame him. "He thinks I should have used the engines all the way back, that somehow I should have known we couldn't get back before the storm. The man has no romance in his soul. I tried to explain the allure of sails under the moon, pale toes trailing in the dark water, but he's apparently forgotten what that's like."

"Perhaps," she said, thinking of all she could tell him of his brother's romantic nature, but, of course, that was nothing she would ever share.

"Where is he?" she asked instead.

"Working. Of course."

"And you're not?" she teased, smiling.

"Not today. Too long a night. I wanted to see you and make sure you were all right, and to say I'm sorry. I am so terribly sorry. You know that, don't you? I wanted to tell you last night, but the women wouldn't let me disturb you."

"I know. I was just so tired."

"You managed to swim a remarkable distance. You are a much stronger lady than you look. All that fragile blond beauty seems to hide steel."

She laughed, but she liked the thought that she had been strong, that they had talked about, perhaps, and admired that she had survived. She wanted Julien to know that. She knew why it had become so important out there in the darkness to survive. He wouldn't know, but she acknowledged it to herself. What she felt for him had kept her alive.

"If," she spoke aloud, "you will just remove yourself from my bedroom, I will attempt to remove my slightly dented and scratched steel body from this bed. Surely it must be time for some meal. I feel as if I've missed a few."

"Lunch," he said unthinkingly, before he added, "but I don't think you ought to get up. Julien's given instructions that you're to be brought a tray. They've already begun preparing it in the kitchen."

"Tell them not to bother. I'm going to shower and then come downstairs. I really feel like I need to get up or nothing is ever going to work again. I'm all right. Just stiff and sore. Ask them to give me thirty minutes."

"I'll tell him, but I leave you to deal with his displeasure. I've had my fair share today."

He unfolded his long length from the chair, moving across the room to take the slender hand that was resting on top of the sheet. He studied the pattern of scrapes and bruises a minute. His mouth lowered, caressing the torn skin.

"I really am so sorry. I wish—"

"I'm all right. I promise. Just go away."

She pulled her hand from his fingers and smiled at the concern in his eyes.

Finally he was gone. She lay a moment, thinking about last night. She threw the sheet off her body, realizing that someone had found a loose cotton nightgown and dressed her in it. She wished she could remember Julien's hands doing that, but she supposed she had been too deeply asleep to be aware of it. Another memory lost.

She moved carefully, but she knew, as she had told

Andre, that it really wasn't bad. She was sore, but nothing was broken or permanently damaged. She couldn't resist walking to the long mirrors that covered the closet doors. She looked pale, and her hair was dark, hanging in twisted threads. She grimaced and pulled the gown off over her head. She carefully unwound the cloth they had wrapped around the abrasions last night. They were as ugly as she had thought they would be, raw and red against the white of her breasts and stomach. Nothing was deep. There would be no scars. It was just ugly. She turned to look over her shoulder at the yellowing bruises of her back. She could almost see in the deeper brown of their fading where the stair edge crossed, but in spite of the picture reflected in the mirror, she smiled.

She jumped when the door opened. Julien stepped inside, and she could see him listening to find her. He turned his head slightly, and she regretted making him hunt for her.

"I'm over here," she said, watching the glasses track to her voice. "Admiring the merchandise. The heavily damaged merchandise."

"They said it was only scratches. They promised."

"It is," she reassured, laughing, "but like a road map. Red and crisscrossed on the front and then in the back... Don't get me wrong. I don't regret any of those on the back. The front, however, were not quite as pleasant in the acquiring."

"Andre said you insist on coming downstairs," he said, ignoring her reference to what had happened on the stairs.

"Won't I be welcome?" she teased, but the response on his face was not what she had expected. Something was different. Something had happened to change him between the time he had left her and this.

"What is it?" she said, and his face tightened. He didn't answer, so she asked again, demanding against his silence. "What's happened?"

"Andre's account of last night differs in several significant details from what you told me."

He was waiting for her denial. She could see him swallow whatever else he had intended to say in response to that denial. The muscles in the brown column of his throat moved, and she watched the movement disappear into the neck of the blue work shirt he wore. The long lines of his legs were clearly outlined against the loose material of the white pants that the breeze blew flat and then slightly fluttering.

"I see," she said finally. "Sound effects." Knowing the uselessness of anything else she might say, she began to gather up the gown and the cloth she had dropped on the carpet.

"Would you like to tell me what really happened?"

"I *told* you what happened. I don't have anything to add to what I told you. There was nothing else."

She moved to pass him to reach the bath, but his voice stopped her.

"I want you to leave."

"Today?"

"No, of course not," he said. "As soon as you've recovered. Saturday. Andre will make the arrangements for your flight."

"Whatever you want," she said. She took another step toward the bath, the soft carpet masking any sound.

"Are you really all right?" he asked. He reached for her, his hand unerringly finding her shoulder despite the fact she'd made no noise. By her smell alone he could have found her in any room, picked her out of a thousand women. But he wouldn't tell her that. Not now.

She nodded, unable to speak against the uncertain concern she clearly heard. Of all that she might have expected him to say, of all he could have said after what his brother had probably told him, that was the most difficult for her to understand. Realizing that he couldn't know how she'd responded, she answered him aloud.

"Of course," she whispered and, breaking away from his fingers, she moved into the bathroom. She turned on the shower, so that she didn't realize how long he stood, listening in the brightness of her bedroom.

SHE JOINED THEM in the shadows the house cast over the patio. The maid had directed her to the table outside. They both rose when she neared, and she smiled at Andre's low whistle, as he pulled out her chair.

"From looking like something the fish rejected to something out of *Vogue*," he said admiringly, "is a remarkable transformation."

"Thank you. It is, perhaps, remarkable what one can accomplish given enough paints and powders," she agreed and smiled at him. She had worked hard for the effect she had just achieved. Her hair was clean and shining, carefully French braided to reveal the shape of her face. Her green cat eyes had been highlighted with more makeup than she usually wore. The light tan she had acquired here was right against the shimmer of the bronze silk shirt that hung loose over white slacks. She had unbuttoned first one and then another of the pearl buttons down the front. Apparently, the result was all she'd intended.

She couldn't resist a glance at Julien's face, but he was in the act of sitting, so she couldn't read the down-turned features. She wondered what she hoped to accomplish by this charade he couldn't see. Andre was his brother, a relationship of long-standing love and affection to be measured against his mistrust of her.

The conversation flowed between the two men, discussing the condition of the decking in the back, the cook's cousin's skills as a carpenter, the most ordinary of subjects. Her eyes again were fascinated by the sure movement of Julien's long, dark fingers over the china and silver or resting on the whiteness of the cloth. It was not until they had finished eating that Andre spoke of last night.

"I think the food at Tatie Babette's was even better than the last time we went, Julien. You would have liked the langoustes. Caroline kept tasting everything I ordered, as well as her own meal."

"You insisted," she said, and then knew she was doing exactly what he wanted—putting them together and Julien set apart, alone. "But if you don't mind, I prefer not to talk about last night. You seem to remember things I don't," she said calmly. The dark face on her right turned toward her voice for the first time. She could read Julien's surprise.

"I don't understand," Andre said. She had to admire the puzzlement in his voice. It was really very good.

"Whatever you told your brother that happened between us." She was surprised at how impassively she was able to say it.

"I'm sorry," Andre said finally. "I really don't understand what you're talking about." The sense of embarrassment was thick in the humid air.

"I think you do. I just don't understand why you feel that's necessary. Nothing happened between us, and you know it. Why did you tell him differently?"

"This is very embarrassing," Andre said finally into

the heavy silence. His brother had not moved since that first focus on her face.

"Yes, it is. And it's not necessary. You are a very attractive man. I'm sure you've made many sexual conquests. It's probably very easy for you, given your looks and your wealth, but *I* am not one of them. I think you should tell your brother that. Tell him you lied about whatever you said happened last night."

He smiled slowly at her calmness, and his voice had not changed, but something shifted in the clear blueness of his eyes. "If that's what you want. I would never wish to displease a guest. I'm sorry you were distressed."

He turned to his brother and spoke in the same reasonable tone which one would use to placate a demanding child, one adult to another. "Julien, forgive me. I lied about last night. She is not, after all, very good. I told you before that she's too easy. I really do prefer to work a little harder. She was so ready she was like a hundred-franc whore in Marseilles."

She gasped with the viciousness of the last words, and watched speechless in shock as Andre rose and threw his napkin into the tureen of bouillabaisse in the center of the table. He walked quickly across the flagstones and into the house. The door slammed so hard that the glass shook again all along the front as it had at the height of the storm.

"My God," she whispered in disbelief. The fury was foreign to the laughing serenity Andre had always displayed. She lowered her head and felt the nausea rise in her throat at his description of her. She couldn't even look at Julien's face, didn't want to know what thoughts might be reflected there. They sat a long time, it seemed to her. Finally she could hear again. The vacuum of horror his words had created eased so she was aware of the sound of the birds and the boom of the surf and even the noises of the servants working in the kitchen. She began to force herself to breathe naturally. She knew that she needed to leave. She slid her chair back and rose on legs that trembled.

"Excuse me," she said, a remembered function of mores Andre had just shredded. There was no response from the man still seated at the table. Finally she turned and walked back into the house and up the stairs. She didn't know where Andre had gone, but it didn't matter. As long as she never had to see him again.

SHE STAYED ALL DAY in her room. The smiling maid brought her a tray after the sun had left the garden, so that she could no longer see the colors of the flowers. She answered all the concerned questions about her condition and lyingly reassured the girl that she had applied more salve to the cuts and that nothing was becoming infected. The infection on this island was not festering in the scratches she had acquired last night. She knew now that it had been growing, instead, a long time.

She had thought of packing her bags, but she didn't want to ask Andre to take her to Guadeloupe. She knew she couldn't get into the boat with him after the scene on the patio. She had spent a long time during the afternoon trying to understand his motives. She should never have openly challenged him in front of Julien. That had been her mistake.

Finally she ate the meal the maid had brought. She had thought at lunch that she might never be able to eat again without the sickness she had felt then interfering. However, the food was good, and afterward she felt better. She lay on the bed in the darkness, listening for movement in the house. She rose when she thought of it and locked the door to her room. Long after all the sounds had ceased, she got up again and took off the silk blouse and slacks and lay down in only her underwear.

She was asleep when the sound she had expected came, but apparently sleeping lightly enough that, in spite of its softness, it woke her. The push against the handle of the locked door and the wait. She could hear when he turned it again, but she lay silent, not answering even when he spoke her name. It was the voice she had expected. Andre's voice. She was pleased that she was so sure of that. She had been afraid that it would be difficult to tell, but in spite of the softness of his tone, she knew.

She slept again long after he had gone away, and the trembling wail of the baby's cry that came through the darkness was nothing unexpected, either. Nevertheless, her flesh crawled against the sound, as it had in school when someone deliberately scraped nails over a blackboard. She still wept, hard sobs that she buried into her pillow. The cry echoed three times, each fainter than before, and she didn't sleep again after that. She watched, as she had last night, daylight touch the cracks of the louvers and then grow to fill the room.

She dressed as carefully as the day before, having learned in the past few years the value of looking, at least, as if composure were natural. She walked finally into the bright kitchen and spoke to the cook and the maid.

"Oh, *mademoiselle,* you look so much better this morning," the cook greeted her, pouring coffee and even cutting fruit for her breakfast. They let her sit there at the central island in the sun and eat, surrounded by their everyday conversation, and here she felt safe.

When she had finished, she asked her question and knew by their expressions that they had heard nothing of what had happened yesterday afternoon on the shadowed patio.

"Is Andre here? I wanted to ask about getting to the airport."

"Oh, no, *mademoiselle*. He is at the distilleries. At work. But surely you're not leaving?"

"I think that's best," she said easily, knowing she didn't owe them any explanation, but they had been kind. "Since Madame Rochette is away."

They had no answer to that, not knowing when the mistress might return, so they shrugged and expressed the hope that her ordeal was not making her want to leave.

"No, I just think it's best," she answered. "Is Julien here? *Monsieur le duc?*" She didn't know what these women called him, and "Mr. Gerrard" could mean either.

"In his office. He's working, too. He was very concerned about you. That night. You are his guest, of course. It was so fortunate that you were found," the cook said, crossing herself.

"Yes," she agreed and nodded. "Yes, it was very fortunate. I think I'll ask him about the flights. Thank you for breakfast. It was delicious." She smiled at them both, grateful for the genuineness of their concern.

She walked across the long room, never looking out the wall of glass to the patio table. She knew he could hear her sandals against the tile and, warned of her approach, would have time to gather his defenses. He would be once again contained and careful, mocking and disbelieving. Only when he touched her, held her, the long years of containment and reserve crumbled. But she thought that now, after what his brother had said, after its ugliness, he wouldn't want to touch her again.

She knocked and he answered, giving permission, so she entered the room she had been in only once before, the day she had brought him the tray.

He was standing now beside the windows that looked out on the garden pool. It was very beautiful in the morning light, the reflection of the sun on the water playing on the blue of the tiles and flickering in the shadows.

He turned at her entrance, but the glasses blocked the full view of his face. She knew that was by design, and she supposed it made no difference now.

"I'd like to talk to you about leaving. I think I should go as soon as possible. Is there some way to ask one of the fishermen to take me? Today if he could."

"Why one of the fishermen?" he asked. "Andre will take you. Today if you like, but you'll have to wait until he gets back from Marie Galante, some time in the early afternoon."

"I don't want Andre to take me. I can't..."

She realized that he had turned back to the window, no longer making a pretense of focusing on her face. She thought for the first time how difficult that must be and wondered why he tried, maintaining the illusion of normality as much as possible.

"I'm sorry he said what he did to you. He'll apologize when he returns."

"Because you'll make him? I don't think that's necessary."

"My brother is a grown man. I can't make him do anything he doesn't want to do. He really is sorry for what he said. He wanted to tell you that last night, but

I asked him to wait. I thought that you would be, perhaps, more willing to listen to him today.''

"I don't think he's sorry for what he did—" she began, but he broke through what she was saying.

"You angered him by denying what he had said. Or maybe you embarrassed him. I don't know why he thinks that I'm interested in his recounting those sorts of stories, but he always has. It wasn't a personal attack on you."

"Lying about sleeping with me is certainly personal to me. Just exactly what do you think he should apologize for? The lie, or his denial of that lie at lunch? Or do you still believe him? How can you still believe him?"

He turned back to her and said very distinctly, "Because he's my brother. And because I love him."

"And what am I?" she challenged. "What do you feel about me?"

"Why don't you tell me who you are? I know who you're supposed to be, but why don't you tell me the whole. I think you're in a situation here where you're unsure of whom to trust anymore. In spite of your intentions in coming here, I promise I won't hurt you. I don't want you to be hurt. I'll even help you get home. I think I owe you that."

"Because I slept with you?" she asked. "Because of the two of you, you are the one I chose? The one I would always choose."

"Because you slept with me? Perhaps. But let's not pretend that there was any free choice involved. That was the intent when you came. I don't understand your motives or his. I don't pretend to. But I think we all must be aware that in spite of how or why this all began, it has turned into something very different. So I think it's time to end it.''

"There was nothing more to my coming than I've told you. I was interviewed by Paul Dupre in Paris and hired to be your sister's social secretary. He made all the arrangements. Andre met me at the airport on Guadeloupe and we came here. I don't know why that's so difficult for you to believe.''

"Because Paul Dupre never interviewed you. Your name was given to his people by a man my brother has used in the past for certain activities that the family solicitors would never have become involved in. The pretense was that *my* staff had discovered your sterling credentials and were recommending you to my sister. Your hiring would probably never have been questioned except Paul Dupre is a very careful man, extremely protective of Suzanne. He ran his own background check of you, which turned up information that caused him some rather natural concern. He took that information to Suzanne, who was inclined to take my recommendation in spite of it, but who was curious enough to ask me why it had never been mentioned. I think you know what I'm talking about.''

"Of course. I've made no secret of my illness. I told you. I told the lawyer. *Whoever's* lawyer he was. I was ill. For a long time.''

"Eighteen months in a state hospital," he said quietly.

"My," she said, bitter against his calmness, "aren't we all so enlightened. What does that mean to you? Do you think I'm insane? Is that why you believe Andre? I'm supposed to be so crazy that I've forgotten all about making love to him, about having sex with him,'' she said.

She could hear the anger building in her voice, but

surprisingly there was no pain to block it. "Wherever the hell that was supposed to take place. You think I'm insane, so I sleep with anyone who comes across my path? Who's next? The boy who does the yard work? Is that why you don't want to ask one of the fishermen to take me? Afraid I'll attack him on the way to the airport? I didn't sleep with Andre, last night or ever. I only met him when I arrived here. In spite of what you may think, I am not in the habit—"

She stopped because he had turned back to his pretended contemplation of the scene through his windows, back to the peaceful pool and the thick foliage.

His voice was very quiet in the heat of the afternoon, even kind in its accusation. "Then explain to me why, less than forty-eight hours after our meeting, you were very willing to have me make love to you. To take you under the most brutal of circumstances. To hurt you by taking you again and again."

"You never hurt me," she whispered, not a defense or an explanation, but an avowal. She saw him lower his head against its force.

"You deny making love to Andre who is young and attractive and physically perfect. You react with outrage to the very idea that you might be accused of having spent a romantic night with him. I should think, given the sexual mores of your generation, you wouldn't even bother to deny what he said. It can't matter. Only the three of us will ever know. I don't understand your continued resistance to admitting what obviously happened, and it really is none of my business. You don't owe me any explanation." He stopped just before she thought she could bear his reasoned tone no longer.

"'The mores of my generation.' old man," she said

tauntingly. "You really *have* let yourself become an old man. You've let your blindness do that to you."

"Don't," he said, and she could hear his bitterness. "I will tolerate a great deal, but I have warned you that there are some things that you may not use in this game. There are weapons that I won't allow you to employ."

She was momentarily defeated by his anger. She waited, and then said it because, whatever happened between them, she needed to tell him this. "I'm sorry I mentioned your blindness, but you've removed yourself from life because of it. No one cares if you stumble. No one will laugh. You can't just cease to exist because you can't bear to have anyone see you make a mistake."

He laughed suddenly, and it was unpleasant, painful. "I don't care if you *say* I'm blind. Do you think I don't know? Do you think if you don't mention it, I'll forget about it? I don't care if you shout that I'm blind. That's not what I'm talking about, and you know it. Just for once admit that you know what you're doing and that you know it's wrong."

"I *don't* know what you're talking about," she said, frustrated by his stubborn insistence. "What do you want me to admit? What am I supposed to have done?"

Finally he moved from the window and walked around the desk with its scattering of papers and the computer. He came to stand before her and removed the glasses she hated. Unable to prevent the motion, her hand reached for his face, to touch his chin and then move slowly up his cheek to his eyes. Her thumb found the ridge of scar nearest to the corner, and she traced it gently.

"I haven't done whatever it is that you think I'm guilty of. And you know why I slept with you. You have to know," she whispered.

His eyes were very still and very blue. She thought suddenly that he was trying to see her, and she felt a loosening of the fear that had held her all day. Until he spoke.

"When I first understood what you and Andre were up to, I wanted to strangle you with my bare hands. The cruelest thing you've done to me is that now I don't want to hurt you, couldn't bear to hurt you, or to see you hurt." He stopped and then forced himself to continue. "If causing me pain was the intent of this entire masquerade, you should tell Andre that he's succeeded beyond whatever he might have hoped. The ultimate cruelty, the ultimate triumph for you, and I suppose for him, is that I no longer want to hurt you." She watched him smile at her, and that twisted movement hurt her, too. "Dear God," he whispered finally, "I only want to believe you."

She didn't understand what he meant, why he was linking her with Andre, but she heard clearly the pain and answered only to assuage it, to wipe it out of the beautiful scarred face before her. She said, "Then do, my love. Please, when it is so important, please do."

His eyes closed, and she waited. When he opened them, he said, "I think you'd better go. I need to think, and I can't do that with you here. I want to talk to Andre."

"Oh, God," she said. "No. My God, Julien, why? You know what he'll say. Please don't do this."

"I think you'll have to trust me. That sword cuts both ways, and you have, I believe, less reason to doubt than I. Please try to understand. He *is* my brother."

"You shouldn't do this. I don't like it and I don't like him. If you had seen his eyes—" She stopped, realizing what she had said.

His voice was still calm and reasoned. "But I didn't. As I haven't seen yours. So I am doing the best I can. It's more difficult than you can imagine."

"All right," she said finally, recognizing the futility of arguing with him because he had always protected his younger brother, but she dreaded whatever Andre would tell him. She could imagine, and she ached with the thought. "Let me stay. I want to hear what he says."

"No, it's better that we talk alone. Trust me. He's my brother, and despite whatever— We love each other. Please."

"Will you come and tell me when you've talked? No matter what you decide? Will you promise me that, at least?"

"I'll come," he said. "I promise. No matter what, I'll come." Finally he smiled at her. "I don't think I really have any choice about that. I've tried, but I haven't succeeded at that self-deception. You know I'll come."

She nodded and didn't remember this time that he wouldn't know. Then she turned and left his office and once more locked herself in her bedroom.

Chapter Eight

The afternoon was endless. She tried to read, but found that she was only staring at the pages, the words making no impact on her brain. Finally she closed her eyes and simply lay on her bed, listening to the noises, trying to identify each and to locate it. She could hear the servants laughing and clattering dishes in the kitchen, the surf beating relentlessly against the rocks, the scream of the birds, all the sounds of the house. She thought about his world, this world of only sound and smells, and she couldn't imagine living imprisoned there forever.

She opened her eyes when clearly, even upstairs, the sound reached her of the downstairs door slamming with the same violence as yesterday, the glass banging again in the long windows that looked out over the landing.

She wouldn't let the maid in with the tray, but she had begun to question the fear that held her here in her bedroom alone, begun to worry whether she were in danger of slipping back into the darkness that had held her so long ago. She waited even after night fell because he had said he would come. When he didn't, she finally fell asleep, exhausted by her tears. She had cried a long time, admitting in despair that she had lost.

The knock was soft, whispering against her dreams,

but she knew his voice, so she hurried to unlock the door. He slipped in, turning the lock again behind him. He stood with his back against her door. She could make out his outline, but his features were so shadowed that she couldn't read his expression.

"You didn't eat," he said finally.

"I thought you weren't coming." As if that alone could explain why she had ceased to function.

"I told you I'd come. I told you I didn't have a choice."

"We always have choices," she said and waited again.

"I don't." He put both hands on her shoulders, pulling her against the hard warmth of his chest. "I don't have any choice about wanting you," he breathed against her hair. His mouth lowered to find her throat. She could feel her body reacting to his first touch, the lift of her breasts, the moisture.

She resisted the lure of that sweet escape, knowing that it was reality she had to examine, that they had to examine together. She put her palms against his chest and pushed. He released her, but she could feel the reluctance and clearly his physical response to simply holding her.

"Talk to me," she whispered.

"Wrong choice," he said, but he smiled at her. She could barely read the movement of his lips. She wanted to see him, to know what he thought and felt. To know if, in spite of his presence here, Andre had won.

So she moved, turning on the low lamp beside the bed. When she took his hand, he followed her. They sat together on the edge of the bed, but he didn't touch her now. He didn't pretend to look at her, so she had to ask.

"What did he say? Did he tell you—" And saw the

negative movement of his head before she had completed the question.

"Damn him, damn him to hell," she whispered, feeling her eyes fill against the injustice. "Why? Why is he doing this? Why is he lying? What did he say?"

"No," he said, and she watched the movement of his head again. "*That* you don't want to know."

"My God, what else? What could be worse?" He didn't answer, but she could see the shiver he couldn't quite control, so she knew that whatever had been said, it had been worse.

"I thought...I let him talk because I thought that there might be something... That I could say, 'No, that's wrong.' But of course, whatever he said, I had no way of knowing how... Making love between two people is—"

"God, Julien, stop it. Stop this. I can't believe you listened to that. What is he? What is he that he could say those things?"

"He's a liar," he said softly, each word spoken distinctly.

"But you said that there was nothing—"

"Not in that. Not in what he said about that. And after a while, I stopped listening. But I asked him about the other. About what I knew. About Paul Dupre and whether he had hired someone to find you."

"And?" she said, hoping.

"And he lied to me. About something I know he did. He lied to me about it as innocently and as believably as he did about making love to you. So I knew that he was lying, was capable of lying, about the other."

It hurt that he had reached that conclusion not because she had told him, but because he had decided that if his brother were lying about part of his involvement, then he might be lying about the rest.

"I know what you're thinking," he said. "I don't blame you. You have every right to feel the way you do. I should have believed you. I wanted to. You'll never know how much I wanted to." From the pain that filled his voice, she thought she did know. In spite of her own hurt, she found she only wanted to ease his guilt, and then he spoke again, "But he's my brother. He was the one who was always there. When this first happened..."

She waited a long time for him to continue, waited, knowing that he must tell this, must destroy these ties, in his own way. Knowing that if she attempted to bring about that destruction, it would always be between them. So she forced herself to be silent, and finally he continued.

"When I reached out, when I couldn't stand the darkness any longer, it was always Andre whose hand was there. When I didn't think I could take another step, couldn't endure another visit to the burn tank, it was always Andre who was willing to go and endure with me, to hold me, to let me lean on him. Always."

She remembered the look she had seen in his brother's eyes when he talked about that endless agony, and what she had seen there had not been compassion. She thought she understood now, but would never say, never put into words, the sickness of the reason Andre was always there, always so willing to be the one to help his brother.

"And I wasn't," she whispered instead, a truth she was learning to bear, could now, finally, acknowledge.

"He's my brother. And I love him. I don't understand what he's doing. None of it makes sense to me. It hasn't from the beginning, but I can't just—"

"I know," she soothed, leaning to kiss the side of his face. "I know, and I'm sorry. I would do anything to keep you from being hurt, but I've told you the truth about how I was hired and why I came. I had no other motives. I swear to you."

At her touch, he turned and pulled her against his body, and this time she didn't move away. "I don't want to talk about this, even to think about it," he said. "I don't want to think about anything. I just want to hold you. Can you understand that?"

She nodded, knowing he could feel the movement against his chest. She moved away enough to put her hands between them and begin to unfasten the buttons of his shirt. She watched him shrug out of it, watched the movement of the muscles against the brown of his skin, against the burns and scars, and thought about what he had said. Andre had been there. Andre of the twisted motives, but not she.

She moved her palms against those marks and felt the movement of his skin against her hands, as the skin of a horse ripples at the touch of the crop. She swallowed against that pain, leaning to kiss and caress with her mouth and lips the mottled, telltale discoloration.

She touched him a long time, feeling his response building in the changed breathing, in the very texture of his skin, its warmth against her lips.

He pulled her down finally to lie with him in the sheets that smelled of lavender and of her skin when it was warm with his lovemaking. His face lowered over hers, seeking her lips, but she reached instead and removed the glasses. This time he didn't flinch away. He waited while her hand found the bedside table and laid them there. He could hear the soft noise of the metal against the wood. And he thought about something else Andre had told him.

Her mouth reached for his, but he stopped her because he had to ask. "You told me there was no reason to wear the glasses?"

Seeing the taut control in his face, the fear, she answered lightly, "That's what I said. No reason to hide behind anything. Not for me. I've seen everything you've got, old man." She smiled and brushed her fingers through the dark hair that curled as if alive against her hand.

"Tell me about my eyes," he commanded softly.

In spite of the lack of emphasis, the careful neutrality of his tone, she knew that this was important, and she was suddenly afraid she'd do it wrong. She hesitated, trying to think of what to say to him, finally settling for the truth.

"There are scars. Like little cuts. Nothing big. Nothing that— It's not bad, I swear, Julien. Just a lot of little white lines."

"I can feel those. Tell me about the other," he said tightly.

"I don't understand," she said, searching his face for some clue. At her continued silence, his lids dropped, covering the clear blue, and so she said again, "That's all. Just the scars. There's nothing wrong with your eyes. They're blue. They're beautiful, but right now they're not looking at me."

She watched as he opened and focused his eyes deliberately on the face he couldn't see.

She finally whispered, "There's nothing else to tell you. There's nothing wrong with your eyes. They don't look wrong. They don't look damaged in any way. Surely Suzanne or somebody has told you that."

"Suzanne told me," he said.

"But you didn't believe her? Why? Why would you think Suzanne would tell you that if it weren't true?"

"To protect me. To make me feel more normal. Not a freak. I don't know. I just always wondered what people saw when they looked at me. I don't think I'm vain, but I'd hate to send everyone running in horror if they're grotesque or—"

"Don't. They look like eyes, like anybody's eyes. Except sometimes they're just a fraction off-focus," she said carefully, trying to tell the absolute truth, to let him hear and believe the reality.

When he laughed, she took the first deep breath since he'd started this. "Just a fraction?" he asked, and she relaxed against the gentle mockery.

"That's what I said. Just a fraction. You do all that pretty well—"

"—for a blind man," he finished, smiling at her.

"What happened to your eyes?"

"I thought Andre told you. I was in an automobile accident. Six years ago."

"He told me that. I guess I just wanted to know how they were damaged."

"The car exploded. Some spark from the metal, something, caught the dead leaves. And the gas tank had been ruptured. Eventually it exploded."

"Someone said...someone told me that you came back to the car to get your wife. Is that when it happened?"

She waited, but his face was so closed, she knew he wouldn't answer.

So she said it into the silence, "If you hadn't gone back for her... That's true, isn't it. If you hadn't gone to get her out, then..."

"Then I wouldn't be blind. Is that what you want to hear? Then, yes, if I hadn't gone back to the car, I wouldn't have lost my sight."

The words were brutal, but nothing that she hadn't expected. It was the obvious explanation she had already accepted with her brain. Now he had simply put it into words, and they, too, must be accepted, dealt with. Finally he spoke again, his tone free of the dark bitterness she had heard before, "I thought you'd decided that I do pretty well. Considering. Only a fraction off-focus?"

"I know a couple of other things that you do pretty well," she said, smiling. "For a blind man. For any man. But maybe..."

"Maybe what?" he whispered as he lowered his mouth to her neck, breathed against the fragrance of her hair and skin and knew that what he had said about choices was the truth. He could not have chosen to stay away from her.

"Maybe you might want to practice. Just to be sure that it's perfect."

He slid the straps of her gown off her shoulders and found the peak of her nipple, hard and distended, aching for his mouth.

After a long time of searching lips against her body, of hard hands caressing with a gentleness she had forgotten, her voice whispered again above his head, "Not that it's not already."

He had forgotten what she had said before, had forgotten everything except her response, the movement of her body against his hands.

"What?" he asked, not understanding.

"Perfect," she breathed as his tongue trailed down to worship her stomach. His hands discarded the nightgown, and she lay finally against his long length and could feel every movement of warm skin and smooth muscle of his arms and chest against her body.

"Take the rest off. I want to feel all of you. Please."

She waited while he unfastened the jeans and pushed them off his long legs. She helped with the briefs and then they were together, holding against all the doubts that they pushed away, holding at bay everything but need and the satisfaction of that need.

He was gentle with her, leading, guiding. The driving intensity of his passion was this time overlain by tenderness and concern. As always when he touched her, she was instantly ready for him, welcoming, accommodating his hard body as naturally as she accepted the air that gathered around her skin. As unable to deny him whatever he wanted as she would be unable to deny the need of her body to breathe, to eat, to sleep.

They lay together finally, relaxed and spent, their legs tangled still. Her head rested against his chest, and the rise and fall of his breathing and the slow, steady rhythm of his heart lulled her to sleep. This was safety and peace and freedom to dream without horror or regret. And finally, in Julien's arms, it was becoming freedom to remember without fear.

The sound jerked her from the peace of his strength surrounding her, so she fell again, shivering, into the dark mists of the nightmares, crying against the pain. Then he was over her, his hand pressed against the sobs, his chest and arms sheltering, pulling her back from the fear.

"Shh...don't. I have you. Don't cry, my love." His lips whispered against her ear, a breath of sound that had the power to drown out the other, to force back the darkness and the terror. She opened her eyes to see his face raised now, limned against the faintest light of dawn. He was listening. She held her breath, afraid suddenly that it wouldn't come again. Afraid that it had been, as it had long before, only the betrayal of her mind. So when it echoed hollowly, the sickly wail, which had always before filled her with such dread, was now an answer to prayer.

He whispered, "My God," and she saw his eyes widen uncontrollably with what he, too, heard. She began to breathe again. He felt the movement, and his understanding of her fears brought his eyes back to her face. He removed his fingers from her lips, and he smiled at her.

Somewhere in the midst of the jumbled emotions that tightened her throat and pressed sudden tears against her lids, she found the strength to smile back and to whisper, "You heard it, too? Tell me, Julien, that you heard it, too."

"I heard it. Son of a bitch, of course, I heard it."

The harshness of that whisper should have warned her, so that she might have stopped him. The sudden bunching of the hard muscles that had been resting against hers, holding her a willing prisoner under his body, was a surprise. He was out of the bed, pulling on his jeans as he crossed the room to throw open the door, before her shattered senses could call him back. She shouted his name, but he was gone into the darkness of the hall and to whatever waited there.

She found her gown and slipped it on, listening, paralyzed the vital minute she might have made a difference. The sounds that came were unmistakable, although not the ones she had been waiting for. Instead of that imagined horror, the reality of the noise that came were more terrifying than any she might have created. She thought she heard him cry out, but if so, his voice was lost in the crash of his body down the wooden stairs to the unyielding tiles below.

She screamed his name as she threw herself into the hall, unthinking now of who or what might be there, uncaring of anything but finding him. She saw, clearly outlined against the dawn that touched the wall of glass downstairs and climbed into the darkness to lighten the stairs, what he had not seen, could not see. Stretched tautly as a rope across the stairs was the the ripped lime shell she had worn the day he had made love to her on these very steps. Stretched and tied at a level designed to cause exactly what had occurred.

She sobbed as her fingers struggled to remove it, wasting precious seconds. Finally, the silk released into her hands, freeing the passage of its obstruction. She ran down the remaining stairs to the crumpled figure at their foot. So still, so still, just as before.

She knelt beside him, afraid to touch him. She lowered her face to feel the comfort of his warm breath against her cheek.

"Julien," she whispered, touching his face, gray under the tan. She brushed his hair off his forehead and watched, like a miracle, the blue of his eyes revealed by the slow rise of his lids.

"Are you all right? What can I do?"

His lips parted, and she recognized the slight lift for what it was. He was trying to smile to ease her fears. His hand reached, and this time it was her fingers that closed against the darkness. He gripped too hard as he tried to move, to straighten.

"Just wait," he breathed, and examined what that cost, carefully, before he spoke again. "I thought…" he tried, gasping at the breath required for the effort.

"What, my love?" she whispered, stroking his face again. "What did you think?"

"That I'd learned how to fall." The short laugh broke with the pain. He said, when he could balance the required air against the agony, "Ribs. And all the old ones."

"I don't understand," she said, wondering why no one had come. The house was absolutely silent. She thought that the noise of his fall had been great enough to wake everyone, but they were still alone.

He moved suddenly, unrolling onto his back. She heard the sharp exhalation and the gasp he tried to control. He hurt her hand again, but when he realized what he was doing, he loosened his fingers, forcing the blind eyes to open. They made no effort to find her face, drifting uncaring now to stare instead into his unremitting darkness. She knew the pain had driven all thought of that subterfuge from his mind.

"I don't think I'm going to be able to get up on my own, and I'm too heavy for you. You're going to have to get someone. Angeline or the maid."

"I don't want to leave you," she said. She had done that before and it had been wrong, so wrong. She saw understanding on his drawn features. He smiled at her, meaning to reassure, but the gesture was more grimace than smile. She knew she would have to do as he asked. She moved her hand against his face and could see even in the dim light the swelling over his temple.

Concussion, she thought. *Fractured skull. God, who knows.* She bent to kiss him and watched him close his eyes. He was breathing in small rapid breaths, almost panting.

She ran to the kitchen, which was dark and held no

welcoming fragrances of coffee or bread baking for the day. There was nothing. No one.

She turned and hurried down the short flight of steps that led to the lower level, to the maids' rooms, but they were open and empty, the beds all made, smoothly undisturbed. There was no clutter of personal belongings. It was all as empty as the kitchen. She stood a moment not understanding, and then the fear began to grow again. There was no one here. No one had come to investigate the noise because they were all gone. She was alone, and Julien was hurt. Again. As she thought that, the pain tightened viciously against her temples, but she fought its debilitating effects. She had no time for that weakness.

He had managed to straighten his body further while she had been gone. He had taken the opportunity, used her absence to move against the pain he didn't want to reveal. He lay almost on his back now, with his good left leg drawn up slightly. His arms were crossed over his chest. He opened his eyes as she leaned over him.

"There's no one there," she said, not knowing what to do next.

"They have to be," he whispered. "They were there last night." She could almost see the thoughts moving behind the unfocused blankness of his eyes, so she was quiet to let him think. "The boat. You have to see if the boat's there. Andre's boat. The top of the steps. You can see from there. Can you do that? Can you go there and see?" He knew what he was asking, but, as he had, she realized there was no other choice.

"Do you think he's here?" she asked, her mouth dry with fear.

"I don't know. Just to the top of the steps. Leave the door open. I'll be here. I can hear you if you call." He tried to focus on her face. The effort to reassure her of normality brought tears so strongly that, for a moment, she couldn't see him. She touched his face and knew that if she called, he would come to her, no matter the cost. She also knew that she had to match that courage, that promise, with her own. She wouldn't fail him again.

"All right," she whispered and pushed up from her knees to stand over him. His eyes followed the sound of her movement, so she smiled at him, although, of course, he wouldn't know.

The tile was cool and pleasant against her bare feet and the doorknob turned easily under her fingers. The patio had retained more warmth from yesterday's sun and the texture of the flagstones was rougher against her skin. She concentrated on those sensations and not on what she was seeking. She reached the steps and saw that the dock was empty. She looked carefully along the beach, but the boat wasn't there. There was nothing. In spite of the need to get help for Julien, her immediate reaction was sharp relief. Andre was not here.

When she returned, she saw that he had managed to push himself to prop against the bottom step. If possible, his face was even grayer than before, showing her the effort that had gone into achieving that short distance. The swelling over his temple was already beginning to discolor, but he was smiling at her.

"The boat's gone. There's nothing there."

"Then Andre must have taken the servants back. There must be something I've forgotten. Some religious holiday. Something."

"You don't believe that," she said more harshly than she had intended and watched him swallow, but he didn't answer. When he spoke again, it was something different.

"If you bring a chair, maybe I can use it—"

"No, you're too badly hurt."

"Just ribs," he said again. "And everything that was broken before is using this as an excuse." She could hear the self-derision as he tried to make light of his injuries.

"You should see your head," and realized then the cruelty of that expression.

"I can feel it," he said, trying to laugh.

"Don't," she said, recognizing the pained reaction he couldn't quite control from that effort.

"You're right," he whispered, almost panting again. "That was definitely a mistake. No more laughter." He held out his hand as he had before, and she caught it and caressed his fingers.

"What happened?" he said, but she didn't understand until he asked again. "What did I fall over. There was something—"

"My shell," she whispered, knowing what he would think.

"Your what?"

"The blouse I was wearing that day. The one you tore. It was tied across the stairs. Halfway down. I never even wondered what happened to it. I never even thought about it. Do you suppose he found it? My God, Julien, he found it and realized what we had—"

"No," his harsh voice broke across her horror at Andre's knowledge of that intimacy. "I found it. They were coming in, so I hid it in the laundry hamper under everything else. I didn't think of it again."

"Then how…" Her voice faded because there was only one explanation, one she knew he would never accept.

"I have to get up," he said with grim determination.

"We have to try it with the chair. Do you understand?"
Again she knew he was right, and so she nodded.

"Caroline?" he asked. Only then did she realize what
she had done.

"Yes," she whispered and went to do as he had
asked.

The whole operation was as terrible as she had feared
it would be. By the time he was finally upright in the
heavy armchair she had dragged across the room, he was
drenched with sweat and too frighteningly white around
the lips. She had thought he might faint and once his
head had dropped loosely, but he had rejected that escape, and they had finally managed. She was crying, but
she had managed to keep that from him. If he could do
this, then she could, too. She would show him that she
could be as strong as he.

When he spoke, his voice was hoarse, but determined
again. "My room. In the chest. There's a back brace.
Top drawer. It should work as well for the ribs as strapping. We can tighten it."

She didn't question or hesitate this time. There was
no one here to fear. Her only fear was for him. She
changed quickly into shorts and a knit top in her own
room. She found the brace where he had said and compared the perfect organization of those drawers to her
own chaotic housekeeping. But she could be this neat.
She could remember the necessity for this strict order
because, like Suzanne, she cared so much that he might
fall.

His eyes were closed, and he was sitting carefully
straight and tall against the pain of the broken ribs.

"What do I do?" she said.

He raised his arms, grimacing openly. "Just put it
around me. The opening in the front."

She followed his instructions, the brace fitting his back smoothly, the metal ribs hugging the contours of his body. She began to fasten the straps across the front.

"Tighter," he breathed. She raised her eyes to his face, but there was nothing to read there. She tightened the strap until he nodded, and then she moved on to the next set, there, too, following his directions. Finally when she was done, his eyes opened and once again he smiled at her.

"Better?" she asked and saw him nod, a minimum of motion.

"Now let's see what we can do about getting me vertical. Are you willing to lift again?"

"Not right now. For now you're going to rest. Do you have anything for the other? Any pain medication?"

"Upstairs," he said, knowing that she was right. "My bathroom."

When she returned this time, he had leaned back in the chair. She thought he looked better, less ashen and perhaps in less pain. She got water from the kitchen and put the two capsules in his hand. She could see that it shook, but he quickly gripped the pills to prevent her seeing that telltale evidence of shock. He took the medication and leaned back again, his head resting against the cushioned back of the chair. She sat finally at his feet, laying her face carefully against his left knee.

"It's all right," he said. "Give me a few minutes. I promise the ribs are the worst. The other will ease. Stop worrying."

"I just thought..." she said.

"What?"

"I shouldn't have given you anything with a head injury. God, I'm so stupid."

He laughed, and then cursed softly, another colorful string of French oaths, a few of which she didn't know.

"I told you to quit worrying. If you're going to react like this every time I fall—"

Whatever he had been about to say was deliberately halted. She waited, but he didn't finish the thought. Finally she turned her face against his knee and let his long fingers tangle in her hair while she tried to believe him.

Chapter Nine

She waited until she could feel the relaxation of the hard muscles of his thigh against her face, until his hand forgot to caress her hair, instead resting limply against it. She raised her head then. He was lying back against the chair, his eyes closed. She realized suddenly that she had let him go to sleep with a head injury. She couldn't do anything right. Not even after all this time. Not with him.

"Julien," she whispered, relieved when his eyes opened immediately. "Is there any way to contact the main islands? Someone with a boat?"

"The radio," he said, beginning to straighten carefully.

"I don't understand."

"A shortwave radio. We use it for emergencies. Storms. When we're cut off and can't take the boat out."

"Where is it?" she asked, trying to think if she had seen it.

"My office."

"We have to have help. We have to call the authorities." She was afraid he would deny that, would suggest they simply wait until Andre returned, but he nodded, and then she worried, because of his easy agreement, that he was hurt more seriously than he had admitted.

"What can I do?" she asked as she saw him ease carefully to the front of the chair. His knuckles whitened against the chair arms.

"Nothing," he said, gathering his resolve. "This either works or not." Suddenly he was standing, in one strong surge of motion, lifting with his arms, but she heard the soft sigh of effort or pain, and he swayed slightly before he balanced.

"Let's go," he said and waited. She didn't understand, but she could hear the bitterness when he spoke again. "You'll have to let me hold your arm. I don't think I can manage to count the steps. This throws everything off."

She hurried to press against him. She felt his left hand reach and find her arm, but then she moved too suddenly. He swayed, his delicate balance upset.

"I'm sorry," she whispered and waited instead for him to lead.

His hand tightened against her upper arm, and she turned to watch the emotion move across his face. He said only, "Slowly. You'll have to wait. And I'm the one who should be sorry."

"For what?" she asked, caressing his fingers that were still biting painfully into the muscle of her upper arm. "What do you have to be sorry for? We'll manage. Just be patient with me. I'll get it right. Eventually."

He moved carefully, putting as little weight on the right hip and thigh as he could, leaning heavily against her. She wondered what the cost of this maneuver was on the damaged ribs, but she didn't ask. She matched her stride to his halting progress, the whole procedure made more difficult by his reliance on her guidance, so that she was forced to both lead and follow.

They had moved almost halfway across the room when she felt him stop, his head hanging, exhausted with the effort he had made.

"One minute," he whispered.

"Do you want to sit down?" she asked. He raised his head to smile, again focused only vaguely in the direction of her voice.

"I'd never get up again," he said.

They were silent a long time, and then he spoke, "You're finally seeing the reality, and you don't like it." His voice was neutral, stating the obvious.

"Of course, I don't like it. I hate knowing that you're in pain. Why would anyone like this?"

"I didn't mean that," he said.

"Then what? What reality?"

"Of who I am. What I've become. What she always called me is true now."

She knew what he meant and wanted to say it again, teasing as always, against his strength and sure maturity. She knew that he no longer saw himself as strong so she didn't know what to tell him. She let the silence stretch too long, and then it was too late. Nothing she could have said would make it right. He moved finally, and they began the journey again.

She opened the door of the office and was shocked, although she should have anticipated something like this. The chaos was total, even to the computer, the disks, papers, everything mutilated, destroyed. She wondered when and how it had been done without their hearing. During the long hours he had spent in her bed perhaps. While she had slept in his arms, imagining that she was finally safe, she had instead been bringing this chaos into his ordered world.

"What is it?" he asked, sensing through her body the scope of whatever had happened.

"It's destroyed. Everything. The office, the computer. I don't know where the radio was."

"Far wall, under the seascape."

"It's not there. There's nothing there. If there's a radio here, it's like everything else. Destroyed."

He released her arm and commanded because he could hear the unraveling control in her tones, "Find it. It's here. You just have to find it and see what shape it's in. Maybe I can—"

She laughed in despair, and then knew he would misinterpret that laughter as a response to his hope that he could repair whatever had been done.

"You don't understand," she said, not knowing how to make him see the totality of the hostility that had been let loose in the room.

"Tell me."

"There's nothing that's in one piece. Or even ten pieces. It's just mutilated. Even the paper is torn into shreds," she whispered.

"Why? My God, why?" he said. The question was not addressed to her, but because she thought she understood, she answered.

"Because of me. Because you came to me last night. And he knew."

"Everyone was asleep last night before I came to your room. I made sure."

"You thought."

"God, you think I'm a fool." His anger lashed her. "You think I'm incompetent because I'm blind. I listened at his door. He was asleep. Do you think I'd chance—" He stopped, unwilling to admit even now what he feared.

"Chance what?" she said. "Tell me."

"I thought that after what he had said had happened between you, he might be jealous. He was always—"

"Tell me," she demanded, knowing now that he knew far more about his brother than he had ever acknowledged, even to himself.

"He was always jealous of anyone I was seriously interested in. When it was over, he always tried to move in. Then he would tell me about it. I thought at first he was only trying to follow in my footsteps. Some sort of misguided admiration, imitation. 'The sincerest form of flattery,' Suzanne reminded me, but she didn't know. I didn't tell her. He was cruel to them. There was something wrong in the way—"

"The way he treated women," she guessed, suddenly sure of that knowledge.

"Women I cared about," he said softly. "As if he were punishing them for becoming involved with me. He'd ask them things. More than one person warned me, but I didn't listen. He was my brother. I thought it was just part of his growing up. Maybe something to do with his mother's death. Some sort of sexual adventurism. But I wondered, even then, and I was careful. After I knew, I was careful that my relationships were private. Hidden. I suppose on some level I knew what I was doing, but—"

"But you never admitted it," she said. In the revealing silence, she knew that he would not admit it even now.

"He was so young. And in the years since, there's been *nothing* like that. He's been my eyes, always willing to do the countless errands that allow me to function in the business world. He would fly from here to Paris at a moment's notice. If I even suggested that I needed him, he was there. To talk, to discuss plans, to do whatever made it easier for me. He would drop whatever he was doing and come. The other was all over. I'd forgotten it. There's been nothing wrong, not in all these years.''

''Since your accident?''

''More than six years. He outgrew the need to have whatever I had had.''

''Because you had nothing,'' she said softly, knowing it had been true. She saw the realization break across the dark face and move into his eyes. ''Or am I wrong? Were there women?''

''No,'' he admitted, shaking his head slowly to reinforce the denial that was also admission. ''There were no women.''

''Why?'' she whispered and touched the corner of his mouth. ''Why in six years was there no one?''

She felt the slight rise of his mouth, the smile, but he only shook his head, again refusing to put into words things that were too painful to admit. She was bringing chaos here, too, she knew. Chaos into the carefully controlled world where he hid his emotional needs. But she, who had never been certain of anything, knew with certainty now that it was necessary that she destroy, as his office had been destroyed, the barriers and artificial successes he had erected around his blindness, around the emptiness of his life.

''Until me,'' she said and watched the memories move in the dark face. Suddenly he swallowed hard and leaned to kiss her. She lifted on tiptoe to find his mouth, to protect him. Then his lips were over hers, his tongue seeking her response. When she broke the kiss, he straightened carefully away from her body. She left her hands resting lightly on his shoulders.

"You think this is all because of that?" he asked.

"Don't you? You know it is. It's the only explanation."

"No," he said quietly. "There is another explanation." She could tell from his tone what he meant.

"God, you're not going to start that again. Why won't you believe me? I haven't done anything. You think I did this? Why? And when? You were with me. Did I slip out of bed and come down here and do all this? That doesn't make any sense."

"And the other does? I haven't seen 'all this.' I have only your word for whatever destruction is here." He heard her quick breath and anticipated her answer. "It wouldn't take long for you to throw enough things around in here to make me believe it's all as you say. I can't go charging in to investigate. I can't risk another fall, and you know it." His voice was harsh and bitter.

"Do you understand what you're accusing me of? Did I tie my shell across the stairs, too? Did I do that, too?"

"The maids would have brought it to you when they found it. How would anyone else know where it was? And damn you, you know I have no way of knowing if that's what was there. You could tell me anything, and I have no way..."

He controlled the anger carefully. When he spoke again, it was there, but he was trying to be reasonable. "Do you understand what you are asking me to believe about my brother? That he tied something across the stairs to make you fall? That he used a tape recorder to create that crying baby to deliberately lure you out of your bedroom and to those stairs, to make you fall?"

"To make *me* fall?" she said, incredulous that even now he didn't understand. "Not to make *me* fall. I could see it, Julien. Anyone could see it. The tape must have been operated by a timer, set for an hour when there would be enough light that anyone could see…''

His face was stone, denying what she was saying. He turned so sharply back to the door of the room that she was afraid he would stumble.

''Wait,'' she said and walked to stand so he could touch her arm.

''Get out of my way,'' he said quietly.

''Julien,'' she began, but he moved past her, pulling away from her hand that slipped off his bare shoulder.

He spoke as he limped painfully into the next room, but she could hear every word. ''I don't know why you're here. I don't know what you really came for, but it's over. I don't want you around me again. We'll wait for Andre. You can tell him whatever you think he's done. Until then, you stay the hell away from me. Just go upstairs and leave me alone.'' His voice broke on the last and she heard and understood perhaps for the first time the pain she was causing. ''I can't stand any more of this. Whatever it is, is over. No more, sweet God, please, no more.''

She watched him grope until his hand encountered the tall chair that he had sat in the first night. He eased down into it. He finally put both hands over his eyes and lowered his head into them. She watched a long time, but he never moved again. She knew that in spite of what he had said, she couldn't leave him alone, so she sat down and leaned back against the wall and waited with him for Andre.

IT WAS A LONG TIME before she dared to speak. She didn't want to hurt him again, but she knew that the morning was well advanced. If Andre had just gone to work, it would still be only a matter of an hour or two until he would be back. If he were somewhere else, she had no idea how long, or how short, a time until he came.

"Even if," she began and saw the response to her voice in the slight movement of his hands. At least he was listening. "Even if I have done whatever you think I've done in coming here, you must know that I would never make you fall." She waited for him to answer, but he didn't move again. "I would never deliberately hurt you. You have to know that."

"You've done nothing but hurt me since you came. You had to know how this would hurt."

"What? How what would hurt?"

"God, you do that so well. Are you an actress? Where did he find you? But even if you are, you are also so right," he said softly. "Your size, your smell, your voice. You even feel right, move right under me. That's what—"

"Julien, tell me. Who do you think I'm pretending to be? Tell me."

He raised his head at that and turned to the sound of her voice. "My wife, of course. You're supposed to be my wife. I don't know how he found out all the things he told you. They never met. He and I were not on the best of terms then. We'd had a misunderstanding, and I was too angry at him to listen to any explanations, too involved with her. I couldn't think of anything but her. And I'd banished him here." He laughed softly, perhaps at his own banishment, and then realized he'd moved away from the point. "You are so damn good. And you know so much. The little-girl-lost quality. The baby. God, that was ingenious. I could hear the pain. Whatever he's paying you isn't enough. You could make more on stage. You are very talented."

"Then why didn't you believe?" she whispered.

"Because I *know* better. Did you think I wouldn't investigate? Was the old woman part of it, too? Or did her story just necessitate this?"

"I don't know about an old woman. I don't know anything about that."

He shook his head and leaned back against the colorful print of the chintz upholstery. And his eyes closed.

"But I'll tell you what I do know," she said. He didn't respond, but his lips moved into a slow, knowing smile.

"He's going to kill me," she said softly and saw his eyes open at that. It was clearly not what he had expected her to say. She was perversely glad she had shocked him. "And maybe you. He tried before. This time he's going to succeed because you're going to let him. We're going to sit here and wait for him to come back, and then there'll be another accident. And do you know something, Julien? In spite of whatever you just said, in spite of whatever you believe, or say you believe, about my motives, I don't think you want me dead."

"Again," he said, and his laugh was bitter.

"No," she denied, shaking her head, and realized that he couldn't see. But this time it didn't matter, so she simply waited.

"There's a boat," he said after a long time. "In the boathouse. It was mine. It's supposed to be taken care of. You should be able to lower it into the water and leave. Surely you can find one of the other islands. Have you ever driven a boat?"

"I don't know," she said. "You tell me. What's the right answer?"

"Don't," he said against her mockery, and she was

sorry. As angry as she was with him, she didn't want to hurt him anymore. None of this had been his fault, nor could she blame him for the bitterness.

"I don't think I have," she said finally. "You can help me."

"You don't understand. The boathouse is on the beach. I can't get down the steps. There's no way. But you can go. No matter what you believe," he said, mocking her again, "Andre won't hurt me."

"He already has. He brought me here. Arranged it. And he tied the shell across the stairs."

"No," he said, "but that doesn't matter now. Perhaps you really believe that. I can't tell what you really think or feel. But if you believe Andre intends to harm you, I realize it must be difficult for you to sit here and wait. Maybe you're confused because—"

"Because?" she asked, but she knew what he meant, and she understood suddenly that this, too, was part of whatever diabolical plan Andre had devised.

"Because you were sick. Because of the baby," he said softly, but his voice didn't condemn.

"I think Andre's going to kill me because I'm insane? Is that it?"

"Confused about what's happening here. About why you're here."

She wondered bitterly if he could be right. The flood of doubt was so intense her throat ached against the sobs his words had almost released. She struggled against the darkness of the mists and the easy retreat they offered, but she knew better now. "If you really want something…" her grandfather had always said, but because the sweetness of his memory could weaken her, she blocked that thought, too.

"It's not paranoia if someone's *really* trying to kill you," she said reasonably. "Anyone will tell you that."

She saw him smile at her argument, and she suddenly wanted to hit him for treating her like a child. He always treated her like a child. As if she couldn't think. As if she were stupid. She recognized the old refrain and stopped it. That wasn't true, and she knew it now. She finally knew better than that. Those were only her insecurities, her needs, that she had always forced him to fight against. With that realization, she felt the pain begin to tighten against her temples, and its darkness was familiar and even comforting somehow. She closed her eyes, waiting for the confusion to clear.

She opened them to find he was turned toward her face, so she knew that she must have been quiet a long time, lost again in the darkness. But she wasn't confused any longer.

"You have to come with me," she said. "Whether you want to or not, whether you think you can or not, whether you trust me or not. You *have* to come. Do you understand? If you don't come with me, I won't go. I really believe he intends to kill me. He had to get rid of the servants, so he took them somewhere. He's probably on his way back now. I think he's the one who's insane, and I think you know that somewhere deep inside. If you put it all together, all the little pieces of the puzzle and the clues through the years, I think you know that."

"I can't do the steps," he said softly. "It's not a matter of wanting to or even of believing you. I would do it if I could because I know you believe what you're saying. And I know that you're afraid. I know what it feels like to be afraid. I'd come with you if I could. But I can't. So you better go. I want you to go because..."

''Because?'' she whispered as before, and she felt the tears scald at what was in his face and voice.

''Because I don't want you to be hurt. Or to be afraid.''

''Why? Why don't you want that?''

He shook his head and turned away, and she knew he wouldn't tell her.

''I'm going to find the boat,'' she said. ''To see if it's all right. You could try the stairs. Maybe sitting. One at a time. You have to try,'' she said, watching his averted head.

''I'm going.'' She rose on legs that were stiff and painful from sitting on the floor these hours. They made her think about how he must feel. ''You have to try. Promise me you'll try. I'll come back when I have the boat in the water. I won't even know how to start it. If you're not on the beach when I finish, I'll come back here for you. But you have to try. Promise me.'' And finally she saw the slight nod.

She made the journey again across the patio and down the long steps. There was still no sign of Andre's boat. She took a deep breath and walked across the expanse of beach to the boathouse. The hot sand made her hurry, or at least that's what she told herself as she jogged across the openness of the beach. She prayed that she could lower the boat and get it into the water. Julien had said the boat was his, and that meant no one had used it in six years. She wondered what that would do to a boat. He couldn't know whether Andre would have taken care of it or not since Julien would never use it again. What if they had sold it without telling him? A thousand possibilities flew through her mind as she crossed the few hundred feet of sand. Then her fingers were struggling with the door. There was a padlock, but

it had not been fastened. It was large and the chain it
held was rusted slightly and unyielding. She finally
forced the metal to give and placed the lock carefully
back through the links.

She opened the doors, but the sudden darkness of the
interior after the bright, reflected light of the beach
blinded her so she had to wait for her eyes to adjust.
Gradually it took shape there in the darkness. It hung
above the water, swaying gently, and the flashing lights
off the water under the gray planks of the dock reflected
against the gleaming wood of its bottom. She ran her
hand over the tight boards and thought that it looked all
right. By now she knew with certainty that she didn't
know anything about boats. There had been no soft
clearing of the mists that still blocked parts of her memory, no instinctive feel of what to do. She had nothing
to go by here.

She found the handle that would winch down the
hanging boat, but like the lock on the door, it was stiff
and unyielding. She tried a long time in the dimness of
the boathouse and even pushed with her bare foot against
the crank. Nothing. She found a tool she didn't recognize
on the bench and began to beat against the handle, but
the too-loud echoing clanging made her afraid. She wondered how long she had been here. God, she couldn't do
anything right. The old familiar inadequacies threatened
to swamp her effectiveness, but she gritted her teeth
against the lure of giving in, of giving up.

"You son of a bitch," she said softly and pushed
against the metal shaft with both hands, taking out all
her frustrations with him and with herself on its unyielding resistance. She felt it move, give slightly against her
determination. She pushed again, adding her bare, sand-
covered foot to the effort and heard the grind of metal

against metal and saw the slight rocking movement of the boat as it edged downward. She felt a sense of triumph and bore down all her slight weight against the handle and it turned again under her hands. With each revolution, the groaning metal moved more easily. The boat was gradually lowering toward the flickering surface of the water. She was covered with sweat when it was accomplished, but it was down.

She found the cap of the gas tank. When she opened it, she knew that it was dry and had been for a long time. She was glad she had thought to check, but still she was probably going to do all this, and the damn thing wouldn't start. Dead batteries or whatever. She would get him down here, and they would simply be stuck on the beach. Then she realized the boat was rigged like Andre's for sails. They could always sail her out. She could row it out of the boathouse and raise the sail and be gone. When Andre had done it, it had all looked so easy. And Julien would be with her.

She filled the tank from a can she found stuck in a corner of the dark shed. The sharp smell of gas in the close space almost made her sick. There were already paddles in the boat, and she pulled two life jackets from the hooks on the wall and threw them into the bottom. She walked to the back of the boathouse, the side away from the house, and pushed against the double doors. They opened easily until the blinding noontime sun lit every corner of the building.

She turned to start back to the house to bring Julien, and the life jackets were already afloat, drifting softly on the water that had quickly filled the bottom of the boat. It was only what she had expected. She didn't know why she was so bitter. This would have been too easy. Nothing was going to be this easy. Andre wasn't that careless. All the time wasted. All the effort. She should have known. Whatever he had planned, it did not include their sailing peacefully away from the island before he returned.

She stepped out of the boathouse and was perhaps halfway across the beach that stretched between it and the steps before she saw the boat. It was tied to the end of the dock of the sheltered cove, drifting gently on the waves that moved under it to break slowly across the sand. Andre was back.

The boat was empty, so she looked up the long steps to the patio that lay silver in the sun. She couldn't see into the room from here. Whatever was happening between the two brothers was hidden. Whatever was happening or had already happened. She hoped she was wrong and Julien was right. God, she hoped she was wrong.

She ran to the side of the house, toward the boathouse, and began to climb the rough slope that led to the end of the patio. She watched the stairs to see if Andre descended, but they were empty in the hot sun. The patio was deserted when she reached the top, and she lay quietly along the rim of the rise and looked through the long windows. There was no movement. She could see the chair that Julien had been sitting in, but it was empty now. She heard in the blinding stillness feet pounding against the wooden stairs, and she couldn't remember what she had done with the torn piece of silk.

She didn't move until she heard Andre calling and knew by that that Julien had gotten out of the house. He must be down on the beach somewhere. While she had struggled with the boat, he had done what he had promised and made it down the steps to the cove below. He would be waiting for her there. Maybe Andre would think they were gone. Maybe she could make him believe that.

She slid down the slope she had climbed, cutting and bruising her legs on the rocks. Andre was still occupied with searching the house, so she had a few minutes.

She ran to the boathouse, which would be hidden by the angle of the house unless Andre came down to the beach. She opened the doors, hoping that Julien had managed to find his way here, but it was as empty as she had left it. She released the chains that held the boat, knowing it would sink. Perhaps Andre would think they had left in it. She pushed it to the open outer doors and through them, trying to get it into deeper water, but the current caught it, and she realized, too late, that it would be carried to the beach. There was nothing else she could do. Maybe he still would think...

She could hear Andre calling his brother as he came down the patio steps. She slipped into the water under the boathouse dock and began to swim strongly out the doors and around the far side. She dived, hoping the clear water would be deep enough and dark enough to hide her body. She held her breath as long as she could and swam hard under the surface. She could see the bottom quite clearly and knew by the light in the water that it wasn't deep enough.

A darker, colder current moved over her suddenly, and she followed it, twisting to find the dark mouth that loomed out of the blue depths surrounding her. She didn't have time to wonder what it was. She surfaced only long enough to breathe deeply, praying that Andre wasn't looking this way. She dived down and tried not to think about what she was about to do as she moved with the current into the blackness.

Chapter Ten

The blackness she had entered stretched far enough in front of her that she began to be afraid. The only decision left seemed to be to drown here in this enclosed shaft she had found or to struggle back the way she had come in order to surface, gasping for air, right under Andre's nose.

Just as her lungs began to burn and her mind to command her mouth to open and breathe, to breathe anything, even the brackish death that surrounded her, she realized there was a lightening in the distance. She kicked fiercely, fighting the urge to surrender. She reached the end of the rock tunnel and fought upward to the gleaming brilliance of the surface, uncaring who might see her. She used the last of her strength to pull herself from the water. She lay against the rocks and took in air in great gulping lungfuls, and when she had fed her oxygen-starved body, she finally looked at her surroundings.

She had apparently swum through a break, a fissure near the end of the volcanic rock that made the island. She was now on the other side of the narrow ridge, where the sheer rock face of the cliff that the house was built on met the unrelenting pounding of the surf. She could tell by the exposed rock that the tide was out. The cliff appeared to be deserted, but her presence was brutally exposed here to anyone who might look out the windows of the house or walk out onto its back deck.

She scrambled up the rocky face, angling toward the house, using handholds that tore her clinging fingers. The entrance to the cave loomed before her and, almost without a conscious decision, she found herself sheltering in its dark depths. Surely this was better than having Andre find her, alone and defenseless.

Although Andre's boat was deserted in the cove, she couldn't leave without Julien. She knew, even if he wouldn't admit it, for whom the trap on the stairs had been intended. She knew that Andre was perfectly willing to injure, perhaps even kill, his brother to bring about whatever it was he had hoped for by arranging for her employment, for her presence here. Like Julien, she didn't understand his original motives, but that was no longer important. Or not important now. What mattered was getting safely off the island and away from whatever Andre's plan had now become. She had made it easy for him that night on the boat because she hadn't known what he intended. But he wouldn't find her unprepared again. She knew that he would stop at nothing, not even hurting the brother he professed to love, to carry out whatever it was he had now decided was necessary.

She lay a long time on the damp, rocky hardness of the cave floor. She gathered every ounce of her remaining strength, trying to marshall her mental forces as her body was almost automatically gathering physical resolve. She had to think where Julien might have hidden, find him and then get them both to Andre's boat that lay calmly drifting in the gentle waves on the other side of the island. Or would it be better to simply hide here, hoping that Andre would eventually give up his search for her and his brother and leave? But she was afraid for Julien. He was in no condition after his fall to deal with Andre.

The hand that touched her out of the darkness was totally unexpected. She barely managed to stifle the scream that would have given away her hiding place. His approach had been hidden by the pounding of the waves against the rock below, but she recognized the voice.

"Are you all right? My God, Caroline, what's happened? Why are you here?"

She sat up to face him, trying to think clearly in spite of her exhaustion. "I swam through a fissure at the end of the island, a tunnel in the rock. Near the boathouse. And came out here."

"We played there as children," he said, and she could hear the memories threaded through his voice. "We dared one another to swim it. Of course, no one could refuse and be forever branded a coward. I always hated the darkness, hated the way it made me feel when it closed around me." The horror of that remembrance was fully exposed, although the words were ordinary enough. A childhood game that had scarred.

"I know," she said softly. "I felt the same way. As if I'd never reach the end. As if I'd swim there in the blackness until—"

"Until you died," he finished for her. "I hated it. But I did it. I thought I had to. To prove something. God knows what."

"That you weren't afraid," she whispered. "That you could do everything..."

"Everything my big brother could do," he said bitterly. "My whole life long. My whole damn life."

"Andre, you never had to prove anything to him. He loves you. He didn't care if you did what he did, accomplished all that he had. He loved you for what you were. You never understood that." She waited, but he didn't answer that truth. And finally, because she had to know, she asked about his brother.

"Andre, do you know where Julien is?" she asked quietly, hoping that he hadn't found Julien before he came to find her.

"No," he said, "he's hiding from me. I suppose I have you to thank for that. What have you told my brother about me? More lies?" He laughed again, and that sound raised the hair all over her body. She crossed her arms over her breasts and rubbed at the coldness that caused her to shudder involuntarily. She was alone in the cave with the man who had already tried to kill her, and who, she was sure, intended to succeed this time.

"I never lied about you. I don't know what you're talking about," she said, deliberately injecting calmness and certainty into her voice.

"You denied what I told him. About that night."

"But that wasn't true," she said, trying to force him to acknowledge it. "You know it wasn't true."

"I know you're a lying bitch. You're in love with him, aren't you? He came to your room last night. In spite of what I had told him. He believed you rather than his own brother," he said, the venom plain in his tone.

"Is that why you made him fall? Because he came to me last night?" she asked calmly, but she wanted to scream at him, to force him to admit what she knew.

"I don't know what you're talking about. Did Julien fall? Is he all right? Is that why he didn't answer me?"

His hands grasped her shoulders, gripping painfully, biting into the soft flesh of her upper arms, and he shook her suddenly. "Tell me about my brother, damn you. Is he hurt?"

"Leave her alone," Julien ordered, and they both jumped at the unexpectedness of that command. She could see him outlined against the light, the surf creaming around his bare feet and ankles as he stood, leaning against the rocky entrance to the cave. He had pulled on a shirt, but he hadn't taken time to button it, so she could see the white brace strapped tightly across the tan of his chest. She wondered at the nightmare the climb down the rocks must have been. Far worse than the steps he had doubted he could manage.

"Julien," Andre said, relief in his voice. "She said you'd fallen. Are you all right or was that another of her lies?"

"I fell, but there's nothing broken. Maybe ribs. The other is just—" He paused, cautious, perhaps, of revealing more than was evident about his injuries.

"What happened?"

Andre's concern grated because she knew he was lying, that he was well aware of what had caused his brother's accident, but she waited, needing to see and hear Julien's reaction.

"Caroline says there was something tied across the stairs," Julien answered calmly. His tone was neutral, bearing no accusation, but the information was, of course, accusation in itself.

"Tied!"

Andre's disbelief sounded as genuine as his other lies had. He was so good at this. Maybe he really believed it. Was it possible that he could do these things, lie as he did, and convince himself of their truth?

"That's insane," Andre said, breaking into her speculation. "No one would tie something across the stairs.

Do you mean that you think that was done so you would fall?''

"Caroline believes that," Julien said.

"My God, who do you think would deliberately cause my brother to fall?"

She waited for Julien to tell Andre of her accusation, but finally she realized that he wasn't going to speak. He had pitted her against his brother, deliberately, and now he was going to sit back and listen and decide whom to believe.

"There was no one else who *could* have," she said into the silence.

"No one else who could have? No one other than... My God, do you mean me? You think I tied something across the stairs to trip my own brother? God, what do you think I am?"

His fury communicated itself starkly in his distorted features and she was again afraid. She was too close to him. He had obeyed his brother and released her when Julien stepped into the cave, but he was standing there before her. Too close. He could kill her before Julien could stop him.

She moved away from him as she answered, as far as she could until she was against the cold seepage of the far wall. Still, only a few feet separated them and that was as far as she could go.

"I think you are what you've always been—a jealous little boy. Trying to be something and someone you can never be." She watched his face and his hands, to anticipate whatever move he might make. She swallowed against the nausea that crowded her throat, but she knew that she had to go on. She knew she was right. These were old truths that these brothers both knew and had denied. "I think you've always been jealous. Julien was so much better than you at everything. And he had so much more. The firstborn. His father's favorite. The one who could do everything so well. Sports. The businesses.''

''So because I'm jealous, I devise traps to make my blind brother fall. My brother who has been hurt so much…'' His voice broke as he tried to control his emotions, but she was unmoved by his denial. She didn't believe in that pain. She knew clearly now what he was. ''My God,'' he whispered, ''you must think I'm insane.''

''Perhaps,'' she acknowledged. She was glad her voice sounded so calm in the darkness. ''I know what I saw on the stairs this morning. And I know now that what happened on your boat that night wasn't an accident. You deliberately knocked me into the water. You tried to kill me that night, Andre. I *know* that. I just don't know why you would go to all the trouble to bring me here, halfway around the world, to kill me.''

''You're the one who's insane,'' he suggested. ''Julien, are you hearing this? Now I'm supposed to have tried to kill her. This is crazy. She's crazy.''

''Then why did you have the sail up in the storm?'' she asked, trying to remember Julien's questions that night. ''Why weren't you using the engines to get us back here as quickly and as safely as possible?''

''I was taking the damn sail in when you did your stupid maneuver into the boom. I had told you to sit still. If you'd done what you were told, you could have saved us all a lot of trouble. You've been nothing but trouble since you arrived.''

''Then why did you arrange for me to come here?'' she asked again. Apparently her accusation about the boat had driven all thought of her second remark from his mind. Or he had been busy deciding on the most convincing lie.

"*I* didn't arrange for you to come," he said incredulously. "You're *Suzanne's* secretary. Her lawyer made the arrangements. I'd never set eyes on you until I picked you up in Guadaloupe. You know that."

"That's true. I'd never seen you before, but you arranged for my name to be given to Paul Dupre. Julien knows that."

He turned to his brother, and she saw the deep breath he took before he spoke. When he did, he sounded like someone reasoning with a child, or with someone not very intelligent, and she was suddenly furious with him for that.

"Look," he said, "I explained that to you. I never had any connection with the search for Suzanne's secretary. I thought we had that all straightened out. Did she tell you that I did? Is she where you got that idea?"

Julien made no explanation. He was still outlined against the outside light, only a dark shadow who apparently had chosen to listen, but not participate in the resolving of this conflict. She felt deserted by his failure to answer. In that pain, she was not aware that Andre had turned back to her until he spoke again.

"Why would I suggest your name to Dupre? What possible motive could I have for interfering in the search? And why you? My God, why would I arrange for *you* to be sent here?" he said angrily.

The question seemed to echo in the dank air of the cave, and she knew this was the most dangerous moment. She was about to open up all the long-healed wounds. Except none of them had ever healed. They had only closed over with the infection of his long-ago treachery still festering under them. He had been so sure he'd won. So triumphant. Triumphant as he had watched the brother who had always been better at everything requiring physical prowess struggle those long months simply to drag his broken body across the room. Triumphant anew each time Julien had to ask for his help.

But he was wrong. So wrong. Because with blinding clarity she knew. Everything was clear, unshrouded suddenly as it sometimes had happened here, breaking through the pain and the mists like sunshine through the morning fog.

"Because I look like her," she said softly, almost whispering the words. "Because I'm like her."

"Like who?" he mocked, laughing. "Who are you supposed to be like?"

She smiled because she could hear the fear. She wondered if Julien could hear it, too.

"Like his wife. Julien's wife. That's why you chose me. Why your lawyers found me. Your ad must have been written with me in mind. The flyer posted where I was working as a temporary. I'm sure they told you how desperately I needed a permanent position. You knew I'd apply. And I did. I wondered why, out of all those women who showed up for the interview, I was the one. It seemed like a miracle. But of course, it wasn't. It was something you'd arranged. Hadn't you done enough to him? Or was he coping too well? Was that it? 'He does it all so well,' you said. And you couldn't stand it. So you brought me here. The physical torture had ended, had been overcome. And now you provide the mental anguish. Isn't that what this is really all about?" she questioned, as gently reasonable as he had been.

"I don't know what you're talking about. I don't intend to stand here and listen to you tell lies about my relationship with my brother. I don't know why you're doing this. I had nothing to do with bringing you here," he said, and then his tone changed suddenly. "And I never even knew my brother's wife. I never met her."

"I know," she said softly. "And that was your error."

"My error? How many times must I say it—"

"You don't understand even now, do you, Andre?" She smiled at him. "I suppose that's the ultimate irony. That you still don't know."

"Know what?" he shouted at her, his reasonableness of only a short time ago breaking down suddenly and violently. "What the hell don't I know?"

"That your lawyers succeeded too well," she said, waiting for the impact of that to reach his brain. She sensed rather than saw in the dimness here at the back of the cave his sudden stillness. So she spoke again, to confirm what she knew he now must understand. "They didn't find someone who looked like Julien's wife. They *found* his wife. They found Kerri."

The silence stretched until she thought she had to speak, to say anything that would ease the tension that vibrated in waves between the three of them. She had seen Julien's head lower against what she had just said, what she had claimed, and she wondered what he was feeling.

She had finally put all that had been between them, all that she had begun to feel but hadn't understood, into words, and in a situation in which she had no opportunity to seek his reaction. She had made her claim in the most brutal way possible. She supposed in doing that she had helped Andre succeed. This was surely as agonizing for Julien as even he could have hoped.

"My God," Andre whispered, drawing her attention back to him. That was dangerous. Letting her feelings about what they were doing to Julien make her relax her vigilance against Andre. He was the one she must watch. She must be aware of his every move if they were going to survive.

"You *are* crazy," Andre spoke again in that same carefully shocked whisper. "They said you were crazy, but I didn't understand. 'Just a little off,' they said. You think you're Kerri. You poor crazy bitch. You came here, and we all told you the tragic story of my brother's wife and, you insane little fool, you bought into it. You think you're her. God, that's so pathetic. I could almost feel sorry for you if I didn't know what you're doing to Julien. Has she been telling you this, Julien? Trying to make you believe that? You can't believe her. You have to know…"

His brother didn't move. His head was still lowered against what was happening here. And still he refused to participate.

"*Who* told you, Andre?" she asked quietly, recognizing his error. She watched his gaze come back to where she was leaning against the wall of rock. "Who told you I was crazy? Your lawyers? The same ones who *didn't* find me?"

She saw him try to think what had been said, but he didn't give in that easily. "I don't know. I don't remember. Maybe Suzanne. Dupre had been concerned about it. Maybe someone in his office told me. About your baby. That you'd killed it."

She had thought that pain had been conquered with the destruction of this part of the drifting mists that had obscured her memories, but it tightened now against her forehead. She almost cried out against what he had said, against the lie.

"I didn't kill my baby," she whispered, but she could

hear the strain in her own voice as she tried to convince them. "That's a lie. He died because he was born prematurely. He came too early because of the wreck."

"Is that why you were caught up in the story? Julien's wife lost her baby, tragically, blamelessly, and you thought if you became her, you could give up the guilt that makes you hunt for the child you killed, that makes you hear him crying in the night."

"I didn't kill my baby. It wasn't my fault."

She found that in spite of her efforts to be calm, in spite of her need to do this rationally, she was crying. What he was doing was so unfair.

"You are *so* pathetic," Andre said again. "I could almost feel sorry for you, but you're not my brother's wife. I know that, and Julien knows that. That's why whatever you were doing, whatever you were pretending, could never work. I'm sorry for you because I think you might really believe it. But it's not true. Your name is Caroline Evans, and you killed your baby. You killed him when he was born because he was the product of a particularly brutal rape. Your family was Catholic and wouldn't allow an abortion. And so, when the baby was born, you—"

"No," she whispered again, but the band of the pain was so tight she was blind against its onslaught. She had heard this before. *Déjà vu.* His words echoing against the words that someone had said to her so long ago.

"No," she said again, desperate against the accusation, "that's not true. It wasn't true then, and it's not true now. I didn't kill my baby. There was something wrong with the brakes. That night. They didn't work. God, I remember that they were—there was nothing. I pushed and nothing happened. The car didn't even slow. I tried to tell Julien, but it was too late. I remember that now," she said, so sure. And into that clarity came another truth. It all fit. "Did you try there, Andre? Just like you tried here. If you could get rid of Julien's wife, everything would go back to how it had been before. But instead of killing me, you hurt Julien, and you hadn't really intended to do that, had you?"

She began to run down, her excitement about remembering suddenly not so important in the face of what that meant. "But it worked out well, anyway, and you enjoyed his pain. I could see it in your eyes the day you told me about the wreck. You enjoyed his dependence on you. You finally got your revenge for all the times you were dependent on him, unequal to his strength, to his perfection. You blinded your brother and found that it was the perfect revenge. One that's lasted for six years," she whispered finally, the horror she had discovered overcoming her own triumph in breaking through the darkness surrounding that night. "Until his strength defeated all you had done, and you had to find some other way to make him suffer."

"That's enough," Julien said, the command clear, although his voice was not particularly loud even in the enclosed space. When she looked at him, she could see that the rising tide was pushing above his knees now and around her calves here at the very back of the cave. "That's enough," he said again.

"But it's true, Julien. I remember it all now. I remember looking down on you in the road and thinking I had to go for help. And I left you. That's when you went back to the car. If only I had stayed," she said softly, the tears beginning again, tears of regret for what could not be undone. She had left him there, and she would always have to live with that.

"I'm sorry," Julien said, his voice very gentle. "I'm

sorry you've become involved with this because I know that you're going to be hurt. I know that you really believe what you've just said. That you are…my wife.'' He hesitated, but when he spoke again, his voice was as filled with certainty as hers had been. "But you aren't. And rationally I've known that since this began. I'm sorry I've let it go on as long as it has. I believed at the start that you knew, that you were in on some kind of elaborate trick to make me think…to make *me* believe what you believe," he finished softly.

"But it's true," she whispered again. "It's true and I remember everything. Everything we did together. How we met. The day the baby was conceived. You remember. You have to remember," she whispered, willing him to answer her.

"She's dead," Andre said so brutally that she cried out against it. "Dead and buried at the convent of the Sacred Heart. Her grave is there. You're not Kerri. I don't know who the hell you are, but you're not my brother's wife."

"Julien," she begged against the pain of Andre's words. "Please, Julien," she said his name like a prayer.

"She's dead. I went to her grave," he answered finally. His voice was clear even against the rush of the rising water, and she closed her eyes to shut out that reality of his answer, wondering how she could be insane and not know. But of course that was the classic answer. *If you thought you were insane, you probably weren't, and if…*

She squeezed her eyes closed tighter as if she could block the sound of what he had said as easily as she blocked the vision of his lowered head. She had been so sure. She had remembered it all. If those memories were not true, then perhaps what Andre had said was. Perhaps she had killed her baby and that was why he haunted her sleep. But Julien had heard the baby, too. Or had she created that memory as she must have imagined all the moments of their life together? That was even the term psychologists used—created memories. Was it possible that she *had* become Kerri because she wanted to, because she loved Julien so much.

As the pain of Julien's denial tore through her soul, she sought, again, the comforting darkness where she didn't have to think about anything she had done. The darkness where she had hidden so long. She mentally closed her ears and her mind. She wouldn't listen to any more. She had been so sure. So sure. And Julien's words to his brother simply washed over her in the darkness of the cave and were lost in the matching darkness that she created to fill her mind instead.

"I went to the convent after the old woman came. In spite of what you'd told me. I had to know. I think you have more to explain than Caroline demanded, and I won't be as easily put off by your lies as she was," Julien said. "Several questions, Andre, but we can take them one at a time. Think carefully before you lie to me again. I always knew. You could fool everyone else, even Suzanne, but you could never lie to me."

"I don't have to answer your questions. I haven't done anything. Don't patronize me, big brother." Andre's voice was suddenly filled with hate. "You thought you always knew everything I did. You were always trying to be my father. I'm grown up now, Julien, and I don't need you checking up on me. I don't intend to answer anything. I haven't *done* anything."

"Then you should have nothing to hide," his brother said reasonably. "Why did you bring her here? You had Beaulieu find her and you gave her name to Dupre's office and led them to understand it came from me. They weren't suspicious until they checked her background. Why did you send her?''

''I don't know what you're talking about. I had nothing to do with her being hired.''

''This isn't speculation. I can prove it. You know me well enough to know I don't bluff. Tell me the truth.'' Julien's command was as obvious as it had been before.

''I refuse to stand here and be treated like a child,'' Andre shouted as he faced his brother. ''I'm leaving and there's nothing you can do to prevent it.''

''Perhaps not, but I wonder how long you can manage to live on your salary from the distillery. I've always thought the division of our father's holdings between us was unfair, but now I wonder if he didn't know far more about you than I have ever suspected. Far more than even I knew.''

''I don't know what you're talking about. What do you think you know about me?'' Andre said, but his fear tinged the question, betraying him.

''More than I wanted to,'' Julien said quietly, the pain obvious in his voice. ''Things I denied and tried to explain away. Through the years. Things I covered up and fixed. And that was wrong. But I loved you. And I thought that Father's indifference and your mother's death were burdens that had caused you to rebel. I tried to understand and to help. But I want the truth about this. It's too important to me too. Tell me, Andre. You tell me, damn it, why the hell you brought her here.''

Chapter Eleven

He waited a long time for his brother's answer, and when it came, it was the same gently reasoned tone as before.

"I was wrong. I can see that now, but I was only trying to help. I lied to you after the old woman came. I was afraid you'd find out the truth and blame me. I couldn't face that. You were right, of course. I was the one who had her sent to the convent. It was my decision. I thought I was protecting her and the baby. I was wrong, and they died. I let you think they died in the car because then you wouldn't blame me. When the old woman came, I couldn't face your knowing that I'd let you down. I told you she hadn't died. It was stupid. Something I said so you wouldn't be angry with me. We've always known it was all her fault, but I was afraid you'd blame me. Don't you understand? Can't you see that it was all finished years ago? Why should you blame me when it was her fault?" Andre's voice was pleading now.

Julien steeled himself to the pain in the voice of the man he had always protected. He heard the echoes there of the child who had thought Julien could fix anything.

Andre had always wanted his approval, and so perhaps he *had* lied to keep his brother from being angry.

"But that doesn't explain why you brought her here. Why you tried to find someone so much like Kerri and arranged to bring her here. You must have known..." The pain broke through the careful control. "Even *you* must have known what that would be like for me."

Julien heard his brother's soft sigh and knew that he was moving across the distance that separated them. He felt Andre's arm around his shoulders, but he resisted the pressure to lean against that strong young body. Even the touch of the smooth muscles against his shoulder evoked the first painful days when he had begun to try to walk again. Those memories brought back Caroline's words about what she had seen in Andre's eyes.

Finally Andre must have realized his brother wasn't going to respond. He stepped away and spoke again, allowing emotion to color his soft voice.

"You were so lonely. So alone. I had watched you isolate yourself from everything. There were so many things your blindness robbed you of. All the sports you'd loved. Driving. Riding. But you even stopped the things that you could *still* have enjoyed. The opera, the symphony, plays. You had nothing, and I thought that if I could find someone who reminded you of her..."

Andre's voice faded into the darkness, but the last of Julien's questions had to be asked. He knew that the tiny seed of hope that she might be Kerri, the hope which had begun to grow so slowly in his darkness, in spite of all his efforts to deny it life, would be killed, poisoned by Andre's answer.

"And the things she knew? About what we did together? My God, Andre, she knew so many things. Or she seemed to know. Things that made me believe—"

"I'm sorry. I never meant to hurt you. Just the opposite. I guess I wasn't thinking clearly when I started all this. It made sense just to find someone for you. When I found Caroline, she seemed so perfect. I *wanted* her to be perfect for you. I asked people who had known you then, who had known you both. I found out everything I could and—'' He stopped suddenly. "God, Julien, I'm so sorry. I know now how wrong I was in helping her pretend to be your wife. I thought that if she could be enough like Kerri, you'd fall in love with her. I only wanted you to have somebody, something. I knew how lonely you were. I thought I could ease some of the pain of her death. I have watched you grieve over her for so long. Caroline thought she could carry it off. She wanted to. Even more after she came here, after she met you. I realize now what a mistake bringing her here was, but I couldn't know that her illness would make her believe she really *was* Kerri. It was only a game. I could never have foreseen that. I'm sorry for her, but I'm not responsible for—''

"Damn you, you're never responsible for anything," Julien said bitterly. "You hurt and damage and there's always some excuse, some reason why you're not to blame. Do you have any idea what you've done here? To me? And to her? Who *is* responsible if not you? For once accept the responsibility for your own actions. For once be man enough to say, 'I did it. It's my fault.' Just once. Just once, let me hear you say it."

"All right, damn you, all right. I brought her here. I'm responsible for this."

"And the baby? Why the baby, Andre? What were you hoping to accomplish by the crying baby?"

As he asked, Julien found he was angrier about this cruelty than he had been about what his brother had done to him. She was so fragile, so anguished with guilt about the child's death, and Andre had played on her pain. "You knew her baby had died, so you made it cry here for her. To remind her? Is that why? Not content to torture me with the memories of what I had been, what I had had, you had to torture her, too."

"Oh, no," Andre said. "You're not blaming that on me. I'm not responsible for that. She has nightmares. I had nothing to do with those."

"Except I heard the baby. And it was no nightmare. I went to investigate, and the blouse was stretched across the stairs. I thought that was to make her fall, but it wasn't at the top. It was more than halfway down. You couldn't take a chance on killing me, could you, Andre? You couldn't kill the goose that lays the golden eggs you so enjoy? You tried running the businesses before, when I was hurt. And you failed at that as you have failed at everything. All your life," he said, his anger snapping his remaining control. He had known he must have command of every faculty in this confrontation, but in his fury over what his brother had done to her, he had forgotten.

Andre's voice echoed his anger when it answered, "And you, you bastard, you never failed at anything. My father never even *looked* at me. I wasn't you. Why would he want another son? He had the ultimate one. The son everyone would want. I could never be anything but second best. God, even my own mother preferred you. She couldn't stop talking about you, comparing me. It's all I heard. How perfect her precious Julien was. *I* was her son. Not *you*. Damn you, you took my own mother away from me. Made her hate me."

"No," Julien said, his whisper barely audible against

the force of the tide that had begun to pound now against the opening of the cave as the level rose over the cliff face. Soon, he knew, the sea would flood the cave. Already the force of the waves against the rocks would make swimming dangerous. They needed to leave now, and instead, he could hear the loss of control in his brother's voice. Whatever else Caroline had been mistaken about, confused about, she had understood Andre's hostility, and she had been right about his instability. It explained so much through the years.

"That's not true and you must know it, Andre. Your mother adored you. You were her whole life. She was kind to me because I loved you as much as she did."

"No," Andre said, shaking his head. "You won't deny what I saw, what I know, what you have *always* known. You were the golden boy—everyone's golden boy—but not now. Now *you* call Andre. It doesn't matter that I made mistakes. You need me. You hate it, but you call. It's Andre that you need now. The golden boy is broken. No more perfection. I thought it was enough, would be enough. But you—" The painful exposing triumph died as he realized what he had revealed. Nothing would ever be the same.

"We have to go," Julien said quietly, working at making his voice soothing, confident. "The tide's coming in. You know how quickly it fills the caves. We have to get Caroline and leave now. It's becoming more dangerous by the second."

As he spoke, he began to move into the cave, his hands outstretched toward his brother. The water lapped against his chest, pushing strongly enough to make him stagger with the force of each driving wave that broke against the cliff and into the opening behind him.

"No," Andre's voice came clearly out of the darkness

before him, and he knew what the single word meant. As Caroline had earlier, he felt the hair at the back of his neck begin to rise against that malignant syllable. "I'll help you, my *dear* brother. My dear, blind, helpless brother. Grope your way to me, and I'll get you out. I'll guide you to safety, golden boy." Andre laughed viciously. "But not her. Not her. I don't like her, Julien. I never did. You and I, brother. But not her."

"We have to find Caroline and help her swim against the tide. You have to, Andre. You know that. There's nothing to decide. You *have* to help her. I'm afraid that I won't be strong enough to hold her against the surf. Not with my—" Julien stopped, wondering if he should remind Andre of his injuries.

He knew then that he was afraid of his own brother. As afraid as she had been, and he tried to control the dark thoughts. This was Andre. Whatever mistakes he had made had, as always, been impulsive, unthinking. Not malicious. But still he didn't finish the confession of his injuries.

"I'm depending on you again, Andre," he said calmly, washing the fear and anger from his voice. He was determined to act as if he knew that Andre would do the right thing. As if he had never doubted it. That usually worked. It had so often worked in the past.

"I told you I'd help you," his brother answered, so close that even above the sharpness of the brine that surrounded them, he could smell the pleasant familiar cologne. He felt Andre's hand take his reaching one, and then his body moved close beside him.

"We have to find Caroline. You know that. She's farther back in the cave. Help me find her."

"I don't want to find her," Andre said calmly, as if that answered all his demands. "She has driven a wedge between us. Or tried to. As far as I'm concerned she can find her own way out. I don't know why you're worried about her. She survived that night. In the storm. And she swam through the tunnel at the end of the island. She's a good swimmer, and she's stronger than she looks."

"Caroline," Julien shouted, denying the calm rationality of his brother's statements. "Caroline, you have to answer me. Come here, and let us help you. We have to get out. The cave floods at high tide."

They waited together, but the boom of the surf echoed against the walls of the cave, distorting, so that his straining ears heard nothing but the water. There was no answer, and then his brother laughed.

"I don't think she wants to come with you. Maybe you weren't as compatible as I thought you would be. Maybe she's already tired of your stupid blind groping, your everlasting fumbling and falling. Did she see you fall today, Julien? Maybe that's why she doesn't answer you. Or perhaps she's already gone. You wouldn't know, would you, my perfect brother. Not with the noise of the water. What if she left while we talked? You'd never know. Admit it. You don't know where she is, and I don't intend to help you look. So unless you come with me now, you can play blindman's buff here in the dark until you drown."

"You don't mean that—" Julien began.

"Now," Andre said, shoving viciously against his chest.

Julien fell into the churning water, the pain bursting into a thousand different agonies. The blow to his ribs took his breath so that he choked under the water. His leg twisted beneath him and buckled, a burning shaft invading the long bone of his thigh. Andre was right. Why should she come....

He pushed that thought away and fought to the surface, burying the pain, locking it in a compartment in his head and denying its hold on him. This was something he had learned long ago—control of pain. So his little brother would not have to see how much it cost to respond to his gentle coaxing.

"Now," Andre said again. "Do you understand? You and I will go *now*. We have to leave. You know the surf. Now or never."

Julien didn't speak again. He didn't want to warn him in any way. He dived awkwardly into the next wave that rushed through the rapidly filling cave, away from Andre's voice and toward what he hoped was the back of the cave. He swam as deeply as he could, not worrying about direction now, knowing that the wave would carry him farther into the cave, trying to judge by his memories of childhood hours here when to break surface. He misjudged it, and his body slammed into the rock wall at the back. His left shoulder took too much of the force, so it was numb when he finally struggled to the surface as the wave retreated around him. His eyes burned with the salt, and he wondered if there was enough light that Andre could see him here. He prayed that he was hidden, knowing that his prayers had been answered when he heard Andre begin to call his name.

He listened for too many long minutes as Andre reasoned with him to come. He could hear the fear begin to grow and knew that his brother would leave him soon. Self-preservation had always been Andre's strongest motivation.

Just go, he thought, praying again. Finally the begging voice stopped, and he still waited until the waves pounded against his chest even here. Their force pushed him into the wall behind his back, each another blow to his damaged ribs. The cave angled up the cliff, of course, the elevation higher here at the back, so he knew that the entrance where Andre had been was underwater. He must have gone. There had been no noise for a long time. And he had no choice.

"Caroline," he said softly and then knew she couldn't hear him against the noise. "Caroline," he shouted. "Answer me, Caroline. Tell me where you are. We have to go. I'll get you out, but you have to answer me so I can find you."

He waited again, but there was only the pounding of the sea. There was no voice, no movement that he could hear. God, had Andre been telling the truth? Had she left?

But he knew she hadn't. He knew that she was here in the darkness with him. He had never been as certain of anything in his life as he was that she was with him, so he was afraid again. She had chosen not to answer him, and he knew what that meant.

He took a breath against his own fear, feeling his heart pounding in his ears. Not this way, he thought. Not like this. Alone and in the dark. He shook off the terror and began to grope before him, using the wall against his shoulder to guide him. The surging waves forced him again and again into the rock wall, and still his reaching fingers found nothing.

"Caroline, please. Answer me. Tell me where you are. Talk to me." He forced himself to be still again, but there was nothing he could hear above the sounds that had filled the cave since the beginning.

Suddenly he knew what to do. He had been such a fool.

"Kerri," he said, pitching his voice calmly into the darkness. "You made me a promise. You promised that you would never again elude me. I'm trying to touch you, darling, to find you, but you've got to help me. You promised. Do you remember? 'Never again, Julien,' you said.''

He waited, still hoping, and closed his eyes when she didn't speak.

Her hand found his shoulder and then touched his face, and he was holding her too hard, hurting his ribs in his need to hold her. She put her arms around his neck. He lifted her with the movement of the next wave, turning her body to protect her as it drove him again against the wall.

''I thought I'd lost you. I thought you weren't going to answer me,'' he said. The cold, wet strands of her hair wrapped against his face as the wave broke over them. ''God,'' he whispered, ''I was so afraid that you didn't want to answer me.''

He heard her laugh, and she said softly, ''I didn't hear you. I didn't know you were looking for me. I would have come. You know I would have come to you.''

''I know,'' he whispered. And then, ''We have to go. You have to trust me. I can get you out. You have to do what I tell you. Will you trust me?''

''Of course,'' she said easily. He wondered worriedly how much she understood of the danger. Of any of this.

''There's a tidal blowhole. At the top of the cave. I used to ride it out of the cave as a boy. You just have to ride the wave. It will carry you to the cliff above the cave. You don't have to do anything but time it. If I push you into the wave, can you ride it out? Can you do that, my love?''

''Yes,'' she said, and he heard the conviction and was grateful that she did trust him. ''I'll do whatever you tell

me. You'll come with me?'' she asked, realizing perhaps
that he had said nothing about getting himself out.

"The next wave," he said softly. "So as soon as
you're out, you have to climb up, above the level of the
tide, and you have to do it quickly, before the next swell.
The force could carry you back into the sea otherwise.
Do you understand?'' he asked, wishing he could see
her face, that he had some way to judge what was going
through her mind now. She seemed so passive, accepting
everything he told her.

"Promise me," she said. "Promise me you'll follow.
The next wave."

"I promise," he said and knew that he couldn't tell
her the truth. She understood something was wrong. And
he *would* try. So the lie was not really a lie. He doubted
that the force of the wave would be enough to lift his
far heavier body against the ceiling of the cave and
through the narrow opening. He didn't even know if he
could make it through the hole anymore. More than
twenty years had gone by since the last time.

"Julien," she whispered, putting her cold cheek
against his. "Something's wrong. What's wrong? What
are you not telling me? You are coming? Promise me.
Swear to me."

"I'm coming. I swear," he lied. If he didn't make it
through, what would Andre do to her? But this was the
best he could do. To get her out and then try to join her.
To get them away from the island. If not this, then he
would try against the surf. He would try until he died.
Because he wanted to live. He wanted to hold her again.
Suddenly he lowered his head and found her lips. They
tasted of salt and the cold and they clung to him. Sweet
and familiar. Known and loved. Like echoes of a song

whose melody teased the memory with words half forgotten, half remembered.

He pulled his lips away, but she lifted against him, reaching, her mouth feeling the stubble of his beard, his breath over her cheek. So dear. So loved.

She whispered it finally, knowing that whatever happened, whatever the truth of all that had been said today, she had to tell him. "I love you. You must know that. I love you so much."

The urge to tell her was so strong he had to fight against it. Instead of what he wanted to say, he commanded, "Then do this. Because I want you to do it. I'll help you. When I tell you, kick as hard as you can, and the wave will carry you through. You can do this," he said, reassuring.

"I know. I'll try. But you have to come. There are so many things..." She stopped, knowing there was no time, but wanting him to know.

"Kerri," he said softly. And nothing more. She waited, but he didn't speak what she had hoped. When he spoke again, it was to tell her to breathe with the rise and fall of the cold water that was trying to separate them again.

"The next one," he said finally. He was lifting her now to allow her to breathe against the rush of water that filled the cave almost to the top even when it was ebbing back to the sea. As tall as he was, his head was barely above the receding water. She felt his hands on her waist, ready to push her upward when the next surge broke over them, and then it was there. He threw her into the rush of the water, and she extended her body to ride the lift of the wave through the opening. The movement was strong enough that she had to do nothing. Only to ride as he had said and she was suddenly free, lying on the rocks and the water was running strongly down the cliff, foaming against her clinging body.

She remembered what he had told her and began to climb, desperately moving over the sharp rocks to give him room. Afraid that, in spite of what he had promised, he wouldn't come. There had been something wrong in the cave.

She climbed a long way and then turned to find the water shooting out of the opening in the top of the cave in a great gush. Like a fountain. She thought that she saw something in the heart of the plume, but then it was gone. The water ran down whitely against the gleaming blackness of the rocks to join the sea, and the foam fell back into the hole. He had not come. She waited for the next wave, her breath gasping agonizingly through her heaving chest. *Please, God,* she thought, watching as the column began to crash through the vent again. When it retreated this time, she could see Julien clinging to the rim of the opening, trying to pull himself up with his hands.

His face was distorted with the effort. She was afraid that he wouldn't be able to lift himself through and climb to the rocks above. She slid carefully down the rock face that separated them and spoke his name.

"Julien, what can I do?"

"Pull," he said, reaching for her, locking his left hand in her trembling fingers. "When the next surge comes."

He bent his elbow, and she saw the fingers of his right hand whiten against the rim of rock. He lifted with the push of the water beneath him as she pulled, and he finally was free. He lay on the wet rocks, fighting the pain and the exhaustion, but she knew they had to hurry.

"Julien," she whispered, bending to kiss the dark bearded cheek that was so cold beneath her mouth. "We have to go. To the boat. Andre's boat. You have to move.''

She watched as he forced himself to his knees, his head bowed like an animal with the effort. He raised his arm, and she fitted her shoulder under his. Together they got him to his feet.

''Across the ridge,'' he gasped. ''Not the house.'' She knew that he was speaking as little as possible to spare breath for the climb. Even as she dreaded that ordeal for him, she knew he was right. Andre would have headed to the house.

They hurried as much as they could, staggering. The farther they went, the more of his weight she was forced to carry. When they finally reached the top, she eased him down against the rocks.

''I have to rest,'' she gasped, brushing the wet hair off his forehead. He was white around the lips, the area around his closed eyes sunken and dark. She wondered if he were going into shock. She had to get him to the boat and then to one of the other islands. He couldn't endure much more. And neither could she. She turned, looking for the first time into the cove. The boat drifted as peacefully as she had left it. It seemed as if that had been days ago, but she knew it had been a matter of perhaps an hour, if that long. She was so grateful that it was there, and that Andre didn't seem to be.

''Let's go,'' she said. He tried to rise and fell back to his knees. ''Now, Julien,'' she commanded, willing him to find the strength. She watched him open his eyes and his head moved once in negation and then again.

''Yes,'' she said. ''Yes, you can. You must. He's going to kill me. And you know it now. We have to go.''

She watched him will his muscles to move, and he moaned against the agony this time, but she knew she was right. They had to do this. He didn't speak again, not even when she held him to let their bodies slide down the long sandy slope that led to the beach.

She again let him rest there against the white heat of the sand while she scanned the patio and tried to see into the long windows. There was nothing. No sign of Andre and now that worried her. Was he planning to let them make this nightmare journey, almost reach the boat and then stop them? Planning to hurt Julien again?

She rejected the scenario she was imagining and helped Julien to his feet. His progress, in spite of her support, was only a slow stagger, his limp pronounced. His breath had begun to catch with each limping step and then finally they were there.

"Hold on to me and step into the boat. We're here, my love. Help me get you in and then you can rest. I promise. Just this last part," she said, easing him carefully into the boat.

He lay against the side, crowded painfully into the narrow space. She took one final look across the deserted beach and up the long curve of the stairs and still there was nothing. She reached to untie the lines and turned to find Julien's hand moving to start the engine. It caught immediately, and she listened to its throbbing noise with more gratitude than she could ever remember feeling in her life.

"Make sure it's in Reverse," Julien's voice spoke harshly. "Back away from the dock and then turn the wheel slowly. Keep the sun before you and let me know when you see one of the islands. Just find a cove, a shallow beach, and run her aground like the fishermen do."

She could hear the pain, but she did as he told her. It was as easy as he had said.

She had lost all track of time long before the island began to grow against the horizon. She followed Julien's instructions until she found a cove that had a scattering of fishing boats resting against its white sands. Julien cut the power when they entered the breakers, and she simply guided the boat between the other vessels until they both felt the scrape of the sand against the bow.

"Tell them…" Julien began, and then his eyes drifted shut. He forced them open again. "Tell them d'Aumont," he said, and his head fell forward on his chest. She knelt and touched her lips to his face. She knew he was right. It was a name that would bring the help she needed, and so she left him and stepped out of the boat to run, calling, across the sand until several of the men had come to see what the commotion was. They hurried with her back to the boat, and she listened to their expressions of dismay and answered their questions with as little information as possible.

"An accident," she said again and again. "I know he has broken ribs. I don't know what else."

Finally someone brought a battered pickup, and they lifted him gently into a bed they had made in the back with some of the nets. They helped her climb beside him, never questioning her right to be there.

She settled into the coarseness of the nets and saw that he had lifted his hand. She caught the searching fingers, his long brown ones closing around hers.

"It's all right," he whispered. "You're safe. They won't let anyone bother you. Tell them—" He stopped so suddenly she thought he must be in pain with the lurching of the truck on the rutted road.

"Tell them what, my love?" she asked, stroking his hair back from his face, which was gray under his tan.

She waited a long time for him to speak again.

"Tell them..." he finally whispered, knowing that it was the best protection here he could offer her, the only protection he could give her now, "that you are my wife."

She didn't answer the soft command, but her eyes filled with how much it meant to hear him say it. He had given her all that she could ever want. She held his hand through the long journey, her back propped against the sway of the truck.

Finally there were other hands lifting him, as concerned as the fishermen and as kind. They would see that he was cared for. His fingers had grown limp long before they loaded him into the small plane. She still held them and stroked against the moaning breaths he took, but she knew that he was not aware of her at all. He could not know that this time it was her hand that reached into the darkness and would never let go.

Chapter Twelve

She released him to be cared for at the modern hospital to which the ambulance that had met the plane carried them. The nurses showed her to a staff shower. When she had finished, she found that one of them had left well-worn slacks, a cotton top and sandals outside the stall. Although the clothing was too large, fitting loosely on her slender frame, it was clean and she was grateful for their thoughtfulness. As she dressed, she tried to think what she should do, whom to notify.

She finally called the one name she had, the one place she was sure to reach. The international operator put her through quickly to the Paris offices of Paul Dupre. She left a message for Suzanne, worded to cause as little alarm as possible, but urgent enough to bring her to Guadeloupe. She tried to think if there were anything else she should do, but she knew he wouldn't want the authorities involved, no matter what he now knew about his brother's actions and motives.

She was waiting when they brought him into the quiet room with its starched white sheets and dim lighting. She watched them lift him carefully into the narrow bed. The bruises that covered his arms and chest extended, darkly purpling, above the tight strapping. His leg was

encased completely, rigidly immobilized against whatever damage he had done to the old injuries.

When they had covered him, she moved beside the
bed and, lifting the battered fingers, kissed them gently.
He slept with the drugs they had given him, no longer
sighing against the pain as he had in the plane. His lips
were slightly parted, the dark stubble on his cheeks a
contrast to the pristine white of the sheets. The skin
around his eyes looked bruised, too, as abused as the
long, tanned body they had handled so tenderly. She was
still watching his face when the doctor entered and put
his clipboard on the hook at the end of the bed.

"He's all right," he said, seeing her fear clearly reflected in her eyes. "Broken ribs, abrasions, exhaustion,
concussion, and he's done a lot of damage to that leg.
Do you know what originally happened to that?"

"A car wreck," she answered, but her eyes had already returned to the dark face on the pillow. "Six years
ago. I don't know any details of the injury."

"The X rays revealed the extent of the original damage. I was simply curious. We'll have a specialist tomorrow. There's nothing else we can do tonight. He's
not in danger. He's strong and fit. Why don't you get
some rest? You look almost as worn as he. The nurses
will check on him frequently, and you'll be fresh when
he's awake tomorrow. There's no need to exhaust yourself while he's here. You'll have enough to do to care
for him once you get him home."

What he said was only reasonable, but he was not
surprised when she shook her head. Her eyes had not
moved from her husband's face even while he talked,
and so he left her, having seen the same kind of determination in the past. Perhaps she would be better off
here where she could watch over him.

When the doctor had gone, she moved the chair beside the bed and laid her face against the fingers that had already begun to twist against the sheets where she'd placed them. She wondered if he were in pain again and thought about calling the nurse, but when her cheek touched his hand, it stilled, and he began to breathe evenly once more. The sound lulled her until she drifted into the sleep her mind had denied she needed. She awoke when he spoke her name. She turned to find his eyes open and fixed upward into the darkness.

"Caroline?" he whispered. She touched the back of her hand against his temple, feeling for fever. He turned against the caress, his whiskers brushing her fingers, and she smiled to feel how heavy his beard was in this short time. He had always shaved twice a day because her skin was so sensitive.

"What is it? Do you need something for the pain? I can call a nurse."

"No," he said, and she waited. "Where are we?"

"The hospital on Guadeloupe. You were right about the ribs. And your leg. But nothing serious. I left a message for Suzanne. I couldn't think what else I should do."

"Andre?" he asked finally.

"I don't know. I don't want to know."

"You were asleep and I woke you. Why are you here? You need to rest. I'm all right."

"I know, but I want to be here. I want to stay with you. Please, Julien, let me stay."

"You can't sleep here. You can't be comfortable sitting in a chair all night. It is night, isn't it?" he asked suddenly, wondering if he could be so wrong about how much time had passed. He hated to have to ask, hated to reveal how easily confused he could be by any change in the routine. He felt out of control as always when in an unfamiliar environment. In spite of what he had told her, he was grateful when her fingers touched his face again.

"It's night. Almost midnight, I think. I've lost track of time."

He relaxed against her admission, and they were silent again. He tried to think what else they should do, and finally he decided that until Suzanne arrived there was really nothing. He couldn't call the police and say, "My brother refused to help a guest out of a tidal cave. He wanted to get me out first." He knew they would look at his blindness and think it made sense. They wouldn't understand the insanity, the cruelty, of his refusal. Its intent. And there was nothing else that he could prove, nothing that was criminal. Andre's motives could be as he had said, and no one would believe what she said. Poor Caroline. She was Andre's victim more than he. He had suffered the physical hurts, but she...

He must have sighed or moved his head to deny what had happened to her, for her voice came again close to his face.

"What's wrong? They said you could have something else for the pain. I can call—"

"No," he denied, "I'm all right. It's not that. You need to rest."

"I'm fine. I want to be here."

"Then come here. Beside me. There's room. Stay with me. Tonight. Sleep beside me," he whispered, wanting it so much he ached just to think about holding her against him.

"I'll hurt you," she argued, but he could hear in her voice that she wanted to.

"No," he answered, smiling in the direction of the

whisper. "Only if you won't. That would hurt. For to-night. We have tonight. Please."

He listened to see if she would obey, but she was moving gently against his side before he knew she had agreed. She was cool against his hot, aching body, but she didn't hurt him, and he relaxed when he felt her weight settle. He put his arm around her, drawing her to him, and eventually her breathing slowed. She moved her head once against the muscle of his chest, and he turned his face into her hair. It didn't smell of her shampoo, so he supposed she had washed it here with some-one else's. But it was right. Her size and shape. And having her here was right. *God, so right.*

He didn't sleep for a long time, trying to decide what to do for her, what was the kindest way to handle it. He knew what he wanted to do, but that was so unfair. He couldn't take advantage of her confusion because he wanted her so much. She needed to be helped to under-stand, to cope with the reality, not allowed to move into his fantasy, into his darkness, simply because he loved her, because he couldn't stand the thought of letting her go. He didn't know that dawn was touching the windows before he slept, but the nurse who found them together had enough romance left in her soul, despite the pain in her tired feet, to quietly close the door and leave them alone.

CAROLINE HAD GONE to shower the next morning, again invited to use the staff facilities, when Suzanne arrived. She was with Julien, they told her when she came back to the room. His sister, they reassured.

She waited in the hall, leaning against the wall and wondering what Suzanne would say to her when he had told her. She didn't want to interrupt anything they

needed to talk about—Andre, her reappearance after
these lost years. She knew there would be hostility. She
had seen it in Suzanne's eyes when they had talked
about Julien's wife over lunch on the island. A hundred
years ago.

The woman who finally opened the door to his room
was not the friendly employer of the island. Her suit was
classically cut, obviously from one of the Parisian designer houses. She was still small and her hair still the
gleaming dark cap, but there was nothing casual about
her. She was in control, and when her eyes found the
bedraggled figure leaning against the hospital wall, it
was not hostility Caroline read there. It was an emotion
she couldn't identify, so she wondered suddenly what
Julien had told her. And how much.

"Caroline," she said softly, "are you all right?"

"I'm fine. I know how I look, but it's not due to
injury. The staff has been kind, but I don't have any
clothes or makeup. I know I look like something the cat
dragged in, but really, I'm fine."

Suzanne studied her face a moment and then smiled
at her. "Julien was concerned. I want to be able to give
him an accurate report. He was afraid you were hiding
some injury from him."

"I wouldn't do that," she said quietly. "I don't think
it's fair to lie to him. Not even to keep him from worrying."

"You're right, of course, and I won't have to, if
you're really all right. He wanted a doctor—"

"No," Caroline interrupted sharply. She took a deep
breath and calmed her sudden panic. "That's not necessary. Really. I'm fine. I'll tell him."

She began to move past Suzanne to open the door.

She felt Suzanne's fingers catch her arm and hold, gripping too tightly. She turned in surprise.

"What's wrong?" she asked, suddenly afraid. "Is he all right?"

"Yes." Suzanne saw the concern and was sorry. "He's fine, but the doctor's with him, the specialist. Besides, we have to talk. Come with me. I need some coffee, and we can talk while we drink it. He's fine, I promise," she reassured as she watched the green eyes drawn again to the closed door. "You can't go in now, so come with me. We need to get better acquainted."

Because it was the right thing to say, Caroline was suddenly hopeful, agreeable to walk with her to the hospital cafeteria that was crowded with the lunchtime throng. They found a table after getting their coffee. Caroline drank hers, grateful for the soothing warmth. Grateful, too, that Julien's sister had sought her out.

Suzanne watched her sip the coffee and noticed the slight tremor in the slender fingers. The hands were cut and scratched, and she knew from what Julien had told her what had caused that. Caroline didn't look strong enough to have survived all they had been through, but of course, she hadn't been. The damage Andre had done was not visible in the bright sunshine of this noisy, crowded room. It was more insidious than the injuries Julien was dealing with today and far more painful. Suzanne didn't know how to begin what he had entrusted her to do. It was so difficult.

"I've arranged for your things to be sent from the island. They should arrive this afternoon."

"I appreciate that. I should have thought of sending someone. Julien will need things, too. I just couldn't think past calling you."

"Of course not. You were both too tired. You did the

right thing. It was clever of you to call Paul. He handled
everything.''

"They were very kind to me when I called. Concerned
and efficient. You're very lucky to have them to look
after you. And to have Julien.''

Suzanne smiled at her and knew that the rest was going to be so painful. She was doing this only because
she didn't want Julien to have to deal with it. He had
dealt with enough.

"I have a friend I want you to meet,'' she began carefully and watched the green eyes come up to her face,
confused by this divergence from what they had been
talking about. She plunged on, talking rapidly now, as
if she could make it less distressing by doing it quickly.
"He's offered to take care of you for a while. He's very
good, and I think you'll like him. Julien wants you to
have the very best of care. He's so concerned about you,
about what Andre did.''

"I don't understand,'' Caroline said softly. "I told
you I'm all right. I was frightened, but as soon as Julien
is released, we'll go to Paris. I don't want to go back to
the island. I don't think Julien will, either, but I don't
need a place to stay. Or are you trying to tell me Julien
will be here a long time? It's his leg, isn't it?''

"No.'' Suzanne shook her head. "I realize I'm not—
Look, Julien wants you to stay at the clinic and talk to
Dr. Simone. He can help you understand what's happened to you. It's not your fault. Julien feels responsible
for what Andre has done, and so do I. We only want to
help you.''

"And what do you think has happened to me, Suzanne? Why do you believe I need to talk to your
friend?'' Caroline bitterly emphasized the last word.

"This doctor. Why have you and Julien decided I need a doctor?"

She waited, but she knew the answer even before the sympathy flooded the blue eyes. Sympathy. That had been the emotion in Suzanne's carefully controlled features when she came out of his room.

"Julien told me what you believe. Who you believe you are."

"Who I believe— My God, he still doesn't know," Caroline breathed softly. "How can he not know? He told me to tell them that."

"Tell who?"

"The fishermen. I thought he knew. I thought he finally believed me. And in the cave." She thought about what had happened then and understood what he had done. How he had cheated her. "But that was because he knew I wouldn't come. I didn't want to come if he didn't believe me. So he tricked me. Damn him. Damn him for tricking me."

"I don't understand," Suzanne said. "How did he trick you?" She watched the woman opposite her smile bitterly and then shake her head.

"It doesn't matter," she said finally. "He lied to me. I told you I'd never lie to him, even to protect him, but apparently he doesn't play by the same rules. I'd like to talk to him."

"He..."

Caroline waited and then knew the bitterness of this, too. "He doesn't want to see me. Is that what you don't want to say? That's true, isn't it? You can tell me. At least you can tell me the truth."

"He thinks it would be better."

Caroline laughed suddenly. "Just ship the poor deluded creature to some sanitarium until she forgets everything again.''

''He's only trying to help. He cares so much that you've been hurt. We're both so sorry…''

''Nothing Andre did to me was like this. You tell him that. Nothing hurt like this. Will you at least tell him that for me?''

''I'll tell him. He doesn't mean to hurt you, but you can't go on believing that you're Kerri. It's not true, and it's so hard for him. You don't understand how he felt about her.''

''Oh, God,'' Caroline breathed harshly, lowering her head. She finally raised her eyes, and Suzanne could see the tears. ''I understand. Believe me, I understand,'' she whispered. Her lips tightened, her eyes fixed on a spot over Suzanne's shoulder. Finally they came back to find the concerned blue ones, so much like Andre's, locked on her face.

''Will you give him another message for me?''

''Of course,'' Suzanne said, willing to do anything to get this session over.

''Ask him about the rock on the beach of the villa at Monte Carlo. And the rain. And about the picnic under the hedge of roses. Wild roses. Pink. And the fragrance. Ask him. Ask him who else would know.''

''Don't do this to him,'' Suzanne begged. ''I know that Andre told you a lot of things…''

''Ask him who else would know those things. Who could tell Andre so that he could tell me. Make him answer you, Suzanne.''

She waited until Suzanne nodded, compelled by the determination in the green eyes. She stood then and asked very calmly, ''When can I expect my things to arrive?''

"Perhaps by two. Three at the latest. I asked Angeline to have her brother take her. Angeline will find everything and pack. They'll bring them here."

"Thank you. I appreciate that. I'll be downstairs."

"Will you at least think about the other? Julien wants you to," Suzanne said, thinking that perhaps she would agree to do it for him.

"Why should I care about what Julien wants me to do? I think he has forfeited any right to be concerned about my welfare. I can take care of myself. But you ask him about the other. Promise me, Suzanne. If you care that Andre did what he did, then do this for me. Promise me."

"I promise, but not today. He can't deal with any more. Even this."

"I understand. There's no hurry. Just ask him. I wish I could hear what he tells you. I'll be downstairs waiting for Angeline."

Suzanne watched her walk across the crowded room, composed and dignified even in baggy, borrowed clothes. She had mishandled it, and she didn't know what to tell Julien. Caroline had not been as Suzanne had expected, had not reacted in any way that suggested what her brother believed. She wondered suddenly in the face of that quiet conviction if Julien could possibly be mistaken. At that thought she tried to find Caroline's figure, but she had been caught up in the crowd. Suzanne sat a long time over the cold coffee. She didn't know what to tell her brother. Only that she'd failed.

CAROLINE KNEW she had to leave. There was nothing now to stay for. But of course she didn't have the money for the flight. And no credit cards. That had not been her life-style. She wondered bitterly if she would be stuck here, dependent on his charity until he arranged for her to be sent to another hospital, to be told another story by more doctors who didn't know, didn't understand.

"No," she said fiercely. "Not again. Not ever again." She tried to think who to call. Who to ask for help. But there was no one. She wasn't like Suzanne. No one had ever rushed to take care of her. Her grandfather. And, of course, Julien. But that had been so long ago. There was no one in her world anymore who cared if she lived or died. She felt the sting of tears and shook her head against the self-pity.

Lucky Suzanne. The secretaries in Paul Dupre's office had certainly rushed around to see to her needs. To make all the arrangements to locate her and for the flight. They had started the efficient handling of Suzanne's business without even talking to her. Without any questions....

The thought was sudden and inspired. It flashed complete into her mind like a blueprint. *Without any questions.*

She used the desk phone again, reversing the charges. Madame Rochette's secretary for Mr. Dupre's office in Paris. God, it was so easy. Inspired.

"Madame Rochette's brother has been injured in an accident," she found herself explaining to a different secretary.

"Of course. We have been informed and are taking care of the situation," the Parisian voice assured her. Caroline was amused at the pretentious assumption of authority.

"Madame Rochette wants you to make arrangements for my flight back to Paris. This afternoon. As early as possible. There are some personal matters I need to attend to while she makes arrangements for her brother's care. There is some urgency involved."

"Of course, Ms. Evans. We'll have you on the first flight out of Guadeloupe. You have only to get to the airport."

"Would you arrange for a cab? I'm tied up with helping Suzanne," she said, hoping that the use of the Christian name would establish a closer relationship than Dupre's secretary enjoyed. She was praying that they would be as cooperative and unquestioning as before. "I really don't have time to make those arrangements and handle these responsibilities, too. I can be ready to leave the hospital by four. If you'll have the cab here and the flight arranged."

"That's no problem. Please assure Madame Rochette that we will handle everything. Leave it all to me, Ms. Evans. You just help with the arrangements there, and we'll handle everything else. Shall we have a cab meet you in Paris?"

Why not? A cab to take her to her apartment. An address if Julien wanted to trace her. She smiled at the self-deception that made her think he might care that much. Enough to try to find her.

"If you would," she said.

"Then your cab will pick you up at four. Thank you for calling. And Ms. Evans?"

"Yes."

"How is Madame Rochette's brother? It's so tragic what happened to him before. I only hope..."

"Thank you. I hope so, too. I'll tell Suzanne you asked."

She broke the connection and put her forehead against the wall, closing her eyes. All she had to do was wait and then leave. Go back to what her life had been before. At least this time she could remember. She could think about him and all that they had had, both years ago and on the island before Andre. Suddenly she wasn't sure that remembering was better than the blankness of the mists. This emptiness hurt so much because she knew, this time, what she had lost.

SUZANNE CAME DOWNSTAIRS to check on her twice while she waited. She was foolish enough to hope the first time that he wanted to see her. Instead they only wanted to try to convince her to go to the clinic. She listened with part of her attention to Suzanne's arguments and, when she had finished, thanked her for her concern. She was trying to be fair in spite of the hurt. They were genuinely concerned. They were just wrong. He was wrong and wouldn't listen. A grave had convinced him. At the Convent of the Sacred Heart.

She wondered vaguely whose grave was there with her name, but it didn't really matter. It wasn't hers. He and Andre were wrong. The more memories that crowded her mind as she tried to relax and wait calmly for Angeline, the more convinced she was. So many memories.

It was almost four when she saw the cook's figure hurrying across the street in front of the hospital and in through the glass doors. She was clutching her handkerchief, and the redness of her face and eyes betrayed recent tears. The man following her carried Caroline's bags.

She rose and walked toward them, and Angeline began to cry again when she saw her. She didn't understand, but eventually the words the cook muttered became horribly clear.

"Ms. Evans, it is so terrible. It's Monsieur Gerrard. Monsieur Andre. My brother found his body caught in the rocks at the foot of the cliff. Henri was waiting for me and walked out on the deck to look down and saw him. First *monsieur le duc* is hurt and now this. He must have fallen from the deck. We thought he had been swimming, but he was dressed. Do you suppose he was looking for his brother? After you had left the island with *monsieur le duc?* Afraid his brother had fallen on the rocks or that he was swimming there? *Monsieur le duc* did swim there sometimes, although Monsieur Andre warned him again and again. I don't know how to tell them. To tell Madame Rochette. You must help me. Come with me," she pleaded, grasping Caroline's hand.

"I can't, Angeline. I'm sorry. So sorry for them all, but I can't come with you." Through the glass doors she saw the cab pull into the loading zone and the driver climb out, and she knew he was here for her. "I have to go. Madame Rochette asked me to handle some business for her. You must tell her and let her tell her brother. Perhaps he was looking for *monsieur le duc* when he fell. I don't suppose anyone will ever be sure of what happened," she said softly, knowing this was best. "It's very tragic, but you'll have to tell her."

By that time her driver was talking to the receptionist at the desk. Caroline saw the girl point her out and, turning, she gave Angeline a quick hug and patted her shoulder. The cook's tears began again with her sympathy. "I have to go," she said finally, and the woman nodded as she wiped her eyes.

The driver took her bags. She followed him to the cab, and she never looked back.

Chapter Thirteen

It was almost a month later that the letter arrived, the return address stopping her breath. She carried it into her apartment, sat down on the couch and slipped off her heels. She waited a long time, knowing that she was hoping too much, that she was counting on it being what she thought, what she had dreamed of through the long days. She had imagined the scene in her mind through endless hours of sleepless nights. Suzanne would tell him what she had asked, and then he would realize. He would know that she was right and that he had only to admit it for everything to be as it had been before.

She turned the envelope finally, breaking the seal, and pulled out the rich, heavy business stationery. Even the letterhead of his business. A paper fluttered out when she unfolded the sheet, but she was too intent on the letter itself to notice. Her eyes dropped to the signature and read the destruction of her dream. His secretary. She laughed bitterly at her fantasy. This was not personal. When she finally remembered that someone would have to write it for him, her eyes skipped back to the top.

It was only after she had read it all that her fingers found the check on her lap. That was what had fallen out of the letter, what she had ignored in her rush to see if he wanted her, if he were asking her to come to him. And instead…

For services rendered. She was suddenly furious with him, as angry as she ever had been. When they had first married, she had been so insecure that she had always been afraid he was making fun of her if he smiled at something she said. She had thought then he was ashamed of her because there were so many things about his world she didn't know. She had reacted to her own insecurities with anger directed against him. Now she was again so angry over his rejection that she wanted to strike out as she had in those days.

She glanced at her watch and then back to the address on the letter. She thought if she hurried she might have time. She had had a half day at work today, so it was only two o'clock. Perhaps he would still be at the office, and she could throw this in his face. She slipped her shoes back on and crammed the check into her purse. She tried to think about the routes she should take, but instead she simply walked until she flagged a taxi and gave him the address. She allowed her anger to build and realized that, even with the fury, there was no pain around her temples, and there had not been since her return. Of course, the pain had been to prevent her remembering what was too traumatic to face. She had finally faced what she had done, her role in the accident and the baby's death, so there was no longer any need for that protection.

She thought about what she wanted to say to him for sending her money. *Services rendered.* She wondered what services he was trying to pay her for, so she practiced the scathing comments through the Paris traffic. Somewhere deep inside she knew the truth. This was a way to see him again, to know that he was all right, and that he had recovered from all that had happened.

She was unprepared when the driver stopped. It was too soon, but she paid him, and was then standing on the street before the elegant building she had never before entered.

She was directed pleasantly enough to his office, on the top floor, of course, but the real barrier would be that she had no appointment. She knew that no one would be allowed to simply walk into his office unannounced, so she tried to think what she should do.

She took the check from her purse and held it crushed in her hand as she stood before the desk of the man she was sure had written her the coldly condescending letter. He even looked like someone who would write that kind of letter.

"I would like to see Mr. Gerrard. Julien," she said, watching the movement of his eyes toward the central one of the three heavy oak doors.

"I'm sorry, but Mr. Gerrard is in a meeting. He has no appointments scheduled for this afternoon. Perhaps there has been a mistake," he said.

"Tell him his wife is here," she said, perversely enjoying his shock.

"I don't know who you are, but I know that you aren't—" His voice faltered at whatever he saw in her eyes. It took him several seconds to compose the next thought. "Monsieur Gerrard is not married. I think you are making a grave mistake."

"Is that supposed to be a pun?" she said, allowing herself a slight smile at his confusion. "Tell him," she demanded again.

"I can't do that," he began. All at once she was tired of the argument. This was not why she was here.

She walked across the thick carpet and opened the middle door. In spite of her anger, she was suddenly unsure as faces turned questioningly toward the open door and her intrusion. A meeting, he had said, and he hadn't lied about that.

Her eyes found Julien, his head now tilted slightly, that familiar listening posture she remembered so well, trying to identify whatever had disturbed the calm of his afternoon. She swallowed against the pain and joy of seeing him again. He was so compelling, so much in command here, in spite of the dark glasses she hated.

She began the long journey around the table and across the bare parquet, her heels echoing sharply. The sound seemed to fuel her anger with him. *Money was all he had to offer her, all he was willing to share of who he was.*

"What is it?" he said softly to the white-haired man on his right.

"A woman." Caroline heard him answer. "No one I know."

"It's your wife," she said too loudly, ignoring the scattered gasp that ran into the silence of the group at the huge conference table.

She watched the impact break across his face, and something twisted her heart, biting into the anger, when he reached for a ebony cane and pushed himself to his feet, using the stick and his hand on the polished surface of the table. She watched his knuckles bend and whiten against the wood, as he used the table to take some of the weight off his damaged leg.

"Caroline?" he said softly. "What is it? What's wrong?"

She caught his hand, and he let her lift it, but she was aware that as a result he was forced to lean more heavily against the cane. Now, instead of what she had intended, she wanted to ask about his leg, to tell him how much she cared. But she did only what she had come to do.

"I don't want your damned money," she said, opening his fingers to push the crumpled check into them. She saw the sudden frown and knew he was struggling to understand. She realized that he didn't know what it was.

"I didn't want your money even at nineteen, and I don't want it now. That was never what I wanted. Don't you ever send me money again, Julien. That's not what I want from you."

His fingers closed tightly over the check, crushing it, and she knew she had his full attention and, of course, the attention of every fascinated listener at the table.

"Caroline," he said again and then nothing.

"You know what I want," she said. "You've always known. Why are you doing this? What did you tell Suzanne? How did you answer my questions?"

"Suzanne?" he said. "I don't understand."

"Did Suzanne give you my message?"

"Yes, of course, at the hospital." He stopped suddenly, swallowing, thinking of what she'd said about his actions hurting her far more than Andre's. He whispered, "I'm sorry, Caroline. More sorry than you can imagine."

"You bastard," she said softly, but she didn't hit him. Perhaps she had, after all, learned some restraint in the long years. She turned and saw the secretary at the door with a security guard.

She walked deliberately to them through the absolute silence of the room and spoke very distinctly, "Get out of my way." She waited until they moved. She didn't see Julien's gesture that directed them to step aside. She

walked across the office and knew that she would probably never see him again.

THE LONG DAYS stretched before her and, although her
depression made even rising every morning an effort,
she was determined that her mind would not choose
again the escape it had found the first time she'd lost
him. She was stronger than that now.

She rose and dressed in the clear dawn light and went
every day to the secretarial pool where she had found
temporary work. She tried not to think about him at all,
but sometimes the most insignificant thing, an aroma,
the impression of dark hair and broad shoulders, of a
head turned at a certain angle, let the memories rush
back so strongly she would be forced to stop and close
her eyes against their assault. And then gradually, after
she had endured the string of painful days and endless
nights, she knew that she had something that would insure her survival and even the survival of all the memories she had once destroyed.

SHE HAD MADE IT back to the comfort of her bed and
pressed her face against the coolness of the spare pillow
when she heard the knock. She knew that if she rose
again to answer the door, the nausea that had eased with
the last trip to the bathroom would again attack. She had
to go to work today. She had already given in to the
queasiness twice this week. She could not afford to lie
in bed today because she couldn't afford to lose this job.

When the knock came again, she tightened her lips
against what she knew would occur and, pulling on and
belting her robe, she walked carefully to the door and
opened it.

She would not have been more surprised had Julien

himself stood outside. In the month since she had embarrassed him before his business associates, she had relived that painful episode again and again, until the humiliation of the memory had faded somewhat. It had simply retreated into the pain of all the other episodes she'd at last remembered, when her childishness and temper had disgraced the name he had given her. No wonder he had rejected her. He was, at least in that way, free of her presence, a constant reminder of all she had done to him.

"Suzanne," she said and saw again, as at the hospital, the distance between her sister-in-law's carefully groomed elegance and her own appearance. This time she could smile at the proof of Andre's claim. She would be only an embarrassment to these people. She had been trying to distance herself from that pain through these long weeks. She thought the contrast between herself and the woman who had knocked on her door was the best illustration of the breadth of the gap.

"I have to talk to you," Suzanne said, so she moved away from the door and led the way into the shabby sitting room.

She eased down on the couch and, uncaring now of what Suzanne might think, put her feet up and leaned back against the arm. As the nausea receded, she took a brief breath of relief.

"How are you?" Suzanne asked softly, her voice holding only what sounded like genuine concern. Caroline knew how she looked. Before she had left the unpleasantness of the bathroom, she had carefully studied her pale face in the mirror. The shadows around her eyes made them look like Julien's after the fall and the cave, and she was too thin. But this would pass. It had before and then she had bloomed with health. Of course, before...

She blocked that thought and answered truthfully, "I'm all right. I've been sick this week, maybe a virus, but it's nothing."

"I called you at work yesterday. They said you had missed the past two days. I was concerned."

"Why did you call?" she asked carefully. In spite of all she could do, the tiny flame that her reasoning could not fully extinguish leapt again to life. He wanted to see her.

"Because I was wrong—we both were wrong—and because I need your help."

"I don't understand. You were wrong about what?"

"About you. About the possibility, at least, that you are who you claim to be."

Caroline couldn't speak against the emotions that tightened her throat as she watched the beautiful blue eyes search her face.

"But he said—"

"I went to Monaco," Suzanne interrupted. "I had the bodies exhumed. I had no authority to do that, but I used his name and his money to ease the way."

"And?" she asked carefully, not really knowing what to expect.

"The baby's there. Julien's son. I had tests made." Suzanne paused at the flash of pain in the clouded green eyes. "Forgive me, but I had to know."

"And the other grave?"

"An old man. The stones said Tremaine, nothing else. Both stones. When he asked about the graves before, the nuns told Julien only that the old man had made all the arrangements. He thought it was your maiden name. It was how you had signed the marriage license, so he

assumed the graves were yours…and his son's. It hurt
him that the baby's grave didn't even bear his name, but
he understood your grandfather's bitterness, so he left it.
But Tremaine was your grandfather's name, your
mother's name, not yours. Was your grandfather buried
in the other grave? Was it his grave and not yours Julien
found that day?''

Caroline shook her head, trying again to remember.
This had never come back, only vaguely in dreams perhaps, but she could never recall enough of them to be
sure of what had occurred after the wreck. Looking
down on Julien's face in the moonlight. The sound of
the baby's thin wail. Dark figures glimpsed against the
agony of the birth. A jumble of impressions from the
most painful part of the past her mind had buried. So
devastating that she had begun to believe it would never
come back.

"I don't know. I can't remember the convent at all.
Nothing after the wreck. I've tried. Believe me, I've
tried. I thought it would be the key, the explanation that
would make him finally believe. But I can't remember.''

"Would your grandfather have come to you after the
accident? Would he have taken you to the convent for
some reason?''

"He would have come. He was angry that I'd married
Julien. Angry about the baby because he thought Julien
had seduced me.'' Suzanne watched the tenderness of
the smile that touched the pale, thin face. "I couldn't
explain that it was really the other way around. I'd never
met anyone like Julien. And he wanted me. I knew that
and so I—'' She took a deep breath and continued, denying the pull of the memories. "My grandfather
thought Julien was just a playboy with too much money.
It was what my mother had done. She married an Amer-

ican playboy, and my father had turned out to be everything my grandfather warned her he was. She committed suicide when I was eight. My father sent me away to school, a very expensive school in Switzerland, and I never saw him again. He paid the bills and that was it.''

She stopped the painful narration and wondered why she was opening all the old wounds to this woman she barely knew. She had told no one but Julien about her adolescence, about the fact that nobody had ever wanted her or cared what she did. She had acted out her frustration and anger over the desertion of both parents with increasingly serious escapades, until the school had no choice but to send word to her father that she was no longer welcome there. Still he had made no move to come for her. She could feel, even now, the humiliation when the headmistress informed her, as gently as she could, given the nature of her message, that her own father didn't want her. They had finally called her grandfather after the episode that followed the conference in the headmistress's office. He had come, of course, and he had loved her, had understood, as had Julien, the bitterness that made her doubt and demand proof over and over of the security of the love they both had offered.

''The accident made the news,'' Suzanne's voice broke through her contemplation of the past. ''Julien's reputation and the location were glamorous enough to insure that. If he had heard...''

''My grandfather would have come, but he would never have sent me to the convent. It was too far away from the hospital in case the baby came early. He would have taken me home perhaps, but never to Sacred Heart. There was no reason.''

''Maybe he thought the nuns could oversee the birth.

Old people sometimes have different ideas about child-birth.''

Caroline laughed, and then, seeing the confusion on Suzanne's face, explained, ''My grandfather was a doctor. He practiced in a small town, but he was very competent, very up-to-date. It had been an obligation to his patients. He subscribed to every journal, attended countless conferences. He would *never* have sent me to the nuns,'' she said with certainty.

She paused because she knew who had. He had even admitted it to Julien. Whatever role her grandfather had played in all this, he was not the one who had arranged for her to be sent to the convent.

''Andre made those arrangements,'' she said aloud. ''He admitted it to Julien. But if my grandfather came to the hospital, and he would have had no trouble finding out where we would be taken, given the location of the accident, perhaps someone at the hospital might have sent him from there to the convent.''

''The old woman said you were dying, hemorrhaging. The nuns had sent for a doctor, but she knew he couldn't arrive in time. Perhaps if your grandfather came—''

''I don't know. I don't remember any of that. I'm sorry. Don't you know that if I could explain all of this, I would? Don't you know how important it is that I make Julien believe me? If I knew anything that might convince him, that might shed some light, I would have told him. I would tell him now,'' she said. ''I gave him the best proof I had that I *am* Kerri.'' She was forced to blink away the tears that had formed. ''And he rejected it. I don't have anything else. There was a necklace he'd given me, but I don't know what happened to it. I don't know when or where I lost it. Perhaps where they sent me. The sanitarium. Maybe someone there took it. The staff or another patient. But I have nothing. Except what I remember. And he won't believe me because of what Andre told him. Andre's poison.''

"I told him about the grave," Suzanne said when the silence grew and stretched.

"And what did he say? How did he answer that fact?" Caroline asked bitterly.

"You don't understand," Suzanne said softly. "He wants so much to believe, and maybe he does, but...even if he knows, I think he would reject that knowledge."

"Because I was to blame for it all? For his blindness? For the baby? I told him about the brakes. I was angry. I was driving too fast, but there was something wrong with the car."

"I didn't know that. He didn't tell me. I think he forgave her long ago, if he *ever* blamed her. It's not that. He wanted you before I told him about the grave. I told him that I believe your grandfather's buried there. I think your grandfather came to find you, arriving at the convent in time to save your life. Perhaps when he realized that your mind...that you were confused...maybe he told the nuns you were dead and arranged for you to be taken secretly to the hospital in France. When you didn't recover for so long, he thought you never would. He had already arranged for the two graves at the convent to make us believe just what we did believe—that you were dead and safely out of Julien's reach. When your grandfather died, before you recovered, he was buried, according to his plan, in the empty grave at the convent. Buried in your place. I don't suppose we'll ever know for sure. Whatever happened, Kerri isn't buried at the convent, and Julien knows it, but he won't acknowledge the possibility that *you* are Kerri. He doesn't believe that it would be fair to accept what you're offering.''

''I don't understand,'' Caroline said, trying to follow a line of reasoning that made no sense. If he didn't blame her, then why—

''He's blind, he's older than you, and there are other effects from the wreck. I told you.''

''He was using a cane when I went to his office.''

Suzanne heard and answered the unspoken question. ''He had surgery, some repair work on the old injury to his leg.''

She waited a long time and finally said what she believed to be the truth, ''Even if he believes you, even if he has accepted that you are Kerri, I don't think he'll ever come to you. I saw his face when I told him what you said about the roses. After you came to his office, he asked about the message you'd given me at the hospital. I hadn't told him before. I didn't want him to be hurt any more by what I was so certain then was just more of the pain Andre had planned, but the look on his face convinced me that he knows. What you remember had some significance to him. That's when I began to investigate the story Andre had told him. I tried to find the old woman, but no one had taken down her address.''

''Julien mentioned an old woman. I don't understand what she has to do with it all.''

''She told him about the convent. She said you died there.''

''I don't have any more proof. I don't know if my grandfather is buried there. I don't know who the old woman was. *I don't know.* And I have nothing else. I've examined everything. Anything else I remember, someone could say that Andre told me, but what I told you to ask Julien...those are things no one would share. The most private of our times together. If he rejects those, if he doesn't believe me, then I have nothing else. What do you want me to do? I don't understand why you're here if you know he's refused to accept those memories.''

"I want you to go to him. I want you to tell him *all* about the roses. Remind him of whatever happened between you there and of what it meant to him. Tell him about the rock on the beach. Anything that will bring those events back to him so strongly that he can't deny what he knows. I want you to break through that wall he's put up around himself. Make him admit that he loves you.''

Caroline read the sincerity in Suzanne's eyes and wanted to believe.

"Do you think he loves me?" she said softly.

"He's grieving again, as much as he did before. You were again within his reach and, because of his view of himself, because of his pride perhaps, he felt he had to let you go. I can't guarantee that's his reason. He would never tell me that, but it's what I believe. Isn't it worth a chance? Isn't he? Or is your pride and fear as great as his?"

Suzanne watched the tears spill over the emerald eyes that had locked on hers and, for the first time since she had mentioned the roses to her brother, she began to hope.

Chapter Fourteen

She stood before the door of his apartment and tried to stop the trembling of the hand she had raised to knock. Suzanne had cleared her with the building's security, so he wouldn't be able to deny her access to his door, and so he would have no warning, no opportunity to become again contained and careful. It was late enough that his man had left. She knew from Suzanne that no servants slept here. He had refused that, in spite of his blindness. He was alone, and she knew he would answer the door.

She took a deep breath and knocked. It seemed a long time until she heard his steps.

"Who is it?"

Suzanne had suggested that she lie, that she use his sister's name to gain admittance, but she knew that she couldn't trick him. She didn't want any deception between them.

"It's Caroline," she said and waited.

When the door opened, she could see the concern in his face. He wasn't wearing the dark glasses, his eyes the same crystal blue she had seen so often in her dreams. They were unfocused now, so she spoke to let him know where she was and watched them track to her face.

"I need to talk to you. If you'll let me. Suzanne said that she'd told you everything. I don't understand how you can still doubt what we all know."

"And what do we all know?" he asked softly.

"That Kerri isn't buried in the grave at the convent. That I know some things only you and Kerri could know, things she would share with no one. Don't you think we should talk about what that means? Or don't you care anymore what it means?"

She watched the resignation on his features. Finally he shook his head, but he moved back and let her step into the apartment. When she entered the room, the memories washed so strongly over her that she thought she might not be able to move against their force. She had lived here with him. They had come here often during the brief months of their marriage.

She shivered and walked into the room, turning back to see him standing still beside the open door.

"What is it?" she said. "What's wrong?"

"Nothing." He smiled at her concern and blocked the images that the fragrance of her hair had caused to move through his mind and into his body. "Nothing's wrong."

"Then come away from the door," she invited. "Come and talk to me. Or don't you want me here? Suzanne thought—" She paused carefully, wondering how much to tell him of what his sister believed.

"What does Suzanne think?" he asked. He closed the door and limped to stand before her. He was as casually dressed as on the island, jeans and a soft cashmere sweater against the chill. The sweater's blue was the same as his eyes. He was so beautiful to her, in spite of the faded scars and his eyes slightly off-focus.

"Suzanne thinks that you know who I am, that you know and won't admit it?"

"Why would I deny you're Kerri if I believed you were?"

"I thought because of what I had done. Of all I'd cost you. Your son. And your sight."

She watched him smile at her and shake his head. "If you were Kerri..." he began softly, and then stopped. His throat moved with whatever emotion crowded it at even voicing the words. "If you *were* Kerri," he began again, "then you would know it wasn't her fault. She wasn't to blame for the accident."

She thought about what he was saying and tried to understand. "I told you there was something wrong with the brakes. I told you that."

He shook his head, lowering it as he had in the cave.

"What is it?" she asked. "I don't understand what you mean. I was driving. Too fast. I always did. And I was angry."

"Why were you angry?" he said, and his eyes came up. She could see the strain clearly etched into the spare planes of his face.

"I was jealous. Some woman at the reception. I wanted you to tell me how much you loved me. How much you wanted me, despite the pregnancy and my stupid jealousy. I wanted you to reassure me, as always. I'm so sorry. I didn't mean for it all to end that way. You know how much I loved you. You had only to touch me and I was always— I was only trying to make you tell me, to say it again. I *never* tired of hearing it. I needed to hear it so often." She heard the apology for that long-ago need in her voice. "You understood that."

"Yes," he said, his fingers touching her hair gently,

perhaps in comfort. "But that's not what I said. Not what I told her. Not that night."

"You told me you'd wanted to make love to me all evening. To touch me. We argued about the dress. I'd spent so much and I still looked..." She stopped and shook her head. She had been as much a child then as Andre had said. "And the gown was ruined. Someone had spilled a drink down the front, a man I bumped into as I ran out of the reception." She shivered at the memories. "I could smell the whiskey the whole time we were fighting. I couldn't stop screaming at you. You said you didn't care what I spent, and I knew you didn't, but I couldn't stop screaming at you because I was afraid. I was always so afraid I would lose you," she whispered.

His face was hard set. As unyielding as when she had accused his brother of trying to murder him, and still she didn't understand.

"You asked me if I regretted marrying you," he whispered, and finally she remembered the last, insignificant words of their argument, returning clearly now out of the confusion of that night.

"And you said, 'Only at times like these,'" she breathed softly, and his eyes closed. Unlike Suzanne, who couldn't know her story, she understood it all. "So you thought you'd failed me. That it all was your fault," she said it for him. "All your fault," she whispered, finally understanding why he had allowed Andre to bring his "impostor" to the island. She touched his face, brushed her hand over his cheek and up against his temple and then ran the sensitive pad of her thumb over the scars and the closed lid.

"My God," she whispered again when he said nothing, "you've *always* thought it was your fault. That you deserved this. That you deserved it *all*."

He moved his head away from her hand. "Expiation," he said softly and turned to walk, limping slightly, back into the hall.

"No," she whispered. She saw that it stopped him, but he didn't turn back to face her. "I knew you didn't mean that. Don't you think I knew? I was angry, but I knew how you felt. I was a child perhaps, but not a fool. You were angry. Out of all the scenes, all the embarrassments I had caused you, you finally lost your temper. I knew that. I never blamed you."

"Because you didn't remember what I'd said. But I did. They were my last words to...Kerri," he finished quietly. But the name was enough. Suzanne was right. Although he knew, he still intended to deny.

"Why are you doing this?" she demanded. "Why are you denying what you know? Why are you rejecting what we had?"

He turned back to her then and the look that was burned into the harsh tautness of his mouth was warning. "Because we can't go back. I *destroyed* what we had. We can't ever put it together again. I prefer to remember it as it was, rather than trying to build it again with broken pieces." The calm voice was unemotional, contained, and very sure.

She walked across the room and touched his face before she asked, "And what about what *I* prefer? Or don't you care? Don't I matter to your decision?"

"You don't know it all," he said, the careful neutrality of his tone painful to hear.

"Then tell me. Let's get it all out so I can understand why you don't want me. Why you don't want to make love to me anymore when I want you so much I ache. When I dream of you touching me and wake up wet and aching and alone. Always alone," and her voice broke with that aloneness.

"I killed our son because I couldn't control my tongue—" he began, and she broke through the softness of his words.

"No," she argued harshly. "I told you about the brakes. You must know..." she began and watched the denial of her certainty in the pain on his face.

"All right," she said finally, "if one of us must bear the blame, let it be me. I've already lived with that guilt so long." She swallowed and deliberately repeated his words, "I killed our son because of my need to be re-assured that someone *finally* loved me. But must I be punished forever? It's been so long. And I love you. And I can give you other sons," she begged. Her tears had begun with her confession, but through them she saw that the painful admission with which she had tried to ease his guilt had instead done something else. Something terrible. She watched it move into his face and was frightened by what she saw.

"What is it?" she whispered. "What is it, Julien? What did I say?"

"No," he said, and his hand moved to touch her throat and then to her breast as it had that day under the roses. "No," he said again and caressed her gently so that she waited. "I can't give you a son to replace the one I killed. I can't give you children, my love. Not ever. I suppose that's only fair, but I know how you felt about the child. I even understood. Someone who would always love you. I couldn't seem to convince you of my love, but I thought perhaps after a while...but that hope was something else I destroyed that night."

"You don't want children?" she said, not understanding. "Because of your blindness? Julien, that's something that—"

"No," he said too loudly and turned away from her. "No," he repeated, modifying his tone. "I'm sterile. Part of the injuries. It didn't matter before. It's so ironic that this seemed the least of all the things...until now. Until you came back and then I realized...it's just one more reason."

"Who told you that?" she said furiously. She pulled his shoulder until she could see his face and the confusion her anger had caused. "My God, who told you that? Tell me, damn it," she demanded and watched him struggle to remember.

"The doctors," he said finally. "After the wreck."

"Which doctor?" she said harshly. "Tell me which one. His name."

"I don't remember. I was—" He shook his head. "I can't remember who told me. I think that they asked Andre..."

She laughed into the sudden silence. "I thought so," she said. "I thought so. That bastard. He had so much to answer for, and he escaped."

"He's dead," Julien said.

"I know. I hope it was very painful. I hope it took him a very long time to die. That lying bastard."

She could see the shock on his face and heard it in his voice when he whispered, "He was my brother."

"Who *always* lied. About everything. You aren't sterile," she said, catching his hand and holding it hard against her belly. "Say hello to this son," she said. "Tell him how much you love him. Like you did under the roses. It won't be the same. Only the smell of lies and treachery will surround this memory. But you have another child, my love. Andre is dead. He won't destroy this baby.''

"Don't," he said, removing his hand, suddenly and violently. "Why are you doing this? Why would you say that?"

"Because it's true. I'm pregnant. I haven't been to a doctor. But I am. I know. And soon you'll know, too. You'll feel him move and turn and kick. Like the other baby.''

She saw his face then and ached for what was reflected there. Her voice softened, "Did you ever ask? Ever confirm what he told you?"

She waited, and after a long time watched the negative movement of his head.

"Then why won't you believe?" she asked softly. "Why can't you accept this? Another chance. And nothing is going to happen to this baby. Nothing.''

"Too much has changed," he said finally. "We can't go back.''

"No," she agreed. "And why would we want to? I don't want to be the person I was then. I don't want to hurt and embarrass you as I did then. I don't want to be reckless with my child's life. I don't want to go back, but I want very much to go forward.''

A muscle jumped in his jaw, and then his lips tightened. "But I can't," he said, "and unlike you, I *want* to be what I was. And I can't be.''

"So, because you're blind, you're going to reject me. And your child.'' He didn't answer and she laughed softly into the silence. "No wonder *Lear*'s your favorite play. 'Dark and comfortless,''' she mocked. "You are as proud and unbending as they, and like them, you are losing everything. Throwing it away for pride.''

"No," he said suddenly, "that's not true. Not pride.

I have none left. I ask strangers for help now. Don't accuse me of pride," he said, and she could hear the bitterness. "Blind men give up their pride very early. Pride, privacy, independence..."

"Companionship, love, children. Are you adding those to the list? You should. You're giving them up because...I don't even know why. Why does your blindness have anything to do with being a father? With wanting me? Explain to me why you can't love me if you're blind."

"I love you," he said, bitterly. "Would you like me to grope my way to your side and be led into a bedroom to prove it?" he asked, suddenly furious with her lack of understanding.

"Yes," she said simply. "Yes, of course." And waited for his answer to her certainty.

She watched him shake his head. When she spoke again, he could hear her despair. "Do you remember how I tried to hide from you when I was pregnant? I didn't want you to see me because I was so heavy. Do you remember, Julien?"

In spite of his earlier anger, she saw the memory of those days play over his lips in a tender smile.

"Did you love me any less? Did you ever find me repulsive or disgusting or any of the things I called myself until that day—"

"Under the roses," he finished softly, and she felt the sting of tears again.

"Until you told me how you felt and made me believe. What can I do to show you, my love, that I don't care? Your blindness hurt me at first. I thought of you as suffering, enduring...I don't know. But now...I only think of you. I only want you. Don't you want us, the two of us, enough to be able to—"

"Forget that I'm blind?" he asked simply.

"Enough to stop being a martyr, to stop enjoying your martyrdom," she finished and knew she had hurt him. God, she hoped she had hurt him enough. "Or do you enjoy too much being alone? Haven't you punished yourself enough? And me? Must you punish your child, too?"

"That's not true," he said, but she didn't answer. He waited, and finally she saw the familiar movement of his head. Listening for her. Trying to find her by the sound.

"Then do you want me to go or to stay?" she asked. "You just have to say. To decide."

She hardly dared to breathe while he thought about what she'd told him. She waited a long time, watching him, and still she couldn't tell what he was thinking.

When his answer came, it wasn't words. He held out his hand to her, waiting until she took the reaching fingers. He tucked her hand against his arm and led her to the bedroom where everything was exactly as she remembered it.

She stood a minute after he had released her arm and felt the atmosphere of this room, of its memories, invade her senses. He had stripped off the sweater and was removing the faded jeans. She watched the muscles move and the low light reflected against the mottled brown of the scars, the blue-black highlights of his hair. She had made no move to take off her clothes, but he was already undressed and removing the spread from the bed. He moved confidently around the room, familiar tasks, everything in its place, his clothes carefully folded on the dresser.

"Are you all right?" he asked. She realized he was waiting for her. "Kerri?" he questioned softly when she didn't answer.

"My name really *is* Caroline," she said, wondering why she had told him that. "I thought it was boring," she admitted and watched him smile.

"What do you want me to call you?" he asked, still smiling.

"I have thought these weeks, since I remembered, that I would give anything—" she paused because, thinking of the baby, she knew that wasn't true, so she amended "—*almost* anything to hear you call me Kerri again. And now…"

"And now?" he echoed, urging her to go on.

"I wonder if I want to go back to being Kerri. I'm not sure I don't prefer the Caroline you called me on the island. At least Caroline didn't…"

He waited, but she didn't finish the confession. "I think that perhaps I'm not the only one who can't let go of the pain. That, too, is a sword that cuts both ways," he said finally.

Because he cared so much that she regretted even a small part of their time together, he offered what he believed wouldn't cause her pain.

"I have something that belongs to you," he said softly. She watched the searching fingers find and remove an object from the box on his dresser. "I'm sorry," he said when he turned back to her. "I can't put it around your neck again. I had trouble enough with the clasp before."

By that time she had taken the delicate chain from his hand. When she had fastened it around her neck to rest as it had so long ago between her breasts, she brought his fingers to touch the roughness of the emeralds that he had said matched her eyes.

"Do you remember when I gave you this?" he asked.

She nodded as that memory tightened her throat and then remembered that he couldn't see her.

"Yes," she whispered, moving into his arms. She felt him catch his breath with the touch of her hand over his body.

"Yes," he echoed. His was a different affirmation. Just as necessary. And as cleansing. She smiled as his fingers moved easily to remove her clothes. Finally his arms were carrying her to his bed, their bed. She reached for him when his body lifted away from hers, and he smiled to feel her fingers catch and hold his arm.

He touched the bulb of the bedside lamp and knew by the heat it was on, and then he said, "I want you to see, to watch how much I love you. How much I want you and my son. I know there'll be problems and adjustments, but I want you. Never doubt that."

He stopped too suddenly, but she saw the emotion he was trying to mask. He lowered his mouth as he had so long ago to kiss and caress her body where it guarded his child. He welcomed this soul into existence as gently and as reverently as he had the baby they had lost.

When he lowered over her body, she closed her eyes with the anticipation of his first movement and joined him in his world of touch and smell and sound. His hands over her breasts and against the heart of her desire. His mouth and lips, warm and unhurried. Caressing, tantalizing in their selectiveness. And the sounds he made deep in his throat when she moved in response, lifted and strained to answer the need he so easily aroused in her. The smell of his skin. The texture of his beard against her throat, her breasts, her stomach and then her thighs, making her arch and twist to find the release offered by his mouth and hands and hard, sure strength. Until there was no more need, no more passion, only the tenderness of stroking fingers and trembling skin. No more driving force, but only softly spoken questions and sighing answers, releasing tensions built by months and years of aloneness. There was no loneliness tonight. And there would never be again, they promised each other silently. Each sure that he or she was taking the most, and that love was the only barter accepted in this exchange. Finding that its value was enough and more than enough.

She awoke with her face against the hard muscle of his chest and his thumb slowly moving up and then down her arm. His eyes were open, and she watched him a long time before she reached and kissed the scars. His lips lifted, and his hand tightened on her shoulder, pulling her closer to the lean strength of his body.

"I've been thinking," he said, but because he didn't turn to face her, she felt the sudden fear jerk through her heart.

"About what?" she asked carefully, hearing her own unease in the question. He turned then to smile at her and found her lips with his.

"Don't," he said softly. "Don't be afraid. That was what last night was all about." Finally she nodded against his face, and his voice when he spoke again was normal and strong.

"You have to see a doctor."

"I know. I will. It was only because I was afraid they'd say all those things again, and I knew they weren't true."

"Then today," he said and waited.

"Will you go with me?" she asked, smiling to see his concern.

"Of course," he whispered, touching his lips to hers again.

"Into the examination room?"

"Do you think they would allow that?"

"If you wanted to? Do you think they could keep you out?"

"Why do you say that?" he asked, laughing. "I'm only the father. I have no rights there."

"I don't believe you," she said, laughing with him. "I've never seen anyone refuse you anything you wanted. You browbeat everyone. That blue-blooded, icy stare."

When the laughter was wiped suddenly from his face, her smile faded. She knew that she would never remember all the ways she might hurt him. She still thought of him as the same. She knew he was. But he didn't.

The sudden noise from the front of the huge apartment surprised her, frightened her. She sat up too quickly. The nausea moved into her throat, and she closed her eyes against it.

"It's Emile. I'll tell him to leave. That I don't need him today."

He threw off the sheet and rose to pull on the carefully placed jeans. She heard him pad barefoot into the other room and the low murmur of voices. She lay facedown across his pillow and tried to will her sickness away. Not this morning. Nothing could be more humiliating than this.

She heard him come back into the room and the smooth slide of sound as he removed the jeans. His weight disturbed the bed, and then his lips were on her spine, tracing each vertebrae, following the curve to her buttocks and then he was lifting her, moving against her, positioning her prone body. His hands were cupping under her breasts. She could feel the hard length of him between her thighs.

"Don't," she said harshly, breathing in light rapid breaths through her mouth. She had read about that somewhere and it did seem to help. She felt him still and was suddenly too sick to even explain. If he touched her again... She closed her eyes against that thought. She had never denied him anything.

He moved to lie beside her on the bed. She turned her head to look at him and saw the faint furrow between his brows.

"I'm sick," she said softly. "Morning sickness. Just wait."

She watched the wrinkle disappear as he smiled at her. "I thought you were tired of me already," he said and pressed his lips to her forehead. He found her hand and held it. Finally the palm of his other hand began to move in soothing circles against her shoulders and back until she drifted into sleep, comforted with the touch of his fingers.

GET 2

HOW TO GET YOUR
2 FREE BOOKS AND FREE GIFT!

1. Peel off the MIRA sticker on the front cover. Place it in the space provided at right. This automatically entitles you to receive two free books and an exciting surprise gift.

2. Send back this card and you'll get 2 "The Best of the Best™" novels. These books have a combined cover price of $11.98 or more in the U.S. and $13.98 or more in Canada, but they are yours to keep absolutely FREE!

3. There's no catch. You're under no obligation to buy anything. We charge nothing – ZERO – for your first shipment. And you don't have to make an minimum number of purchases – not even one!

4. We call this line "The Best of the Best" because each month you'll receive the best books by some of today's most popular authors. These authors show up time and time again on all the major bestseller lists and their book sell out as soon as they hit the stores. You'll like the convenience of getting them delivered to your home at our special discount prices . . . and you'll love your *Heart to Heart* subscriber newsletter featuring author news, horoscopes, recipes, book reviews and much more!

5. We hope that after receiving your free books you'll want to remain a subscriber. But the choice is yours – to continue or cancel, anytime at all! So why not take us up on our invitation, with no risk of any kind. You'll be glad you did!

6. And remember...we'll send you a surprise gift ABSOLUTELY FREE just for giving "The Best of the Best" a try.

SPECIAL FREE GIFT!

We'll send you a fabulous surprise gift, absolutely FREE, simply for accepting our no-risk offer!

Visit us online at
www.mirabooks.com

® and TM are trademarks of Harlequin Enterprises Limited.

BOOKS FREE!

Hurry!

Return this card promptly to GET 2 FREE BOOKS & A FREE GIFT!

The Best of the Best ™

> Affix peel-off MIRA sticker here

YES! Please send me the 2 FREE "The Best of the Best" novels and FREE gift for which I qualify. I understand that I am under no obligation to purchase anything further, as explained on the back and on the opposite page.

385 MDL DNHR   185 MDL DNHS

FIRST NAME	LAST NAME

ADDRESS

APT.#	CITY

STATE/PROV.	ZIP/POSTAL CODE

◄ DETACH AND MAIL CARD TODAY!

(P-BB3-02) ©1998 MIRA BOOKS

The Best of the Best™ — Here's How it Works:

Accepting your 2 free books and gift places you under no obligation to buy anything. You may keep the books and gift and return the shipping statement marked "cancel." If you do not cancel, about a month later we will send you 4 additional novels and bill you just $4.49 each in the U.S., or $4.99 each in Canada, plus 25¢ shipping & handling per book and applicable taxes if any.* That's the complete price and — compared to cover prices of $5.99 or more each in the U.S. and $6.99 or more each in Canada — it's quite a bargain! You may cancel at any time, but if you choose to continue, every month we'll send you 4 more books, which you may either purchase at the discount price or return to us and cancel your subscription.

*Terms and prices subject to change without notice. Sales tax applicable in N.Y. Canadian residents will be charged applicable provincial taxes and GST.

Chapter Fifteen

When she woke again, she could tell by the quality of light in the room that it was very late. She was alone. She experimented with sitting and the queasiness didn't resurface. She moved carefully to his huge bathroom, showering a long time under the luxury of enough hot water. She had no clean clothes to put on, so she found his robe, belting it around her still-slender waist.

She had smelled coffee, gently permeating the apartment, but he wasn't in the kitchen. She poured a cup, pleased that the strong aroma didn't bother her this morning. Too often lately it had been the catalyst for the nausea. But not today. Perhaps she just needed the luxury of being able to sleep until noon to conquer this effect of her pregnancy. After all, it *was* called morning sickness.

She leaned against the counter and thought about all he had said to her last night. All the words she had thought she would never hear again. The promises. She knew he would never break them. That was his real strength.

He wasn't in his office or any of the other places she looked. She finally opened the door of what had been a spare bedroom when she had last lived in this apartment.

Now it was a gym, and he was here. He was leaning against a padded station, pushing the damaged right leg against a weighted apparatus. She could see the concentration on his face and watched his lips count each straining movement. She didn't interrupt until his head dropped, resting against the exertion.

"What are you doing?" she asked softly.

She saw him turn, smiling, to her voice. His hair was damp and curling. The muscles that corded his arms and chest, when he pushed away from the machine, gleamed softly with perspiration.

"Just exercises. For my leg. I had surgery six weeks ago. Just rehab," he explained easily, moving away from the machine. He limped confidently through the maze of equipment to stand before her. He was wearing only a pair of navy shorts. She could see the scars that traced paths down the right leg, white against the tan. One that was newer and redder than the others extended only an inch or two below the hem of the shorts. He used the towel around his neck to wipe his face and hair and then realized she was still standing silently, simply watching.

"Are you all right?" he asked, worried by her stillness.

"Of course. I've decided sleeping until noon is really the cure," she said, laughing. "I can even enjoy my coffee now."

"I'm glad you're not sick any longer."

"I'm sorry," she whispered and caught his hand to press it against her throat. He turned his head slightly, the faint crease moving between his dark brows.

"For what?"

"For this morning."

"For being sick? If there's blame to be placed for that,

it's more my fault than yours,'' he said, smiling at her. ''I seem to remember some stairs.''

''For denying you,'' she said, and saw his face change again.

''Denying me?'' he repeated unbelievingly. ''You were sick. Do you honestly think that I would want you—'' He stopped suddenly, his lips tightening. ''I wish I could see your face, see what you're thinking. What you're feeling. Are you afraid I'll be angry if you don't let me make love to you? Afraid to say that you don't want to, don't feel well, or just don't want me? Are you afraid that if you 'deny' me, I'll stop loving you? God, Kerri, you can't *still* be afraid. Is that why you were always so willing? Was it only because you were afraid?'' he asked harshly.

''No,'' she said, touching him, caressing him through the soft material of the shorts. ''You know that. I have *always* wanted you,'' she said, feeling his quick response to what she was doing, ''as much as you could want me. That wasn't fear. But I thought you might think something had changed. Because I'd never done that before.''

''Has anything changed?'' he questioned, needing her reassurance now. She recognized that need in his voice. She had heard it often enough before in her own. ''Does this all really not matter to you?''

''Not like you mean. I'm not sure I can explain it to you and make you see.'' In her concern over making him understand how she felt about him, she didn't even notice what she had said. Nor did she notice the small lift of his lips that recognized and accepted her choice of words.

''You were always so perfect, Julien,'' she began and then hesitated. ''Perhaps I understood Andre's evil before anyone else because I, too, had cringed before that perfection.'' She watched him shake his head, but she ignored that and went on. "I needed you so much, wanted you. But I could never understand why you would want someone like me. Someone 'so worthless.' Andre said that, and he was right. Why would someone like you want someone like me? You had everything. And I had nothing. I had *never* had anything. Nothing that mattered. Until you. And I didn't understand why you loved me. I never trusted that love because I didn't deserve it.''

"Don't," he said. "I told you last night. I don't want to hear this. Those insecurities are in the past, dead and buried."

"Dead and buried? Because you're not perfect any longer? Because you're blind?" she asked softly. "You're the one now who feels that you have to deserve this. And it turns to gall. It will turn what we can have to gall. I know.''

When he didn't speak, she told him the rest.

"Perhaps there is some part of me that feels safer with your imperfection. I would hate that part of me, but I can't deny that it might exist. Now *I* have something to give *you*. If you'll let me. In exchange for all you have always given me. But if my hand on your arm offering guidance through somewhere unfamiliar becomes bitter to you, then we'll be back to where we were before. To the anger and the accusations.''

She saw the denial move into his face.

"I can't help being angry over what happened to me," he said. "My life is so changed. You don't know yet, and when you do, you may not want to live with my limitations. That's a chance you convinced me to take last night. And I'm willing. But are you asking me to give up being angry, to give up resenting the fact that I now and forever *must* be guided? That I will never do any of the things I did before? Is that what you're asking?''

"I don't think so," she said. "I think I'm saying that if you *are* angry, don't let it be because I want mine to be the hand that guides you. Because some part of me doesn't mind having to guide you. Because some part of me likes being able to do something for you. To give you something. I never had anything to give you before. That's why the baby was so important. You thought I wanted him so much because he would love me, and that was true. But I also wanted to give you a son. I could do that, I thought. Sometimes when people said I'd trapped you into marrying me, I knew, even if there was some element of truth there, it didn't matter because you really wanted the baby. I never doubted that.''

"No one thought that," he said, and she laughed.

"*Everyone* thought it. Everyone but you.''

"I want you here," he said suddenly. "Under any condition. However you feel about my blindness. I won't resent your hand. As long as it's yours. As long as you want it to be on my arm.''

"Are there beds here, old man?" she asked softly and saw the slow smile.

"You never used to want a bed. You used to—'' He stopped as her hands pushed against the waistband of the shorts, moving them down over his lean hips and the muscles and scars of his thighs. She let them drop to his feet, and then she was kneeling before him on the carpet of the sunlit room. She lifted her fingers to touch him and saw his reaction, as strong as last night, as strong as always. She looked up to watch the lids drop to cover the blue of his eyes. She lowered her face then to touch against his body and didn't see his head fall back in response to what her lips were doing to him. But she felt his response. So strong, so hard.

Suddenly he was kneeling with her, and she opened her eyes as his dark fingers struggled briefly with the knot in the belt of his robe. His hands moved to her shoulders when he had succeeded, and he pushed the open edges over and down her arms. She was as exposed to his lips and hands as he had been to hers. He lifted her breasts, cupping strong fingers under their fullness and lowering his mouth to pull against each taut nipple. She felt the force of that suction between her legs and then the rush of moisture that signaled how much she wanted him there. She turned her face against the softness of his dark hair and put her hands on his shoulders for balance.

"I want you," she whispered into the fragrance of the curling blackness.

"Not enough," he said gently. "Not yet."

"Yes," she argued and took his hand and placed it between her legs that moved to open and welcome him.

He smiled at what he felt there. He cupped the heel of his hand against the bones of her body that were liquid with wanting him. She gasped to feel his fingers invade, as hard and demanding as she knew he would be.

"Yes," she said, lowering to meet their touch, feeling the breath sigh out of her lungs at what he was doing.

"Yes," he echoed and turned her body to lie under his. Her legs moved with the surety of long habit, never forgotten by bone and muscle, never betraying the memory of this as her mind had. They opened to welcome his long muscular body between them, and then closed hard around him as he moved into the wetness that surrounded him, hot and tight and slick with her desire for him. For only him. And he wondered suddenly.

"Have you ever…" he began and felt the wrongness of that question move between them, softening his surety.

"What?" she asked, wanting nothing but the movement of his body farther into hers. Not understanding the sudden cessation of his invasion.

"Made love to anyone else?" He knew he was spoiling this, felt it in the sudden stillness of the arching body beneath him, in the loss of his own driving strength.

"How can you think that?" she asked angrily. "You know. You were the first. On the beach at Monte Carlo. You know."

"And in these years?" he asked softly, hating the need to know, but acknowledging it, and he felt finally the release of her anger, the relaxation of the tight muscles against his body.

"I'd forgotten. These long years," she said softly. "I'd forgotten that they were between us. And that you couldn't know."

He was listening very hard to read her voice, to understand what she was telling him. Afraid suddenly because she hadn't said it. Because she hadn't denied what he had asked her to deny.

When her mouth moved against his, in spite of his doubt, his need to know, he opened to her tongue, and knew that even if she couldn't deny what he had asked, he still wanted her. He was hard and tight again, suddenly filling her with his need, pushing into her soft yielding with the force of his passion. Knowing that it didn't matter.

She pulled her lips from him and watched him lower his head to follow their withdrawal, and she spoke against the touch of his tongue, reassured by his response that he no longer cared. But knowing this was something else she could give him, as she had given him before.

"No one," she whispered. "There has never been anyone else." She watched his eyes clench tight against his sudden tears. "I never wanted anyone to touch me. Not the doctors. No one. They weren't you. I didn't know it was your hands I wanted, but I knew no one else's were right on my body. I remembered that much. Until the island. And the nightmare." She wondered if she should tell him about that, but this was Julien, and she could tell him anything. That, too, was part of his strength.

"I let Andre kiss me. I didn't understand why I wanted his lips, but it was because he reminded me of you. His eyes. The same blue and I thought..."

Her voice faded at the sudden hard, deep fullness of his body, driving against the walls of her soul, and instead of moving away from the pain, she moved into it and felt it become something else, something different, something that was theirs. She felt his release begin long before she was ready, but she only smiled into the hard shoulder that was against her face. She listened to what he said, the rush of words she knew he would not even be aware of having spoken. When the pressure grew too great under his shuddering body, her teeth found the dark skin. She gave him back the pain and felt him convulse in response.

The spiraling journey began again immediately and that had never happened before, but he carried her with him this time. Able to wait, to judge her responses and to meet them. She felt his fingers guiding her to join him and finally the answering movement in her own body. Because he had gone there first, he was able to control his need, so that she arched against him time and again, driven by the sure assault of his body against hers. Driven until she dug her nails into the hard buttocks and begged for the relentless demand he was making to stop, to give up its strength and loose its need in the warm, dark wetness of her body. When he did, it was stronger than she ever remembered. She held him a long time then, shivering against the force of what he felt for her.

He touched his lips finally to her throat, gentle again. Caressing.

"Are you all right?" he asked. "I didn't mean to hurt you. I didn't mean..."

"No," she denied, lifting his face with both hands to kiss him. "You didn't hurt me. You can't hurt me by wanting me."

"The baby?" he questioned softly, moving his lips under her jaw, against the soft skin until he found the beating pulse that echoed still the movement of their bodies.

"The baby's safe." She laughed. "Well-protected from a father who wants too strongly. At least for now, well-protected. And perhaps by the time we have to be careful, you won't want me that much."

"You know—" he began and shook his head. "You have to know that how I feel about you never stops. Through all the long years," he echoed her words. "I never wanted anyone else. I thought that was be-cause—"

He stopped, and she nodded, understanding what he was telling her without the pain of putting it all into words.

"I know," she said softly. "I know it all."

He held her there on the floor of the bright room a long time, not wanting to release her, as he had wanted to hold her at the top of the stairs. Finally she spoke into the silence.

"You went to his grave," she whispered. "Suzanne said that you went to the convent."

"Yes," he said.

"I want to go. Will you take me there? I want to see it."

"It's very quiet," he said, "and peaceful."

"Can you go there again, my love? I'll go by myself if you want, but I'd like you to go."

He smiled and said softly, "Of course. There's nothing there to make me not want to go. I'll take you. Whenever you're ready."

When he felt her nod against his chest, he tightened his hold on the slender body, moving his hand to rest against the soft curve of her stomach. They lay in the quiet sunshine, content again only to hold and be held.

IT WAS SEVERAL WEEKS before he made the arrangements, and she wondered if he were regretting his promise to take her back to Monaco. Suzanne teased that he would never leave the business at this time of year, but Caroline only smiled at how little she understood. He had never taken a real holiday before because he had nothing to pull him away from how he had chosen to fill his long dark days, and that was no longer true.

He had arranged for the villa to be reopened and they spent the night there. She wondered if he would expect her to drive to the convent, but of course, he had made arrangements for that, and the driver waited below with the car as they made their way slowly up the gently sloping hill to the stand of trees that sheltered the two graves.

After they reached the top, she didn't remember when

he removed his hand from her arm, freeing her to seek what she had come here to find. She gradually became aware that she had been kneeling beside the grave for a long time. It was so small, and in spite of the years, the tiny stone looked too new and raw. It needed the softening of lichen and time and the rain to make it at peace, but the hilltop was very peaceful, just as he had said.

She looked for him and found him leaning against one of the trees, relaxed, his face lifted into the breeze that stirred the leaves above his head. She listened to see what he heard, becoming aware for the first time of the birds and the movement of the branches and, from somewhere in the village below, the sound of church bells floating on the wind. He had been right. There was nothing here to fear or to dread.

"It's very peaceful," she said finally and saw him smile, but he didn't answer or turn to her voice. There was no longer a need for that between them.

"My grandfather *is* here," she said softly. "Suzanne was right. I don't know when or how. I don't understand how I know, but I do. He came to sleep beside our son. To protect him."

"From what?" he said, smiling at her again. "There's no need for protection here. To keep him company, perhaps. To hold his hand into eternity. He was too small to find his way alone."

She felt the tears flood her eyes at his words and wiped them with the back of her hand. He'd know she was crying. He always knew everything.

"Don't cry," he said softly. "There isn't anything to cry about."

"I know. Pregnant women cry. You should know that after these weeks," she said, laughing through her tears.

She watched the memories of all the easy tears move

across his face. She had cried to see his dark hand rest again against the growing fullness of her body and when he had brought home the rocking horse. It was like a carousel horse and like the one he had brought home before, but then he had smelled of sweat and horses from a polo game she hadn't wanted to attend because she was always afraid he might be hurt. This time he hadn't talked about teaching their son to ride. It hadn't been mentioned, but they had both remembered, and he had held her while she cried.

"I don't want to move them. I thought I might want him closer, but this is right. I want to leave them here together. Do you want to change the stone?"

She watched him think about her question, and finally he shook his head. "It doesn't matter. I took you from the old man. So perhaps…"

They were silent then. Finally she rose and moved across the shaded grass to stand beside him. When she touched his face, he turned to smile at her again.

"I have one more question. I know—" She stopped, and then forced herself to continue, hating the tension she saw move into his peace as she talked. "I know you don't want to talk about this. And I'll never mention it again. But I need to know. I need so *much* to know."

The birds quieted against the shadow of the cloud that blocked the sun, and he waited.

"How did Andre's mother die?" she asked, but it was a long time before he answered.

"The brakes failed on her car," he said into the stillness, and she felt the weight lift from her heart.

"Why?" she asked simply, but he understood.

"Andre had been sent home from another school. My father and I were in Paris. He came here to his mother.

I don't suppose we'll ever know what Camille said to him, but whatever it was—''

''Didn't you ever think—''

''Not until you said that in the cave that day. After that it began to grow like a cancer in the back of my mind.''

''Then you believe—''

''Don't,'' he said. ''I've told you what you asked. No more, Kerri. Despite it all, he was my brother and I loved him.''

She saw the pain in his face and was sorry for this last agony. She leaned against him, and he opened his arms to let her body relax against his length. He lowered his mouth to move tenderly against the brightness of her hair. He closed his eyes with the force of the emotion that had grown to fill all the long-empty spaces of his soul. She took his hand, placing it to rest against her body. He waited and finally felt the soft movement of his child that was growing there, loved and protected.

''I love you,'' she said, touching his face to turn his head to her.

''I know.'' He smiled. ''I know you do. And you must know how much I love you. How much I have always loved you. All the long years.'' His voice broke, and he was silent.

She lifted to find his lips and kissed him gently. ''Let's go home, old man,'' she whispered.

He took her arm, allowing her to guide him, and they walked together down the hill, leaving the two graves shadowed with the softness of the leaves that moved eternally in the breeze above them.

* * * * *

THE SECOND MRS. MALONE

Amanda Stevens

Chapter One

The woman was covered in blood. The drying crimson splashed across the front of her expensive white tank dress like globs of red paint. Her pale face was streaked with dirt and mascara, and her blond hair hung to her waist in damp, matted clumps. She looked as if she'd been to hell and back, and Sergeant Troy Stoner of the Houston Police Department couldn't take his eyes off her.

He turned to the patrol officer who had picked her up earlier in the evening after spotting her wandering down a busy street and brought her to the emergency room at St. Mary's.

"Who is she?" Troy asked over the noise and chaos of the ER. Thunder boomed outside, and somewhere down the hallway, a baby cried incessantly while a man with a gunshot wound in his leg screamed obscenities in Spanish at one of the nurses.

Officer Dermott shrugged his damp shoulders, oblivious to the general confusion around him. "Hell if I know. I couldn't find any identification on her, and she was pretty disoriented when I picked her up. Didn't say one word the whole way here." He paused and tapped his left temple with his fingertip. "I figure they'll take her up to the bin after they check her out here."

Troy frowned at the derogatory term for the psychiatric ward, although to be honest, he couldn't say it had ever bothered him before. But something about this woman brought out something in him he didn't care to analyze. Unable to tear his gaze away, he stared at her through the curtained partition.

Who was she? What the hell had happened to her? She hadn't been seen by a doctor yet, but the nurse who had spoken briefly with Troy a few moments ago assured him that her injuries appeared to be minor, a few scrapes and bruises, nothing to warrant the amount of blood on her clothing. So whose blood was it? And how had it gotten on her?

As if reading his thoughts, Dermott said, "She's damn lucky that blood isn't hers. It's a wonder some drunk didn't splatter her all over the pavement."

Somehow *lucky* wasn't a word Troy would ascribe to the pale, frightened woman sitting on the very edge of the hospital bed, as if poised to flee the moment she sensed danger.

He wondered if she had any idea she was being watched. He and Dermott stood just outside the curtained partition, speaking loudly enough to be heard over the din of the ER and the storm that raged outside, but the woman gave no indication that she was aware of their presence. She sat stone still, staring at some distant point in space that only she seemed aware of.

He should have gone home, Troy decided wearily. His shift had ended hours ago, but he'd been delayed at the hospital with a prisoner who'd sustained serious injuries after a botched convenience-store holdup. Just as he was about to leave, hoping to beat the rain, his lieutenant had called him to tell him as long as he was still there he might as well stick around and talk to another suspect who was being brought in.

But the moment Troy had seen the blonde, he'd been experiencing a myriad of regrets. He didn't need this. Not tonight. He wished he'd told his lieutenant to go take a flying leap. Let somebody else handle this case. But it was too late now, and with another weary sigh, Troy pushed the curtain aside and stepped through.

He hardly made a sound, certainly nothing that could be heard over the groans in the next cubicle, but the woman's gaze shot up, panic flashing in her blue eyes before she glanced away, as if wanting to shield her emotions from him.

But in that moment when their eyes met, Troy felt an odd little tremor in the pit of his stomach, a sensation not unlike the ones he experienced in times of keen excitement or extreme danger.

Damn, he thought. He *really* didn't need this.

He walked toward her, but she didn't look at him again. Except for that brief moment of eye contact, she'd retreated into that distant place that made her appear so unreachable. So…fragile.

Troy guessed he ought to be relieved she wasn't his type. He didn't like fragile women. He wasn't like his brother, Ray, who needed to be in control, or his other brother, Mitch, who needed to be needed. Troy liked strong, secure, independent women. Women who knew the score as well as he did.

What he didn't like was a woman who brought out his protective instincts. He'd found out the hard way that a woman like that could be a dangerous thing for a man like him.

He cleared his throat, trying to draw her attention

without causing her further alarm. "I'm Sergeant Stoner," he said gently. "I need to ask you a few questions."

When she didn't answer, he said, "Let's start with your name."

Still no response.

Taking out his notebook and pen, Troy tried not to let his eyes wander to the slender bare legs revealed by her short hemline. He concentrated instead on the bloodstains. "The nurse said you didn't appear to be seriously injured, but you have a lot of blood on your clothing. Can you tell me what happened?"

Silence.

Troy moved to the end of the bed, giving her a little more space. He studied her profile and wondered what she was thinking. He could almost feel her sinking deeper into that place where no one, least of all him, could reach her.

But he wanted to try anyway. He wanted to take her by those thin, tanned shoulders, gaze into those crystalline eyes and, by sheer force of will, bring her back to a place where he *could* reach her. Touch her...

He broke off his thoughts abruptly. "What were you doing out alone this time of night? Officer Dermott said he found you on Westheimer, walking down the middle of the street. What happened to you? Were you running away from someone? Were you assaulted?"

Her hands were clasped in her lap, and Troy saw they were trembling. He took that as a good sign. At least she wasn't completely unaffected by his questions.

A scream erupted down the hallway, and the woman flinched. She looked around, as if suddenly aware of her surroundings. The groans in the cubicle next to her grew louder, and her blue eyes widened in despair.

''Where am I?'' she whispered.

''The emergency room at St. Mary's Hospital. Don't you remember?''

She looked around again, as if seeing the cubicle for the first time. Judging by the quality of her clothing and the heavy gold bracelet around her wrist, these stark surroundings were hardly the accommodations she was accustomed to. But she was damn lucky it was Sunday, Troy thought. On Friday and Saturday nights, beds were lined up in the hallway.

''What's your name?'' he asked again.

She lapsed back into silence, her blue eyes again staring into space.

He walked toward her, recapping his pen and putting it away. ''Look, I want to help you here. Your family must be worried sick about you—''

At the mention of the word *family,* her gaze darted up to his. Her eyes widened, giving her the appearance of an animal trapped in a headlight. Troy found himself leaning toward her, wanting to shield her from whatever terror had driven her out into the rainy darkness.

Her left hand fluttered to her neck, and for the first time, he saw the faint shadow of a bruise marring her forearm, as if someone had grabbed her roughly. He also saw the glitter of diamonds around the third finger of her left hand.

She was married, a suspect, completely off-limits. But before he could stop himself, Troy reached out to touch the bruise on her arm. She gasped and jerked away, wrapping her arms tightly around her middle as if she could somehow ward off whatever threat he might pose to her.

Troy let his hand drop to his side and said, ''I won't

hurt you. I only want to help you. Your husband...did he do that to you?''

The blue eyes flooded with tears, but she still said nothing.

Troy swore under his breath. He'd seen it before. A battered wife refusing to press charges against an abusive husband. Refusing to admit what had really happened until it was too late.

"Look," he said impatiently, running a hand through his damp hair, "I can't help you unless you level with me. Tell me what happened. What's your name? Where do you live?"

One tear spilled over and ran down her cheek. Troy had to forcibly restrain himself from reaching out to wipe it away. She looked so young, sitting there with a teardrop drying on her cheek and bloodstains drying on her dress.

Troy's temper surged at the thought of any man committing an act of violence against any woman, but especially one who was as defenseless as this one.

Or was she?

He let his gaze drift back to the bloodstains. "You don't have any identification on you. Did you lose your purse? Did someone steal it?" When she still didn't respond, he sighed. "This is getting us nowhere fast."

He started to turn away, but her blue gaze met his again, and in those crystal depths, he saw a plea for help that touched him all the way to his soul.

He took a step toward her in urgency. "Won't you at least tell me your name?"

"I...can't."

Her voice floated across the distance separating them and wrapped around him like a sweetly provocative perfume. Her blue eyes held him enthralled, mesmerizing him with the secrets hidden within. Troy had the sudden mental image of a gossamer spiderweb, so deceptively beautiful, so potentially deadly...

"What do you mean, you can't?" he asked. "Are you afraid to tell me your name?"

"I mean...I can't." Her voice quavered with emotion, and her eyes brimmed with tears. Troy thought he'd never seen a face so haunted. So terrified.

"I can't tell you my name," she whispered in anguish, "because I don't know it. I don't know who I am."

"HEY, DOC, WAIT UP!" Troy hurried to catch up with the man he'd been waiting to see.

Dr. Timothy Seavers, tall, lanky, with a plain face and a disarming smile, strode down the hospital corridor, his lab coat flapping behind him like the wings of some giant white bird. When he heard Troy's voice, he turned, the blue eyes behind the wire-rimmed glasses lighting up in recognition. "Troy! How's it going?" He pumped Troy's hand vigorously.

He hadn't seen him in years, but Troy had known Tim Seavers for a long time, ever since he'd attended medical school with Troy's younger sister, Madison.

"Not bad," Troy said. "How about you?"

"Busy. You know how it is." Tim ran a harried hand through his light brown hair. "So how's the family? Not a Sunday goes by I don't think about your mom's fried chicken."

"You should drop by sometime. She still cooks enough to feed a small army. She'd be thrilled to see you, and so would Dad. He's retired now, you know."

Tim's eyes widened in mock surprise. "You're kidding. I didn't think your old man would ever quit the force."

"Neither did I. Look, Tim, I need to talk to you about the Jane Doe who was brought in earlier tonight. Blond hair, blue eyes, about so tall." Troy measured the air with his hand. "The one who says she doesn't remember her name."

Tim glanced at the chart in his hand. "What do you want to know?"

"I need for you to explain to me just exactly what her condition is. In layman's terms."

"She's only had a preliminary examination in the ER. None of the test results are back yet, including the blood work."

"I know all that," Troy said impatiently. "But you checked her out, right? What's your guess?"

Tim frowned. "I don't like to guess."

"Come on," Troy urged. "Just between you and me. Off the record. It would be a big help to me to know exactly what I'm dealing with here."

Tim sighed. "Okay. Like I said, I haven't seen all the test results yet, but my best guess, in layman's terms, is that she has hysterical amnesia."

"In other words, there's no physical reason for her memory loss? No bump on the head or anything like that?"

"Other than a few minor bruises, she appears to be perfectly healthy."

"She wasn't sexually assaulted, then?"

"No."

The woman's trauma, along with her almost palpable fear, had led Troy to the obvious conclusion. He felt a moment of intense relief before asking, "Is there any chance she could be faking the memory loss?"

Tim glanced at him curiously. "Anything's possible. It's also possible that by morning her memory may be restored, at least in part."

"Could the amnesia be drug related?"

"I can't say for sure until we get the blood work back, but I don't think so. I'm guessing she received a tremendous shock of some kind tonight, something so traumatic her mind couldn't cope, so she blocked out whatever it was she saw or heard."

"Or did," Troy added, almost to himself. "Her dress was covered in blood, and yet you say she only has minor injuries. The blood had to come from somewhere, Tim. From someone. I'll need that dress, by the way, along with the rest of her clothing."

Tim nodded. "I know the drill. We'll bag it up, along with all her other personal effects. That is, except for her wedding ring. She became quite agitated when the nurse tried to remove it. Under the circumstances, I felt it best not to upset her. Who knows? Her ring may be the one thing that can trigger her memory."

"Let's hope so." But Troy had a feeling it wasn't going to be that easy. "In the meantime, I'll get everything over to the lab. Hopefully, in a day or two we'll have some answers about Jane Doe one way or another."

"I feel sorry for her," Tim said suddenly. When Troy glanced at him in surprise, he shrugged. "I know. I'm a doctor. Like you cops, we aren't supposed to have feelings, but there's something…haunting about her. I can't explain it."

He didn't have to. Troy knew exactly what Tim meant, but he kept his opinion to himself. The last thing he needed was to be having feelings for a suspect, one who couldn't remember her own name, let alone how she'd come to be covered in blood. Troy had learned a long time ago that when it came to women, he was a lousy judge of character.

He said so long to Tim and then retraced his steps down the hallway. After she'd been examined in the ER, the woman had been moved to a room on the seventh floor. Troy stood outside the door, wondering if he should go in and talk to her again. Demand some answers. Find out if she really was faking her amnesia.

But it was late, after one o'clock in the morning. The caffeine kick had long since worn off, and exhaustion was setting in. Troy couldn't remember how long it had been since he'd seen a bed. It seemed like a lifetime. He'd been working too damn hard, he thought. Seen too much going down lately. He didn't like closing his eyes anymore. Didn't like dreaming about the bullet that might have his name on it.

He wondered if his brother Gary, who had been killed in the line of duty five years ago, had had those same nightmares before he died. He wondered if Mitch and Ray, who were also cops, had them now, and knew he would be relieved to learn that they did.

But there was no way Troy would ever ask them. No way he would ever reveal to his brothers that being a cop sometimes scared him. He was the daredevil of the family. The thrill seeker. The Stoner who didn't give a damn about tomorrow. His brothers would be shocked and not a little disappointed to learn that Troy had nerves after all. And that he just might be losing them.

Maybe he wouldn't go home, he decided. Even on a Sunday night, there were still places where he could find plenty of warm bodies and lonely souls who would be willing to share a few drinks and whatever else he might crave. Maybe he'd just go drink himself into a stupor so that when he finally did fall asleep, the doubts would be held at bay. For a few hours of blessed oblivion, he wouldn't have to think about mortality and betrayal and the woman from his past who had almost killed him.

SHE WOKE UP, choking on a scream. Someone was leaning over her bed, whispering to her.

Her eyes flew open, straining to see in the darkness that surrounded her. A scent lingered. Something familiar.

Fear exploded inside her, and she bolted upright, sweat pouring down her back. Her heart pounded in terror as she peered into the darkness, afraid to call out, afraid to even breathe. Someone was in here. Someone who wanted to hurt her.

A flash of lightning revealed that she was alone. No one was lurking in the shadows, but her terror did not lessen. She had to get out of here. She had to run away. Find someplace to hide where they would never find her.

An image of a small, dark room appeared in her mind, and an overwhelming sense of panic engulfed her. She couldn't go back *there*. They would find her. They would lock that dark room and never let her out. They would say she'd done bad things. Terrible things.

But before she could get out of bed, light flooded her room, the door opened and a middle-aged nurse with a kindly face bustled into the room. "What's the matter, hon?"

She looked at the nurse blankly. "Wh-what?"

The nurse nodded toward the bed. "You pressed the call button several times. Do you need something? Are you in pain?"

She uncurled her fist and found the call button inside. She hadn't even been aware of holding it, much less pressing it to summon help. "I think someone was in here."

The nurse took her by the shoulders and pressed her gently back against the pillow. "You probably had a nightmare. God knows, this weather is enough to give anyone the heebie-jeebies."

It wasn't a nightmare. She was sure of it. Someone had been in here with her. Someone—or something—evil.

"Someone was here," she said again.

"No one was here," the nurse soothed. "I've been at the desk all night. I would have seen if anyone had come into your room."

What about the scent? she wanted to ask. But the fragrance, so tantalizingly familiar, had already faded away. She put her hands to her face. "What's wrong with me? Why can't I remember?" she whispered.

"You will," the nurse assured her. "The doctor said your tests so far all appear normal. More than likely, your memory loss is only temporary. In a few days, everything will start to come back to you."

No! She didn't want everything to come back to her. What if they took her away again? What if they locked her in that dark room again?

But even as those thoughts flitted through her mind, a flash of memory caught her by surprise. A man's voice screaming *Andrea!*

Her heart started to pound again. "Andrea," she murmured. "My name is Andrea."

The nurse brightened. "There, you see? You're starting to remember already. What you need now is rest." She straightened the covers with an economy of motion. "Do you want me to bring you something to help you sleep?"

No drugs! The idea filled her with terror.

The nurse patted her arm. "Very well, then. Do you need anything else before I go?"

I need to know why I'm so afraid! I need to know who wants me dead!

She needed to know about the dark room.

But she said nothing.

"Get some sleep now," the nurse said, turning toward the door. "Everything will seem better in the morning."

But Andrea didn't think so. She didn't think daylight would bring an end to her terror.

Chapter Two

When she awakened again, sunlight streamed in through the hospital window. She closed her eyes and lay there, hovering pleasantly between sleep and wakefulness. She'd been dreaming about Mayela. The two of them were walking in the park, laughing and talking and having a wonderful time. She always had a wonderful time with Mayela—

Who is Mayela? a voice in the back of her mind asked.

And with that question, the terror of last night returned. She sat up in bed and gazed around frantically. Where was she?

The hospital. She dimly remembered being brought to the emergency room. She'd talked to a police officer, hadn't she?

Her hand flew to her mouth. Oh, God, what had she told him? What if he found out about the dark room? About all the blood? What if he sent her back? What if—?

You didn't tell him anything, the little voice assured her. *Because you don't remember anything.*

There was safety in not remembering.

She did a quick survey of the room. A window, one

door that led to the hallway, another door that led to the bathroom and a sink with a mirror.

Andrea got up and padded over to the window. The parking lot was far below. No one could have gotten into her room through the window. She crossed to the door and peeked out. The elevators were at the end of the hallway, near the nurses' station. No one could have come that way without being seen. The nurse had been right. The intruder last night had been nothing more than a product of Andrea's imagination. But somehow that thought did not make her feel any better. Far from it.

She let the door close and moved to the sink to examine her reflection in the mirror. Blond hair, blue eyes, oval face, full lips, high cheekbones. A model's face, she thought without pride, for the face in the mirror belonged to a stranger. *Was* she a model? A wife? A mother? Was that who Mayela was? Her child?

But surely she would be able to remember her own child. What kind of mother would forget her child?

And her husband? She searched her mind frantically for an image, then lifted her left hand to stare dispassionately at the impressive glitter of diamonds in the mirror. If she had a husband and a child out there somewhere, why did she feel so lost? So lonely? Why did she feel as if she didn't belong anywhere?

Why wasn't her husband looking for her? Why hadn't he come forward to claim her?

A sudden explosion of memory caught her by surprise. A voice deep inside her mind screamed, *I hate you. I want you dead.*

A red mist covered her vision.

Andrea's right hand curled at her side, as if gripping a knife. She lifted the imaginary blade to the mirror and struck at her reflection.

I hate you. I want you dead. Dead! Dead! Dead!

Gasping in horror, Andrea grabbed her right wrist with her left hand as if to physically restrain the slashing motion. What had happened to her?

What had she done?

BY MIDMORNING, she had been poked, prodded, X-rayed, stuck with needles, her blood drawn, her head examined, her vital signs checked and rechecked, and all because she couldn't seem to remember who she was.

"Well, Andrea, I have good news and I have bad news," Dr. Seavers announced as he strode into her hospital room later that day. "The good news is, I can't find anything wrong with you."

"And the bad news?"

"I can't find anything wrong with you." He pulled up a chair beside her bed and sat down. "The MRI and the CAT scan have turned up nil, and the blood work so far is clean, which is pretty much what I expected. Your memory loss appears to be psychosomatic."

"Meaning I can't remember because I don't want to." She studied the doctor carefully.

He took off his glasses and rubbed the bridge of his nose with his thumb and forefinger. "It's usually not quite that simple."

Wasn't it? "Will I ever remember?"

He slipped back on his glasses, gazing at her with earnest blue eyes. "There are no guarantees, of course, but I'd say the chances are excellent your memory will return."

"All of it?"

"Probably not all at once. Bits and pieces will come back to you, sudden flashes maybe. Eventually you may remember everything."

"When?"

"That's what I'd like to know," said another voice from the doorway. Andrea's eyes darted to the figure standing just inside her room. He looked vaguely familiar, but she couldn't place him. There was something disturbing about the way his dark eyes studied her so intently. Something frightening about the way she seemed to respond to him.

For a moment, she wondered if he might be her husband. Was that why he seemed so familiar to her? A thrill of excitement raced up her back. A memory darted through her mind.

A man was kissing her. A man just as tall and dark and handsome as this man.

But he wasn't this man.

Disappointment shot through her as she quickly tore her gaze from his.

Dr. Seavers said, "You remember Sergeant Stoner?"

The policeman who'd questioned her last night. *I don't like cops,* she thought suddenly, though she had no idea why.

She flashed him another glance, and he smiled at her. Andrea's pulse fluttered in her throat. He really was quite attractive, she thought, and wondered why she hadn't noticed last night.

Maybe she had noticed. Maybe she'd forgotten.

She didn't see how she could forget this man, though.

But she'd forgotten her husband.

I want you dead!

She looked away, unable to hold Sergeant Stoner's probing gaze.

"I'm glad to see you're looking so much better this morning." He crossed the room to her bed.

Dr. Seavers stood up. "I'll stop by later, and we can talk more. I'm sure you still have a lot of questions."

"As do I." Something in Sergeant Stoner's voice made Andrea tense, and she realized that his smile had only been a ruse. He wasn't to be trusted after all.

"Have you remembered anything?" he asked when Dr. Seavers had left the room.

"My name." She was still unable to meet his gaze. "It's Andrea."

"So I heard. That's a very pretty name." He paused, then said, "And your last name?"

"I don't know." Andrea didn't know why she felt so afraid to look at him. Guilt, maybe? Was she afraid he would see something in her eyes that even she didn't know about?

She wondered if she should tell him about the intruder in her room last night. But why should he believe her when Andrea wasn't even sure herself? He might think her crazy. He might want to send her to the dark room.

"What's wrong? Have you remembered something else?"

"No, nothing." With an effort, Andrea willed herself to relax, forced her gaze to meet Sergeant Stoner's. His eyes were a dark, impenetrable brown and fringed with long, curly lashes. He was tall and lean, but Andrea knew that beneath his suit coat, the muscles in his arms and chest would be powerful. She could almost feel them flex and bunch beneath her hands—

She stopped her thoughts cold. Was she remembering how it felt to be in a man's arms? Or was she experiencing wishful thinking, because of this particular man?

Just what kind of woman are *you?*

Obviously one who wasn't to be believed, she

thought, if the shadow of doubt in Sergeant Stoner's eyes was any indication.

"Let's go back to last night," he said. "What's the first thing you remember?"

Andrea closed her eyes, straining for recall. "The emergency room. There was so much noise. Someone screamed."

"Do you remember talking to me?"

She flicked him a sidelong glance. "Vaguely."

"Do you remember being examined?"

A blush of humiliation touched her cheeks. The examination had been thorough. "Yes."

"Dr. Seavers said he could find nothing physically wrong with you."

"So he told me."

"Your amnesia appears to be—"

"Fake?"

Something flashed in those brown eyes. "I didn't say that."

"But you have your doubts about me, don't you? I can tell."

"I'm not a doctor, I'm a cop. We tend to see things in black-and-white. We're naturally wary of terms like 'hysterical amnesia' and 'psychosomatic.'"

Hysterical amnesia? *Was* she hysterical? Andrea didn't think so. Right now, she felt amazingly calm. Completely in control. She began to relax because she knew as good a detective as Sergeant Stoner might be, he wouldn't find out anything she didn't want him to.

"Do you have any idea why you might have been walking down the middle of a busy street at ten o'clock at night in a thunderstorm?" he asked suddenly.

Andrea's poise slipped a little. She shook her head.

"Were you trying to get away from someone?"

That struck a note of truth, but Andrea forced her expression to remain placid. Safety lay in keeping her mind a blank. She shook her head again.

Sergeant Stoner took a deliberate step toward her. He towered over the side of her bed, and his dark eyes probed her face, searching for the truth. "Where did all that blood come from, Andrea?"

"Wh-what?"

He bent toward her, his eyes intense. Andrea found she wasn't quite as calm as she'd thought. "You had blood all over your clothing, but it wasn't yours. Whose blood was it?"

"I—I don't know."

Sergeant Stoner stared down at her. "You have to admit, your memory loss seems just a little too convenient. You're found wandering down a busy street in the middle of the night, covered in blood. Yet you can't remember why you were on that street or how that blood got on your clothing. You can't even remember your last name. Our hands are tied, Andrea. We don't know if a crime has been committed or not. We don't even know where to start looking. And if a crime was committed, by the time your memory returns, the trail will have undoubtedly grown cold. Do you see what I mean?"

She saw, all right. She knew exactly what he was driving at. "Just what is it you think I've done?"

"I don't know." He sat down in the chair next to her bed and took out a black fountain pen, twirling it between his fingers. "All I know is that you had a great deal of blood on your clothing when you were brought to this hospital. Type O-positive, the lab tells me. Does that mean anything to you?"

"No. I don't even know what type my own blood is."

"It's A-negative, as a matter of fact."

"It seems you know more about me than I know about myself." She didn't think she was usually so flip, but Sergeant Stoner frightened her, and she had to hide behind something.

"I doubt that," he replied. "I doubt that very much."

When she didn't answer, he tried another tack. "Would you be willing to talk to a psychiatrist?"

An image of the dark room rose in her mind, and Andrea's heart pounded in terror. *No!*

She didn't want to talk to a psychiatrist. That was the last thing in the world she wanted.

She forced herself to stare at him coolly. "Will my talking to a psychiatrist alleviate your doubts about my amnesia?"

He shrugged noncommittally. "Will you talk to her?"

"Her?"

"Someone I know. She's very good. You'll like her."

"I suppose I'll have to take your word for that, won't I?" Andrea said, wondering just who the woman was and what she meant to Sergeant Stoner.

Those dark eyes studied her carefully. "You do want to remember, don't you?"

"Of course I do. Why wouldn't I?"

"That's a good question, Andrea. A very good question."

TROY FROWNED as he stood in the hallway outside her hospital room. The interview hadn't gone quite as he'd expected. She was too damn cool, for one thing. What had happened to the poor, helpless girl he'd seen in the ER last night? The woman he'd just spoken with seemed completely in control of her faculties, and not nearly frightened or confused enough for someone who couldn't remember her own name.

A chill of foreboding crept up Troy's spine. What kind of game was she playing? And what the hell did it have to do with him?

WHAT DO YOU THINK you're doing, Andrea? The woman with the haunted blue eyes stared back at her in the mirror.

I couldn't let him see how much he frightened me. Then he would know something was wrong.

He already knows something is wrong, her reflection scolded. *You were found wandering down a busy street with blood all over your clothing, and you don't remember who you are or what happened to you. What is he supposed to think?*

That I'm guilty.

Of what?

I don't know.

Yes, you do. You know. You know.

She raised her left hand and stared at the diamonds twinkling on her finger.

I want you dead! Dead! Dead! Dead!

"THE LAB FOUND TRACES of a mild sedative in her bloodstream," Tim said.

"A sedative?" Troy frowned. "What do you make of that?"

"Parvonal C is sometimes used in sleeping medications, completely harmless in the amount we found in Andrea's blood. It might have contributed to her disorientation, but it wouldn't have caused her memory loss. Everything else appears normal. Under the circumstances, I won't be able to keep her here much longer. We're just too understaffed and too short on beds."

''Where will she go?'' Troy asked, but he knew the answer as well as Tim did.

Tim shrugged, not in indifference, but in resignation. ''Judging by her clothing and jewelry, she doesn't appear to be destitute. Maybe someone in her family will turn up to claim her. If not, there's always the shelters.''

Troy tried to picture Andrea in one of the homeless shelters downtown, but the image was too incongruous. She obviously didn't belong in a shelter, but just where did she belong? So far no one had filed a missing-persons report fitting her description, and Troy was having a hard time believing that no one in her family had missed her yet. But it hadn't even been twenty-four hours. Andrea's husband might yet turn up to claim her.

And what if he did claim her? What if he was the reason Andrea had been found wandering alone at night, bruised, disoriented and frightened? What then? Troy would have no recourse but to turn her over to him. If Andrea couldn't remember what had happened, if she couldn't file a complaint against him, there would be nothing Troy could do to help her.

What makes you think she wants your help? Or needs it, for that matter? he asked himself as he thought about the cool, collected woman he'd spoken with earlier. It was almost as if he'd interviewed two very different people. One vulnerable and frightened, one calm and controlled.

He wasn't sure which one of them was the true Andrea. Or which one of them was the most dangerous.

''I'd like Madison to talk with her,'' he said. ''Do you have any objections?''

Surprise flashed in Tim's red-rimmed eyes. ''I have no objections. In fact, it'll be nice to see your sister again.''

IT WAS LATE AFTERNOON and Andrea had just awakened from a troubled sleep. She'd dreamed about Mayela again. The name had been fresh on her mind when she'd opened her eyes, but when she'd tried to put a face with the name, the tenuous image vanished.

Was Mayela even a real person or another figment of her imagination?

A knock sounded on her door, and she called out, "Come in," expecting to see either Dr. Seavers or one of the nurses. But the dark-haired young woman who stuck her head around the door was someone Andrea was sure she'd never seen before.

"Hello," the woman said pleasantly. "Up for a little visit?"

Andrea shrugged, immediately on guard. But the woman's smile was infectious, and Andrea soon found her uneasiness fading. The woman was tall, at least five-eight or five-nine, and very slender, with short, glossy black hair and dark brown eyes that tipped slightly at the corners. She wore faded jeans, a yellow T-shirt and a pair of running shoes that had definitely seen better days.

"I'm Madison Stoner," she said. "It seems we have a mutual acquaintance."

Andrea looked at her in surprise. "You mean Sergeant Stoner? Are you his wife?"

The brown eyes twinkled. "No, thank God. I'm his sister, which might have just as many disadvantages, come to think of it." She set her macramé bag in the chair and came to stand beside Andrea's bed. Not too close, though. She was careful to keep an unthreatening distance, Andrea noted.

"You're the psychiatrist he told me about," she said with sudden insight.

Dr. Stoner gave her a mock frown. "Am I that transparent?"

Was she? Andrea wasn't sure how she'd identified the woman so quickly. How she had associated that calm voice and nonjudgmental expression with those of a psychiatrist.

She'll lock you in the dark room if you're not careful. "I don't know what your brother told you, but I'm not crazy," Andrea said, moistening her dry lips. "I just can't remember."

Dr. Stoner smiled sympathetically. "Yes, I know. That must be pretty scary."

Scary? Her amnesia was terrifying, but Andrea knew remembering would be worse. Remembering would be the death of her.

She couldn't afford to let Dr. Stoner help her regain her memory, and she couldn't let Sergeant Stoner suspect her resistance. It was all so tricky, this deception. So nerve-racking. Andrea felt the onslaught of a terrific headache. She massaged her temples with her fingertips.

"Are you in pain, Andrea?"

"No, I'm okay."

"You sure? I could ring for the nurse."

"No, I'm fine. Just tired."

"I won't stay long," Dr. Stoner assured her with another warm smile. "But as long as I'm here, we might as well get acquainted. Do you mind if I sit?"

"Of course not."

Dr. Stoner tossed her purse onto the floor and sat. "So." She crossed her long legs and smiled at Andrea. "What do you think of my brother?"

The question was so unexpected that Andrea found herself blurting out the truth. "He's very good-looking."

Madison laughed. "You aren't the first woman to

have noticed that. He's quite the lady-killer, my brother.''

Andrea wondered what Sergeant Stoner would say if he could hear the way his sister talked about him to a complete stranger. Dr. Stoner wasn't like any psychiatrist Andrea had ever known, but then, she had no idea how many she had known.

She fingered her wedding band. "Is…he married?"

"Troy? Please. He has an aversion to commitment. But then, all the Stoners seem to suffer from that affliction. None of my other brothers are married, either."

"How many brothers do you have?"

"Three. Ray's the oldest, then Mitch, and then Troy. They're all cops, and so is my dad. Or he was, until he retired last month. Can you imagine what my social life has been like?" She laughed without rancor, and her brown eyes tilted even more.

"An entire family of cops," Andrea murmured. The notion intrigued her for some reason.

"Oh, you have no idea. My family's fascination with law enforcement goes back a long way. Both of my grandfathers were police officers, and one of my great-grandmothers was a county sheriff," she said with obvious pride.

"Why didn't you go into law enforcement?" Andrea asked.

A wistful smile touched Dr. Stoner's lips. "I almost did. Up until I went to college, I had every intention of following in the Stoner tradition."

"What happened?"

The smile disappeared. "Oh…that's a long story. Anyway, I've found being a psychiatrist has its distinct advantages in my family. My brothers usually steer clear of me because they're afraid I'll try to psychoanalyze them. No cop can stand that.''

Andrea glanced at Dr. Stoner's hands folded in her lap. Her fingers were long and graceful, like those of a pianist, and unadorned with rings. ''You aren't married, either, then?''

''No. But I see that you wear a wedding band. It's very beautiful,'' Dr. Stoner said.

The transition was made so skillfully, Andrea was hardly aware of it. She lifted her hand and studied the diamonds.

''You don't remember your husband, do you?'' Dr. Stoner asked softly. ''That must be very troubling.''

If you only knew.

''Have you had any flashes of memory at all?''

A dark room. A knife. Someone named Mayela. What did it all mean? ''I don't think so,'' Andrea said. ''At least nothing that makes any sense.''

''It probably won't for a while. Everything will seem hazy at first, but then your memories will become clearer and clearer until eventually, everything will click back into place.''

''You make it sound like a puzzle.''

''It is, in a way. Almost all of the pieces are missing right now, but as you find each piece, the bigger picture will start to take shape.''

''How do I find the missing pieces?'' Andrea asked fearfully.

''You may not have to. They may find you. But if they don't, there are certain procedures that might help you.''

''Such as?''

''Regressive hypnosis, for one thing.''

''Hypnosis?'' Why was that idea so terrifying? Be-

cause she was afraid to remember what had happened? What she might have done? Andrea shivered.

"Does the idea of hypnosis disturb you, Andrea?"

"No, it's just..."

Dr. Stoner smiled. "I understand. Everything is very confusing for you right now. But try not to worry. I'm willing to bet your memory will return on its own in a few days. All you need is a little time."

But how much time did she have? Andrea wondered. How much time before they found her?

Who's they? her mind screamed in frustration.

Dr. Stoner picked up her purse and stood. "I can see you're getting tired. Why don't I let you get some rest and we'll talk again later. That is, if you want me to come back." When Andrea hesitated, she said, "It wouldn't have to be as a psychiatrist, you know. I could come back as a friend."

Sudden tears filled Andrea's eyes. The loneliness and fear were suddenly overwhelming. A deep despair settled over her. "I'd like that," she said, almost in a whisper. "I think I could use a friend right now."

Chapter Three

Forty-eight hours had passed, and still no missing-persons report had come in on anyone fitting Andrea's description. Lieutenant Lucas seemed particularly put out by this turn of events.

"We need to get this thing cleared up, Stoner. I don't like loose ends."

"I'm all over it, sir," Troy assured his superior on Wednesday morning. "I've got the lab reports right here, but unfortunately they're not all that useful at the moment. We don't have any unsolved homicides in the last two days with type O-positive blood, so for the moment, that's a dead end. Her dress, however, is by a fairly unknown but pricey designer whose label is only carried in two stores here in Houston. I'm going in to talk with the managers this afternoon."

"What about her jewelry?"

"I've taken the bracelet around to a few upscale jewelry stores that specialize in custom pieces, but no luck so far."

"She was also wearing a wedding band, right? Any leads on that?"

Troy looked away. "Uh, no. Actually she's still wearing the ring. She got pretty upset when the nurse tried to remove it, so under the circumstances, her doctor felt it best to let her wear it. He thinks her ring may be the one thing that can trigger her memory.''

Lucas scowled. ''Might be an inscription inside, though. Have you thought about that?''

Of course Troy had thought about that. *To My Beloved Wife…*

He shrugged. ''When her doctor says the time is right, I'll ask her to take off the ring.''

Lucas nodded. ''Well, stay on it. I want this thing cleaned up.'' He dropped a stack of folders on Troy's desk. ''We've got bigger problems than some chick who can't remember her own address.''

Troy didn't figure it necessary to point out the fact that that same ''chick'' might have been involved in a crime. That there might be a little more going on with Andrea whatever-her-name-turned-out-to-be than just memory loss.

But he didn't say anything. He didn't want Lieutenant Lucas thinking he might have a little more interest in this case than was warranted. He didn't want Lucas remembering the rumors about Troy's involvement with a certain murder suspect named Cassandra Markham, and he sure as hell didn't want Lucas remembering how that involvement had almost cost Troy his badge. Not to mention his life.

Five years ago, right after Troy had first made detective, the Markham case had been his first major homicide investigation. Cassandra Markham had been the chief suspect in her husband's murder, but her sweet smile, her youth and naiveté had convinced Troy she was innocent.

His brother Gary had just been killed a month earlier, and looking back, Troy guessed he'd been vulnerable.

And gullible. He'd fallen in love with Cassandra Markham, and she'd played him for the fool he was. He'd learned the hard way that looks, more often than not, were deceiving, and he'd vowed he would never make that same mistake again.

And yet here he was, attracted to another suspect.

But he was older now and wiser, and a hell of a lot more cynical. It would take more than killer blue eyes and soft blond hair to turn his head this time.

BY THE END of the third day, Andrea was becoming accustomed to her memory loss. She no longer awakened frightened and disoriented, and she found herself looking forward to Sergeant Stoner's visits in a way she didn't understand. She instinctively knew he could be dangerous to her, and yet the effect he had on her was undeniable.

Of course, there was no way she could ever let Sergeant Stoner—Troy, as she had begun to think of him—know of her feelings. He'd remained so aloof, so impersonal with her that she knew he only thought of her as a suspect.

And therein lay the danger. He thought of her as a *suspect*. Someone who may have committed a terrible crime. If he had even an inkling of her feelings for him, he would question her motives even more. He would begin to wonder what kind of woman would be married to one man and attracted to another.

A woman who couldn't be trusted, that's who.

And she needed him to trust her. If she were to have any chance at all, she had to somehow make him believe in her.

She got up and padded to the mirror, gazing critically at her reflection. She looked much better today, with her hair clean and combed, and a touch of makeup complementing her features. Madison—as Dr. Stoner had insisted she call her—had dropped by earlier this morning and brought Andrea a pale blue silk nightgown along with an assortment of toiletries and cosmetics. Andrea had been overwhelmed by the generosity and thoughtfulness of the gift. It was amazing what getting out of a hospital gown could do for one's spirits.

But as she walked to the window and stared out at the early-afternoon rain, her spirits once again sagged. Did she have a family out there somewhere, loved ones who were waiting anxiously for some word of her whereabouts? Why hadn't they come forward, then? Why hadn't they been looking for her? Was there no one out there who missed her? Who cared about her?

Loneliness tugged at her heart, the emotion all too familiar. Instinctively she knew she'd experienced this feeling before. The sensation settled around her like an old, comfortable shawl. She'd learned to deal with her loneliness years ago, hadn't she? When she'd lost her mother and father. When she'd been sent to that dark room—

The door of her hospital room opened, and Andrea swung around. It was the first time she'd faced Troy, standing up, and she wished that it made her feel less vulnerable to him, but the impact was the same. Her heart beat an excited staccato inside her.

"I'm sorry," he said. "I knocked, but I guess you didn't hear me."

She lifted her chin, swinging her long hair over one shoulder in a move she hoped appeared casual. "It's okay. Come in."

He let the door close behind him, but his eyes never left her. Suddenly she realized he was seeing the differences in her, too. The blue silk nightgown, the combed hair, the makeup. His gaze was oddly intense.

She picked up a fold of the nightgown. "Your sister came by this morning and brought me a CARE package. I feel like a new woman."

"Madison's thoughtful that way." His gaze lingered just a fraction too long on the delicate lace neckline of her gown.

"She's very nice," Andrea agreed, wondering if her voice sounded as breathless to him as it did to her. "You were right. I like her a lot."

"Good. I'm hoping she'll be able to help you. In the meantime, I may have a lead."

A fist of panic closed over Andrea's throat. Her hand crept to the tender skin on her arm, where the bruise was now almost invisible. "What kind of lead?"

"Your dress." His gaze dropped for a fraction of a second to the nightgown she wore. "The label is from a designer whose line is carried in only two stores in Houston. Alaina's in the Village and Zoë's on Post Oak near the Pavilion. Both shops are fairly small but very exclusive. Do either of those names ring a bell for you?"

Andrea closed her eyes, searching her mind. Her dress was a designer original from an expensive shop, and she knew that the heavy, ornate bracelet the police had taken from her the first night in the hospital was solid gold, worth a small fortune, as was the diamond wedding band that sparkled on her finger. Her nails bore the evidence of a professional manicure, and her long hair was so precisely cut that every strand fell into place by a simple shake of her head.

And yet...she didn't feel rich. She didn't feel pampered. Far from it. Andrea had the distinct impression that she had worked very hard all of her life. That at times mere survival had been an extraordinary struggle.

So where did her expensive jewelry and clothing come from? A wealthy husband?

The memory came so blindingly fast that Andrea had no time to prepare herself. She saw him so clearly, an older man with gray hair and a careworn face. *I'm a rich man, Andrea. As my wife, you will be entitled to certain privileges, anything your heart desires....*

You little gold digger! Who do you think you're fooling? I'll see you in hell before you get a penny of his money!

I want you to know that I've changed my will, Andrea. When my time comes, you will be well taken care of.

I hate you. I want you dead!

In her mind's eye, Andrea saw the gray-haired man fall to the floor, blood gushing from the stab wounds in his chest.

Andrea's knees buckled as she followed her vision to the floor.

SHE WEIGHED no more than a dream. Troy lifted her easily and carried her to the bed. As he bent over to lay her on top of the sheets, a strand of her hair curled around his arm, and once again the image of a spiderweb formed in his mind. But he shook it off and reached for the call button.

The nurse, an enormous Hispanic woman with hips the size of a battleship, stormed in and hustled Troy out of the way. She quickly felt Andrea's pulse and took her vital signs, all the while muttering in Spanish under her breath, something that Troy thought translated roughly to, "Stupid cops. Stupid men. God give me strength."

She removed the stethoscope from her ears and

glanced at Troy. "She fainted." Her voice was distinctly accusing. "What did you do to her?"

"Nothing."

"She faint for no reason? I don't think so. Women don't faint for no reason. Men maybe, not women."

"I didn't do anything to her," Troy said. "We were just talking."

The nurse's dark eyes narrowed on him. "Cops like to talk too damn much, I think. Now, get out of my way," she said as Troy started toward the bed. She lifted both hands as if to shove him back, and Troy retreated a safe distance away.

"Is she going to be all right?"

"Maybe, if you let her rest." She pulled the sheet over Andrea and tucked it about her shoulders.

"I'm just trying to do my job," he said defensively.

She gave him a "Humph" that told him exactly what she thought of his job.

Andrea moaned and her eyes fluttered open. The nurse's expression immediately softened. It was amazing how quickly Andrea had managed to assemble her troops. *She'd* come into the hospital covered in someone else's blood, and Troy was suddenly the villain of the piece.

"What happened?" she murmured.

"You fainted," the nurse said gently as she lifted Andrea's wrist and felt her pulse again. "Almost back to normal."

Andrea's brows drew together. "I...fainted?"

"Yeah," Troy said, coming to stand by her bedside. "You gave me quite a scare."

Andrea's gaze flew to his, as if she'd forgotten his presence. He said quickly, "You seemed to have remembered something that upset you."

She lifted a hand to her forehead. "I just felt so weak suddenly. So dizzy…"

"I think it was more than that," Troy insisted.

The nurse shot him a warning glance. "She needs her rest."

"If I go now, I'll just have to come back later. Wouldn't you rather get our talk over with?" he asked Andrea.

"I don't remember anything. What more is there to say?" She turned her head toward the window.

"Oh, I think we'll find something to talk about."

The nurse shook her finger at him. "Ten minutes, no more. You understand me?" She marched across the room and opened the door. "I'll be back," she said in a voice that sounded alarmingly like Arnold Schwarzenegger with a Spanish accent.

When the door closed behind her, Troy turned back to Andrea. "You've got yourself quite a champion there. Do you always make friends this quickly?"

Andrea frowned at his tone. "I don't know what you mean."

Troy shrugged. "You seem to have a knack for making people want to go out of their way to help you. My sister, Dr. Seavers, the nurses." Who else had she put under her spell?

"Is that a crime, Sergeant Stoner?" Her beguiling blue eyes, even more startling against her now pale face, trapped him with her stare. He couldn't look away and Troy found himself wondering if he was becoming her next victim.

In a bloodstained dress with wet, matted hair, she'd been dangerous enough, but in a blue silk nightgown that was hardly more than imagination, and her hair—an intriguing shade of silvery gold—curling down her back,

Troy thought her positively lethal. She was a knockout, a woman that would be noticed in a crowd of beautiful women, and yet no one had come forward to identify her. No one had reported her missing. Why?

It didn't make sense. Nothing about this woman made sense, least of all the way his body was responding to her in that blue silk nightgown.

"What did you want to talk to me about, Sergeant?" Andrea asked softly.

Her voice sent a shiver of unease up Troy's spine. He deliberately turned away from her and walked over to the window. The drizzle of early afternoon had turned into a full-fledged downpour. He could hardly see beyond the parking lot.

"Are you in the habit of taking sleeping pills?"

"What?"

He turned back to her. Her eyes were wide with shock. "Dr. Seavers said the lab found trace amounts of a mild sedative in your blood, a drug called Parvonal C. It's usually found in over-the-counter sleeping medications."

Andrea frowned. "I don't think I would take sleeping pills."

"But you can't know that for sure, can you? Since you can't remember?"

Their gazes met and held almost in challenge, and then Andrea glanced away. "No." She took a deep breath and released it. "Is that what you wanted to talk to me about?"

"There's something else," Troy said. "I'd like to run a picture of you in the newspapers and on television. There must be a reason why your family hasn't come forward. Maybe they don't realize you're missing."

"How could they not know?" Her blue gaze tracked

him as he turned away from the window. "It's been days. If there was someone out there who cared about me—" she fingered her wedding ring "—he would have already come forward, wouldn't he?"

Although it was hard to argue with her logic, Troy found it even more difficult to believe a woman like her would have no one. "Not necessarily. There are any number of reasons why you might not have been missed. Your husband may be away. Or he may think *you're* away. The best way to get the answers we need is to run the picture."

"Dr. Seavers and Madison both agree that my memory will probably return on its own in time."

"But how much time?"

Her gaze dropped.

Troy stepped close to her bed, staring down at her. "I don't think we *have* that kind of time, Andrea. I don't know how to explain it, but I feel some urgency in this matter. I think we need to find out who you are and what happened to you as soon as possible." It was imperative, in fact, that he return her to her real life, to her husband, before it was too late.

Before he, too, got caught in her web.

"I'M SERGEANT STONER," he said, showing his ID and badge to a clerk who appeared to be no more than seventeen or eighteen. "I'd like to talk to the owner."

The girl look unimpressed by the badge. "Zoë's my aunt."

Which probably explained how a girl who wore black lipstick and nail polish, not to mention hot pants and white retro boots, managed to snare a job in a swanky joint like this. She looked like an escapee from the seventies, and Troy wondered what kind of familial persua-

sion had been brought to bear on poor Zoë to give the
girl a job. "Is your aunt here?"

The girl examined the black nails, which were so long
they'd begun to curl under, giving her hands the appearance of claws. "She's out of town and won't be
back until the end of the week."

"What about the manager?"

"Called away on a family emergency. No one's here
but me."

"Are you in charge, then?" Troy asked carefully.

She shrugged. "Yeah, I guess so."

"I called yesterday about a particular dress you carry
here. I talked to someone named Carol."

"She's the manager, but she's not here."

"So you said. Look, I'm going to need your help..."

"Star," she supplied, flipping back her straight, white
blond hair. "My name's Star."

"Star, the dress I'm looking for is by a designer
named Tamara Casey, and I'm told Zoë's is one of two
shops here in Houston that carry her line." He'd already
bombed out at Alaina's, the shop in the Village, and was
hoping for better luck here. "Are you familiar with that
designer?"

Star shuddered. "We carry Tamara Casey, all right,
but I wouldn't be caught dead in any of her clothes."

Troy fervently hoped Star wasn't planning on making
sales her lifelong career. "The dress I'm looking for is
short, white, sleeveless. Real nice. Do you know the one
I mean?"

"Maybe." The girl tucked a strand of hair behind an
ear that was pierced no less than five times. She led him
to the front of the store and pulled a dress from the rack.
"Is this it?"

Troy fingered the fine fabric, remembering the way

that dress had looked on Andrea. Remembering the bloodstains. "That's the one."

"We've only had this style a few days," the girl told him. "If it was purchased in here, it had to have been since last week."

"That should make tracing the purchaser a little easier," Troy said.

Star shrugged. "Yes and no. If the dress was charged to an account, Carol could probably use the computer when she comes back to find out who bought it, but if someone paid cash for it..." She shrugged again in dismissal.

"Does that happen often?" Troy asked. "Someone paying cash? I didn't think that was done much anymore."

"It is if some rich old geezer doesn't want his wife snooping in his business."

In other words, men buying presents for their mistresses wouldn't want a record of the transaction that their wives might run across.

"I see what you mean." Troy fished in his coat pocket for a card. He handed it to Star. "Why don't you give me a call when your aunt gets back from her trip or Carol gets back from her emergency?"

"Sure." The girl glanced at his card. "There's not like a, you know, a reward or anything involved, is there?"

FOUR DAYS AFTER she'd been found and brought to the hospital, Andrea's picture was shown on TV. She was watching the news when she first saw it. One moment they were talking about a tropical storm in the gulf that had just been upgraded to a hurricane, and then in the next instant, the radar map gave way to her picture with the lead-in, ''The police are searching for the identity of this woman....''

Andrea stared at her picture, trembling uncontrollably.

The fear that had been kept under control came storming back, stunning her with its intensity.

She should never have let her picture be shown on TV. But how could she have stopped it without arousing Troy's suspicions? She knew he already doubted her. She couldn't afford to make him even more suspicious. She needed him on her side. When everything came out—

It won't. As long as your memory is lost, no one will find out anything.

But how long could she keep the memories at bay?

How long could she keep pretending she was an innocent victim?

Chapter Four

It was dark by the time Troy got back to the hospital to see Andrea. She was sleeping with the light on, and Troy flipped off the switch, letting the soft illumination from the corridor filter in. He started to turn away, but something about the way she stirred in her sleep drew him to her bed. He stood in the dark, staring down at her, wondering what secrets her dreams would reveal if he could see them. Wondering if he would ever find out the truth about her.

She muttered something in her sleep, a name, and Troy stepped closer. Her head thrashed from side to side. She was obviously in the throes of a powerful nightmare. Troy took her hand and shook it lightly.

Her eyes opened wide and she screamed, bolting upright in bed. She slashed out with one hand. "No! Please don't lock the door! It's so dark in here—"

Troy caught her thrashing arm in his hand. He tried to calm her. "Andrea, it's me, Troy. It's okay."

Her frantic movements ceased. "Troy?"

"Sergeant Stoner."

She clung to his hand. "I'm so glad to see you. I thought—" Her grip tightened. "Why is it so dark in here?"

"I turned off the light. I thought you might sleep better in the dark."

"I hate the dark!"

"Yeah, I got that. I'm sorry."

He was about to ask her why she was so afraid of the dark when the door to her room burst open, and a deep, masculine voice demanded, "What's goin' on in here?"

The light came on, and Troy found himself staring into the angry face of a burly male orderly. The man's eyes narrowed. "Who the hell are you?"

"Sergeant Stoner, HPD. Who the hell are you?"

He ignored Troy's question. "Is this man botherin' you, Miss Andrea?"

"No, it's okay, Calvin. He's a policeman. He's here to help me. Aren't you, Sergeant Stoner?"

Her gaze was a bit too challenging. Troy frowned. "I'm doing my damnedest."

"Well, you sure do have a funny way of helpin', that's all I know. Comin' in here, gettin' Miss Andrea all upset." Calvin's gaze went past Troy to fix on Andrea. "You sure you're okay?"

"I'm fine. Thank you for coming to see about me."

Calvin nodded. "If you need anything else, you just press that there call button." He pursed his lips disapprovingly as he shouldered his way past Troy.

After Calvin left, Troy turned back to Andrea, shaking his head. "How do you do it?"

"What?"

"Have everyone eating out of your hand like that."

"*You're* not," she said, her gaze meeting his.

Wasn't he? Why else was he here instead of going home when he had the chance if he wasn't falling under her spell, just like everyone else?

''What *are* you doing here?'' she asked, as if she'd read his mind.

Good question. He glanced at his watch. ''It's still early. I don't suppose you feel like taking a walk?''

''Where to?''

Troy shrugged. ''I don't know. There's a coffee shop on this floor. I haven't eaten yet, have you?''

Her blue eyes widened almost imperceptibly. ''Are you asking me to dinner?''

''I need to talk to you,'' he clarified quickly.

''All right.'' Was it his imagination or did she seem a little disappointed? ''Would you mind waiting for me in the hallway? I'll just be a minute.''

''Sure.'' That would give him plenty of time to ask himself just what in hell he thought he was doing.

Troy stepped outside and leaned against the wall. This wouldn't do. It wouldn't do at all. He couldn't afford to screw up again. His involvement with Cassandra Markham had almost cost him everything. What the hell was the matter with him?

He could just hear what his old man would say if he could see his son now. And what about Ray and Mitch? What would they say if they knew their little brother was about to get in over his head one more time? Would they be so quick to try to bail him out this time? Or would they decide to let him sink or swim on his own, just as Gary had done when he'd thrown Troy into the creek behind their grandparents' farm?

Swim, kid! Give it all you got!

Somehow Troy, only three years old at the time, had managed to make it back to the bank, and then he'd lit into ten-year-old Gary with a vengeance. Gary had just laughed, shoved him away like a pesky fly and said, ''Now I don't have to worry about you getting yourself drowned when you follow me and my buddies down here.''

Thanks to his brother, Troy had turned out to be the best swimmer of them all and a competitive diver, even getting a full scholarship to the University of Houston. But he wondered what Gary would think if he could see the way Troy was floundering now, and all because a woman who didn't know her own name had caught him completely by surprise.

He sighed, scrubbing his face with his hands. He was a damn fool and he knew it.

After a few minutes, the door opened and Andrea stepped out. She was wearing a blue satin robe over her nightgown and blue quilted slippers. Her hair was pulled back and fastened in a loose braid down her back, making her look incredibly soft and feminine, incredibly desirable.

"I'm sorry," she said. "This is all I have to wear."

"Don't be sorry," he murmured. "You look... beautiful."

His words seemed to catch *her* by surprise. She started to say something, but the light in the hallway ignited the diamonds in her ring as she moved her hand up to smooth back her hair.

Her hand stopped in midair.

The diamonds flashed with cold fire.

And a warning sounded somewhere in Troy's brain. *Back off, you idiot. Back off before someone gets hurt.*

"Uh, the coffee shop's this way," he said, motioning with his hand.

They started down the hallway, each of them careful to keep a distance between them. But as they approached the coffee shop, Troy's arm brushed against hers when he reached out to open the door for her.

A thrill of excitement shot through Andrea. She wondered if she had ever been so aware of a man before. Surely she'd been attracted to her husband. Hadn't he made her heart beat this fast, her knees grow this weak, her stomach flutter like a thousand butterflies had taken flight inside her?

Somehow Andrea didn't think so.

The coffee shop was almost empty. They took a table for two near the windows, and Troy went to get their coffee and a sandwich for himself. While he was gone, Andrea stared out the window at the downtown skyline, picking out the buildings she recognized. It was strange. She knew what the Texas Commerce Tower looked like, could pinpoint the neoclassical lines of the Esperson Building, but she had no idea what her own home looked like or where it was located. She knew she lived in Houston, though. Knew she had been born here. There was no doubt in her mind about that, except…

Something niggled at the corners of her mind. She'd been sent away once, hadn't she? Lived where the winters were long and brutal and the summers much too short. She'd been very unhappy back then, her father dead and her mother—

Abruptly her thoughts cut off, as if a curtain had dropped inside her mind. *Don't think about your mother,* a little voice whispered. *Think about surviving. Think about getting out of here. Think about helping Mayela.*

"Sure you don't want something to eat?" Troy asked as he dropped down in the chair opposite her. He handed her a cup of coffee, then finished unloading his tray.

Andrea shook her head. "No, thanks. I'm not hungry."

"Well, if you're sure." He picked up his ham-and-cheese sandwich and began to eat.

After a few bites, he wiped his mouth with a paper napkin and shoved his plate aside, grimacing. "Hospital food never changes."

"No, I guess it doesn't." She put her coffee cup down, careful to avoid his gaze. "You said you wanted to talk to me."

When he didn't answer, she was forced to glance up. His dark brown eyes studied her with an intensity that took her breath away. Her hands began to tremble, and she clasped them in her lap so he couldn't see.

"What's the matter?" she asked. "Why are you looking at me that way?"

He shook his head slightly. "I can't figure you out."

"What do you mean?"

"Look at you. You're gorgeous, a real head-turner. A face that would be almost impossible to forget, and yet no one has recognized you from your picture. No one's called in about you. No brother or sister, no mother or father. No one."

"Maybe I'm an orphan," Andrea said. "Maybe I don't have parents." As she said it, she knew it was true. She didn't have parents. Not anymore. Somehow she knew her father was dead and her mother was lost to her forever. Andrea felt the sudden heat of tears behind her lids. "Maybe there's no one."

"There must be *someone*," Troy said. "What about your husband?"

"What about him?"

"Why hasn't he come forward?"

Andrea fingered her wedding band. "You said yourself, he may be out of town. Or he may think I'm out of town." That was true, wasn't it? He *could* be out of town....

Yes! She remembered now. The gray-haired man

bending down to kiss her on the cheek. It had been a brotherly kiss, completely lacking in passion. *Goodbye, Andrea. I'll see you when I get back. Take care of Mayela for me.*

You know I will. Please don't worry. She'll be safe with me.

A spurt of fear shot through Andrea. She knew as surely as she was sitting there that someone named Mayela was in terrible danger, but Andrea was powerless to help her because she didn't know who Mayela was or where the danger came from.

Andrea thought about telling Troy everything she had remembered, begging him to help her solve this terrifying riddle, but another memory stopped her. Or was it her sense of survival?

I hate you. I want you dead! Dead! Dead! Dead!

She looked down at her robe, almost expecting to see bloodstains covering her hands and spreading over the blue satin of her robe. But her hands were clean, her clothes spotless. The bloodstains were only a memory. But of what?

Andrea's hands began to shake even harder. "I'm tired. I—I think I'll go back to my room."

Troy was watching her carefully, that shadow of suspicion clouding his dark eyes. "We haven't finished our talk."

"There's nothing I can tell you." She pushed herself up from the table. "I don't know anything. I don't remember anything."

Troy stood, too. "Who're you trying to convince, Andrea? Me...or yourself?"

"I know you don't believe me," she said with a desperate edge to her voice. "But I really don't remember what happened. I don't remember anything."

She tried to brush by him, but he snared her arm with his hand. "Then who is Mayela?" he asked, his eyes growing even darker with suspicion.

"Wh-what?"

"You were whispering her name in your sleep. Who is she, Andrea?"

"I don't know."

"I don't believe you." His eyes turned so cold Andrea felt chilled to the bone. "I don't believe you *can't* remember. I think you don't *want* to remember. I think you're *afraid* to remember. What did you do, Andrea? Whose blood was on your dress?"

His hand on her arm sent a thrill of awareness through Andrea, but she kept her expression even. She didn't want him to see how much his touch affected her. "Why don't you just charge me with something if you're so sure I've committed a crime? Why don't you put me in jail and throw away the key?" Despite the bravado of her words, her mind screamed in denial. *Don't lock me in the dark room! Don't leave me by myself!*

As if he'd glimpsed the terror in her eyes, he dropped his hand from her arm. "I'm sorry. I didn't mean to hurt you."

"You didn't hurt me." And he hadn't. Not the way he meant. His grip on her arm hadn't been tight. She could have gotten away from him at any time, but he'd hurt her just the same. Hurt her with his doubts and suspicions.

But who could blame him? If Andrea didn't have doubts about herself, she would have confided in him days ago, wouldn't she? She would have told him about the flashes of memory she was experiencing, about her nameless fear, about the man with the gray hair and the girl named Mayela. She would have told him about the knife...

He lifted his hand and drew his fingers through his hair. "I don't know what came over me," he muttered. "I'm really sorry."

"Forget it. I have." But she hadn't. She would never forget that look of suspicion in his eyes, the accusations. She would never again let herself forget that Sergeant Troy Stoner wasn't a friend, no matter how much she might wish him to be. He was a cop who would do whatever necessary to find out her dark and deadly secrets.

And she would do everything she could to make sure he didn't. Because that was the only way she knew to save herself.

"Come on," he said. "I'll walk you back to your room." He was still looking shaken by what had happened. She suspected his loss of control was out of character for him, and the notion that she was responsible was more than a little frightening.

"Don't bother," she said. "I think it's time we call it a night."

He stopped, gazing down at her. Something flashed in his eyes. Disappointment? Andrea wished she could believe it was so. "Maybe you're right," he said slowly. "Maybe I should have called it a night a long time ago."

And with that, he turned and walked away, leaving Andrea to wonder about this dark and dangerous man who wasn't her husband.

MADISON CAME BY to visit Andrea the next afternoon. It was a strange visit. One minute, Madison was telling Andrea about her mother's cat, which had triggered a memory of a kitten Andrea had had as a child. The next

hing Andrea knew, Madison was patting her hand.
'Wake up, Andrea.''

Andrea opened her eyes and yawned. ''What happened?''

''You fell asleep.''

''I did?'' Panic curled inside her. Andrea moistened
her lips. ''Did I…talk in my sleep, or anything?''

''No. You were sound asleep.'' Madison smiled, but
her usually open gaze looked a little reserved. ''You
obviously needed the rest.''

''I do feel refreshed,'' Andrea said. She felt as if she'd
just awakened from a full night's sleep, except for the
persistent notion that she'd been dreaming about something important. Something revealing. It was like peek-
ing through a piece of cloth. She could see shadows, but
nothing concrete. Nothing real.

Her forehead knitted as an image began to clarify.

There he was again, that gray-haired man with the
careworn face.

''I can see him,'' Andrea murmured.

''Who?''

Andrea put out her hand, as if to touch the image. He
was looking at her, his eyes shadowed with pain.

An overwhelming sense of sadness came over her.
She felt like crying.

''What is it, Andrea? What are you remembering?''

As she continued to watch, the memories unfolded
like scenes from a movie. As if in slow motion, the gray-
haired man crumpled to the floor. Blood oozed through
his fingers where he clasped his chest, and someone
screamed, *I hate you! I want you dead!*

A tear rolled down Andrea's face. She felt Madison
touch her hand, and she wiped the tear away with her
fingertips.

"You remembered something, didn't you?" Madiso
asked quietly.

"No, it was just—" What? A man dying? A ma
being murdered? Who had killed him? And why?

*I've changed my will, Andrea. When my time comes
you will be well taken care of.*

I want you dead. Dead! Dead! Dead!

Andrea's heart thundered in her ears. She looke
down at her nightgown, seeing the blood-splattere
white dress.

Dear God, what have I done? she wondered franti
cally. *What have I done?*

"SHE FELL ASLEEP," Madison said.

"Fell asleep? Just like that?" Troy sat across the tabl
from his sister in the hospital cafeteria.

Madison stirred lemon into her tea. "It was reall
strange, almost as if…"

"What?"

"I don't know. Almost as if she'd fallen into a hyp
notic trance."

Troy frowned at his sister. "Did you hypnotize her?'

"No. At least not intentionally."

"Can you do that unintentionally?" His tone wa
skeptical.

"Not unless there's some sort of trigger that's bee
implanted in her subconscious that I might have stum
bled upon purely by accident."

Troy's frown deepened. "I don't follow."

"Once a patient becomes comfortable with hypnosis
a therapist will sometimes use a word or a phrase, ofte
an image, that triggers instant relaxation. The patient ca
fall almost immediately into a deep trance."

"You think that's what happened with Andrea?"

"Not necessarily. I'm only speculating. It's curious, though, because the other day when I mentioned hypnosis to her, she seemed frightened by the notion."

Troy sat back in his chair and studied his sister thoughtfully. Something was bothering her. He could tell by the way her dark eyes were having trouble meeting his. "Just tell me one thing," he said. "Do you believe her memory loss is real?"

Madison shrugged. "It doesn't take a brain surgeon to fake amnesia, but honestly? I'm inclined to believe her. I think she may have had flashes of memory, bits and pieces that have come back to her, but Troy...it's what she *can't* remember that worries me. What she won't let herself remember."

Troy nodded. "It worries me, too." It worried him that she had been found wandering down a busy street, with O-positive blood covering her clothing. It worried him that she had a bruise on her arm and a wedding band on her finger, and it worried him that he couldn't seem to get her out of his mind, that he dreamed about her at night and woke up thinking about her each morning.

It worried him that he didn't know what the hell he was going to do about her. His choice should have been clear. In fact, there shouldn't even *be* a choice. She was a married woman. Therefore, no matter what she might or might not have done, she was off-limits to him.

Troy liked to think of himself as an honorable man. A man who didn't go after someone else's wife. But Andrea had gotten under his skin as no other woman ever had. Not even Cassandra Markham, who had almost gotten him killed.

Just then, Troy saw Tim Seavers walk into the cafeteria, and he raised his hand and motioned him over.

"Pull up a chair," he invited when Tim had walked over to their table.

Tim sat down. "I'm glad I ran into you," he said to Troy. "I've been meaning to call you, but I haven't had a chance. I'm releasing Andrea tomorrow."

"Releasing her?" Madison asked with a note of alarm in her voice. "Where will she go?"

"I don't know. But there's no physical reason for her to remain hospitalized, and we don't have enough beds to keep her any longer than necessary."

Madison turned her dark eyes on Troy. "Where will she go, Troy?"

He shrugged carelessly, but he was wondering the same thing himself. Where *would* she go? She had no money, no credit cards, and she still didn't know her last name. He supposed she could hock her bracelet and wedding ring, but those funds wouldn't last forever. What if her memory never came back?

Not your problem, a little voice warned him. The same little voice that cautioned him each and every time he was about to do something stupid. For all the good it did.

"I have an idea," Madison said.

"I don't like it," Troy said.

"You haven't even heard it yet!"

"I know, but I don't like that gleam in your eyes."

"Don't be ridiculous," Madison scoffed. "My idea is perfectly feasible. Andrea can come stay with me."

"Isn't that violating some sort of doctor-patient thing?" Troy asked skeptically. In truth, he wasn't sure how he felt about Madison's proposal. On the one hand, it would keep Andrea close by, so that he could keep an eye on her. On the other hand, it would keep Andrea close by.

"I'm not her psychiatrist," Madison reasoned. "I'm trying to be her friend. Under the circumstances, I think it's the perfect solution."

"She's right, Troy," Tim said. "Otherwise, where else would she go? I'd hate to think of her living in the shelters."

Madison looked appalled. "You can't send her to a shelter. She wouldn't last a day."

Troy didn't want to think about Andrea in the shelters, either, for any number of reasons, but he had a feeling she was a lot tougher than any of them thought.

"Okay," he said. "I see there's no talking you out of this. I just hope you know what you're doing."

Madison smiled at him in reassurance. "Don't worry about me. Don't worry about Andrea, either. We'll be fine."

But Troy couldn't help worrying. His sister had a habit of picking up strays, and sometimes those strays had a tendency to bite the hand that fed them.

BEFORE GOING HOME that night, Troy decided to swing by the hospital to see how Andrea had taken the news of Madison's proposal. It was late, and the hospital corridors were all but deserted. No one was manning the desk at the nurses' station, and Troy supposed whoever was on duty had been summoned by a patient. He turned the corner and started down the hall when he noticed a doctor wearing green scrubs standing outside Andrea's room. He was pushing open her door with one hand while holding a syringe in the other. It seemed awfully late for a doctor to be paying a call on a patient, and as far as Troy knew, Andrea wasn't receiving any medication.

He called down the hallway. "Tim?"

At the sound of Troy's voice, the doctor's head jerked toward him. Troy was still some distance away. He had only a brief impression of a surgical mask and cap covering most of the face before the doctor whipped around and took off running down the hallway.

"Hey!" Troy bolted after him, but the green-clad figure was already disappearing around a corner. Sliding on the polished tile floor, Troy took the same corner seconds later. A service elevator was located halfway down the next corridor. Just as Troy reached it, the doors slid closed, and the car began to descend.

Pounding the doors in frustration, Troy turned and located the entrance to the stairwell. He slung the metal door back so hard, it bounced off the wall, then slammed with a bang behind him as he charged down the stairs two at a time. Halfway to the bottom, he jumped over the railing to the lower level and continued down six more flights.

There was something ominous about the way the green-clad figure had been lurking outside Andrea's door. Something dangerous about the syringe he held in one hand. Troy had no idea who the figure might have been, but he damn well intended to find out.

Panting hard, his heart beating like a piston inside his chest, he reached the ground floor and slammed open the stairwell door just as the elevator bell sounded outside. Troy raced down the corridor toward the elevators, automatically reaching for his revolver. He got himself into position just a split second before the doors slid open.

There was no one inside.

Chapter Five

Madison's west-side town house was situated in a deeply wooded cul-de-sac a few blocks over from Memorial, in a quiet, elegant part of town. As Madison fished in her bag for the key, Andrea took a moment to look around.

Although the complex was modest in appearance, there was no mistaking the exclusivity of the neighborhood. The postage-stamp front lawns were emerald green and lushly landscaped with crape myrtle, hibiscus and scarlet bougainvillea. No cars were parked along the street. No trash cans lined the walkways. The scene was almost surreal in its tranquillity and a direct contradiction to Andrea's inner turmoil.

She'd talked with Troy earlier that morning before being discharged from the hospital, and he'd told her about seeing someone outside her hospital room last night. Someone dressed in green scrubs and a mask, so that his or her identity was protected. Someone who ran away when Troy called out.

Andrea's heart tumbled inside her as she thought about her first night in the hospital, when she thought someone had been in her room. She'd managed to convince herself her imagination had been playing tricks on her, but now she wasn't so sure.

Who had been lurking outside her door last night? Not a friend, surely. No friend would have tried to visit her so late, hiding his identity. No friend would have run away.

Then who? An enemy? It was staggering to think that someone out there might want to harm her, that someone could actually hate her enough to want her dead. Even though she didn't remember why, Andrea had absolutely no doubt whatsoever that she was in danger. And now so was Madison.

Andrea had been so touched last evening by Madison's invitation to stay with her and so relieved because she really didn't have any place else to go. But now Andrea wasn't so sure they were doing the wise thing. Was it fair to put Madison's life in danger, as well?

But Madison wouldn't take no for an answer, even after Troy had told them about last night. She'd insisted Andrea come home with her, and that was the end of it.

Troy, however, had looked less certain. He, too, had his doubts about this arrangement, and Andrea knew it wasn't just because of the man outside her hospital room last night. Troy still had his doubts about *her*. He still wasn't convinced she was an innocent victim in all this, and truth be told, Andrea couldn't say she was all that sure herself. The images she'd been seeing, the feelings she'd been experiencing—to put it mildly, it was all less than reassuring.

She still didn't know what kind of person she'd been, but she knew one thing about herself. She hadn't told Troy or Madison about the flashes of memory she'd been having, so she knew she was capable of deceit.

What else was she capable of?

Madison finally got the door open, and the two of them stepped into the cool interior of the town house. A tiled entry led into the large living area, which was light and airy, done for the most part in peach, cream and teal green. Several oil paintings hung from the walls, and when Andrea went to examine them more closely, she noticed they had all been signed by someone named Beverly Stoner.

"My mother," Madison explained, coming to stand beside Andrea. They were staring at a scene that seemed vaguely familiar, a paved courtyard and stone fountain. The picture seemed so real that Andrea could almost feel the spray from the water on her face.

"It's very beautiful," she said softly, the beginning of a memory tugging at the corners of her mind. And then it burst upon her with the force of a juggernaut. Andrea stared at the painting as the images rushed through her.

"Do people really live like this? It's like a palace!"

Someone laughed. A young woman with jet black hair and onyx eyes. Her voice sounded like music. "Oh, Andrea, you're so much fun! This place is far from being a palace. It isn't even the biggest house in River Oaks."

"But it's so beautiful!" Andrea let her hand trail through the cool water that splashed from the stone fountain. The spray misted her face, and she closed her eyes. "I love it here. I wish I never had to leave."

"Why would you have to leave? Mayela adores you. We all do."

An almost unbearable sadness came over Andrea because she knew sooner or later she would have to leave. She didn't belong in a place like this. She didn't belong anywhere....

And then the memories seemed to fast-forward, and another scene played out in Andrea's mind.

The same fountain splashed in the same lovely courtyard, but a different woman was speaking to her this time. She, too, had dark hair and black eyes, but she was older, and instead of a soft, lilting voice, her tone was icy with scorn.

"My daughter felt sorry for you, took pity on you. She brought you into her home, treated you like a friend, and look how you repay her. By betraying her memory. You're nothing but a cheap, backstabbing, little gold digger. If Richard thinks I'll stand by and see the two of you married, with my Christina not even cold in the ground—"

Andrea broke off the memory abruptly. She didn't dare take the scene any further, because she had a terrible premonition of what that would do to her. Any illusions she might have had about herself, about the kind of person she had been, would be shattered forever. There would be no deluding herself once the memories returned. No pretending. Just cold, hard reality.

A reality she wasn't sure she was ready to accept.

The burst of memory seemed to have gone on forever, but in actuality lasted only seconds. Madison appeared not to have noticed Andrea's silence. She was still talking about her mother's paintings.

"...often wondered what she might have done with her talent if she hadn't had so many kids to take care of. Then after Gary died, she stopped painting altogether. It's been five years, and as far as I know, she hasn't picked up a brush since." She caught herself then and glanced at Andrea. "Listen to me rambling on like that. You don't even know who I'm talking about, do you? Gary was my brother. He was killed five years ago."

"I'm sorry," Andrea murmured. She had begun to think of Madison Stoner as someone who led a perfect life. She seemed professionally successful, came from a big family and had a past that Andrea doubted very seriously would ever come back to haunt her. But Madison had known grief in her life. She'd known pain, and Andrea realized that nothing was ever as it seemed on the surface. There were always undercurrents, some not so strong, but others so treacherous they would pull you under if you let them.

Those were the undercurrents Andrea worried about. "I'm not sure this was such a good idea after all." She turned to Madison. "Aren't you afraid to have me stay with you? What if that man Troy saw outside my door last night comes looking for me here?"

"Look." Madison tucked her short glossy hair behind her ears. "In the first place, we don't even know if that person was a man or a woman, and in the second place, since he or she was dressed in surgical scrubs, it could very well have been hospital personnel."

"Then why did he run away? Why did he disappear like that when Troy chased him?"

"Maybe *because* Troy chased him. Or her," Madison said. "My brother's not always subtle."

"Still, the person's actions were suspect, you have to admit," Andrea persisted. "And I can't help thinking that if he found me in the hospital, he could just as easily find me here. I don't want you to get hurt because of me."

"You're assuming that the person's intent was to harm you. You don't know that for sure, do you?"

The brown eyes, so like her brother's, studied Andrea intently. Andrea had to remind herself that Madison Stoner, regardless of her kindness and generosity, was a trained psychiatrist, and she was the daughter and sister of cops. Andrea knew it wouldn't be easy fooling her, day in and day out, pretending that her mind was still a complete blank. In spite of the danger lurking outside these walls, there was danger inside, as well. Maybe she would be better off just to leave. Maybe they all would be better off if she simply disappeared.

"Andrea?"

She forced her attention back to Madison. "I'm sorry. What did you say?"

"I said I don't think you have to worry. The complex has a security guard on duty twenty-four hours a day, and no one is allowed through the gates without the access code. My brothers made sure this place was secure before I moved in. You're safe here."

Was she? Was she safe anywhere?

All you have to do is remember, Andrea. Then you'll know where the danger is coming from. You'll know who your enemies are. All of this will finally be over.

But it wouldn't be. Somehow she knew that when her memory returned, the real nightmare would begin.

She rubbed a hand across her forehead, willing away the gnawing doubt that she had done something wrong. Terribly, terribly wrong. Why else did she have these flashes of remorse? This almost overwhelming feeling of guilt?

Why else had she been found covered in someone else's blood?

"You look tired," Madison said. "Why don't I show you to the guest room?"

"No, I'd like to stay out here for a while, if that's okay." She didn't want to be shut away somewhere. She wanted openness, at least the illusion of freedom. She gazed around, admiring the simple yet elegant furnishings. "This room is so soothing."

"I'm glad you think so." Madison smiled and sat down on the couch, curling her feet beneath her. She waved Andrea to the chair facing her. "I like to think of this as my sanctuary, a place where I can get away from all the problems of the world, mine as well as everyone else's."

"But you can't do that with me here, can you?" Andrea's fingers clutched the arms of her chair, but she willed them to relax.

"I don't think of you as a patient," Madison said. "I think of you as a friend, Andrea."

Andrea was touched beyond words. She instinctively knew she didn't make friends that easily, had had maybe one or two really close friends in her whole life. But she'd felt an instant bond with Madison from the first and had to resist the urge to confide in her, to tell her everything she'd remembered. And everything she feared.

Andrea had felt that instant connection with Troy, too, but the bond with him was very different from friendship. What she felt for Troy was an emotion she didn't dare analyze too closely. There was no such thing as love at first sight, was there?

She twisted the ring on her finger, but didn't take it off.

"Can I ask you something, Andrea?"

"Of course."

Madison's gaze was direct, but nonjudgmental. "There's something between you and my brother, isn't there?"

Her insight was terrifying. "No," Andrea said quickly.

Madison sat forward, her dark eyes troubled. "I don't mean to put you on the spot. It's just that…I worry about him."

"Why?"

"This isn't the first time he's been attracted to the wrong woman." She looked immediately contrite. "I'm sorry. I didn't mean it like that."

Andrea shrugged. "It's all right. I understand what you mean."

"I don't think you do." Madison paused. "You see, several years ago Troy became involved with a woman who almost destroyed him. She was a murder suspect, and he was the detective assigned to the case. She convinced him that she was innocent, and that all she needed was for someone to help her prove it. When Troy tried to help her, she turned everything around, accused him of everything from police misconduct to planting evidence to make her look guilty, and it worked. Her lawyers got her off, but afterward, when Troy confronted her, she went off the deep end, pulled a gun and tried to kill him. It was all a big mess, a terrible scandal, and Troy was suspended pending a formal hearing, which eventually cleared him. But his reputation took a pretty bad beating, and he lost faith in his ability to judge a person's character, both in his professional and personal relationships. He doesn't trust easily, and if he seems a little harsh with you at times, that's why."

"I understand." But in her case, he had good reason not to trust her, Andrea thought sadly. She didn't even trust herself.

"I just thought you should know," Madison said softly. "Troy was hurt very badly once. I wouldn't want to see that happen again."

"I don't want to hurt him." Andrea hoped she didn't sound as defensive to Madison as she did to herself.

"Of course not. But you're married, Andrea. If my brother falls in love with you, someone is going to get hurt."

Fall in love? Why did that notion send such a burst of excitement spiraling through her? Why did the thought of a man like Troy Stoner falling for someone like her make her want to shout with joy?

Because she was having feelings for him, too, Andrea admitted. She knew, without knowing how she knew, that she'd never felt this way about anyone else. In spite of his doubts and suspicions about her, Troy Stoner was someone very special.

But Madison was right. Andrea couldn't afford to let her feelings get out of hand. Not only because she was a suspect. Not only because she might have done something wrong, and not even because Troy had once been badly hurt.

She couldn't let her feelings for him show because she wasn't free to love him.

A terrible yearning came over her. A part of her knew he was the person for whom she'd been searching all of her life, but she'd found him too late. If she had any decency left inside her at all, she would sever the bond between them, before it was too late.

Before anyone got hurt.

TROY SAT AT HIS DESK, staring at the stack of files in front of him, and decided he wouldn't call his sister to find out how things were going with Andrea, no matter what. By all indications, Andrea was a married woman, and what's more, a suspect. He couldn't afford to let his attraction go any further. Hadn't the past taught him anything?

But his affair with Cassandra Markham had been different. He'd been a lot younger for one thing, and he realized now the fact that she'd been taboo had been the strongest part of her appeal. Troy had always been somewhat of a rebel, and in Cassandra Markham, he'd sensed a kindred spirit that had drawn him as surely as a moth to flame.

It was different with Andrea, although the similarities couldn't be denied. She was a beautiful, desperate woman in a whole peck of trouble. Troy's natural inclination to be the rescuer had been struggling like hell to get out. But it wasn't just that. It wasn't that he sensed a dark and dangerous quality about her, although he did. But after Cassandra, that no longer had the appeal it once did.

No, what he felt for Andrea was something different, something deeper, something harder to define. The fact that she was off-limits to him was not an attraction but a frustration. She was a married woman. What if he got involved with her, and then when her memory returned, she suddenly realized she was deeply in love with her husband? Where would that leave Troy?

Best to stay away from her, he decided, wadding a phone message and tossing it toward the trash can. Best to keep his distance. Because if he didn't stay away, he might start to think that she was attracted to him, too. He might start to wonder if that subtle light that ignited in her eyes when she looked at him was desire. And if that happened—

God help him, if that happened, he might start to forget that she was forbidden.

SHE KNEW she was dreaming but she couldn't make herself wake up. Andrea lay helplessly in the throes of her nightmare, watching the scenes play out before her as if she were looking through the keyhole of a door.

She could see the gray-haired man with the careworn face, the dark-haired young woman with the musical voice, the older woman with the hate-filled eyes and someone else Andrea couldn't quite make out. Someone who stayed in the shadows.

Where was Mayela? She seemed to be the central figure in the drama, but she had yet to take the stage. Was she the one who waited in the wings for her cue? Somehow Andrea didn't think so. The shadow who prowled offstage was a dark figure, an ominous apparition that frightened Andrea, although for all she knew, that lurking presence could have been herself.

Disturbing thought, that.

The young, dark-haired woman with the musical voice said, "Please say you'll stay, Andrea. Your being here has been a godsend for all of us. I don't know what I'd do without you. You're the only one I can talk to. I've been so depressed lately. I've had such terrible thoughts. At times I've actually wondered what it would be like to...do away with myself."

The older, dark-haired woman with the hate-filled eyes said, "My daughter is dead. The police say it was suicide, but I don't think so. I think you had something to do with Christina's death."

The gray-haired man with the careworn face said, "I've changed my will, Andrea. When my time comes, you will be well taken care of."

Suddenly the scene became even more dramatic, but Andrea was no longer watching through the keyhole. The door had opened, and she was there, with the gray-haired man as he clutched his heart and fell to the floor. Blood was everywhere. All over her.

"I hate you! I want you dead!"

An overwhelming sense of guilt washed over Andrea, stronger even than the horror that lay before her. But even as she stood staring at the blood on her hands, a little voice inside her screamed, *Run, Andrea. Find a place to hide! If they find you, they'll take you away. They'll say you've done bad things, terrible things. They'll lock you in the dark room!*

And then a child, a little girl, screamed, "You killed my daddy! You killed my daddy!"

The focus changed, and Andrea was now watching the scene through the child's eyes, experiencing the child's emotions. She thought for a moment she *was* the child, but then she thought the child must be Mayela. From the child's eyes, she saw a woman bend over the dead man. Blood covered her hands as she lifted them in front of her.

Then Andrea was behind the door once again, observing both woman and child through the keyhole. The child was sobbing, screaming in terror. The woman turned her head toward the sound and smiled, her expression demented.

With deepening horror, Andrea saw that the woman's face looked like her own.

WHEN ANDREA WOKE UP, she was gasping for breath. She felt as if someone were choking her, and for a moment, her arms flailed in the air.

But there was no one in the room with her, and as her heart settled down, the images in her dream began to come back to her—the gray-haired man, the young, dark-haired woman, the older woman with the icy voice and the unseen presence lurking in the shadows. Who were these people?

The gray-haired man worried her especially because Andrea knew in her heart he was dead. But *how* did she know? How could she possibly know, unless...

She got up and walked to the window, staring out

blindly into the darkness. It was all coming back to her, just as Madison and Dr. Seavers had predicted. Andrea was finding the pieces to her puzzle one by one, and the bigger picture was starting to take shape.

Someone had died, and someone from her dream was the murderer and someone was the victim. But just what role Andrea had played in the grisly tableau was yet to unfold. She wondered how much longer she could prolong the ending.

As long as you have to, said the little voice of survival.

But Andrea was no longer listening to that voice. She was listening to her heart, and it was telling her that the longer she delayed her confession to Troy, the more he would despise her when the truth came out.

Somewhere outside, a shadow moved and Andrea's heart stopped. A tree limb blowing in the breeze, she tried to tell herself, then realized there wasn't a breath of air stirring. The night was still and silent. There was a three-quarter moon, but a lacy filigree of clouds hung over the pale light. Madison's tiny yard lay in darkness. Andrea peered anxiously through the window. Outside, nothing stirred. Nothing moved.

Inside, Andrea's breath was suspended in her throat. Her heart hammered against her chest. He was out there, she thought. Somewhere among the shadows, the figure who had been in her hospital room and the malevolent presence in her dream were waiting. But for what?

For a moment, in spite of her terror, Andrea experienced a brief stirring of hope. If someone was watching her, if someone wanted to harm her, didn't that mean she wasn't the killer? Didn't that mean she was an innocent victim? Couldn't she go to Troy and tell him everything she knew?

But what if he doesn't believe you? whispered the little voice of reason. *What if he locks you away in the dark room? What would happen to Mayela?*

Who is Mayela? Andrea wanted to scream. Why couldn't she remember her? Why was Mayela in danger, and why was Andrea so sure that she was the only one who could save her?

Andrea couldn't explain it, but the feeling was so strong inside her she was forced to accept it. She had to remain free. She couldn't be sent away. She had to pretend she remembered nothing, because only then could she help the little girl named Mayela.

Chapter Six

By the time Madison got up the next morning, Andrea had fixed them both breakfast. She'd set the table on the tiny patio out back and brought in the paper from the sidewalk. She didn't open the paper, though. She didn't want to see her picture, didn't want to think about the fact that no one had come forward to identify her. Except for that figure outside her hospital room, and the malevolent presence last night.

She suppressed a shiver as she poured freshly squeezed orange juice into two glasses and carried them to the table.

Madison came outside, yawning widely. She gazed at the table in amazement. "This is lovely, Andrea, but I didn't invite you here to be my maid. You didn't have to do this."

"I don't mind. Besides, it's the least I can do." She took a seat across the table from Madison and unfolded her napkin.

Madison took a bite of the scrambled eggs and closed her eyes. "Heavenly! Where did you learn to cook like this?"

From my aunt, Andrea almost said, but then realized

she had no idea who her aunt was, or why she had taught
Andrea to cook.

*You must be self-reliant in every respect, Andrea. Not
only do you need to learn to cook and keep house, but
you need a profession. A respectable way to earn a living. Never depend on a man—for either your support or
your happiness. Look what happened to your poor
mother. If she'd never met your father, she wouldn't be
locked up in that awful place today, and I wouldn't have
been forced to take in her wayward child. Not that I
mind, of course. I've never been one to shirk my responsibilities. But I'm not as young as I used to be, and
you can be a handful at times, though I'm sure you always mean well. I just pray you haven't suffered any
permanent damage from that horrible ordeal, and you
won't suddenly become unhinged one day....*

"Andrea?"

Andrea blinked. "I'm sorry. What did you say?"

Madison blotted her lips with her napkin. "Where do
you go when you drift off like that?"

"I beg your pardon?"

"You do that a lot," Madison said. "Become completely still and silent. You're remembering something,
aren't you?"

"Sometimes," Andrea admitted. "But most of the
time it's nothing that makes much sense. Just then, I was
remembering something from my childhood. I think I
was sent to live with my aunt when I was quite young.
She never married. In fact, I think she hated men, and I
don't think she had much use for children, either. She
was quite happy living alone, and I guess I spoiled her
tranquillity."

"That's quite a burden to place on a child's shoulders,

feeling responsible for someone else's unhappiness. How long did you live with her?''

Andrea closed her eyes. ''I don't know. A long time, I think. I remember being lonely. We didn't have much company. My aunt didn't like to socialize, and I wasn't allowed to have friends over after school.'' That same feeling of loneliness came over Andrea now. A terrible sense of isolation. She'd been different from the other kids at school, afraid to get close to anyone, afraid they might find out why she was so different.

''Where are you from, Andrea?''

''Here. I was born in Houston.''

''Is that where your aunt lives?''

''No, she lived up north somewhere.'' Where it was always cold, always winter.

''You said 'lived.' Is she dead?''

That snapped Andrea out of the dreamlike state that had overcome her. She shook her head. ''I don't know. That's all I remember.''

''Well, that's quite a lot actually.'' Madison smiled at her across the table. ''This is a good sign, Andrea. I don't think it will be long now before everything comes back to you.''

Andrea glanced down at the ring on her finger. Sunlight danced on the diamonds. Memories whispered through her mind, and the morning suddenly turned ominous.

Madison said, ''There is one thing we should talk about. When you do get your memory back, you should be prepared.''

''For what?''

Madison paused, her dark eyes pensive. ''Amnesia is a tricky thing. There's still a lot we don't understand about it, but in cases like yours, where there's no apparent physical reason for the memory loss, it seems to be the mind's way of coping with something extraordinarily traumatic.'' She paused again. ''When this event occurred—whatever triggered your memory loss—you weren't able to deal with the shock and so your mind blocked it out, in order to protect you. In your case, this mechanism was fairly extreme because you blocked out everything, not just the actual event.''

''What does that say about me?'' Andrea asked.

''What do you mean?''

''Does that mean I'm...crazy?''

''Of course not. It means you may be a little more adept at self-preservation than the rest of us, that's all. Your mind wasn't taking any chances. It wiped out everything, letting only tiny pieces filter back in until you're ready to cope. It actually makes a lot of sense, when you think about it.''

Andrea glanced up almost fearfully. ''What kind of trauma would cause such a complete block?''

''I don't know, but because of the extent of your amnesia, it almost certainly had to be something extremely stressful. That's what I mean by being prepared. When your memory does return, you'll still have to deal with whatever it was that happened to you.''

''But what if I can't deal with it?'' Andrea asked. What if she'd done something so terrible, so horrible that her mind would never be able to accept the reality? What then? The dark room?

''You're a very strong and determined woman, Andrea, and your instinct for survival is obviously quite strong. I think when the time comes, you'll be able to accept what happened, work through it and go on from there. I have complete faith in you.'' Madison smiled brightly and laid her napkin aside. ''There. Having said all that, I'm going to turn off the psychobabble, as Troy so charmingly refers to my profession, so that we can concentrate on something a little more pleasant. What are your plans for the day?''

It was Sunday, but that meant little to Andrea. She had no memory, which meant she had no past and no future. What kind of plans could she have?

''Because if you don't have any,'' Madison was saying, ''I'd like you to come to dinner at my parents' house. It's a Stoner family tradition, you see, and none of us—not even my brother Ray, the brooding loner of the family, would dare not show up without one whale of a good excuse. And according to my mother, short of being in a body cast, there are no good excuses.''

Andrea was on the verge of asking her whether or not Troy would be there. But Madison had said everyone was expected, so obviously that included him. Andrea knew what she should do. She should make up some excuse—surely amnesia ranked right up there with a body cast, didn't it?—and stay home where she would be safe from her emotions.

But Madison was right. The memories were coming back, almost too fast, and Andrea didn't want to be alone with them. She didn't want to have to think about what might have happened, prepare herself for what she might have done.

Besides, she'd been alone so much. All of her life, it seemed. To be asked to Sunday dinner with a family that intrigued her as much as the Stoners was an invitation that was almost irresistible.

If Troy was there, she would avoid him.

If her heart started to pound when she saw him, she would ignore it.

If her stomach knotted when he talked to her, she would pretend calmness.

After all, she'd gotten quite good at pretending, hadn't she?

TROY WAS SITTING in the den, talking to his brother Mitch, when Andrea walked in with Madison. Andrea's silvery gold hair was pulled back and fastened in a loose braid down her back, and she wore a yellow sundress that made her look as cool and tempting as a glass of lemonade on a hot summer's day. The dress bared her shoulders with straps that crisscrossed in the back, and several of the buttons in front had been left undone, so that a tantalizing portion of tanned leg was left exposed.

Beside him, Mitch had been in the process of lifting a beer to his mouth, but the bottle froze in midair. Earl, who had been talking quietly with Ray, let his sentence trail off into dead silence. And Ray, who never showed emotion of any kind, turned his head, and one dark brow lifted slightly when he saw Andrea. Their reactions were registered by Troy only because when he'd first seen Andrea, his heart rate had accelerated so alarmingly, his pulse had jumped so erratically that he'd glanced around at his family to make sure no one had noticed.

He needn't have worried. Every pair of male eyes in the room had vectored in on Andrea and remained there. Even his old man couldn't take his eyes off her, and Troy frowned, experiencing a proprietary emotion that was surely unwarranted.

Everyone stood as Madison made the introductions, and Troy glanced around again, wondering this time what Andrea thought of his family—Mitch in shorts and boat shoes without socks, Ray in faded jeans and a T-shirt, Earl in starched khakis and a long-sleeved plaid shirt and Troy himself in pleated trousers and a white collarless shirt. Their attire was as diverse as their personalities, but they all had their profession in common. Troy couldn't help thinking that a family of cops had to be a little intimidating to someone like Andrea.

But she didn't look intimidated at all. She looked completely at ease and in control of the situation as she said hello to everyone and stepped forward to shake their hands. Troy thought that both Ray and Mitch held on to Andrea's hand a little longer than was necessary. He moved forward, claiming the spot beside her.

"Sergeant Stoner," she said, an intriguing little glint in her blue eyes. "Nice to see you again."

"It's 'Troy.' I'm off duty today. We all are." She didn't offer her hand to him, Troy noticed, and he couldn't help feeling a little slighted. "I didn't know you were going to be here today," he said, low enough so that he hoped his father and brothers couldn't overhear, though he knew Earl was straining to.

She trained those blue eyes on him. "Madison invited me. I hope you don't mind."

"Why should I mind?" No red-blooded male in his right mind would have an objection to her presence, especially considering the way she looked in that yellow dress, and Troy was no exception. Like his father and brothers, he couldn't take his eyes off her. He vaguely recalled having seen Madison wear that dress before, but it sure as hell hadn't had the same impact.

As if sensing the direction of his thoughts, Madison swept forward and grabbed Andrea's hand. "Come on. I want you to meet my mother."

After the two of them had disappeared into the kitchen, the men all took their seats again. Earl settled back into his recliner, and Mitch turned on the TV. Ray walked over, and the two of them sat on the couch, watching a basketball game. It was an NBA play-off game, and normally Troy would have been just as engrossed, but today basketball was the furthest thing from his mind.

He wandered around the den for a moment, glancing out the window, thumbing through a magazine, then as he walked by Earl's recliner, his father waylaid him.

"That girl with Madison. She's a knockout."

Troy grinned. "I noticed you noticing."

"Man'd have to be dead not to." Earl took a long swig of his beer. "I know all about her amnesia. And about the blood on her clothes."

Troy figured his old man probably knew a hell of a lot more than that. Even in his retirement, Earl was still better informed than any of his sons. After forty years on the force, he had eyes and ears everywhere.

"All right," Troy said in weary resignation. "What do you want to know, Dad?"

Earl stared him right in the eyes. "You behavin' yourself with her?"

Troy couldn't have been more shocked. The question took him completely by surprise, and for a moment, he had no answer. Then he said, "I'm trying to find out who she is, where she's from and where her family is. That's all."

Earl nodded, but there was a glimmer of doubt in his eyes. "Just thought I'd ask." He didn't mention the Cassandra Markham case, but Troy knew that's what his father was thinking about. "Why don't you go on out to the kitchen and see if you can give your mother a hand?"

Troy was glad to escape. He met Madison in the kitchen doorway, and he snatched a chip from the bowl she was carrying out to the den. His mother was at the sink, rinsing vegetables. He walked over and kissed her cheek. "Need some help?"

"Everything's under control, but thanks, anyway. Just stand here and visit with me, okay?"

"That's easy enough." Troy leaned against the counter, watching his mother work. She was a tall woman and still almost as slender as her daughter, with the same short cap of glossy black hair—hers now sprinkled with gray—and the same dark brown eyes. "Where's Andrea?" he asked casually.

"I sent her out to the back porch for some ripe tomatoes." His mother glanced up. "She's such a beautiful young woman, but then, I'm guessing you already noticed that."

"Couldn't help but," he agreed.

"And 'Andrea' is such a lovely name. She told me it was her grandmother's name."

Troy stared at his mother. "She told you that?"

His mother looked up at his tone. "She said she was named after her grandmother. Nothing unusual about that, is there?"

Troy shrugged. "No, I guess not." He paused, then said, "How much has Madison told you about her?"

"Nothing really, except that she has amnesia. Is there something else we need to know?" His mother's dark gaze eyed him curiously.

"I'm just wondering what else she may have remembered that she didn't tell me. I think I need to have a talk with her."

"Troy." His mother turned to him, wiping her hands on a dish towel. "Can't you stop being a cop for one day? She's our guest. Now's not the proper time to interrogate her."

"I wasn't going to do that," Troy said. "I'd just like to ask her a few questions."

"About what?" Andrea was standing in the back door, her arms laden with tomatoes. The red stood out starkly against her pale yellow dress, and Troy was immediately reminded of another dress, covered with blood.

For a split second, their eyes met and no one said anything. Then the kitchen door swung open, and Mitch walked through with Tim Seavers. "Look who the cat dragged in," Mitch said.

Beverly Stoner exclaimed in delight, "Tim! Where in the world have you been keeping yourself!"

In all the confusion, Troy managed to relieve Andrea of the tomatoes, then took her arm and steered her out the back door.

"Where are we going?"

"You haven't seen Mom's garden yet, have you?"

"No. Just from the porch."

They walked down the steps, into the dappled sunlight of the backyard. The air was filled with the scent of roses and the drone of bees. A breeze drifted through the oak trees, stirring the morning glory vines that clung to the trellised sides of his mother's gazebo. The tree house he and his brothers had built a lifetime ago perched precariously on the wide, lower branches on the oak tree.

Andrea laughed delightedly when she saw it, and the sound charmed Troy. Sunlight glistened like gold in her hair, and a tiny yellow butterfly circled her head, as if weaving an invisible halo.

"It must have been wonderful, growing up in a home like this," she said softly. "Having a mother and father like yours, lots of brothers and sisters to play with. You're very lucky."

"Yeah, I guess I am." It wasn't something Troy thought about much. He'd grown up in this house, surrounded by family, not just brothers and sisters, but aunts and uncles, dozens of cousins. He'd never considered his family anything out of the ordinary, just people sharing a common bond who cared about each other, who watched out for one another. They were like any other family and only extraordinary to someone who'd never had one.

He wondered if Andrea had been an only child, if she'd been lonely growing up. He wondered what her family was like, if she'd ever had anyone to take care of her.

Maybe she didn't need anyone, he thought, but at that moment, he wanted to believe she did. His gaze met hers, and something stirred inside him. Before he could stop himself, Troy reached out to tuck an errant strand of gold behind one delicate ear, and her hand lifted to settle over his. They stood motionless for what seemed like an eternity, her hand capturing his, their eyes meeting and Troy's heart pounding inside him.

What had she done to him? What kind of spell had she cast to enthrall him so completely, to make him forget the hard lessons he'd learned in this life?

What would it take to release him from her spell? A kiss?

Worth a try, he decided, and lowered his lips to hers.

She backed away, dropping her hand from his, and turning to comment on the roses as if nothing had passed between them. As if that brief moment of magic had been conjured by his imagination.

And maybe it had been.

But he had to know. He had to be sure. "Andrea—"

She still wouldn't look at him. "Don't." Not a command but an entreaty, as if she had no strength left to fight him.

He found hope where there should have been none. His heart quickened. "I have to know, Andrea."

"Oh, God." She put her hands to her face. "I've made such a mess of everything, haven't I?"

"What do you mean?"

She shook her head. "It's all so hopeless."

"What is?" He reached for her arm, but she moved away from him again, at last turning to face him.

Her eyes looked bleak, haunted. She held out her hand, and at first he thought she wanted him to take it, but then he saw the flash of diamonds on her finger. "This is my wedding ring," she said.

"I know."

"I have a husband."

"Probably."

"I can't do this, Troy."

"We haven't done anything."

"But I want to," she whispered, squeezing her eyes tightly shut. "Just now, I wanted you to kiss me." It was all Troy could do not to take her in his arms, hold her so tightly she could never get away from him. Never escape him. He wanted to enthrall her, mesmerize her, so that she fell under the same spell she had cast over him.

"Andrea—"

She opened her eyes and looked at him. A calmness came over her features, almost as if a curtain had dropped over her emotions. "Let's not speak of this again," she said. "Let's pretend I never said that."

"You're not asking much, are you?" he said bitterly.

"It's the only way," she said, slipping even farther away. She turned and gazed up at the tree house. "Show me your tree house, Troy,'' she said a little desperately. ''Tell me what it was like to grow up here. Tell me all about your family, everything. I want to hear it all.''

The words gushed from her, as if they could somehow erect a safe wall between them. Troy didn't know what to say, what to do, how to feel. He knew she was right. There couldn't be anything between them.

But to know that she felt the same way he did, to realize that she wanted him as much as he wanted her…

It was as if a fist had taken hold of his heart. To have her so close…and not be able to touch her, kiss her, whisper to her all the things he wanted to say to her.

To have found her too late. To know that she could never be his. To realize that when she got her memory back, she would be lost to him forever…

She was already at the bottom of the steps that led up to the tree house, reading a faded sign that had been hammered to the railing years ago: No Girls Allowed (That Means You Madison).

''No girls allowed. What kind of chauvinistic attitude is that?'' she challenged.

''A stupid one,'' Troy said, coming up behind her.

''Then it's okay if I go up?'' Andrea glanced back over her shoulder, her eyes twinkling with merriment, as if the last few moments had never taken place.

Troy had no recourse but to do the same. ''I won't tell if you won't,'' he said, brushing past her. ''Better let me go first, though. These steps can be pretty tricky. I'll give you a hand up.''

She waited until he'd climbed all the way up, then she bounded up the steps, unmindful of her dress, and ignored the hand he held out to her. She hauled herself up to the wooden floor, stood and dusted off her hands.

''Point taken,'' Troy muttered.

They walked over to the railing and stood staring down at the neighborhood. All the yards and houses were pretty much alike, but the Stoner home still retained a special enchantment for Andrea. Maybe because of the man standing beside her.

"That's the Gilmore house," he said, pointing to the redbrick home behind the Stoner property. "See that window? My brothers and I used to sneak up here at night and watch Lorie Gilmore get ready for bed. I was just a kid, probably not more than seven or eight, too young to know or care what was going on, but I knew it had to be a pretty big damn deal, seeing a girl in her underwear, because of the way Mitch and Gary would carry on."

"What about Ray?"

"Ray was too old for that type of juvenile stuff by then, and besides, he never had to sneak around to get a look at a girl. He always had them falling all over him, the big football jock."

"Did you play football?"

"No. I was a diver."

"You dove off those tall platforms, did all those flips in the air and everything?"

"Yeah, it was great," he said with a grin.

"I'll bet." Especially considering those tiny trunks divers wore. A scene rushed through Andrea's mind, not her memory this time, but her imagination…going wild.

"What was Gary like?" she asked.

"Gary? He was a great guy. The best. He taught me a lot."

"You still miss him."

"We all do. You don't get over something like that. You just get on with your life."

They stood in silence for a moment, each lost in

thought, and then Troy said, "You see that house over there?" He pointed to a white two-story home, half a block away. "When we were kids, a girl named Dana Farrell lived there. The summer he turned fifteen, Gary fell madly in love with her. The two of them were inseparable all through school, and then right before her senior year, her father got transferred to California. She and Gary kept in touch for a long time, but eventually they drifted apart. She went to law school, and Gary became a cop. Years passed, and then one day she got a job in the D.A.'s office down here. She moved back, looked Gary up, and the two of them picked right up where they'd left off in high school. They were engaged to be married when he was killed."

"I'm sorry," Andrea said, not knowing what else to say. But Troy wasn't telling the story as if he were still grieving, or as if he thought it a tragedy. He was telling it as though he were in awe of their love. As if he couldn't quite understand feelings that ran that deep, that could last that long.

"It's been five years since Gary died," he said. "And Dana's never married. I don't think she's even come close."

"Does she still work in the D.A.'s office?"

"Yeah, she's an A.D.A, an assistant district attorney. In fact, she's supposed to be here today. You'll like her."

"I'm sure I will."

Silence again. Andrea could feel his eyes on her, but she didn't dare turn to meet his gaze. Didn't dare let him see what was in her own eyes.

"Your turn now," he said softly. "I've told you all about my family—now I'd like to hear about yours."

"But I don't remember my family," she protested. "I don't have anything to talk about."

"You remember your grandmother," he said. "Her name was Andrea."

She did turn to him then. "Your mother told you."

"Why didn't you?"

She shrugged helplessly. "It just came to me when I was talking to your mother. I didn't have time to tell you." But the excuse sounded lame even to her. She turned her gaze back to the yard below them.

"Is Mayela part of your family?"

Andrea's heart skipped a bit. "I don't know."

"You were whispering her name in your sleep that night. You seemed frightened for her."

"Did I?"

"It's an unusual name," he persisted. "Surely you can remember something about her."

She's in danger, and I'm the only one who can save her.

His eyes darkened, and for a moment, Andrea was afraid she'd said the words aloud. Then when she realized she hadn't, she wanted to. She wanted to confess everything to Troy and let him help her. But what if he couldn't help her? What if he didn't believe her? What if they took her away again?

There would be no one to save Mayela. No one to save Andrea, either.

She couldn't say anything, not until she knew what she was up against. Not until she knew she hadn't done anything wrong.

A voice called up to them from the backyard. "Hey, you two! You'd better get down here fast or Bev says she's going to put you in charge of the cleanup detail!"

Andrea stared down at the young woman in the yard.

She wore a denim skirt and a white tank top that showed off a gorgeous tan. Her hair was light brown, thick and straight and cut bluntly at her shoulders. She waved when she saw they were looking down at her.

Troy waved back. "That's Dana," he said. "Come on. I want you to meet her."

Andrea climbed down the steps behind him, relieved that for the moment at least, she had been given a reprieve.

Chapter Seven

On Monday morning, Troy was at his desk, going through the stack of case files Lucas had given to him last week, when the lieutenant came out of his office and walked over to Troy's cubicle.

"Looks like you're about to get a break, Stoner."

Troy glanced up. "Yeah? On which case?"

"Jane Doe, the one with amnesia."

Troy's heart slammed into his chest. "What kind of break?"

"There's a woman in my office claims to know her."

Troy's head snapped toward Lucas's office. Through the glass partition, he could see a woman seated across from Lucas's desk. "Who is she?"

"Name's Claudia Bennett. *Dr.* Bennett. She's a psychiatrist."

A chill of foreboding came over Troy. "A *psychiatrist?*"

"Yeah. Says Jane Doe's a patient of hers. Thought you might want to talk to her."

He sure as hell did. Troy stood, shoving back his chair with more force than was necessary. It hit a filing cabinet with a loud bang, and Lucas raised a brow. "Sorry,"

Troy mumbled, grabbing his notebook and pen and heading toward the office.

The woman looked up when Troy walked in. She didn't stand, didn't smile and didn't offer Troy her hand when he introduced himself.

He took a seat behind the lieutenant's desk and studied her for a moment. She looked to be in her late forties, conservatively dressed in a navy blue suit, white starched blouse and low-heeled pumps. There was an exotic quality about her, but Troy couldn't pinpoint her ethnicity. Her eyes were tilted at the corners, but they were light, not dark, and her black hair was pulled back into a severe French twist that gave her face a tight, almost masklike appearance.

The impression was further enhanced by the thick makeup she wore, which was several shades lighter than the skin on her hands, making Troy wonder if she was deliberately trying to obscure her origins. Rather than giving her a striking appearance, however, the pale skin and blue eyes against her thick black hair made her look even more foreign. Almost alien.

Troy thought her one of the most intimidating-looking women he'd ever met.

"You say you recognize the woman in this picture?" He held up the photograph of Andrea that had run in the newspaper and on TV.

Dr. Bennett nodded. "Yes. She's a patient of mine. Her name is Andrea Malone."

Malone. The name was like an electrical jolt through Troy. Already Andrea was slipping away from him. Now she had a complete name, a whole identity. A life that didn't include him.

"How long have you known her?"

"Several months."

"Her picture first ran in the papers and on the news four days ago. Why has it taken you so long to come forward?"

Dr. Bennett shrugged. "I've been out of town, on business. I just returned last night, and this morning, when I saw Andrea's picture in the paper, I came straight here. Is she in trouble?"

"She's not under arrest, if that's what you mean."

"I'd like to see her."

"I'm sure that can be arranged," Troy said. "But first there're a few questions I need you to answer for me."

Something flashed in her eyes, a mild annoyance that was quickly stifled. "What is it you wish to know?"

"I need to know about her family, where she lives, if there's someone who can take care of her while she recovers."

"Are you telling me that no one else has come forward to identify her? I'm the first?" Although her tone sounded astonished, her eyes remained calm. Almost too calm, in Troy's estimation.

"Can you tell me about her family?"

"Of course. As I said, her name is Andrea Malone, and she lives in River Oaks with her husband, Richard, and his daughter, Mayela."

Mayela. Troy recognized the name instantly. So Mayela was Andrea's stepdaughter. And Richard Malone was her husband.

"I think there's also a mother-in-law who resides at the estate, and perhaps a brother, but I'm not quite sure," Dr. Bennett was saying. "And as for having someone to take care of her, Andrea has a veritable army of servants who are at her beck and call. Richard is... quite wealthy."

Troy made note of the fact that Dr. Bennett referred

to Andrea's husband by his first name. He wasn't sure what it meant, but it did seem a little unusual. Then again, maybe not. Maybe he was looking for some reason not to believe the woman. Not to trust her.

"You told Lieutenant Lucas that Andrea is a patient of yours."

"That's correct." She glanced at her watch. "Look, I really didn't come down here expecting an inquisition. I'm a busy woman, Sergeant, and I really don't have time for this. If you'll just tell me where I can find Andrea..."

"It's not quite that simple."

"Why not?" A look of alarm flashed in the woman's eyes. "You said she's not in any trouble."

"I said she isn't under arrest."

Dr. Bennett blinked. "Well, I just assumed..."

"There are some questions that have arisen as a result of Andrea's...condition, and I'm hoping you can answer them for me."

"Such as?"

"Where is her husband? Why hasn't he come forward to identify her?"

"I can't speak for him, of course, but he could be out of town. Richard travels extensively. He's seldom home. He may not know about Andrea. And then, of course, it could be because..." Her voice trailed away.

"Because?"

Her blue eyes drilled him. "Andrea is my patient. I cannot violate her confidence. But it's no secret that she and Richard have had their difficulties."

Troy felt a queasiness somewhere in the pit of his stomach, as if he were invading Andrea's privacy, eavesdropping on the most intimate details of her life, but he had no choice. He had to find out just what the hell was going on, whose blood had been on her clothing when she'd been picked up.

"What kind of difficulties?"

Dr. Bennett shifted ever so slightly in her chair. "Richard is a great deal older than Andrea. There are certain problems inherent in that kind of relationship."

"How much older?"

"I'd say at least twenty years."

Troy wondered how he felt about that revelation. At the moment, he was too numb to react to much of anything. Later, when he had time to think, to digest everything Dr. Bennett was telling him...

"Dr. Bennett, are you suggesting the reason Andrea's husband hasn't come forward is because they may have had a fight?"

"If she'd left him, he might not know she was missing, would he?"

"That doesn't explain why he hasn't seen her picture in the paper or on the news."

Dr. Bennett shrugged. "Like I said, Richard travels extensively. He may be out of town, as I was."

"And there's no one else in this city who could have recognized her?"

"I don't believe Andrea has lived in Houston all that long. She'd only recently moved here when she got the job as nanny to Richard's daughter."

Nanny? Andrea was a nanny? Somehow that didn't surprise Troy as much as it might have. In spite of her defensiveness at times, her keen instinct for survival, there was a gentle quality about Andrea that would naturally attract children.

"How did she come to marry her employer?" he mused, more to himself than to Dr. Bennett.

"Richard's first wife died," she said, "not long after

Andrea came to live with them. It was all very tragic. The little girl, Mayela, was devastated.'' Dr. Bennett glanced at her watch again. "I really do have other appointments.''

"Just a couple more questions. You said it was no secret that Andrea and Richard were having problems. Is that why she was seeing you?''

"No.'' A shadow crept over the woman's features, a subtle darkening that sent another chill through Troy. "Andrea's problems were much more serious than that, but I'm not at liberty to discuss them with you or anyone else.''

ON THE WAY TO MADISON'S town house, Troy called his sister and asked her to meet him there. He told her briefly about Dr. Bennett, about the information she'd supplied concerning Andrea and that he was going over to tell her what he'd learned. Dr. Bennett was following him in her car, so that if Andrea agreed, the doctor would be able to talk with her immediately. Dr. Bennett had insisted.

Andrea answered the door wearing a light pink T-shirt and denim overall shorts that must have come from Madison's closet. Her eyes lit with pleasure when she first saw him, then she quickly masked her emotions by gazing past him at the dark car that pulled to the curb behind his.

"Who is that?'' she asked.

Troy glanced over his shoulder. The windows in the BMW were tinted so darkly that Dr. Bennett was obscured behind the wheel. But he knew that she was there, watching Andrea closely, perhaps trying to evaluate her from a distance.

He turned back to Andrea. "Let's go inside.''

Although he tried to keep his tone even, he saw fear leap to her eyes. She cast another anxious glance at the black car as she stepped back for him to enter. Then she followed him into the living room.

"What's wrong?" she asked before he could say anything.

"Maybe we'd better sit down."

"I don't like the sound of this," she said, but she did as he suggested.

Troy, however, remained standing. He went to the window and peered out. Dr. Bennett had gotten out of the car and was standing by her door. She wore dark glasses, but Troy knew she was gazing at the house, at him.

He turned away from the window. "Your name is Andrea Malone."

He heard the sharp intake of her breath. "How did you find out?"

"Someone identified your picture from the paper."

"Who?"

"A woman named Claudia Bennett. She's a psychiatrist."

"Oh, God." It was hardly more than a whisper, but Andrea's words seemed to echo through the room. Her face drained of color, and her eyes suddenly looked hollow. The reaction was strong, and Troy couldn't help but wonder why.

"She says you're a patient of hers," he said carefully.

Andrea didn't say anything this time, but he could see her fingers gripping the arms of her chair. "What else did she say?"

"You have a husband named Richard."

No reaction this time, and Troy thought that odd. There was not even so much as a flash of memory or a glimmer of recognition in her eyes when he mentioned her husband.

"You have a stepdaughter named Mayela."

"Mayela." Her gaze shot up to connect with his.

"Yes. At least that's one mystery solved."

"Is she all right? Is she safe?"

Troy frowned. "I don't know. I haven't had a chance to contact your family yet, but why wouldn't she be?"

"No reason. I…just wondered."

It was more than that, but Troy didn't press. "Dr. Bennett is here," he said. "She wants to talk to you."

"Why?"

"To make sure you're the woman she thinks you are." Troy realized his phrasing was a little strange, but he didn't know how else to say it. "Will you see her?"

"I don't know." Andrea got up and walked to the window, parting the blinds to stare out. "Is that her?"

"Yes."

Andrea glanced at him over her shoulder, her expression bordering on desperation. "Why do I have a psychiatrist, Troy?"

He'd been wondering that very thing himself, almost as desperately, but he forced himself to shrug casually. "Lots of people see psychiatrists for a lot of different reasons."

"But not me. I wouldn't, unless…"

"Unless what?"

"Unless I was scared." She turned back to the window.

"Scared of what?"

She didn't answer him. Instead, she said, "I don't recognize her. She doesn't look familiar to me."

"Maybe when you talk to her, it'll come back to you."

"Maybe I don't want it to." She faced him. "Maybe I don't want to remember."

His heart bounced against his chest at the look in her eyes. "Why not?"

"You *know* why not," she almost whispered. "Troy—"

He put his arms around her and pulled her against him, closing his eyes as he pressed her head against his shoulder and buried his face in her hair. She smelled so good, felt so right...

But it wasn't right. Today he'd learned without a shadow of a doubt that Andrea had a husband. He'd learned the man's name, and soon he'd have a face to put with that name.

But until then...

Until that time, he could almost pretend that Andrea was his. That nothing else mattered except the way they felt about each other.

As if reading his thoughts, she stiffened in his arms, and for a moment, Troy thought she was going to pull away. But instead, she lifted her face, and his lips touched hers, a whisper-soft kiss that burned all the way to his soul. Just for a moment, just for a heartbeat, she kissed him back, and then she did pull away.

"I can't do this," she whispered.

"I know."

"It isn't right."

"I *know.*"

"Troy, I'm sorry—"

"It's all right. My eyes have been wide open from the moment I first met you. Don't blame yourself." *You play with fire, you have to expect to get burned,* he thought bitterly. He ran a hand through his dark hair and looked away.

"She's still out there," Andrea murmured.

Troy glanced back to find that she was staring out the window. "She's not going away, Andrea."

"I have to talk to her, don't I?"

"Sooner or later."

"I guess it might as well be now." She turned back to him, her expression bleak. "The sooner we find out...everything, the better off we'll all be." But her words lacked conviction.

DR. BENNETT FRIGHTENED Andrea. It wasn't just the conservative way she was dressed or the reserved way in which she greeted Andrea. It wasn't even the way she observed Andrea as if she were a specimen under a microscope. What frightened Andrea the most was the knowledge Dr. Bennett possessed about her. The secrets that might have been revealed in their therapy sessions.

Dr. Bennett turned to Troy and said briskly, "Is there somewhere Andrea and I can speak in private?"

"I'll step outside," Troy said. "Take all the time you need."

Andrea wanted to scream at him, *No! Don't leave me alone with her! I'm afraid. So very afraid...* But then she told herself she was being ridiculous. She had obviously trusted Dr. Bennett enough at one time to go into therapy with her. Surely the woman only meant to help her.

Besides, Andrea could no longer rely on Troy. She had a husband, a man named Richard Malone.

She was Mrs. Richard Malone.

Andrea glanced up to find Troy watching her, as if he knew everything she was thinking. An overwhelming sense of guilt came over her. *What have I done?* she thought. So many people had been hurt. Because of her?

Andrea had the horrible premonition she was about to find out.

When the door closed behind Troy, she glanced uncertainly at Dr. Bennett. The woman smiled, but there wasn't the slightest bit of warmth in her eyes. "Shall we sit?"

Like an automaton, Andrea took a seat. She clasped her fingers in her lap, but said nothing.

Dr. Bennett crossed her legs and studied Andrea confidently. "What's this I hear about amnesia, Andrea?"

An odd question, surely. Andrea said, "Didn't Sergeant Stoner tell you? I've lost my memory. I don't remember anything about my life."

"You don't even remember Richard, your husband?"

Andrea shook her head.

Dr. Bennett leaned forward. "Do you remember the last time we talked, Andrea?"

"No. I don't remember you at all."

"Shall I tell you why you were seeing me?"

Andrea nodded, but she wasn't at all sure she wanted to know.

"This isn't the first time you've had an abnormal loss of memory."

Andrea looked at the woman in shock. "What—what do you mean?"

"Much of your childhood has been blocked from your memory. I suspect something violent happened to you in the past."

Andrea's insides were quaking with fear. The woman's words had a disturbing ring of truth about them. "That's why I was seeing you?"

"Partly. And partly because of the nightmares."

"What...nightmares?"

Dr. Bennett glanced away. "You were having dreams about killing your husband."

The woman's words were shattering. Andrea felt their impact as if they were physical blows. "No."

"It's imperative that we continue your therapy," Dr. Bennett said with a note of urgency in her voice. "We have to find the root of those nightmares. We have to find out what you're blocking from your past. If we don't…" Her words trailed off ominously, and Andrea felt sick. The implication was clear: if they didn't find out what was causing her problems, there was no telling what she might do.

She got up and walked to the window to stare out at Troy. Madison had just pulled into the driveway, and the two of them were leaning against her car, deep in conversation. As if he could feel the force of her stare, Troy turned his head, so that he was looking at the window where Andrea stood. Their eyes met, and with an effort, Andrea let the blind snap back into place.

Dr. Bennett stood. "I'm sure you're anxious to be reunited with your family, Andrea, but once everything's settled, we need to talk again. The sooner the better." Her smile was still without warmth. She gathered up her purse, and strode across the room to the front door, pausing with her hand on the knob. "I'm glad I found you, Andrea. You have no idea how worried I've been about you."

Then she opened the door and stepped out.

"DR. CLAUDIA BENNETT, this is Dr. Madison Stoner, my sister."

"Dr. Bennett," Madison said warmly, offering a hand that the older woman seemed reluctant to accept. "Your reputation precedes you. I read your book, *Dark Jour-*

ney, in college. It was a primary factor in my decision to become a psychiatrist.''

Something flashed in the blue eyes, something Troy couldn't quite define. Dr. Bennett tried to smile, but the action seemed more of a grimace. ''I'm flattered. Am I to assume you've been treating Andrea?''

''Not really,'' Madison said. ''I've talked with her, but I've tried to be more of a friend to her than anything else.''

''I take it she's staying in your home?'' Dr. Bennett asked with open disapproval.

''She had nowhere else to go,'' Madison explained. ''It was either here or a shelter. I think you would agree this arrangement is the more preferable of the two.''

''I don't know that I would agree with that altogether,'' Dr. Bennett said sternly. ''This arrangement is most unorthodox.''

''Normally I would agree with you, but every situation is different, every patient unique. I don't think I've done Andrea any harm by giving her a place to stay.'' Madison was obviously about to get her dander up, and when that happened, God help anyone who got in her way. Troy decided he'd better run interference.

''Look,'' he said, ''the important thing here is that now we know her name. We can locate her family and find out what the hell is going on.''

Dr. Bennett gave him a withering look, barely hiding her contempt. ''I'm sure you're right, Sergeant Stoner. Perhaps the best thing would be for Andrea to come with me now. I can take her home, talk with her family and make sure she is not put under any more undo stress.''

Troy glanced at Madison, who was shaking her head behind Dr. Bennett's back. Her eyes told him in no uncertain terms that Andrea would not be going anywhere, at least not yet, and perhaps for the first time in their lives, brother and sister were in complete agreement.

Troy said, "Before Andrea goes anywhere with anyone, *I* need to talk to her family."

"Why?"

"Because there's still an ongoing investigation."

"Into what?"

"I'm not at liberty to discuss the details," Troy said, taking some satisfaction in the irritation that flashed across the woman's face.

She turned to Madison. "I'd like to discuss my patient with you," she said. "May I call your office tomorrow?"

"Please do." Madison extracted a card from her purse and handed it to Dr. Bennett.

Dr. Bennett glanced at the card, then put it in her bag. "I trust we'll be speaking again, Sergeant Stoner."

"I'm sure we will," he agreed, but it was a prospect he didn't look forward to.

ANDREA STOOD by the window when Troy and Madison entered the room. She didn't look at them, didn't move a muscle, and her stillness reminded Troy of that first night when he'd seen her in the emergency room. Had that really only been a week ago?

Madison said, "Andrea, are you okay?"

"Yes, I'm fine," she said without turning.

Madison glanced at Troy. "I'll go make some iced tea."

When she'd exited the room, Troy walked over to stand beside Andrea at the window. For a long moment, neither of them said anything. Then Andrea took a deep, shuddering breath, and said very softly, "I have a husband. His name is Richard Malone."

"I know," Troy said, because there didn't seem to be anything else *to* say.

Chapter Eight

The house in River Oaks was startling in its whiteness, and more imposing than Troy had expected. It was a home built to impress, faintly reminiscent of a style he'd seen in the Caribbean, but more formal with two distinct wings and a colonnaded front entrance.

A uniformed maid answered the door, and Troy showed her his badge and ID. "I'm here to see Richard Malone."

"Mr. Malone is out of town."

"Do you know where I can reach him?"

She shook her head. "I don't know his schedule."

"Who would know?"

"His secretary, I guess. Maybe Mrs. Andropoulos."

"Mrs. Andropoulos?"

"Mr. Malone's mother-in-law."

Andrea's mother? For some reason, Troy had assumed Andrea's parents were dead. "Does Mrs. Andropoulos live here?" When the maid nodded, he said, "Is she home? I'd like to speak with her."

The maid hesitated, casting a quick glance over her shoulder.

Troy said, "It's important. Tell her it's in regard to Andrea."

The woman's gaze snapped back to his. Silently she stepped aside so he could enter, then led him into a spacious living room with a wall of windows that looked out on a lush courtyard and fountain. She told him to wait while she announced him to Mrs. Andropoulos, then turned on her heel and exited the room.

Troy looked around, admiring the almost stark but artistic furnishings. A circular marble stair with a mahogany rail rose to a second-floor bridge that connected the east and west wings, and it was on this bridge a few moments later that he saw a woman staring down at him.

His initial thought was that she looked vaguely familiar, although he knew at once she wasn't Andrea's mother. As she slowly descended the stairs toward him, the familiarity faded, and he realized that she was older than he'd first thought, probably close to fifty. But she was still a handsome woman—tall, slender, with a regal bearing that suited the dark purple silk dress and heavy gold jewelry she wore.

Her hair was thick and black, hanging past her shoulders, and her olive complexion was flawless, her cheekbones high and elegant, her eyes dark and piercing. She had the look and manner of a woman who worked hard to retain her youthful appearance, but the fight wasn't an easy one and the bitter signs of defeat were beginning to tell around her eyes and her mouth.

She didn't smile as she entered the room, regarding him coldly as she crossed the marble floor toward him. "I'm Dorian Andropoulos. Estelle tells me you're here about Andrea."

"That's right."

"What has she done?"

Troy glanced at her in surprise. "Why do you think she's done something?"

Dorian walked over to the mantel and extracted a slender cigarette from a porcelain box, then took her time lighting up. She regarded him through a cloud of blue smoke. "You're a police detective, aren't you? I assume you're here because Andrea is in some sort of trouble."

"Not the kind of trouble you mean," Troy said. "But she does have a problem."

"What kind of problem?" Dorian elevated her chin so that she appeared to be looking down at him.

"She has amnesia."

One dark brow shot up. "*Amnesia?* You mean...she doesn't remember anything?"

"Not much. Nothing that has told us why she was wandering down a busy street in the middle of a thunderstorm."

"Wandering down... What on earth are you talking about?"

"Andrea was found walking down Westheimer a week ago Sunday night, completely disoriented. A patrol officer picked her up and took her to the hospital."

"Is she still in the hospital?"

"No. She's staying with a friend."

A frown flickered between Dorian's brows. "What friend?"

"We'll get to that in a moment, but first I'd like to ask you a few questions."

The frown deepened. "What kind of questions?"

"Did you see Andrea that Sunday night?"

"I was out with friends most of the day. I didn't get home until quite late."

"So you didn't see her that night?"

Dorian flicked him a glance. "I believe that's what I said."

"You have no idea what happened to her?"

"None whatsoever."

Troy paced the room, taking in the elegant surroundings, the expensive furnishings. For some reason, it was hard to picture Andrea in this room, but maybe that was because he didn't *want* to picture her here. Didn't want to consider that she might actually belong here.

But even as the thought settled in his mind, his eyes lit on a framed picture on the baby grand piano near the windows. He walked over and picked it up.

Andrea—wearing a white suit, her hair dotted with tiny white flowers—smiled up at him. The man beside her wore a somber dark suit, white shirt, conservative striped tie. Judging by his gray hair and the deep crevices around his mouth and eyes, he was at least twenty years older than Andrea. He, too, smiled for the camera, but there was a look of sadness in his eyes, a weariness in his features.

Troy turned, still holding the picture. "Is this Richard Malone?"

Dorian's lips thinned. "Their wedding photograph."

"I'd like to borrow this."

She suppressed a shudder. "Take it, by all means."

Troy resisted the urge to look back down at the picture, to stare at Andrea's beautiful face. Instead, he studied Dorian Andropoulos. "Can you tell me how to get in touch with Mr. Malone?"

"You can't. He's leading a team of his top executives on a camping trip through the Rocky Mountains. One of those survival-training missions that are supposed to promote teamwork and leadership. There's no way to reach him."

Great, Troy thought. *Just great.* Another missing piece to an already frustrating puzzle. "What's the name of his company?"

"Malone International. It's a consulting firm."

Troy took out his notebook and pen to jot down the information. "Do you know when he'll be back?"

"Not until next week, I'm afraid."

"You haven't heard from him since he left?"

"No," Dorian said. "But as I understand it, that's the whole point of those kinds of trips. To be completely incommunicado with the rest of the world so that one must rely solely on one's wits."

"When did he leave?"

Something flickered in Dorian's eyes, an emotion Troy couldn't define. "Actually he left a week ago Sunday. He had a late flight to Denver that night, where he was to meet up with the rest of his group."

Troy tried not to react to her revelation. "Do you know if he drove himself to the airport?"

"As I've already told you, I was out all day. Richard was gone when I got home. His car is missing, so I assume it's at the airport."

"What time was his flight?"

Dorian shrugged. "Around ten, I believe."

"Do you know if Andrea was home at all that night? If she and Richard spoke before he left?"

"I'm afraid they're the only ones who can answer that question for you. The maid is off on Sundays, and May-ela, my granddaughter, was spending the night with a friend that night. If anyone *was* here with Richard before he left for the airport, it had to be Andrea."

"Does she have her own car?"

"A white Jaguar."

"Is it still here?"

"Yes, as a matter of fact."

"You didn't think it odd that she'd been gone for days and her car was still here?"

Dorian shrugged. "I suppose I just didn't give it much thought."

"Didn't give it much thought? Mrs. Andropoulos, Andrea's been gone for over a week. Why did no one in this house bother to report her missing?"

"No one reported her missing," Dorian said coldly, "because no one missed her. This isn't the first time she's disappeared, but just like a bad penny, she always turns back up."

The woman's malice toward Andrea was a troubling thing. Once again, Troy tried to picture Andrea in this house, but the image was too incongruous. "Are you telling me you didn't see her picture in the newspaper or on TV?"

"I don't watch television and I rarely read the newspapers. The stories are just too depressing."

An answer for everything, Troy thought grimly. "What kind of car does Richard drive?"

"A Mercedes."

"Does Andrea ever drive his car?"

"Sometimes."

"Is it possible she may have driven Richard to the airport in his car?"

Dorian gave him an odd, probing look. "That would be easy enough to find out, wouldn't it? Couldn't you just check to see if Richard's car is at the airport?"

That was exactly what he intended to do. But Troy wished he could end the investigation here and now, before he found Richard Malone's car, before he found out anything else about Andrea and Richard and that Sunday night. He was beginning to get a sick feeling in the pit of his stomach. "Mrs. Andropoulos, when Andrea was found, her clothes were covered with blood that turned out not to be hers. Do you have any idea whose blood it might have been?''

Dorian gazed at him in shock. ''My God. So she *is* in trouble. I've been so worried something like this might happen—''

''Something like what?'' Troy observed her closely. She appeared to be shocked by what he had told her, but something about her eyes, those cold, dark eyes, made him wonder. He had a feeling Dorian Andropoulos was a woman with her own secrets.

She watched smoke curl from her cigarette. ''Nothing. It's just…I've never trusted that woman.''

''But the maid said you're Richard's mother-in-law. Wouldn't that make you—?''

''I am *not* her mother,'' Dorian said through clenched teeth. Her dark eyes narrowed into twin slits of anger, and her mouth thinned. The fading beauty Troy glimpsed earlier all but vanished.

''What exactly is your relationship to Andrea?''

''We have no relationship. Richard's first wife, Christina, was my daughter.''

''I see.'' Obviously this was a sore subject with Dorian. ''How did Andrea happen to become the second Mrs. Malone?''

A furious drag on her cigarette, another cloud of smoke, and then she tapped ashes into a crystal ashtray with a bloodred fingernail. ''Andrea worked for my daughter. She was my granddaughter's nanny. I warned Christina not to hire her, but she wouldn't listen to me. Andrea had never worked as a nanny before, came with no recommendations except for a friend of Christina's, hardly more than an acquaintance really, who had met Andrea through her son. Andrea was the boy's teacher at a private school here in Houston. The friend knew

Christina was looking for a nanny, and she introduced her to Andrea. Christina was immediately taken with her.''

Troy knew how that could happen. Andrea had charmed everyone in the hospital, including his own sister. Including *him*. She had a way about her. She made people want to help her. Maybe it wasn't a deliberate manipulation—he hoped not a manipulation at all—but the ability was there nonetheless.

''My daughter was going through a difficult time,'' Dorian continued. ''She suffered from severe depression, and the problem worsened after Andrea moved into this house.''

''Were you living here then?''

The barest hint of resentment flashed in Dorian's eyes. ''Not then, no. I came to help take care of my granddaughter after Christina died.''

''But wasn't Andrea still her nanny?''

''Oh, yes.'' Dorian stubbed out her cigarette. ''You couldn't have pried that woman out of this house. She knew what she wanted from the first, and she didn't rest until she got it. Poor Richard was so distraught over Christina's death that he didn't see it coming. Never knew what hit him.''

''How did your daughter die, Mrs. Andropoulos?''

Those red nails toyed with another cigarette. ''She committed suicide.''

Troy made a mental note to check the records when he got back to the station. ''How long have Andrea and Richard been married?''

''Not long. Barely a month.''

Just a month, Troy thought. If he'd met Andrea five weeks ago, would it have made a difference? Could he have persuaded her to change her mind and *not* marry

Richard Malone? He wanted to believe he could have, but as Troy gazed around the magnificent home, he had to ask himself how the hell a cop could ever compete with this.

He glanced back at Dorian. "How soon after your daughter's death did Andrea and Richard begin seeing each other?"

"Almost immediately. They were married almost six months to the day Christina was buried. When I heard the news, I couldn't believe it. I went to Richard and begged him to reconsider. How much did we really know about Andrea Evans? I asked. How much could we trust her? I was worried about Richard and frightened for my granddaughter."

"Frightened?"

Dorian looked up, her cool gaze measuring. There was no trace of grief, no hint of any emotion except anger in those piercing black eyes. "The police ruled my daughter's death a suicide, but I never believed it. I always thought—"

"Telling tales out of school, are we, Dorian?"

The cultured, masculine voice spoke from the entranceway, and both Dorian and Troy turned toward the sound. The man standing in the doorway was tall and slender, well dressed and well-groomed. *Fine tuned,* Troy's mother would say.

"Robert, this is Sergeant Stoner with the police department," Dorian said.

The man's brows lifted in surprise. "Robert Malone," he said, walking over to shake hands with Troy.

"He's here about Andrea," Dorian said.

"Andrea? What about her?"

"It seems she has amnesia," Dorian said. "According

to Sergeant Stoner, she was found a week ago Sunday night with blood all over her clothing.''

Robert's gaze shot to Troy. ''My God, was she in an accident? What happened? Is she going to be all right?''

''She wasn't physically harmed,'' Troy said.

Robert frowned. ''Then I don't understand. If she wasn't hurt, why does she have amnesia?''

''Her doctors believe she may have witnessed something traumatic.''

''Like what?''

''I was hoping someone here could tell me,'' Troy said. ''Where were you that night, Mr. Malone?''

''Let me think.'' Robert was still trying to act casual, but there was a definite look of alarm in his eyes. ''Oh, yes. Now I remember. I drove over to Louisiana to do some gambling for a few days.''

''Anyone with you?''

''I always have better luck when I gamble alone.''

Dorian looked on the verge of saying something, then decided to keep her mouth shut. She lit up her second cigarette and exhaled a thick haze of smoke. ''Aren't you going to ask about the blood, Robert?''

A look of annoyance flickered across his features. ''You said she wasn't hurt.''

''That's right,'' Troy said. ''The blood on her clothing wasn't hers.''

''Then whose blood was it?''

''That's what I'm trying to find out.''

Robert shook his head. ''I don't understand any of this.''

''What's to understand?'' Dorian said. ''Obviously our little Andrea has gotten herself into some big trouble. Right, Sergeant?''

"Not necessarily. Andrea hasn't been charged with a crime. She's free to come and go as she pleases."

Dorian looked startled. "But what about the blood?"

"What about it?"

"You can't just let her get away with it."

"Get away with what, Mrs. Andropoulos? Do you have evidence that a crime was committed? Can you lead me to a body or to a murder weapon?"

"Of course not."

"Then you see my problem." Troy picked up Andrea's wedding picture from the piano, and turned toward the door. "As I said, Andrea is not being held, so I assume now that she knows where she lives, she'll return home as soon as possible." He glanced at Dorian, then at Robert, who had walked over to the bar and poured himself a drink. "Is there any reason why she shouldn't?"

Robert didn't say anything, but he knocked back the splash of vodka in his glass, then turned to replenish it at the bar. Dorian looked as if she'd like to do the same.

"I'll be in touch, then," Troy said. At the doorway, he paused and glanced back again. "By the way, do either of you happen to know Richard's blood type?"

"Why, yes," Robert said, swirling the vodka in his glass. "It's the same as mine, as a matter of fact. O-positive."

Chapter Nine

Before going over to Madison's, Troy swung by the station to check his messages. He riffled through the slips of paper while he put in a call to Malone International. But after waiting on hold for five minutes, then getting the runaround for another ten, he finally hung up, frustrated. According to the staff at Malone International, there was no way to get in touch with their CEO. That much Dorian Andropoulos hadn't lied about.

But how much else of what she had told him could he trust? Especially the things she'd said about Andrea. Dorian had gone out of her way to paint Andrea in the most unflattering light possible—a gold digger who had conned her wealthy employer into marrying her while he was still grieving for his first wife.

And what about Dorian's inference that Andrea might have had something to do with Christina Malone's death? *The police ruled my daughter's death a suicide, but I never believed it. I always thought—* There had been little doubt what she would have said—or at least implied—if Robert Malone hadn't interrupted them.

Troy tried to analyze the information he'd heard at the Malone mansion without bias, but the truth of the matter was, he didn't want to believe any of it. He didn't want to believe that Andrea had had anything to do with anyone's death, or that she had married a wealthy older man for his money.

Troy didn't want to believe her capable of such deviousness, and yet there was definitely a dark side to Andrea. Secrets were hidden inside her. When those secrets were revealed, would Troy still be able to convince himself that Andrea Malone was an innocent woman?

He thought about Cassandra Markham and everything he'd done to convince himself of *her* innocence. He'd wanted to believe in her until the bitter end, and look where that had gotten him.

Sighing heavily, he picked up the computer printouts on his desk and began to pore over the latest lists of missing persons and homicides that Leanne Manning, the department's computer expert, had sent over earlier.

Lieutenant Lucas, coffee cup in hand, came out of his office a few minutes later. He'd been headed for the coffeepot, but when he saw Troy, he veered over to his desk.

"We must have had close to half a dozen calls this morning," he said. "Seems everyone in the city suddenly recognizes Andrea Malone's picture."

Troy glanced up. "Makes you wonder why it took so long, doesn't it?"

Lucas shrugged. He set his empty cup on Troy's desk. "Not really. People don't pay much attention to that kind of thing. I've always suspected those pictures on milk cartons are a big waste of time."

Troy figured that was probably sad but true.

"What'd you find out about the family?" Lucas asked.

"A weird bunch," Troy said. "Her husband's out of town, no one seems to know how to reach him and his former mother-in-law and his brother seem to be pretty well dug in at the mansion. They weren't upset by Andrea's disappearance, and they sure as hell weren't overly anxious to get her back."

Lucas leaned against Troy's desk and crossed his arms. "You talked to Andrea yet?"

"Not yet. I'm heading over there in a few minutes, but I had a few things to check out here first. I've gone over the missing-persons and homicide reports every day since Sunday week, but I haven't been able to find one single thing to connect her with anyone on the lists. Two homicides had the same blood type, but both had eyewitnesses to the crimes and the suspects are already in custody."

"What are you checking, Harris County? Maybe you need to widen the search."

"I doubt it. According to the lab, the blood on her dress was still fairly fresh when Dermott picked her up that night. I don't think she'd gotten very far from whatever the hell it was that happened when he saw her. It's possible she could have been running away from the mansion."

"You think she whacked somebody at the house, then fled on foot?"

Troy shrugged. "No one's missing except her husband, and according to his office, he's away on business." Troy wondered why he didn't mention Richard Malone's blood type, and the fact that it matched the blood found on Andrea's dress. "I keep thinking about the sedative found in her blood. Why would she take a sleeping pill if she was planning to kill someone?"

"Maybe it wasn't planned," Lucas said. "You know as well as I do that drugs affect people in different ways."

"Her doctor said this drug is harmless."

"Doctors have been known to be wrong," Lucas said. "I'll feel a lot better once we locate Richard Malone. Have airport security look for his car, and if they don't find it, put out an APB. Sooner or later, he has to turn up."

Yeah, but in what condition? Troy wondered. The sick feeling he'd gotten at the mansion hadn't gone away when he'd left. Instead, it was getting worse all the time, and he couldn't shake the premonition that Andrea was headed for trouble. Big trouble.

Lucas pushed himself off the desk and picked up his cup. "Keep me posted, Stoner."

"Will do."

Troy cleaned up his desk as best he could, then dropped by Records on his way out. Leanne was there, sitting hunched over her computer terminal, scowling at the information scrolling across her screen. She looked up and grinned. "Hey, Stoner, any luck with your Jane Doe?"

"Some. I know who she is now and where she lives, just don't know whose blood was on her clothes. Or how it got there."

"I sent over the latest missing-persons and homicide reports," she told him.

"Yeah, I got them. Nothing so far, but keep giving me the updates, okay? Meanwhile, I'd like you to run a list of names through the system for me. Anything comes up on any of them, you give me a call."

He handed Leanne a piece of paper, and she glanced at the list of names. "I'll see what I can find out, but it could take a while."

"No problem. Just let me know if anything turns up."

After signing out the Christina Malone file, Troy

walked out of the building, automatically slipping on his sunglasses. His efforts were a long shot, and he knew it. If the computer turned up anything useful on the names he'd given to Leanne, he'd be surprised. But there was nothing else he could do right now. Nothing else to go on. No body, no weapon, no evidence of a crime except for the blood.

He got into his car, turned the ignition, then shifted into gear and drove out of the parking lot. His mind churned with everything he'd learned that day. The whole setup at the Malone mansion worried him. He didn't like Dorian Andropoulos and he didn't trust Robert Malone. Sending Andrea home to them would feel a little like sending the Christians to the lions, but what choice did he have? Andrea belonged with her family, and there wasn't a damn thing Troy could do about it.

The sooner he accepted that, the better off they'd both be.

ANDREA STARED at the picture of herself and a man Troy said was Richard Malone, and a deep sense of foreboding stole over her. She felt weak, dizzy with terror as she stared down at the gray-haired man with the care-worn face. There was no question now. She knew without a doubt who he was.

He was the man she had seen murdered in her dreams.

The image of blood was so strong in her mind that Andrea gasped, dropping the picture to the tile floor in Madison's kitchen. The glass in the frame cracked, and when Andrea bent to pick it up, she nicked her finger on the edge. A drop of blood fell on Richard's face, and the symbolism was almost unbearable.

Troy took the picture from her. "You've cut yourself.'' Though his tone was gentle, his gaze was dark and—Andrea thought—accusing.

"It's nothing,'' she murmured.

"Here.'' Madison took charge. She drew Andrea over to the sink, turned on the faucet and doused the finger in cold water. Andrea cringed but didn't pull away. The pain gave her something else to focus on, gave her a moment or two to pull herself together before she had to face Troy again.

Madison wrapped a towel around Andrea's finger. "Just keep applying pressure. The cut isn't deep. The bleeding should stop in a minute.''

"I'm fine,'' Andrea mumbled. Troy was watching her when she turned from the sink. He still held her wedding picture, and Andrea's heart plunged to her stomach when she saw the look on his face.

He knows, she thought.

Somehow Troy knew about the memories and the dreams she'd been having. He suspected more was going on than she was telling him. That was why he seemed so cold and remote.

So unreachable.

Andrea's heart filled with bitter regret.

"Why don't we all sit down?'' Madison suggested. She led the way to the tiny breakfast alcove, where a white wicker dinette had been placed in front of a bay window.

Andrea took her seat and clasped her trembling hands in her lap. Across the table, Troy couldn't seem to take his eyes off her. Andrea didn't think she'd ever been so aware of someone staring at her, studying her. What did he see when he looked at her? What did he think? What did he feel?

Did he still want her, after today?

"Don't you want to know about your family?" he asked softly.

"Of course." *No!* She didn't want to know. She wanted to go on pretending she didn't have a family. She wanted to just keep thinking about Troy, dreaming about how it might be if—

"I met a woman named Dorian Andropoulos. Does that name ring a bell?"

Reality came crashing in. A vague uneasiness crept over Andrea. She couldn't place the woman's face, but she knew she'd heard her voice. *You're nothing but a backstabbing, little gold digger."*

Andrea shuddered. "Who is she?"

"She says she's your husband's mother-in-law. His first wife's mother."

Andrea glanced up. "She…lives with us?" It was the first time she'd referred to herself and Richard as an *us,* a couple.

Troy's mouth tightened. "Apparently. So does your brother-in-law, Robert Malone. Do you remember him?"

Andrea searched her mind, but she had no recall of a brother-in-law. No masculine image came to her at all except for the gray-haired man with the careworn face. Richard Malone. Her husband.

She took a deep breath. "What did you find out about me?"

"Quite a lot, actually." Troy's expression remained neutral, but something flickered in his eyes. "Your name before you married was Andrea Evans."

Andrea tried not to react, but a shudder wracked her. *You know about the little Evans girl, don't you? It was so tragic….*

Her gaze darted away from Troy, as if he somehow

might be able to read her thoughts by gazing into her eyes. "What else?"

For the next several minutes, Troy recounted to Andrea and Madison everything he'd learned at the Malone mansion. At least, he said it was everything, but Andrea suspected he was holding something back from her.

She listened in horrified fascination as he described Dorian's animosity and Robert's cool detachment, how neither of them had reported her missing because they hadn't missed her. Not only did her family not want her back, but it sounded as though they might actually hate her. Why? What had she done that was so terrible? What kind of person had she been?

Apparently the kind who made a lot of enemies.

The kind who married a wealthy, grieving widower six months after his first wife died.

The kind of woman who could be married to one man and deeply attracted to another.

"I don't think I like what I'm hearing," she murmured. "Could I really have been so bad?"

Something in her tone must have gotten to Troy, because he reached across the table and took her hand. Andrea did lift her gaze then, and their eyes met. And suddenly she forgot all about Madison, sitting at the table with them, and about Richard, a husband she didn't even know. She forgot everything except the way Troy was looking at her.

Something stirred inside her, a longing so deep and so powerful, Andrea felt her breath quicken. She wished they were alone and she was free. She wished she and Troy were the only two people in the world right now.

But they weren't.

And no amount of wishing would change the terrible truth.

Troy said, "Look. I wouldn't put too much stock in what Dorian Andropoulos had to say. She's obviously a very bitter woman. I doubt there are too many people she does like."

Madison, who had been sitting quietly until now, cleared her throat, as if to remind them of her presence, and said, "He's right, Andrea. Don't judge yourself by what someone else says about you. Especially someone who may have a personal bias. You know what's in your heart. You know you're a good person. That's all that matters."

But Andrea didn't know she was a good person. That was the trouble. If she were a good person, why did this awful feeling of guilt come over her at times? Why would she feel so much remorse if she hadn't done anything wrong? But what? What had she done? And what did it have to do with Richard Malone?

Was he really out of town? Andrea didn't think so, and for a moment, she toyed with the notion of telling Troy what she'd seen in her dreams, what she had remembered. She thought of confessing to him that she was almost certain Richard was dead, murdered, but how could she? How could she tell Troy she thought her husband was dead when she might very well be his murderer?

She was the logical suspect, wasn't she? She'd been found with blood on her clothing. According to Dorian Andropoulos, Andrea had married Richard for his money. She was a cold, devious woman capable of anything. What further proof would Troy need?

Andrea remembered just enough to point the finger at herself, but nothing at all that would help clear her. She couldn't tell Troy. If he didn't believe her—and maybe even if he did—he'd have no choice but to arrest her.

She would be locked away somewhere with no way to prove her innocence, no way to defend herself against Dorian's allegations and no way to protect Mayela.

It all came back to the child, although Andrea still hadn't figured out why. She just *knew*. Mayela needed her, and Andrea had to get home to her. Now.

She lifted her gaze to meet Troy's. "When can I go home?"

Something that Andrea wanted to believe was regret flashed in his eyes, but he shrugged, as if her words meant nothing to him. "Whenever you want. I'll drive you there myself."

"SHE TOOK IT PRETTY WELL," Troy said. "Better than I expected."

Madison looked at him in disbelief. "What are you talking about? She was terrified. Didn't you see the way her hands were shaking? She was an emotional wreck."

"She seemed calm enough to me." Too calm and too damn anxious to get back home.

Well, what had he thought? That she would chuck it all, the mansion in River Oaks, the wealthy husband, the expensive clothes and jewelry and say, *I don't want to go back. I'll divorce my husband, leave my family, forget I was ever rich. Those things mean nothing to me anyway.*

Obviously they *did* mean something to her. She couldn't wait to get back to them.

Troy didn't like the bitterness that suddenly rose like a dark cloud inside him, but he couldn't help it. He got up and walked across the room, staring blindly out the window over the sink.

"Troy," Madison said softly. "You knew she had a family. A husband."

"Yeah, I knew."

"I hate to see you this way."

He shrugged. "I'm a big boy. I can take it."

She got up and walked over to him, placing her hand on his shoulder. "Maybe you should talk to her, tell her how you feel."

"You know I can't do that. Besides..." He paused. "She already knows."

"And?"

"And nothing." Troy turned to her, his expression bleak. "If she felt something for me once, it's obviously gone now. She's starting to remember her past. Her husband. Did you see her face when she looked at his picture? Maybe she even remembers that she loved him."

"But you don't sound too convinced of that."

He ran his hand through his hair. "It was a weird setup over there, Madison. Tell me what the hell Malone's first wife's mother is doing living with them in the first place? And that leech of a brother..." Troy glanced at Madison. "I'm worried about her going back there."

"What do you mean?"

"Those people are cold. Cold and greedy."

Madison frowned. "You don't actually think they'd try to hurt Andrea, do you?"

Troy's fears had been nameless until now, but he realized that was exactly what he was afraid of. "Remember the way she was found. Wandering down a busy street at night. Blood all over her clothing."

"Yes, but that blood wasn't hers."

"I know." The blood was O-positive, the same as Richard Malone's. "But what about the guy I saw outside her hospital room the night before you brought her here? I keep thinking about the way he held that needle.

I keep thinking about the way he ran away. He meant to harm her, Madison.''

"You can't know that for sure. You said he was dressed in hospital scrubs and that his face was covered with a surgical mask. In fact, you said you couldn't tell if it was a man or a woman."

"That's true. For all I know, it could have been Dorian Andropoulos."

"You don't really believe that."

"I don't know if I do or not." He gave Madison a hard look. "You didn't see her. You didn't talk to her. There's not much I'd put past her."

"So what are you going to do?"

He shrugged. "What can I do? You heard Andrea. She wants to go home."

"But if you told her your suspicions—"

"I can't do that. I don't have anything but a gut feeling that something is wrong in that house, and lately I'm not too sure I can trust my own instincts. But I tell you what I *can* do." His features settled into grim lines of determination. "I'm going to keep digging until I get to the bottom of all this. I'm not going to let it rest."

"I didn't think you would."

"The first thing I have to do is find Malone."

"And when you do find him, what then?" Madison asked. "What if he's exactly where he's supposed to be? What if there's never an explanation for the blood on Andrea's clothing? Will you be able to let it go then? If you find her husband, will you be able to walk away from her?"

More questions, Troy thought. More questions he couldn't answer. "I don't know," he said honestly. "I just know that neither of us can go on like this."

Chapter Ten

Andrea stared up at the mansion, trying to experience some sense of relief, some feeling of coming home, but all she felt was a deep uneasiness. She didn't belong here. This wasn't her home. How could she be married to a man she didn't even remember?

Not exactly true, she reminded herself. She did have memories of Richard Malone. Memories she wished she *could* forget.

She glanced at Troy as he pulled the car in front of the mansion and stopped. His mouth was set in a harsh line, and his eyes looked hard and unreadable. Andrea shivered, feeling his remoteness.

"Are you ready?" he asked, his tone devoid of any emotion.

"I guess so."

Ever since he'd brought her news of her family earlier, Troy had made an obvious effort to withdraw from her, and Andrea had no choice but to do the same. She was home now, and she couldn't afford to be distracted. She had to protect Mayela from whatever darkness lurked within that house, and Andrea's feelings for Troy—and his for her—couldn't be allowed to matter.

But as he leaned over and opened her door, his arm

brushed against her breasts, and a spasm of desire shot through her. As if he'd felt the shock himself, Troy turned, so that their eyes met. Their lips were only inches apart, and Andrea's breath caught in her throat.

She wanted him to kiss her. Wanted it more than she could remember ever wanting anything in her life. Just one kiss. One last expression of the love they didn't dare admit before she walked into that house and into her past.

Before she could stop herself, Andrea lifted her hand to caress his face. He closed his eyes, as if her touch were almost unbearable, and then he turned his head, so that his lips skimmed along her palm.

And still Andrea could not breathe. Still she could not make herself open that door and get out. Still she could not quite admit that Troy Stoner would never be hers. Could never be hers.

He took her hand and kissed each finger, his mouth warm and urgent against her skin. He gazed down at her, his eyes dark and clear and incredibly sexy as he whispered her name on a hot breath of desire.

Andrea trembled. If he kissed her, she wouldn't be able to resist. If he held her, she wouldn't be able to pull away. If he made love to her, she could easily forget that she had married Richard Malone, and that he might be dead at this very moment.

"Oh, God," she whispered.

"You don't have to go in there," Troy said. His eyes grew dark and urgent. "You don't have to go inside that house, Andrea." He stopped short of asking her to go away with him, but Andrea knew that's what he meant, what he wanted.

She drew a ragged breath, his appeal almost too powerful to resist. But even as the temptation almost overcame her will, the front door of the mansion opened, and Andrea could see a woman in a uniform standing at the top of the stairs. A little girl in a bright red dress appeared at the woman's side.

Andrea couldn't take her eyes off the child. She looked to be about seven, with long black hair and a solemn expression that made her seem older. When the little girl saw Andrea sitting in Troy's car, she shot past the maid and flew down the stairs toward them.

Andrea got out of the car. An overwhelming sense of love swept over her. Without thinking, without analyzing her reaction, she opened her arms, and the child rushed into them. Andrea embraced her, lifted her, and the little girl's arms crept around Andrea's neck, holding her as if she would never let her go. "I knew you'd come back! I knew it!"

"Mayela," Andrea whispered, stroking the child's thick curls. "My little May."

Over the top of Mayela's head, Andrea saw Troy. He'd gotten out of the car and walked around, so that he was standing not two feet away from them. He had to have seen Andrea's unbridled response to the child. He had to have heard her call the child by her nickname. Her actions were hardly those of a woman who couldn't remember her past, but neither were they the actions of a cold-blooded murderer, were they?

Could she feel this much love for a child whose father she had killed?

She put the child down, but Mayela clung to her hand. "Dorian said you weren't coming back, but I knew you would. I just knew it."

"Of course I came back," Andrea said, her response automatic. She was aware of Troy's gaze on her. "I couldn't leave you, could I? Aren't we best friends?"

"Yes, but—" The child's expression grew serious again. Her blue eyes, so striking against all that dark hair, looked troubled as she gazed up at Andrea. "Dorian said you don't remember me."

Andrea knelt beside Mayela and gently placed her hands on the little girl's shoulders. "I've been...sick, May, and I'm not quite well yet. But I'm getting better, and even if I don't remember specific things about you, I still remember how special you are and how much I love you. I could never forget that."

The child looked appeased, but only for a moment. "Do you remember Daddy?"

You killed my daddy! You killed my daddy!

The child's tortured scream drove through Andrea with the force of a lightning bolt. She gasped, putting her hand to her heart as Mayela's face blurred before her. Andrea couldn't distinguish the child's features anymore. Couldn't see the dark hair or the troubled blue eyes, but she could still hear her screams. She could still feel the child's terror.

Andrea stood and backed away from the child. Dimly she was aware of Troy's hands on her arms, steadying her. "Easy, now," he murmured.

His voice brought her back. For a moment, Andrea leaned against him, drinking in his warmth and strength and comfort. Then she saw Mayela's face. The child looked as if she were about to burst into tears.

"I'm sorry," Andrea whispered. She was still too stunned by the force of the memory to do much more than stare down at the child in regret.

Troy said, "Andrea's still not well, Mayela. I've brought her here so you can take good care of her. Will you do that?"

Mayela nodded. Hesitantly she approached Andrea

and took her hand. "Don't worry, Andrea. I'll bring you ice cream and read to you and draw pictures for you, just like you do when I'm sick."

Andrea's throat tightened with emotion. Somehow she knew that Mayela was the first person who had truly cared about her in a long, long time. Ever since Andrea was a little girl and her own daddy had—

Had what? Died? Why was it she could remember that her father loved her, but she couldn't remember what he looked like? Couldn't remember how or when he had died?

But he *was* dead. She knew it just as surely as she knew Richard Malone was dead.

She looked down at Mayela with a sudden rush of despair. The child didn't know yet. No one knew yet except Andrea. And that could only mean—

She started to panic again, started to withdraw from Mayela, but Andrea forced herself to remain calm. She didn't know what had happened to Richard. She didn't know for sure he was dead. She couldn't know. Maybe he *was* out of town. Maybe he would come back and the three of them would be a real family.

But Andrea knew they'd never been a real family, just as she knew she'd never been in love with him. She couldn't feel the way she did about Troy if she had ever loved her husband.

That begged the question, of course, of why she had married him. But as Andrea looked up at the imposing facade of the mansion, she wondered if that answer was all too evident.

She glanced back at Troy. He had stepped away when Mayela had taken her hand, as if purposefully distancing himself from them. He said now, "Do you want me to go in with you?"

Andrea shook her head. "That won't be necessary. I know you have to get back."

It wasn't what she'd wanted to say, but Andrea knew it was time to sever the ties, tenuous as they were, that bound them together. Until and unless she could come to him free of and unencumbered by her past and by her deeds, she had to let Troy go.

He stared at her for a moment longer, then turned and got in his car. A wave of emotion washed over Andrea as she watched him drive away, and she had to blink back her tears.

"Who is that man?" Mayela asked. She clung to Andrea's hand.

"He's a policeman, but he's also a friend." Andrea's eyes were still on the spot where Troy's car had disappeared down the street. She couldn't look away.

"He helped you?" the child wanted to know.

"Yes, he did."

"Then he's my friend, too."

Andrea tore her gaze away from the street and smiled down at Mayela. Then, with a deep breath, she turned and looked up at the house. "I guess we should go in."

Mayela's small hand squeezed Andrea's fingers. "Don't worry," she said. "I'll take good care of you."

DORIAN ANDROPOULOS and Robert Malone proved to be every bit as daunting as Troy had warned her. They were both waiting for her in the large living room that opened up just past the stairs. As Mayela led Andrea inside, she held steadfastly to Andrea's hand—not because of her own fear, Andrea thought, but because the child was trying to protect her.

Against what? Andrea wondered with a shiver.

The question was answered the moment she set eyes

on Dorian. The woman's expression, her whole demeanor exuded hostility, and the chill deepened inside Andrea's heart.

The man seated on the sofa, legs crossed, arm draped over the back in an almost studied pose of casualness, bore a striking resemblance to the man in the picture Troy had shown her. But Richard Malone—both in the picture and in her dreams—wore a mantle of strength and character that this man would never be able to achieve. Though he was smiling at her, there was a kind of covert deviousness in his eyes that was almost more chilling than Dorian's open animosity.

As if sensing her unease, Mayela tightened her grip on Andrea's hand. Across the room, Dorian's gaze narrowed on them both. Her elbow was propped on the arm of a chair, and a cigarette smoldered between two fingers. "So," she said, "I see you two have found each other again. Welcome home, Andrea."

There wasn't a drop of warmth in her tone.

"Thank you," Andrea murmured.

Robert got to his feet. "Shall I fix you a drink? A little vodka always hits the spot after an especially trying ordeal."

Trying ordeal? Was that what she was going through? Andrea thought it an understatement. She declined his offer. "No, thanks. I don't drink."

Robert's brows soared. "So you remember that, do you?"

"Just how much do you remember?" Dorian asked. She, too, got to her feet, so that she was no longer having to look up at Andrea.

Andrea shrugged. "Not much, really. I have flashes of memory, more like impressions, I guess you'd say."

"Well," Robert said, turning with drink in hand.

"This is all very fascinating. Do you have any idea how you came to be suffering from this…problem?"

"The doctor said it appears to be psychosomatic," she explained. "I must have seen something or…heard something that was extremely traumatic."

"Do you have any idea what it was?" Dorian's dark gaze swept over Andrea, as if assessing what other damage might have been done to her. Then her eyes lit on Mayela, and her gaze sharpened. "Mayela," she said, "go upstairs to your room."

"But I want to stay with Andrea."

Dorian stamped out her cigarette. "Do as you're told. This is an adult conversation, and you have no business being here."

Though what she said might very well be true, her words were too harshly spoken. Andrea felt the little girl stiffen in defiance. "I won't! You can't make me! You're not my mother! Andrea is my mother now. Daddy said so."

"*Mayela!*" Dorian turned on Andrea. "This is your doing. She never would have spoken to me like that before you came here. Christina would not have tolerated such behavior."

Christina hated you, Andrea thought with a flash of memory, but she held her tongue. She knelt beside Mayela. "She's right. You shouldn't speak to your grandmother that way. I think you'd better apologize."

Mayela folded her arms and clamped her lips together stubbornly, but only for a moment. Then a spice of mischief twinkled in her blue eyes. She turned to Dorian. "I'm sorry, *Grandmother,*" she said sweetly, drawing out the last word.

Though Andrea couldn't fault the child's tone, she instinctively knew something was wrong. She glanced up to find Dorian's face contorted with rage. "Go to your room at once," she ordered through clenched teeth.

This time Mayela must have known she'd pushed too many of Dorian's buttons, for she whirled without argument and dashed out of the room, pausing only briefly at the bottom of the stairs to call over her shoulder, "Things are going to be different around here now that Andrea's home! You wait and see!"

Andrea wished she could share the child's confidence, but at the moment, she felt vastly overwhelmed.

Robert finished his drink and poured himself another. "Let's get back to this traumatic thing that may have happened to you," he said. "What could it have been?"

"I wish I knew," Andrea said, although she didn't. That was the last thing she wanted.

The doorbell sounded, but neither Dorian nor Robert made a move to answer it. Andrea rose instinctively, then remembered that the Malones had a maid to perform such trivial tasks.

Was she used to being pampered? Andrea wondered. She doubted it. Troy had told her she and Richard had only been married a short time, and before that, she had been Mayela's nanny. One of the servants. Was that why she felt so out of place in this house? Was that why Dorian and Robert seemed to resent her so much?

Shivering, Andrea moved to the glass doors that led out to a walled courtyard with a fountain. The setting looked familiar to her, and she thought about the painting in Madison's living room that had elicited such a strong memory. Was this the courtyard and fountain she had remembered? She closed her eyes, and an image came to her.

Christina was standing by the fountain, her eyes dark with despair. "I don't know what's wrong with me, An-

drea. I can't seem to snap out of this depression. Richard is gone so much. He's never here, and when he is, all he thinks about is his company. He hardly knows our daughter, and I...well, I'm afraid I haven't been much of a mother to her lately. I don't know what we'd do without you. You've been so good for Mayela. She loves you so. Promise me you'll always take care of her, Andrea. Promise me you'll never leave her."

The memory shattered as a masculine voice spoke from behind her. Andrea turned to see a man stride into the living area. "What the devil is going on, Dorian? Some cop's been calling the office looking for Richard—" His voice broke off as his gaze lit on Andrea. "Andrea. You're back."

He'd been heading for Dorian, but now he changed course, quickly crossing the distance to Andrea. He had his back to Dorian and Robert as he put his hands on Andrea's arms and bent to kiss her cheek. His fingers slid over her skin, almost stroking her, and the intimacy shocked her.

She backed away, searching her mind for some scrap of recognition, but the man was a complete stranger to her. He was tall, with the lean, athletic build and the bronzed skin of a man who played tennis several times a week at the club. His hair was brown streaked with gold, and his eyes were a clear, probing gray. He was dressed as elegantly as Robert Malone, but where Robert's appearance was almost a study in fastidiousness, this man wore his expensive clothing with the carelessness of someone who possessed supreme self-confidence. He was handsome and he knew it.

He frowned down at her. "What's wrong? Why are you looking at me like that?"

Andrea tried to answer him, but no words came out.

She stared at his mouth and suddenly remembered how his lips had felt against hers.

Sometime, somewhere, this man had kissed her.

What's more, he was looking at her as if he might do so again.

Who in God's name was he?

Andrea took another step away from him. "Who are you? How do I know you?" she asked a little desperately.

His frown deepened. "What are you talking about?"

"Haven't you heard?" Dorian asked, walking toward them. She came over and linked her arm through his. "Andrea has amnesia. The police didn't tell you?"

"I didn't talk to the police. My secretary said some detective, a sergeant something-or-other, was trying to locate Richard." He turned to Dorian. "What the hell is going on?"

She shrugged. "No one seems to know. Andrea was picked up by the police a week ago Sunday night. Her clothes were covered in blood. But no one, including Andrea, seems to know whose blood it was. Or why she can't remember."

"My God," the man said, gazing at Andrea in fascination. "No wonder you seem so frightened." He looked as if he might make a move toward her again, but Dorian's grip tightened on his arm. "Amnesia," he said. "You mean you don't remember anything?"

"Not much," Andrea said.

"You don't...remember me?" His tone was incredulous, his eyes deep and probing. He made Andrea very nervous.

She moistened her lips. "I'm afraid not."

"This is Paul Bellamy," Dorian said. "Richard's business partner. He was the best man at your wedding."

Something flashed in the man's eyes, a look of anger. Andrea said, "I'm sorry, but I still don't remember you."

He nodded, but his expression told her he didn't believe her. She couldn't have forgotten him.

Dear God, Andrea thought. What kind of relationship did she have with this man? Why could she remember his kiss so vividly?

He'd been the best man at her wedding, Dorian said. Maybe he'd kissed her then. Kissing the bride was a tradition, wasn't it?

But the kiss Andrea remembered hadn't been a chaste peck on the cheek. She could remember him holding her so tightly she could scarcely breathe as his tongue invaded her mouth. She'd felt...what? Excited? Aroused?

No, panicked, Andrea thought suddenly. He'd frightened her with that kiss.

They all frightened her. The walls of the house began to close in on her. She could hear the voices of Richard and Christina echoing through the hallways.

Marry me, Andrea. It's the only solution.

Promise me, Andrea. Promise you'll never leave Mayela.

Andrea massaged her temples with her fingertips, willing the voices away. "I'm tired," she said. "If you'll excuse me—"

She hurried out of the room, feeling their gazes digging into her back as she retreated. But at the bottom of the stairs, she hesitated. She had no idea where she was going.

Robert appeared behind her. "Take a right at the top of the stairs. Your room is the third door on the left."

Andrea turned to him gratefully. "Thank you."

"No problem. Come on. I'll walk up with you. I'm sure Dorian and Paul have a lot to talk about."

Andrea wondered what Richard's former mother-in-law and his current business partner might have to talk about, but if the possessive way Dorian had clung to the man's arm was any indication, their relationship was hardly business.

Paul Bellamy, however, had had eyes only for Andrea.

She shivered as she climbed the stairs beside Robert.

"I imagine you're wondering about Dorian," he said.

"What do you mean?"

He trained his gaze on her. "She doesn't like you, you know."

"I gathered as much, but I have no idea why."

"For starters, you're young and beautiful," Robert said. "That alone is reason enough for Dorian to despise you, but then you had to go and commit the ultimate sin. You married Richard."

They paused at the top of the stairs, and Andrea glanced up at him. "You mean because I married him so soon after Christina's death?"

"No. I mean because Dorian planned to become the second Mrs. Malone herself." Robert turned and headed down the hallway.

Andrea, after absorbing this, rushed to catch up. "She wanted to marry her daughter's husband?"

He shrugged. "Dorian considered him fair game. Especially since she'd seen him first."

"I don't understand."

"Richard was in a relationship with Dorian when he met Christina. He fell in love with her instantly. Think how that must have made Dorian feel—her young, beautiful daughter stealing away her fiancé."

"They were *engaged?*"

"Oh, yes. Dorian was very bitter, as you can imagine. She's always carried a torch for Richard. When Christina died, I'm sure she thought she might have a second chance with him. Then you came along, another young, beautiful woman—and her granddaughter's nanny, to boot."

"I'm sorry," Andrea said, not quite knowing how to respond to all that he'd told her.

Robert grinned suddenly. "Don't apologize to me. You and I have always gotten along famously. You didn't kick *me* out when you and Richard got married."

"How long have you lived here?" Andrea asked.

"Off and on for years. Richard's been a good brother to me," he said, but his eyes didn't quite tell the same tale.

Andrea wondered if, in spite of his words, he resented Richard. Richard was the older, wealthier, more successful brother. It would only be natural if Robert felt twinges of jealousy from time to time.

"How long has Dorian lived here?" Andrea asked.

"She came after Christina died, ostensibly to help take care of Mayela, but she never left. She tried several times to move in before, but it never worked. She and Christina couldn't get along for more than a few weeks at a time."

"I see."

"Well," Robert said. "Here we are. This is your room." He waved toward the closed door in front of them. "Yours and Richard's."

Andrea stared at that closed door. Beyond would be evidence of her marriage to Richard. Proof that she was, indeed, married. A visual reminder that she wasn't free to love another man.

She thought of Troy and wanted to cry.

Instead, she put her hand out to open the door. "Thanks for showing me to my room."

"Will we see you at dinner?"

"I don't know. I may go to bed early," she said.

"Then I'll see you tomorrow. Good night."

"Good night."

She turned and opened the door.

Chapter Eleven

"I made a few calls after Dr. Bennett left this morning," Madison said.

Troy glanced at his sister. He'd gone back to her town house after dropping Andrea at the Malone mansion instead of going home to his empty apartment. He didn't want to spend the evening brooding about Andrea, and yet, no matter where he went or what he did, he couldn't stop thinking about her.

"What kind of calls?" He poured himself a cup of coffee, then turned to lean against the counter.

"Let me back up." Madison tucked her dark hair behind her ears. "After Dr. Bennett left this morning, I went searching through the attic for her book."

"The one you read in college?"

She nodded. "I knew there was something about it that fascinated me back then, but I couldn't remember exactly what." She picked up a hardcover book lying on the counter and handed it to Troy. "Notice anything unusual?"

Troy glanced at the cover—*Dark Journey,* by Dr. Claudia M. Bennett. He thumbed through the pages, skimming passages here and there. "Sounds like the usual psychobabble stuff to me."

"I'm not talking about the text," Madison said. "There's no picture of the author on the jacket."

"So?"

"It's intriguing to me because of what happened to Dr. Bennett. She used herself as one of her case studies in the book."

"Are you saying she was her own patient?" Troy asked skeptically. No wonder the woman had struck him as odd.

"In a manner of speaking," Madison said. "She'd only been out of med school a few years when she was attacked one night leaving her office. Two men dragged her into an alley where they beat and raped her. They left her for dead. After that, she became severely agoraphobic. At the time she wrote this book, she hadn't left her home in over ten years."

Troy glanced up. "She didn't seem to have that problem this morning."

"I know," Madison agreed. "That's why I put in a call to a few of my colleagues. I wanted to find out what I could about her before she began seeing Andrea again."

"Did you find out anything?"

"According to the grapevine, she's lived in Houston for less than a year. She moved here to teach a graduate course in behavioral modification at the university, though she still sees a few patients from an office in her home. Before that, she lived in New York, where she had a small practice, but spent most of her time writing and doing research."

"Any idea why she moved down here?"

Madison shrugged. "All I could find out was that she told the department chair at the university she needed a change. I have no idea how she found Andrea. Or how Andrea found her.''

"I think I might know," Troy said. "Dr. Bennett also treated Christina Malone.''

"The first wife?"

Troy nodded. "I looked over the file earlier. According to interviews conducted at the time of her death, Christina suffered from severe depression and had been seeing Dr. Bennett. She overdosed on prescription amphetamines.''

"Were they prescribed by Dr. Bennett?"

"There was no evidence to that effect, and Dr. Bennett denied giving her any kind of medication.''

"It's not that hard to get amphetamines," Madison said. "She could have gotten them anywhere.''

"Yeah, but what I'd really like to know is why Andrea started seeing Dr. Bennett after that. Christina's suicide was hardly a glowing recommendation.''

"You can't blame her suicide on her therapist," Madison said, automatically coming to the defense of a colleague. "You don't know all the facts, and besides, Dr. Bennett's credentials are impeccable.''

"If they're so impeccable, why did you feel the need to check up on her?"

Madison shrugged. "Just to satisfy my curiosity.''

"That's all?"

She hesitated. Her dark eyes clouded, but she shook her head. "She checks out, Troy.''

"Maybe on paper. But if what you say is true, she lived through a pretty severe trauma herself. She was agoraphobic for at least ten years, yet this morning she didn't appear to have any difficulty being out and about. Could she recover from a phobia that easily?''

"We don't know that her recovery was all that easy," Madison argued. "Or how long it may have taken."

"Still," Troy said. "It's enough out of the ordinary to make me think we should keep digging."

Madison smiled wryly. "That's what I thought you'd say, and that's why I've already got a call into a friend of mine in New York. We should know more about Dr. Bennett in a day or two."

Troy was impressed by his sister's tenacity. "You'd have made one hell of a cop, you know that?"

There was a trace of regret in Madison's voice when she said, "I guess it's in my blood."

ANDREA WALKED AROUND the bedroom at least a dozen times, but there was nothing that seemed familiar to her—not the damask curtains at the windows, not the ivory-colored walls or the jewel green carpet. Not the lamps, not the chairs, not the heavy wood furniture. Not even the king-size bed with the bold paisley spread.

Especially not the bed.

When she'd first entered the room, her gaze had gone immediately to that bed, then she'd quickly glanced away, afraid to look. Afraid to awaken her sleeping memories. Afraid to think about her and Richard in that bed—

But she needn't have worried. When she finally got up enough courage to not only stare at the bed, but to sit on the edge, not a single memory was stirred. Not one. The bed was a sterile place for her.

How could that be? she wondered. She and Richard had been married for a month. Surely they must have spent the night together. Slept together. How could she not have memories of making love with her husband?

As Andrea explored the room further, she thought

she'd found her answer. At least, it was the most plausible explanation she could come up with. The dressing room wedged between the huge master bathroom and the walk-in closet contained a cot. Andrea knew instinctively this was her bed. This was where she had slept.

But why?

What kind of relationship did she and Richard have? Why did they sleep in separate beds?

As Andrea lay down on the cot, her eyes fluttered closed and she found herself wishing that this was all some horrible mistake. She wasn't really married after all. Richard Malone wasn't her husband. She didn't have a husband. She was free to love another man.

She was free to go to Troy and tell him how she felt.

A powerful image swept over her then. Not a dream or a memory this time, but a fantasy. She and Troy, together in this tiny bed, arms and legs entwined, bodies pressed close. She could almost feel his lips at her throat, his hand skimming her thigh, his voice whispering in her ear exactly what he wanted to do to her. And her own heated reply, *Yes. Oh, yes.*

She snuggled deeper into the bed, not wanting to let go of the fantasy, but knowing all the while that it could never be anything more.

A LITTLE WHILE LATER, Andrea stood on the balcony off Richard's bedroom, watching dark clouds gather in the distance. She shivered in the waiting calm. The storm was hours away, but the thought of thunder and lightning crashing all around made her uneasy. Was she afraid of storms? She didn't think so, yet she couldn't shake her disquiet. Bad weather meant trouble.

Feeling unsettled by the approaching storm and by her ominous thoughts, Andrea decided to join the others for dinner after all. Mayela's little face lit when she saw her, and Andrea was glad she'd decided to come down.

But the child's joy was short-lived. By the time they went in to dinner, Mayela's shoulders were drooping and her eyes looked suspiciously bright.

"Don't slump, Mayela," Dorian scolded.

Mayela made a halfhearted attempt to straighten, then let her shoulders fall forward again.

"What's the matter?" Robert asked. "Too much soccer today?"

Mayela shook her head. "When's Daddy coming home?"

"You know very well he's not coming home until next week," Dorian said. "He's away on business."

"Why did he have to go away?" Mayela whined. "Why does he always have to go away?" She turned and gazed up at Andrea. Her eyes looked far too troubled for a seven-year-old. "He *is* coming home this time, isn't he?"

Andrea's heart quickened. It was almost as if the child knew something. "If he's away on business," she said carefully, "why wouldn't he come home?"

"You know why," Mayela said very softly. So softly that Andrea was certain Robert and Dorian hadn't heard her. Mayela turned back to her plate and sighed, as if the conversation had taken far too much of her flagging energy. "I'm tired. May I be excused?"

"You haven't eaten your dinner," Dorian said.

"I'm not hungry."

"Very well."

The child got up and stood beside Andrea's chair. "Will you come tuck me in?"

"Of course."

"Will you tell me a story?"

"If I can think of one." Andrea excused herself and pushed back her chair.

Upstairs, she sat on the edge of the canopied bed while Mayela brushed her teeth and got into her pajamas. Then she came and crawled into bed, and Andrea tucked her in.

"Tell me one of the keyhole stories," Mayela begged.

"I'm afraid I don't remember them," Andrea said. "Why don't you tell me one?"

"There was this little girl," Mayela began solemnly. "She was locked away in this dark room by her evil stepmother or somebody, and the only way she could see the outside world was through the keyhole in her door."

Andrea began to feel uneasy. She wished Mayela would stop, but the child warmed to the story. "The keyhole was magic, see. Every time the little girl would look through it, she'd see something different. One time she saw a beautiful garden with roses and lilies and bright yellow butterflies. Another time she saw great big crystal snowflakes that sparkled like diamonds in the sunlight."

"Sounds like a pretty neat keyhole," Andrea murmured. She was drowning. A cold darkness closed in on her.

"Tell me what the little girl sees now, Andrea. Make up something really neat. Please."

Blood, Andrea thought. *She sees blood.*

In her mind, she could see the little girl kneeling at the keyhole. But she couldn't see what the little girl could see. Andrea wouldn't let herself see beyond that door. She couldn't. Not yet. She wasn't ready.

Mayela waited impatiently. She tugged on Andrea's hand. "What does she see?"

"She doesn't see anything," Andrea forced herself to say lightly. "Do you know why?"

Mayela shook her head.

"Because she's sleeping. Just like you should be."

"But I'm not tired." Mayela smothered a yawn.

"You said you were downstairs," Andrea argued.

"Yes, but I just said that so you'd come up here with me. I don't like the way Dorian tucks me in, and she doesn't know any good stories."

"Why do you call her Dorian?"

Mayela shrugged. "She told me to. She doesn't like to be called Grandmother or anything like that."

"Is that why you called her Grandmother earlier?"

An impish smile tugged at the corners of the child's mouth. Andrea couldn't help smiling, too. She knew Mayela was probably a handful at times, but Andrea also knew that she loved the little girl dearly. She didn't have to remember that. She felt it every time she looked at Mayela's sweet little face. Andrea skimmed the back of her fingers along the child's downy cheek.

Mayela turned serious again, her blue eyes gazing up at Andrea in earnest. "You won't go away again, will you? Promise me you won't."

"I won't. Not if I can help it."

"Daddy said you'd always be here to take care of me. Even when he's not." Mayela hesitated. Her eyes clouded, and for a moment, she struggled with her emotions. "I'll be brave," she whispered, blinking furiously. "I promised Daddy."

"Brave about what?"

But Mayela said nothing else. She turned her head away, so Andrea couldn't see her tears. Andrea's throat constricted. She felt like crying herself. Mayela seemed to know something was wrong, just as Andrea knew.

But *how* did they know? Why were she and Mayela the only ones who knew that Richard wasn't ever coming back?

Andrea gathered the little girl in her arms, and for a long moment, they rocked each other back and forth. Neither of them cried. Neither of them said anything.

But they both knew.

Mayela's daddy wasn't coming back.

Just as Andrea's daddy hadn't come back all those years ago.

ANDREA LAY IN THE DARK, her eyes wide, her heart hammering, as she listened for the noise that had awakened her. It came again, and for a moment, she thought someone was on the roof, trying to find a way to break in. Then she realized the storm had hit, and the sound she heard was tree limbs scraping against the shingles.

She got up and moved to the French doors that opened onto the balcony. The rain hadn't started yet, but the wind was up, whipping the giant trees that surrounded the house into a frenzy. Jagged lightning bolts split the sky in two places, and thunder rattled the windows.

Andrea stood outside, letting the wind tear through her hair. She wasn't frightened by the storm, but as earlier, an uncanny sense of unease plagued her. Something about the weather bothered her.

The rain came suddenly, in great sheets, and Andrea hurried inside and bolted the French doors. She stood watching the water drip down the glass as a torrent of memories buffeted her.

It had been raining that Sunday night. She remembered that now, and something urgent had driven her out into the weather. She closed her eyes, remembering the sound of the rain on her car roof, the almost frantic beat of the wiper blades against her windshield. She'd been running to someone, hadn't she? Or had she been running away?

Andrea strained to remember. Why had she been out driving that Sunday night? And why had the police picked her up walking? What had happened to her in the time in between?

She turned away from the window, distressed by all the questions rumbling around inside her. As she moved toward her bed, a piercing scream stopped her in her tracks.

Andrea's heart leapt to her throat. It was as though the scream had come from inside her, a manifestation of her troubled thoughts and her unnamed fears. But as she stood listening to the sounds of the storm, the scream came again and again.

Mayela!

The child was afraid of the storm. That was why Andrea had been so uneasy all evening. She knew the approaching storm would frighten Mayela.

Andrea flew across the room and threw open her door. Mayela's room was in the east section of the house, across the bridge that connected the two wings. There was no light in the hallway, but Andrea didn't take time to look for a switch.

As she rushed across the bridge at the top of the stairs, she felt something wet beneath her bare feet. Her feet slipped from under her. She fell heavily against the stair railing and clung to the banister to keep from falling.

As she righted herself, she could feel water dripping down on her. The skylight directly over her had been broken by a tree limb, and rain cascaded downward, creating a treacherous puddle on the marble.

As Andrea continued to look up, she heard a terrible

cracking sound. Then, almost in slow motion, the window gave way, and large sections of glass arrowed toward the floor. Toward her.

She had no time to think, to even breathe. Automatically she stepped back. Into nothing but air. For a moment, for an eternity, Andrea hung suspended at the top of the stairs. She was still looking up, and just before she tumbled backward, she could have sworn she saw a face in the gaping hole left by the falling glass.

Chapter Twelve

The drive to the hospital from Troy's apartment normally took twenty-five minutes. He was aiming for closer to fifteen. He made almost all the lights, and the ones he didn't make, he ran. An off-duty cop driving like a bat out of hell was a dangerous thing, and Troy told himself to slow down before he hurt some innocent bystander. His foot eased on the accelerator, but his heart pounded like a piston inside him. It had ever since Tim Seavers had called him from the emergency room to tell him that Andrea had been brought in a few minutes ago.

He hit the ER doors on the run, and the nurse at the desk told him where Andrea had been taken. He tried not to think about that first night, when he'd seen her in the hospital with blood all over her clothes. He tried not to remember the premonition he'd had then that a woman like her meant nothing but trouble for a man like him.

"Tim!"

Tim Seavers was coming out of one of the cubicles, and when he heard Troy call to him, he reversed course and came toward him. They stood in the hallway, oblivious to the noise and confusion around them.

"How bad is it?" Troy asked.

"Not as bad as it could have been." Tim jotted a few notes on the chart he was holding, then looked up. "She has a few cuts and bruises, and she'll be sore in the morning, but other than that, she's one lucky woman."

Troy breathed a sigh of relief. "What happened?"

"I don't know all the details, but evidently she took a tumble down the stairs at her home. She managed to break the fall by grabbing hold of the banister. The EMTs said the place is a mess over there. Broken glass and water everywhere. You might want to talk to him." He nodded toward the waiting room where Robert Malone paced nervously.

"I want to see Andrea first."

"Would it do any good if I said no?"

"Not one damn bit."

Tim sighed. "That's what I figured. Go on, then, but just for a few minutes. I don't want her upset."

Troy had no intention of upsetting Andrea. He told himself as he stood looking at her through the curtains surrounding the cubicle that he would be gentle with her. He wouldn't question her too harshly. But what he heard come out of his mouth when she opened her eyes and looked at him was a gruff "What the hell happened?"

"Troy." There was a small bandage on her forehead, and another on the back of her hand. A faint bruise colored her right cheek, and her hair had been pushed back to reveal a deeper bruise at her temple.

Troy felt a curious sensation in the back of his throat that made it difficult to talk.

Andrea's eyes were shadowed as she looked up at him. "Is Mayela all right?"

He cleared his throat. "Why wouldn't she be? You're the one who fell down the stairs."

"I know, but—"

"But what?" He took her hand and held it in both of his. He could feel her trembling, and he wanted to gather her in his arms, hold her close, tell her everything was going to be all right. But how could he tell her that when he didn't know what the hell had happened?

"Why are you so worried about Mayela?" he persisted.

"Because it could have been her here instead of me," Andrea said softly. "She could have been the one to fall, and if it *had* been her—" She broke off on a wave of emotion, as if she couldn't bear to think of the little girl's being hurt in any way.

"Just tell me what happened."

At first, Troy thought she would refuse. She withdrew her hand from his and turned her head to stare at the ceiling. Finally she said, "I heard Mayela scream. I knew she was afraid of storms so—"

"Wait a minute. How did you know she was afraid of storms?"

"I...remembered."

Troy gazed down at her. What else had she remembered? What else had she not told him? "Go on."

"I ran to her. Her room is on the opposite side of the house from...Richard's. The skylight at the top of the stairs had been broken in the storm. There was water all over the floor. I slipped, and then I saw all that glass falling toward me. I stepped back without thinking and lost my balance. But I could have sworn I saw—"

"What?"

She bit her lip. "It all happened so fast. I was so scared."

She was holding back again. Refusing to tell him the whole story. Frustrated, Troy ran his hand through his damp hair. "Why can't you trust me?"

Her blue eyes shone like stardust. "You don't know how much I want to."

"Then do it, damn it. Let me help you."

"I can't."

"Why not?" he demanded.

"Because it's not just me I have to protect," Andrea said desperately. "It's Mayela. I'm all she has left."

Something clenched in Troy's stomach. He stared down at her. Hard. "What about her father? She has him, doesn't she?"

A look of fear flashed in her eyes before she quickly turned away, so he couldn't see her expression.

"What did you mean by that, Andrea? Have you remembered something else?"

She shook her head. "It's…something Mayela said. I don't think her father is home very much. I don't think he spends much time with her."

"I see." More than she thought he did, Troy thought. She'd avoided using Richard's name. She hadn't called him her husband. Instead, she'd referred to him as Mayela's father. If that wasn't significant to Andrea, it sure as hell was to Troy.

Hope springs eternal, he told himself in disgust.

"You still here?" Tim strode into the cubicle and gave Troy a stern look. "My patient needs her rest, Sergeant."

"When can I go home?" Andrea asked anxiously.

"Tomorrow morning. I'm keeping you overnight for observation."

"But I'm fine," she protested. "I don't need to stay here overnight. I have to get home to Mayela."

"Who's Mayela?" Tim asked.

"My stepdaughter," Andrea said. "She needs me. I have to get home to her."

"You have to do what the doctor says," Troy said. "But if it'll make you feel better, I'll go by the house and make sure she's all right." He'd been planning to go over there anyway and take a look at the situation for himself.

Andrea's eyes were still shadowed with worry. She grabbed Troy's hand and clung to it. "Tell them—tell them you're watching out for her."

"Tell who?"

"Dorian and Robert. Make sure they know you're watching them."

"Robert's in the waiting room now," Troy said. "Did he drive you here?"

"No. He called the ambulance, and then I guess he followed in his car. Dorian stayed home with Mayela."

"Do you want to see him?"

"No!"

Her vehemence startled Troy. He gazed down at her. "All right. I'll go out and have a few words with him before I leave."

Andrea clung to his hand for a moment. "Tell him what I said. Tell them both."

But by the time Troy walked out to the waiting room, Robert had already gone.

What was going on here? Why was Andrea so afraid—not just for herself, but for Mayela?

He told himself on the drive to the Malone house that a broken skylight in a windstorm was not an unusual occurrence and not something anyone could have planned on. But when he walked into the house, saw the location of the window and the amount of broken glass on the marble floor, he had to agree with Tim Seavers. Andrea was indeed one lucky woman. He wondered if she had any idea how close she'd come to being killed tonight.

The window had cracked just enough at first to allow water to puddle on the marble floor. It was a wonder Andrea hadn't fallen the first time she'd slipped. If she'd injured herself then, she might not have looked up. And even if she had, she might not have been able to move out of the way in time to see the heavy glass window falling from the sky toward her. She might easily have been killed.

An accident? Maybe.

Maybe not.

Suddenly Andrea's concern for Mayela took on a whole new and ominous meaning. If a child had come running down that hallway, she would have undoubtedly slipped and fallen. She would have undoubtedly been lying there when the large sections of glass had broken loose.

Troy knelt and picked up a piece of the glass. The jagged point would have made a deadly weapon, and he hated to think what would have happened if Mayela had come along first. Or if Andrea hadn't moved out of the way in time.

He looked down from the bridge to find Dorian and Robert watching him. They were both in robes. Robert held a drink in his hand, and Dorian had lit a cigarette. They looked nervous, Troy thought, as if they had something to hide.

"I'd like to see Mayela," he told them.

"What on earth for?" Dorian asked coldly. "The child's asleep."

"She may have witnessed the accident." Troy stood and brushed off his hands, his gaze lingering on the broken glass. Then he glanced down at Robert and Dorian, and his expression hardened. "I want to find out tonight, from her, exactly what she saw."

WHEN TROY ARRIVED at the hospital the next morning, Andrea was already up, dressed and ready to go.

"How are you feeling?" he asked.

"Not bad. A little sore." She tentatively moved her left arm, which had taken the brunt of her fall. She was lucky she hadn't broken it. Lucky she hadn't broken her neck. "Did you see Mayela last night?"

"Yes. She seemed fine."

"Thanks." Andrea looked around, suddenly uneasy at the effect Troy's presence was having on her. She felt more vulnerable this morning than she had in a very long time. He crossed the room to stand in front of her, and Andrea's breath caught in her throat as she gazed up at him.

"I'm going to ask you a question, and I want you to tell me the truth." His eyes were dark and deep and more than a little suspicious.

Andrea swallowed. "What is it?"

"You don't think what happened last night was an accident, do you?"

She shifted her gaze, unable to meet his eyes.

"Don't do that," he said.

"Don't do what?"

"Look away from me. Try to hide your feelings from me. We've come too far for that, Andrea."

They had come too far. Further than they'd had any right. That was the problem.

She sighed. "I don't know if last night was an accident or not. I don't have any proof that it wasn't. No real proof," she added softly.

"What's that supposed to mean?"

"Just that…" She turned to the window and stared out. "Last night, before I fell, I was still looking up at the skylight. I could have sworn…"

"What?"

"I…thought I saw someone looking down at me."

She waited for sounds of his disbelief, braced herself for his skepticism, but his explosion stunned her. "Why didn't you tell me this last night?"

"Because I didn't think you'd believe me," Andrea said. She turned to face him. "Think about it, Troy. I'm not exactly the most credible witness right now."

He started to argue with her, but stopped himself because there was merit in what she'd said, and they both knew it.

"You still should have told me," he said. "How can I help you if you don't level with me?"

"I'm sorry. But it all happened so fast, I couldn't be sure of what I saw. I'm still not sure."

"Well, one thing's for damn sure," Troy said grimly. He paced the room, deep in thought. "You can't go back to that house. Not until we find out what the hell is going on."

Andrea watched his every movement. "I have to go back," she said. "I can't leave Mayela there alone. She needs me."

Troy glanced up, his expression dark. "Then get her out of that house, too. Bring her with you."

"How? You're a cop, Troy. You know there isn't a judge in the world who would allow me to remove that child from her home in my present situation. I don't have a choice. I have to stay there until…" Andrea trailed off, not wanting to mention her husband's name, not wanting him to come between them once again.

But Troy had no such compunction. "Until what? Until Richard comes home?'' He stopped his pacing and stared at her. ''What happens when your husband does come home, Andrea?''

''What do you mean?''

His gaze deepened. ''I mean what happens to us.''

''Troy—''

''Tell me something.'' An angry glint appeared in his eyes. ''How do you feel when you hear his name? What did you remember when you slept in his bed last night?''

Andrea knew that if she was smart, she would tell him it was none of his business. She would do nothing to add fuel to the fire that had ignited between them, but instead she said very softly, ''I didn't sleep in his bed last night. I slept in my own bed.''

Dead silence fell over the room.

Andrea released a long breath. ''I don't sleep with my husband. We have separate beds.''

Troy's gaze was almost too intent to bear. ''I find that very hard to believe.''

''It's true,'' Andrea whispered. ''I don't love him, Troy.''

''How can you know that? If you don't remember him, how can you know that you don't love him?''

''I don't remember Mayela, either, but I know that I love her dearly.''

An emotion that might have been hope flickered in Troy's dark eyes, but he quickly dashed it away by saying, ''I think what you're experiencing is an amnesia that's even more selective than we first thought. Is it possible you've told yourself you don't love him, made yourself believe it because of…us?''

''I *don't* love him,'' Andrea insisted. ''And I didn't marry him for his money.''

''I never said you did.''

"But you've thought it. You know you have, and I don't blame you. I know how all this must look to you, but...I think I married Richard because of Mayela."

"Mayela?"

Andrea nodded. "She said something last night that started me thinking. Richard isn't home much. He travels all the time, and maybe after Christina died, he needed someone to take care of Mayela."

"You were already taking care of her. You were her nanny."

"I know, but maybe Richard thought she needed a mother."

Troy still wasn't convinced. "That doesn't explain why *you* would agree to something so drastic, unless—"

She cut him off. "Unless I was getting something in return? But I *was* getting something. Don't you see? I was getting Mayela. Maybe I needed her as much as she needed me. I don't seem to have any other family."

"It's possible, I guess." He ran his fingers through his hair. "Hell, anything's possible."

"Then you believe me?"

"I believe it's what you think," he said carefully.

Not good enough. She wanted him convinced. She wanted him to believe wholeheartedly, as she did, that she had never been in love with Richard Malone, and that she wasn't the type of woman who would have married him for his money. She wanted Troy to believe the best about her. It was the most important thing in the world to her at that moment. "I wasn't in love with Richard," she said almost desperately. "Because if I had been, I couldn't feel the way I do about you."

Troy didn't say anything to that, but he took her hand and pulled her into his arms. They stood that way for a very long time, and Andrea wasn't sure if the embrace would have eventually led to more. If she would have had the willpower to stop him from kissing her.

She never had the chance to find out. She became aware of such a strong malevolent presence in the room with them, that at first she thought it might actually be Richard's ghost. Then she looked up to see Paul Bellamy glaring at her from the doorway.

Troy saw him at the same time and released her, but he kept one arm around her waist.

Paul walked into the room, his handsome features like chiseled granite. "What's going on in here?"

Andrea's glance fell to the flowers he carried in one hand. White roses. Her favorite. "What are you doing here?" she asked, not liking the way Paul Bellamy was looking at her. Not liking the memory of his kiss.

"I heard about what happened last night from Dorian. I wanted to make sure you were all right. I can see that you are," he said, tossing the roses onto her bed.

Andrea eased away from Troy's arm and felt him stiffen beside her.

Andrea said weakly, "This is Paul Bellamy. He's Richard's partner."

"I'm Sergeant Stoner," Troy said. "HPD." The two men didn't shake hands.

"So you're here in an official capacity?" Paul asked, but his eyes told them he already knew the answer.

Troy ignored the insinuation and the question. "I've been trying to get in touch with you, Mr. Bellamy, but you haven't returned any of my phone calls."

"I thought you were trying to get in touch with Richard," Paul said, casting a meaningful glance at Andrea, as if to remind them just who Richard was.

"Your secretary said there's no way to get in touch with him."

"That's right. There isn't."

"He doesn't check in with the office?"

"No. That's the whole point of his little trip. There's no way any member of the group can contact civilization. They're completely isolated."

"So actually you have no way of knowing whether Richard is with the group or not," Troy said. "Is that right?"

Paul Bellamy hesitated, as if caught off guard by the question. "Why wouldn't he be with them? The whole thing was his idea."

"Are you in charge of the company while he's gone?"

"I'm the president and CFO," Paul said. "But I really can't see where all these questions are leading, Sergeant. Andrea had an unfortunate accident last night, but as I understand it, that's all it was. Is there any reason why I can't take her home this morning?"

"Maybe you should ask *her* that question," Troy said.

Andrea felt both sets of male eyes on her, and she was about to inform them that she could find her own way home. But just then, Troy's cellular phone rang, and he fished it out of his jacket pocket to flip it open. He turned his back to Andrea, but she heard him say his name into the phone. Then he listened for a moment and finished with a curt "I'll be right there."

He disconnected the phone and dropped it in his pocket as he turned back to Andrea. "I have to go." There was a look of urgency in his eyes, and Andrea couldn't help wondering what the call had been in reference to. Was it something to do with her?

A chill crept up her spine, and she shivered.

"You okay?" Troy asked, still gazing down at her.

Andrea nodded. "I'm fine."

He seemed reluctant to leave. He looked as if he wanted to say something else, do something more, and for a moment, Andrea held her breath. Would he kiss her in front of Paul Bellamy?

A trace of regret flashed in Troy's eyes. "I'll be in touch," he said. Then he brushed past Paul Bellamy and disappeared out the door.

As it turned out, Andrea was forced to accept a ride home with Paul after all. There seemed little point in calling a taxi when he was standing in the same room making the offer. Still, there was something about him that made Andrea extremely uncomfortable. She hated how he kept looking at her and the possessive way he took her arm to help her into his car.

Once they were on the road, Andrea stole a glance in his direction. He was very handsome, with finely molded features and a well-honed body that most women would admire, but there was nothing in the least appealing about him to Andrea. Instead, she found his excessive good looks a little unsettling, as if they disguised the real man beneath.

As if reading her thoughts, he flashed her a smile that should have ignited her pulse, but didn't. Andrea turned to look out the window.

"You don't have to keep pretending," he said. "Not with me."

Reluctantly Andrea turned to face him. "I don't know what you mean."

"This memory thing. I don't know what you're trying to pull, but you don't have to keep up the game with me."

Andrea glared at him. "It's not a game. I don't remember you. I don't remember anything about you."

His features hardened, and suddenly he didn't look handsome at all. "You expect me to believe that? After what we had?"

Her stomach tightened in fear. "We...had a relationship?"

Paul shot her a look. "You couldn't have forgotten. There's no way."

Andrea didn't think she wanted to hear any more, but she couldn't seem to stop herself from asking, "Was it...before....?"

One brow rose. "Before you married Richard? It started before."

She looked at him in disgust. "You mean—"

"You really don't remember, do you? I guess it wasn't as good for you as it was for me." He laughed, a low, rumbling sound that set Andrea's stomach to churning.

She couldn't stand to hear any more. She didn't want to find out anything else about herself, about Paul Bellamy and about what had happened between them.

She'd convinced herself that what she felt for Troy was a once-in-a-lifetime thing. A pure and wonderful thing. The reason she could be married and have feelings for him was that what they felt for each other was so very special. Love at first sight.

But now the thought of her and Paul Bellamy...

Andrea's skin crawled. Whether she'd loved Richard or not, she couldn't stand the thought of having betrayed him, especially with a man she knew she *couldn't* have been in love with.

She felt as if she'd betrayed Troy, too.

At that moment, Andrea hoped she never got her memory back. She hoped she never had to find out the kind of woman she'd been. Because what if she became her again?

Tears stung behind her lids, and she squeezed her eyes closed. But even as she tried to keep the memories at bay, one struggled frantically to get out. The image formed against Andrea's will, and she was powerless to stop it.

She could see the anger in Paul's eyes as he grabbed her arm and hauled her up against him. He kissed her roughly, and Andrea pulled away. She tried to slap him, but he caught her wrist and held it so tightly she cried out.

"I never thought you'd go through with it. I never thought you'd actually marry him. But now that you have, it's only fair I get what I want."

"I don't know what you're talking about," Andrea said, her heart tripping with fear inside her. Paul Bellamy was a monster. He'd do anything to get what he wanted.

"I want what's rightfully mine. You owe me, damn it. You're nothing but a tease," he said in contempt. *"All these months you've been leading me on...."*

"I never led you on," Andrea whispered aloud.

He glanced at her and smiled as he pulled into the Malone driveway. "So you remember that little conversation we had at the reception, do you?"

Andrea felt chilled as she watched him. He stopped the car, cut the engine and turned to her, draping one arm over the steering wheel.

"What else do you remember, Andrea?"

"Nothing." She edged toward the door, felt the handle against her side. "I just know I never led you on. We didn't have a relationship. Why did you try to make me think we did?"

"Oh, we had a relationship, all right. And I'll bet you remember a hell of a lot more about it than you're letting on. Maybe all you need is something to jog your memory."

Before Andrea had time to react, he reached for her, pulled her roughly against him and kissed her, just as he had once before. Andrea shuddered, but not in pleasure. Not with desire. She was frightened and disgusted and she wanted to claw his eyes out. She raked her fingernails down the side of his face, and Paul shoved her away.

"Damn you." He put a hand to the angry red marks on his cheek. He looked furious enough to hit her, and Andrea jerked open the door and tumbled out. She fled up the steps to the front door, pushed it open and ran inside.

Dorian was just coming down the stairs. She paused, her gaze moving over Andrea's shoulder. Her dark eyes narrowed as Paul Bellamy appeared in the doorway. "What are you doing here?" she asked.

"I drove Andrea home from the hospital." Except for the scratches on his face, he might have stepped straight from the pages of *GQ*.

The scratches did not go unnoticed by Dorian. She took in Paul's rigid demeanor, Andrea's disheveled appearance, and a look of cold rage hardened her features.

"Where's Mayela?" Andrea said stiffly. "I'd like to see her."

"She's already left for school," Dorian said. "I drove her there myself."

The thought of Mayela alone in a car with Dorian Andropoulos was unsettling. Andrea said, "Then if you'll excuse me, I'd like to go up to my room."

As Andrea passed her on the stairs, Dorian caught her

arm. "Enjoy it while you can," she said softly. "I have a feeling things are about to change around here."

Andrea shrugged loose from the woman's grip without reply. She had more to worry about than Dorian's cryptic remarks.

At the top of the stairs, Andrea paused, gazing up at the skylight. The window had already been repaired, the glass swept up, the floor cleaned and, she suspected, the tree limb cut up and carted away. Someone had been very efficient this morning. If a crime had been committed, the evidence had all been cleared away. There was nothing left to remind Andrea that she had almost been killed last night.

Nothing except the memory of that face staring down at her from the broken skylight.

Chapter Thirteen

Richard Malone had been shot three times in the chest, point-blank. Overkill, Troy thought, gazing down at the body. The first bullet to the chest had undoubtedly taken him out. The second shot had been insurance. The third, rage. Or revenge.

By the time Troy arrived at the airport parking lot following Lucas's call, the trunk of Richard Malone's Mercedes had been popped and his body, which had been found encased in a plastic bag, had been removed and was lying on the pavement. The CSU team was all over the car, and the medical examiner was busy with the body. A few feet away, a rookie noisily lost his breakfast. Richard Malone had been dead for several days. He wasn't a pretty sight.

"Parking stub on the dash is dated a week ago last Sunday, 8:26 p.m.," Lucas said. "Looks like someone plugged him, bagged him and then drove him here to the airport, where they knew it might take a few days for his car to be found. How does that square with the time Andrea Malone was found that same night?"

"She was brought to the hospital just before midnight," Troy said.

"Plenty of time," Lucas said. "Even if she had to get

a cab back from the airport, she'd still have had time to get dropped off, maybe even change back into the blood-stained dress and then wander around for a few minutes until someone picked her up and took her to the hospital. If she had an accomplice, it would have been even easier.''

An accomplice? An image of the way Paul Bellamy had been looking at Andrea earlier this morning rose in Troy's mind. ''You're assuming she's been faking her amnesia,'' he said. ''You're assuming this was all a carefully calculated plan on Andrea's part.''

''Someone sure as hell calculated it,'' Lucas said grimly. ''You know as well as I do that the spouse is always the number-one suspect.''

Troy stared down at Richard Malone's body. Was it possible Andrea had killed him? Was she capable?

Or, as Lucas had suggested, did she have an accomplice? Someone willing to do anything for her—even commit murder?

Troy didn't want to believe it, and yet he couldn't help remembering the way he'd been taken in by Cassandra Markham.

''I'm sending a team over to the house this morning,'' Lucas said. ''We've got to move fast on this thing. We've already lost over a week. Whatever evidence might have been recovered has probably disappeared by now.''

''Give me a chance to break it to the family first,'' Troy said. ''Malone had a kid.''

Lucas nodded. ''Go ahead. It'll take us a couple of hours to get the warrant.''

TROY WISHED he had been able to be alone with Andrea before he broke the news to the rest of the family, but there wasn't a chance. Dorian and Robert were in the living room when he arrived, and the maid was sent to fetch Andrea. Troy was glad that Mayela was still at school.

Andrea looked a little pale when she appeared in the doorway, and when Troy suggested she take a seat, her face became even more drawn. Dorian and Robert were seated on the sofa, and Andrea chose a chair away from them. She seemed to have a hard time meeting Troy's gaze, as if she somehow knew why he was there.

"There's no easy way to say this," he began. "Richard's body was discovered in the trunk of his car this morning at the airport. He'd been shot. The coroner thinks he's been dead since a week ago Sunday night."

Out of the corner of his eye, Troy witnessed Dorian's and Robert's reactions. Robert grew very still. His eyes closed against the terrible news, while Dorian gasped in shock. She covered her face with her hands and sobbed.

But it was Andrea who captured Troy's attention. She, too, grew very still, but her blue eyes were wide open and they contained not even a shadow of surprise. When she saw that Troy was staring at her, she cast her gaze downward. But it was too late. He'd already seen too much.

Andrea had known, before Troy ever arrived, that Richard Malone was dead.

IT WAS DECIDED that while the forensics team went over every square inch of the Malone house, Connie Perelli, the mother of Mayela's best friend, would pick both girls up at school and take them to her house so that Mayela wouldn't have to witness the police search.

Andrea, looking even paler than she had earlier, told Robert and Dorian that she wanted to be the one to tell

Mayela about Richard, and though Troy saw the contempt glittering in Dorian's dark eyes, she reluctantly agreed. Meanwhile, Robert, looking visibly shaken, accompanied an officer to the morgue to positively identify the body.

By the time Troy and Andrea left the house, Forensics had gathered several dozen packets of evidence, but nothing that looked very promising. Still, Troy thought, you never knew what the lab might be able to come up with.

At the Perelli home, Andrea went upstairs to talk to Mayela alone, and Troy was left downstairs with Mrs. Perelli.

"Call me Connie," she said nervously as she sat on the edge of the sofa, wringing her hands. "That poor child. I can't imagine what this will do to her. First her mother, and now Richard—" She broke off, biting her lip as tears sprang to her eyes.

"How well did you know Richard Malone?" Troy asked.

Connie Perelli dabbed at her eyes. "Not well. He traveled a lot. He was hardly ever home. I'm afraid he was little more than a stranger to Mayela. He never came to any of her school functions. Andrea was always the one who attended the parties and sat through the plays. Even before Christina died, Andrea and Mayela were inseparable."

"You knew Christina Malone?"

"We were good friends at one time. I can't tell you how shocked I was when she committed suicide."

"I understand she'd been suffering from depression for quite a while before her death."

Connie's eyes filled again. "That's true. But she wasn't always like that. I remember a time when Christina was truly happy, full of life. She was deeply in love with Richard, even though he was so much older than her. I think it really hurt her that he was always so wrapped up in his business. She hated the way he ignored Mayela. She told me once she thought the only reason he agreed to have a child with her in the first place was so she would have something to keep her occupied while he was gone.''

"Is that the reason she became depressed?" Troy probed gently.

"Not altogether. At least I don't think so. I think part of it had to do with her mother.''

"Dorian Andropoulos?"

Connie nodded. "They never got along. Christina used to get so depressed after one of Dorian's visits. She'd mope around in a blue funk for days. Then the depression started lasting longer and longer, until, toward the end, Christina hardly ever left her room, except to see Dr. Bennett.''

"You knew about Dr. Bennett?"

"Christina wasn't ashamed of seeing a therapist. She wanted to get help. She wanted to get better.''

"Do you happen to know how she met Dr. Bennett?"

"I don't remember if she ever said.''

Troy paused. "You say you and Christina Malone were once close. How did you feel about her husband remarrying so soon after her death?"

Connie gave him a stern look. "You've been listening to Dorian, haven't you?"

"I beg your pardon?"

Connie's thin lips tightened in disapproval. "Look, I know she doesn't like Andrea. Dorian's accused her of some pretty rotten things, like marrying Richard for his money and all that, but...I don't think it was that way.''

Troy tried to keep his tone professional when he said, "You think Andrea was in love with Richard Malone? Is that why she married him?"

Connie hesitated. "I don't know Andrea very well. She keeps to herself, and she's certainly never confided in me. I don't know whether she was in love with Richard or not, but I can tell you this. She loves Mayela as if she were her own child. There's a bond between them that, in some ways, is even stronger than the one between a natural mother and daughter. I don't know what would have happened to that poor little thing after Christina died if it hadn't been for Andrea. I don't know what would happen to her now—" Connie broke off on another wave of emotion, and Troy gave her a moment to compose herself.

"Before today, when was the last time you saw Andrea?"

She didn't have to give it much thought. "A week ago Sunday night. Mayela spent the night with Lauren, and Andrea drove over to bring Mayela a little teddy bear she always sleeps with. She said she knew Mayela would have a hard time falling asleep without it, but the real reason she came was because of the bad weather. Mayela's scared of storms, I mean really terrified, and Andrea wanted to make sure she was all right."

"How long did she stay here that night?"

"Not long. She left before seven. She said she had to see someone."

"Did she say who it was?"

"No. But if it hadn't been something pretty important, I know she would never have left Mayela."

The picture Connie Perelli painted of Andrea was very different from the way Dorian Andropoulos had portrayed her. Troy wondered if he could trust either view.

"How did she take it?"

"It was so strange," Andrea said. They were sitting alone in the Perelli living room. "She didn't cry, she didn't even act that surprised. She just sat there looking so sad."

Not unlike Andrea's own reaction, Troy thought. He studied her as she sat with her head against the back of the sofa, her eyes closed, her fingertips massaging her temples. She looked indescribably weary, and the tiny lines around her eyes and mouth were more pronounced than he had ever seen them.

He stared at her and thought, *I don't know you. I may be falling in love with you, but I don't really know you.*

He wondered if he ever would.

TROY LEFT ANDREA at the Perelli home, then drove over to Dr. Bennett's house a few blocks from River Oaks. A housekeeper answered the door and ushered Troy inside. She glanced at his badge and ID. "Do you have an appointment?"

"No. But I have some information I think Dr. Bennett would be interested in hearing. Is she in?"

"I'll tell her you're here."

A few minutes later, the housekeeper returned and showed Troy to Dr. Bennett's office. "She'll be down in a moment. In the meantime, make yourself comfortable. Please excuse the paint fumes," she said. "We're in the middle of redecorating."

"So I see." Troy glanced around at the sheet-draped furniture.

"We had a little accident a few nights ago," she told him. "A water pipe broke in the wall. Dr. Bennett's office was completely flooded. I've never seen such a mess."

"Sergeant Stoner?" Dr. Bennett walked into the room, looking very much the way Troy remembered her. She was dressed in a conservative brown suit, a cream-colored blouse and low-heeled shoes. Her dark hair was pulled back from her face, and her complexion was covered with heavy makeup. She took a seat behind her desk and dismissed the housekeeper with a curt nod.

"You're here about Richard, no doubt."

Troy looked at her in surprise. "You've heard?"

"It's all over the news, Sergeant. Apparently someone from your office leaked the story to the press right after the body was found."

Figures. "I guess you're wondering why I'm here."

She smiled slightly. "Not really. Both of Richard's wives were patients of mine. One of them still is. I'm not surprised you'd want to talk to me, although I must remind you of the confidentiality agreement between doctor and patient."

"Christina Malone is dead," Troy said. "You're no longer bound by that agreement."

"Maybe not legally, but I still have a moral obligation to protect my patient."

"And I have an obligation to find out who killed Richard Malone," Troy said grimly. "I need to know why Christina Malone was seeing you."

One dark brow rose. "I don't see how knowing that would help you."

"She committed suicide six months ago, and now her husband has been murdered. There may not be a connection between those two deaths, but then again, there just might be. And if there is a link, you could be the one person who can help me find it. Now, if I have to get a court order to get into your files, I'll do it. But wouldn't it be easier if you just told me what I need to know?''

Dr. Bennett paused to consider what he'd said. Then she nodded briefly. ''All right. Christina Malone came to me because she was experiencing severe depression. Her marriage was in deep trouble.''

''Why?''

Again Dr. Bennett paused. ''She believed her husband was having an affair. With Andrea Evans.''

Troy felt as if someone had punched him in the gut. The wind left his lungs with a painful swoosh, and it was a struggle to keep his voice from giving away his shock. ''That didn't create a conflict of interest for you?''

''Not at all. Andrea didn't come to me for help until after Christina was dead.''

''Did she…tell you anything that bore out Christina's fears?''

''I'm afraid I can't discuss Andrea with you, Sergeant. She's still my patient.''

''How did you meet Christina Malone? Did someone refer her to you?''

''Actually we met quite by accident. We shared an affinity for primitive art, and we met at a gallery last summer. We got to talking, and she asked if she could come to see me professionally.''

''Is that the usual way your patients find you?''

Annoyance flickered in her blue eyes. ''I don't solicit, if that's what you're inferring. I knew something was troubling Christina. I wanted to help her.''

''Did you prescribe amphetamines for her depression?''

''I did not. The police asked me that question at the

time of her suicide. I don't believe in drug therapy, Ser
geant.''

''You didn't prescribe sleeping pills for Andrea?''

''Of course not. Why would you ask?''

''The night she was brought in to the hospital, the lab
found trace amounts of a drug used in sleeping pills in
her blood.''

Dr. Bennett shook her head. ''I'm not surprised. An
drea has a great deal of trouble sleeping. She suffer
from nightmares.''

''Is that why she came to see you?''

A look of alarm flared in her eyes, as if she'd said
more than she intended. Then she said carefully, ''The
nightmares brought her to me, but she had...other con
cerns she wanted to talk about, things that were triggered
by Christina's death.''

''Such as?''

Dr. Bennett swiveled in her chair and stared out the
window for a long moment, as if debating with her own
conscience. Finally she sighed and turned back to Troy
''When Andrea first came to see me, she couldn't recall
much about her past before the age of ten. It was as if
her childhood was a complete blank, with occasional
flashes of memory that were as troubling to her as they
were confusing.''

''What do you mean?''

''Andrea was convinced she'd done something wrong
as a child. That's why she was sent to live with an aunt
who didn't love her. That was her punishment.''

''For what?''

''We were just getting to that.''

''How?''

''By using regressive hypnosis. Little by little, we
were putting together the pieces of Andrea's past, and

then this happened. Her current amnesia is a severe set-back.''

"When's the last time you spoke with her?''

"A few days ago. At your sister's house.''

"I mean before that.''

"A week or two.''

"You didn't see her a week ago last Sunday night?''
She looked surprised. "No.''

"She was going to see someone after seven o'clock in the evening. It was a matter of importance.''

"It wasn't me, Sergeant. I rarely keep weekend hours, only in cases of extreme emergency. Andrea and I always met on weekday afternoons. She wanted to be finished with our sessions before school let out, so she could pick up Mayela.''

"Your sessions concerned only her past?''

Silence.

"She didn't discuss her marriage?'' Troy persisted. "She didn't talk about her husband?''

Dr. Bennett leaned back in her chair and eyed him coolly. "I've already said much more than I should have, Sergeant.''

"I understand. And I appreciate your cooperation. Just tell me one more thing,'' Troy said. "Do you really believe Andrea has amnesia?''

Dr. Bennett considered the question for a long, tense moment. Troy felt as if he were sitting on the edge of his seat, waiting for her answer. He forced himself to relax and observe Dr. Bennett as dispassionately as she studied him.

She smiled, as if reading his thoughts. Or more likely, his body language. "You've been with her more than I have in the past few days, Sergeant Stoner. What do you think?''

Just like a shrink to turn his own question back around to him. Troy got up and walked over to the window. "My sister showed me the book you two were talking about the other day."

"Did she?"

Troy turned to face her. "She told me about your condition. The agoraphobia. At the time you wrote *Dark Journey,* you'd been confined to your house for more than ten years. Is that right?"

She gave him a wry look. "I don't see what that has to do with your case."

"It doesn't. I'm just curious. How did you get over something like that?"

"Are you familiar with the term 'flooding,' Sergeant Stoner?"

"You aren't talking about what happened to your office, I take it."

"In psychiatric terms, flooding is an extreme method of dealing with fear. A patient is forced to confront the thing he's afraid of most." She toyed with a pencil on her desk. "When I was confined to my home, my worst fear was that I would someday be forced to face my attackers again, that if I were to leave the protection of my home, they would be lying in wait for me and they would kill me. If not them, then someone else. The outside world became a very dark and dangerous place for me, a world in which I simply could not cope."

"How did you continue your profession?" Troy asked.

"My office was in my home, much like this," she said. "I saw very few patients back then, and only referrals. I wrote books and papers, and concentrated almost solely on my research into behavioral modification. I had a housekeeper, a wonderful woman, who did everything for me. She was my companion, my friend and my buffer against the outside world. I don't know what I would have done without her, because at the time, I was quite certain I would never again leave my home.''

''What happened?''

''One night a fire erupted in the house. The flames were everywhere, the smoke so thick I could hardly breathe. Even then, with my life hanging by a thread, and the firefighters trying to battle their way inside to save me, I didn't think I could make myself crawl toward their voices. My fear was that great. But in the end, my instinct for survival won out, and I was forced to confront my fear.''

''The housekeeper you talked about,'' Troy said. ''Was she the same woman I met earlier?''

Dr. Bennett glanced away. A look of genuine distress crossed her features. ''No. Marlena wasn't as lucky as me. She died in the fire. In fact, the police said the blaze started in her room. She fell asleep while smoking a cigarette. Ironic, isn't it, that she should be the one to be trapped inside that house instead of me?''

Chapter Fourteen

The autopsy was performed on Richard Malone immediately. Troy met with the coroner, Dr. Nguyen, the next morning to determine the exact cause of death—a technicality in this case, considering the extent of damage wrought by the bullets.

Dr. Nguyen launched into the medical specifics with gusto before Troy held up his hand to stop him. "Just tell me if you found anything unusual in the autopsy. Anything I should be aware of."

"We did find something interesting," Dr. Nguyen said. "Richard Malone's death resulted from the gunshot wounds he sustained to the heart, no question. But if the killer had waited, the victim would have been dead in six months anyway."

Troy glanced up. "Meaning?"

"Richard Malone was dying of liver cancer."

"DID YOU KNOW Richard was dying?"

Dorian stared at Troy in shock. *"What?"*

"Richard was dying of liver cancer. The coroner said he would probably have been dead within six months. Did either of you know?"

Dorian visibly paled. She sat down heavily on the sofa, her eyes dark with disbelief. "That isn't possible."

"It's true," Troy said. He turned to Robert Malone, who had poured himself a stiff drink at the bar.

Robert's hand trembled as he lifted the glass to his lips. "Richard never said a word to me." His voice was raspy with shock. "I had no idea. Perhaps he didn't know."

"He knew," Troy said. "His personal physician corroborated the coroner's report, as did his lawyer."

"Lawyer?" Dorian's gaze suddenly became more alert, as did Robert's. The two of them reminded Troy of vultures, picking at the remains.

"He met with his lawyer shortly after he and Andrea married. According to his attorney, Richard was getting everything in order in preparation for his death. He made Andrea his daughter's legal guardian, and he cleared the way for her to eventually adopt Mayela."

If possible, Dorian grew even paler, but her dark eyes flashed with rage. She jumped to her feet, her long red nails curled into claws. "That's ridiculous. I'm the child's grandmother."

"And I'm her uncle," Robert said. "But I agree with Richard. Mayela belongs with Andrea."

"Over my dead body," said Dorian. "That woman isn't fit to raise a child, certainly not my granddaughter. She may have schemed her way into this house and into Richard's affections, but she doesn't fool me. I know how to deal with her kind."

"Watch yourself," Robert advised.

Dorian ignored him. She pointed a finger at Troy. "Andrea Evans murdered Richard. You know it as well as I do. Why haven't you arrested her?"

"This is an ongoing investigation," Troy said.

"We're still gathering evidence. We have more than one suspect, Mrs. Andropoulos."

"You're protecting her," Dorian accused. "I've seen the way you look at her. You've fallen for her just like every other man who comes into contact with her. You all make me sick."

"Dorian," Robert warned.

She turned on him. "Don't 'Dorian' me. You're no better than the rest of them. I've seen you lust after her, too. Your own brother's wife. But she didn't give you the time of day, did she? And do you know why? Because you're not Richard. You're nothing but a washed-up drunk who'd gamble away his own mother's last cent if you got the chance."

Robert didn't say anything to that. He lifted his glass and took a long drink, but Troy could see that his hands were still shaking badly, and his skin tone had deepened to a dull red. Dorian had humiliated and angered him, but Troy suspected she'd also hit a little too close to the truth.

A movement out of the corner of his eye caught Troy's attention, and he turned. Andrea stood in the foyer, just beyond the doorway. She made no move to join them, but he could tell from her expression that she'd heard everything they'd said, including Dorian's accusations.

Without a word, she turned and walked back up the stairs.

ANDREA STOOD on the balcony off Richard's room and watched Troy drive away. She hadn't spoken to him downstairs because she hadn't known what to say. How to defend herself against Dorian's accusations. How to respond to the knowledge that Richard had been dying of cancer before he was murdered.

A chill of unease crept over her. Had she known? She must have, because Troy said that Richard had made her Mayela's legal guardian, that he'd taken steps for her to adopt the little girl. Andrea had to have known, but who else had Richard told?

Suddenly she remembered something Mayela had said the first night Andrea had been back. *Daddy said you'd always be here to take care of me. Even when he's not.*

Mayela had known, too. That must have been part of Richard's preparations. He hadn't wanted her to experience the same kind of shock she'd gone through when her mother had died so suddenly. He'd wanted to make it as easy for his daughter as possible, even going so far as to finding her a mother.

Andrea's heart tripped inside her. If she had known that Richard was dying, didn't that let her off the hook as a suspect? Why would she kill him if he was dying? If she knew she would eventually get what she wanted?

If you didn't kill him, how did you know he was dead before the police found him? a little voice in the back of her mind asked. *Why were you covered in blood that night?*

THE FUNERAL on Saturday morning was a terrible ordeal. Andrea sat listening to Richard's eulogy, holding tightly to Mayela's little hand and wondering what the child must be feeling. She seemed so resolved on the outside, so stoic. But the world-weary expression in the little girl's eyes broke Andrea's heart. She was all Mayela had left, and Andrea's own resolve strengthened. She would do whatever she had to do to protect her.

But for how long? Dorian was the child's grandmother. Would she have more rights than Andrea? Even though Richard had made her the legal guardian, would a court uphold his wishes? Or would Dorian, the child's next of kin, be awarded custody?

Two days later, on Monday morning, Andrea sat in the lawyer's office with the same fears and waited for the reading of the will. Across the room, Dorian, dressed in widow's black, stared at Andrea through the mesh veil of her hat. The woman's hostility was almost a tangible thing, and Andrea shivered, realizing again how very much Dorian hated her.

Robert sat next to Dorian, but the two were hardly allied. They hadn't spoken since Robert had come into the room a few minutes ago and taken his seat. He stared straight ahead, his hands gripping the arms of his chair. Today he wasn't even pretending to be relaxed. He was as tense as Dorian, and not once had he bothered to glance in Andrea's direction.

Paul Bellamy arrived late and sat behind Andrea. He made no move to touch her or to even speak to her, but Andrea could feel his eyes on her. The skin at the back of her neck crawled, and it was all she could do not to get up and leave. She didn't belong here. What was she doing with these people?

Finally the lawyer walked into the room, took his seat behind his desk and, with a flourish, took out Richard's will. His gaze swept the room, making them all wait breathlessly. Then his eyes lit on Andrea, and he said, "Mrs. Malone, Richard has appointed you as executrix of his estate and as such, you will have full control of all assets, including the partnership in Malone International, until the child reaches the age of twenty-one."

Andrea sat stunned. She'd hoped and prayed that Mayela would be left in her care, but to be put in charge of Mayela's fortune? What did Andrea know about managing an estate that large? What did she know about anything? A few short days ago, she hadn't even known her own name.

The lawyer must have sensed her distress. "Rest assured, Mrs. Malone, that this law firm will help you in any way we can. Perhaps you'd like to come back in a day or two when things have settled a bit and we can talk further."

Andrea nodded, but she still felt numb as she listened to the rest of the will. Richard's legacy was quite simple. Mayela inherited almost everything—the cash, the realestate holdings, the stocks and bonds and Richard's partnership in Malone International.

Dorian got nothing.

Robert got nothing.

Paul Bellamy got nothing.

"And to my wife, Andrea Evans Malone, I bequeath the sum of ten million dollars."

Andrea gasped, the only sound made in the otherwise tomblike office. Ten million! Surely there must be some mistake. She and Richard had only been married a few weeks. Why would he leave her an amount so large? Why would he leave her anything, for that matter? They hadn't really been husband and wife, had they? They'd slept in separate beds.

Why had he made her his daughter's legal guardian and the executrix of his estate? Why had he had so much faith in her?

And why had he been killed?

A dark premonition descended over Andrea. Richard's bequest made her look even more guilty. No one else had benefited from his death. No one except Andrea.

Dorian jumped to her feet. Fury contorted her face

into an ugly mask. Her nostrils flared, her lips curled and Andrea thought the woman looked almost bestial in the cruel overhead lighting.

"You won't get away with this," she said. "I'll fight you for Mayela. There isn't a court in this country that would allow my granddaughter to be raised by a murderess. I'll make sure of that."

She grabbed up her purse and stalked out of the room. Paul Bellamy followed close behind, and Andrea wondered what strategy the two of them might be cooking up.

The lawyer rose, too, and picked up his briefcase. "If you'll excuse me, I'm due in another meeting. Call me in a day or two," he said to Andrea.

For an awkward moment, Andrea and Robert were left alone in the office. She wondered what he was thinking. There was an odd glint in his eyes that disturbed her. Then he shrugged, and the carefree Robert surfaced once again. "Congratulations."

An odd thing to say, Andrea thought, in light of his brother's death.

Robert shook his head. "I never thought he'd cut me out like that. He always threatened to, but I never thought he'd do it. When push came to shove, he was always there to bail me out. I thought surely—" He broke off, shaking his head again.

"What will you do now?" Andrea asked.

Robert shrugged again. "Get a job, I guess. Find an apartment. I'll get by. I always do. Don't worry about me."

"What about Dorian?" Andrea asked.

"What about her?"

"Will she stay in Houston?"

"Oh, she'll stay, all right. She won't give up Mayela

without a fight. Don't make the mistake of underestimating her, Andrea. Dorian can be ruthless. I've seen her in action,'' he said bitterly. ''She won't let anything stand in her way. Not you. Not even Mayela.''

Andrea felt chilled all of a sudden. ''Are you saying she's dangerous?''

''I'm saying she'll do whatever it takes to get what she wants. I wouldn't like to be in your shoes right now,'' he said cryptically before he turned and walked out of the room.

Andrea stood in the empty office, feeling so completely alone. The weight of her responsibility pressed down on her. She was thankful that Mayela would remain with her, at least for now, but the money...all that money was an invitation to trouble.

Maybe even to murder, she thought with a shiver.

She was suddenly glad that Mayela had gone to spend the night with Lauren Perelli and her family. It would give Andrea a chance to make other living arrangements for them, because one thing was certain. She didn't want Mayela going home to that mansion. Not while Dorian and Robert were still there.

In spite of his warning about Dorian, Andrea didn't trust Robert, either. She'd seen the greed and desperation in his eyes today when he learned he'd been cut from Richard's will. How far would *he* be willing to go to get his hands on his brother's money?

A few minutes later, Andrea stepped outside the building into the blinding glare of the sun. She put up a hand to shade her eyes just as someone grabbed her arm and spun her around. Andrea gasped when she saw Paul Bellamy's dark expression. No wonder he'd left the lawyer's office behind Dorian. He'd been lying in wait outside.

"We have to talk." He clutched her arms, his expression more urgent than angry.

"What about?"

"You know damn well what about. The partnership should be mine. I've worked my ass off for that company. If it wasn't for me, Malone International would have gone down the toilet years ago while Richard blithely conducted his little survival missions and executive-training courses. I'm the one who made that company what it is today. Malone International is mine, and neither you nor anyone else is going to take it away from me."

The desperate look in his eyes frightened Andrea. She was glad they were standing on a public street, in plain view of passersby.

"I don't know anything about running a company," she said, trying to appease him for the moment. "There's no reason why things have to change at Malone International. You'll still be in charge."

"I'm glad you're being so reasonable." His expression altered subtly. His gaze deepened and dropped to her lips. "I like it when you cooperate."

Andrea shuddered, hating his touch. Hating the fact that she may have once invited that touch. She lifted both hands to shove him away when she glimpsed a familiar face on the street.

Troy!

Troy looking at her in disgust. Troy seeing her in Paul Bellamy's arms and thinking the worst.

Troy turning and walking away.

TROY HADN'T BEEN ABLE to get the image of Andrea and Paul Bellamy out of his head all day. He stood on the balcony of his apartment and sipped his drink as he watched twilight deepen to darkness. He couldn't help remembering the possessive way Bellamy had acted toward Andrea that day in her hospital room, when he said he'd come to take her home. Troy had sensed something was going on then, but he'd told himself it was probably nothing more than his imagination. His own possessive feelings toward Andrea kicking in.

After today, he wasn't so sure. They'd been standing so close, she and Bellamy. Right out there on the street. And Bellamy had been touching her.

Troy's grip tightened on his glass. He'd hated seeing Andrea like that. He couldn't stand the thought of her being with another man. Not Paul Bellamy. Not Richard Malone. Not anyone but him.

You're a fool, Troy told himself as he refilled his glass from the whiskey bottle he'd carried outside. But that admonishment didn't stop him from wondering what Andrea was doing at that very moment.

Was she alone, like him? Or was she with Paul Bellamy? Were the two of them celebrating tonight? Richard was dead, and Andrea now controlled his millions. For all Troy knew, this had been her game plan all along. Hers and Bellamy's. If they'd been having an affair, that gave them both the perfect motive for murder.

But even as Troy devised the scenario in his head, there was one thing he couldn't quite resolve. The way Andrea felt about Mayela. The way she was so protective toward the little girl.

Could that be an act, too?

Maybe, but he was hard-pressed to believe anyone could be that good an actress. It had been his experience that kids weren't easily taken in. If Andrea was putting on an act, if she wasn't genuinely fond of Mayela, the kid would know it. But Mayela seemed to return her affection wholeheartedly. She obviously loved Andrea as much as...

He did.

Damn. Falling in love with a suspect was never a good idea.

He finished off the last of the whiskey in his glass and poured himself another drink. The doorbell rang, and Troy considered ignoring it. He didn't feel much like company tonight, but then he figured, what the hell? If he stayed out here all night, he'd just get drunk, and then he'd have to drag himself out of bed in the morning and feel like crap for the rest of the day. Wasn't worth it.

But when he drew back the door and saw who stood on the other side, he thought again how a woman like her was nothing but trouble for a man like him.

Andrea saw the drink in his hand and looked at him uncertainly. "Am I...interrupting something?"

"No. Come on in." He stood back while she entered, then closed the door behind her. "Would you like a drink?"

"No, thanks. I don't drink."

"A little something else you remembered?" He knew his tone sounded accusing, but damn it, he couldn't help it. Who did she think she was, coming over here like this, looking all soft and feminine and vulnerable? He wondered if she had an idea the picture she made standing in his living room, wearing a black knit dress and pearls and dark stockings that made him want to—

He shook his head, as if to clear away the sudden image of Andrea in black satin. Andrea in his bed.

The image wouldn't fade. Troy wondered if he'd had more to drink than he realized. If his control had been weakened by the whiskey.

Or by the woman.

Lifting his glass, he took another drink, studying her over the rim. He couldn't figure out how she'd found his apartment, but at the moment, the effort to ask her was just too great. He was tired of asking Andrea questions. Tired of never getting the answers he needed. With Andrea, he felt as if he were always walking a tightrope in fog. He couldn't see where he was going, and one false step could be his downfall.

"I guess you know about the will," she said finally, when the silence had stretched on for too long.

"I'm conducting a murder investigation. It's my business to know."

She nodded. Her gaze dropped to the drink in his hand, and for a moment, she seemed fascinated by the swirling amber liquid inside. Then she said softly, "I didn't kill Richard."

"I never said you did."

"But you must be thinking it. All that money—" She broke off and walked to the open balcony doors to stare into the darkness. "I didn't kill him. I couldn't have. I'm not that kind of person...am I?" She turned to face him then, and her eyes looked haunted, desperate. Troy thought he saw a glimmer of fear in those crystalline depths. Or was that wishful thinking on his part? He'd never been able to tell with Andrea.

He set his drink aside and slowly crossed the room toward her. But he didn't dare touch her. "Why did you come here tonight?"

She wrapped her arms around herself. "I don't know. I needed to see you."

"Why?"

"You're the only person I can talk to." She took a deep, shaky breath. "There're so many things I don't know about myself. I don't know who I really am, or what I might have done in my past. I have these horrible nightmares. I see blood all over my hands. Oh, God—" She broke off and closed her eyes, as if overcome with emotion. A tear trickled down her cheek, and it was all Troy could do not to reach for her and wipe it away.

She opened her eyes and gazed up at him, her lashes starred with tears. "I know I don't have any right to ask you this, but…will you hold me? Just for a little while. I'm so scared, Troy."

The last was said on a whisper, and Troy felt something slipping away inside him, the last vestiges of his control. He wondered why he didn't feel more concerned. Why he wasn't trying to fight his feelings for her. Maybe it was too late for that anyway. Maybe it had been too late the moment he'd first laid eyes on her.

He took her hand and pulled her into his arms.

But if he'd meant to comfort her, that notion fled the moment he touched her. He tunneled his fingers into her hair and tilted her head back, so that for a split second, they were gazing deeply into one another's eyes.

And then he kissed her.

Andrea's lips trembled beneath his, then opened like a flower, inviting him to taste the sweetness inside. Troy groaned, wishing he'd never met this woman. Wishing he'd known her all his life. He was a cop, she was a suspect and they were both headed for trouble. But nothing could stop the heat between them. Not his job. Not her past. Not even the uncertainty of their future.

She pressed her body close to his, and passion exploded between them. Troy didn't think he could ever get enough of her. She was like no woman he'd ever known, and the desire roaring through him was like nothing he'd ever experienced. He wanted her. All of her. Now. And forever.

Her fingers were busy with the buttons on his shirt. Impatient, Troy ripped them loose, tossed the shirt aside, then reached for her once more. They kissed, again and again, breaking apart only when he found her zipper and lowered it. Her dress slipped to the floor. She was wearing stockings with black lace tops, and Troy's heart threatened to beat its way out of his chest.

A little voice in the back of his mind whispered to him this might be a planned seduction. Andrea might have come here to lure him more deeply into her web.

He ignored that voice.

He ignored his conscience and good sense.

He let her perfume, something dark and sultry, wrap around him like a silken scarf, drawing him more and more deeply into the fantasy. Slowly, their gazes clinging, he knelt and lowered her stockings from her sleek legs. She trembled when his fingers skimmed her thighs, touched her softly. Her head fell back, and she whispered his name on a sigh.

Troy stood, then lifted her into his arms and carried her into the bedroom. Moonlight silvered her hair as she lay atop the sheets, watching him undress. Then she held out her arms for him, and he moved over her, staring down at her for a long, breathless moment.

"Is this wrong?" she whispered, her eyes glowing with subtle mystery. Troy thought he could easily drown in those eyes. He could easily lose himself in her essence.

"It's the only thing in this whole damn mess that seems right," he muttered. And then he lowered his head and kissed her. Kissed her until nothing else mattered except the way she came to him so eagerly. The way she clung to him so desperately.

The way she shuddered in ecstasy when he took her.

ANDREA SIGHED. Curled on her side, her head resting on Troy's chest, she could hear the deep, even rhythm of his heart as it slowed back to normal. He had one arm around her, and his other arm was sprawled across the bed. His eyes were closed, and he looked replete. Satisfied. But not quite as relaxed as he might have been, Andrea thought. He still had doubts about her. Even after what they'd shared. Even after she'd given everything to him. He still had doubts.

What else could she do to convince him of her innocence?

Try the truth, the little voice in the back of her mind suggested.

She sighed again, and Troy stirred. His arm tightened around her. "What are you thinking?"

"I was just thinking that...I've never felt this way before. I don't know how I know that, but..." She turned to rest her chin lightly on his chest, gazing up at him. "I do know it."

Troy smiled, but his eyes were shadowed. "Why is it I want to believe you so badly?"

"You do?"

The shadow in his eyes deepened. "You do realize what I've done, don't you? What we've done?"

She lifted her head to stare down at him. "What do you mean?"

He sat up in bed, shifting ever so slightly away from her. Andrea felt chilled by his action.

"When you came here tonight...when I let you stay.

I compromised the investigation, Andrea. My entire career could be on the line because of what we've done.''

Andrea drew the sheet around her, bereft. "Are you sorry we made love?"

His eyes softened a little. He reached for her hand. "No. I'm not sorry. I've never felt this way, either. What happened between us was…incredible. But I have to know…I have to make sure you're being completely honest with me.''

"I am." But she couldn't quite meet his eyes.

He took her chin, gently forcing her to look at him. "You told my mother that you remembered you were named after your grandmother, but you didn't tell me. You told my sister about the aunt who raised you, but you didn't tell me. I can't help wondering what else you might have remembered that you haven't told me.''

After everything they'd shared tonight, the closeness they'd experienced, Andrea wanted more than anything to open up to him, to tell him about the dreams and the memories she'd been having. She wanted to tell him about Richard, how she had known, somehow, that he was dead before Troy had come to the house that day.

And she might have been able to tell him once, but not now. Not after the reading of Richard's will. Ten million dollars was a lot of money. A fortune. People had killed for a lot less. Andrea had to be the police's chief suspect. *Troy's* chief suspect.

If he found out she'd been withholding the truth from him, he'd have no reason to believe her about anything. It wouldn't matter that she knew in her heart she was innocent, because everything else, even her own memories, pointed to her guilt. And even though Troy might have compromised the investigation tonight, he was still a cop. He'd still have to do the right thing. If he thought her guilty of murder, he'd have to arrest her. Take her away, and there would be no one to protect Mayela.

"I've laid everything on the line for you, Andrea. All I'm asking is that you do the same," he said softly.

Andrea had never seen eyes so dark and deep. So very compelling. But God help her, she still couldn't tell him. Not even after tonight.

Not even knowing what it would cost her when he found out the truth.

Chapter Fifteen

The phone awakened Troy the next morning. He woke up groggy, his head filled with cobwebs, his memories of last evening hazy. He'd dreamed about Andrea, about the two of them in his bed—

The phone screamed again, peeling away the last layers of sleep. As he reached to answer it, Troy's memory sharpened and he realized it hadn't been a dream after all. Andrea really had been there. They'd made love.

But where was she now? He gazed at the empty side of the bed as he brought the receiver to his ear. "Hello?"

"Troy, it's Leanne."

"Leanne. Don't tell me you're already at the station." He propped himself on his elbows and squinted at the clock. It was only a little after five. Where the hell was Andrea?

"Don't tell me you're still lollygagging in bed while I'm down here working my butt off," Leanne snapped. "I've got some information for you."

"About the Malone case? What'd you find out?"

"I think you better get down here and see for yourself."

"I'll be there in twenty." Troy hung up and headed

for the shower, but then detoured into the living room and kitchen, looking for Andrea. The path of clothing they'd left from the living room to the bedroom was gone. Even Troy's clothes had been picked up, and he found everything folded neatly on a chair.

Andrea had run out on him.

"WHAT'VE YOU GOT, LEANNE?"

She looked up and smiled smugly as Troy approached her desk. "I hardly know where to begin."

"That sounds promising." He pulled up a chair and sat down.

Leanne retrieved a folder from her desk and opened it, thumbing through the pages until she found the one she wanted. "Let's start with the mother-in-law. Dorian Andropoulos, formerly Dorian Kouriakis. She's Greek American, born in the Bronx, but she moved to Athens several years ago. Worked for the American embassy for a while, then married a shipping tycoon named Dimitri Andropoulos, an Onassis type, who even had a daughter named Christina."

"Wait a minute," Troy said. "You mean *he* had a daughter named Christina? Dorian wasn't her mother?"

"Stepmother. Christina was twelve years old when Dorian and Dimitri married. He died in some sort of freak boating accident two years later. The daughter inherited the fortune, but Dorian controlled the money until Christina turned twenty-one. Dorian moved back to the States almost immediately, and Christina was shipped off to boarding school in Switzerland until she was eighteen, at which time she met and married Richard Malone."

She handed the folder to Troy, and he glanced through the contents with interest.

"Another little tidbit you might find interesting," Leanne said. "While Christina was in boarding school, Dorian managed to go through quite a bit of her step-daughter's inheritance. She'd already hooked herself a rich fiancé by the time Christina found out about the money. Only problem was, the rich fiancé married the daughter, and Dorian was left out in the cold."

"Dorian was engaged to Richard Malone before he married Christina?"

"Bet that didn't sit too well with Dorian." Leanne grinned. She swiveled her chair and picked up another file. "Next on your list was Robert Malone. The brother."

"I can hardly wait to hear this," Troy said, amazed at the amount of information Leanne had managed to dig up. It would have taken him weeks to assemble this much data.

"Likes to gamble," Leanne said. "Vegas, the Bahamas, and now the new casinos over in Mississippi and Louisiana. Rumor has it, he's in pretty heavy with some loan sharks."

"Somehow that doesn't surprise me," Troy said, but it would explain why Robert might be feeling a little desperate, now that he'd been cut out of his brother's will.

Another thought occurred to Troy. If Dorian Andropoulos had been Christina Malone's stepmother, that meant Robert Malone was Mayela's next of kin. In a court battle for custody of the heiress, a blood relative might be given special consideration. Troy wondered if this possibility had occurred to Robert Malone, as well. Somehow he thought it probably had.

"Paul Bellamy," Leanne said. "Partner and CFO of Malone International. One of the employees over there leaked some information to a reporter friend of mine at the *Herald,* who was kind enough to pass the info along to me. It seems Richard started an in-house investigation a few months ago. He suspected someone close to the top at M.I. was embezzling pretty heavily from the coffers."

"Paul Bellamy?"

"The employee didn't name names, but as chief financial officer, he'd certainly have control of the purse strings."

And with Richard out of the way, Paul Bellamy would have a chance to cover his tracks before the feds moved in. Interesting. It appeared more than one person had a motive for wanting Richard Malone dead.

"That brings me to the last name on your list. Andrea Malone." Leanne opened the folder and glanced up. "Boy, Stoner. You sure know how to pick 'em, don't you?"

"What do you mean?"

She pushed the file across the desk toward him. "See for yourself."

Troy opened the folder and stared down at a photocopied newspaper picture of a handcuffed woman flanked by two police officers. The caption read Evans Charged In Husband's Brutal Slaying.

The woman in the picture looked exactly like Andrea.

Troy's heart banged against his chest. Sweat trickled down his back, and for a moment, he thought he might actually be sick. Then he glanced at the date of the newspaper article. It was twenty years old. The woman in the photo looked to be in her late twenties, the same age as Andrea now. There was no way that woman could be her.

He glanced up, wondering if Leanne had noticed his

strong reaction. If she did, she let it pass. "That's Andrea's mother. Julia Evans."

"What happened?"

"She went nuts one night and stabbed her husband twenty-seven times. According to the police report, Andrea was in the house at the time. They found her locked in a closet in some sort of trance. She wouldn't talk for days, and when she finally did, she acted as if she didn't remember anything about the murder. But the cops on the scene suspected she'd witnessed it. The closet was right off the room where her father was killed, and it had one of those old-fashioned locks, the ones with the big keys. They figured she could have seen the whole thing through the keyhole. Can you imagine what something like that would do to a seven-year-old kid?"

Troy could imagine, all right. When that kid grew up, she would have horrible nightmares and visions of blood. She would become adept at blocking memories that were too painful to recall.

As a man, Troy's heart went out to her. As a cop, he had to ask himself what else she might do.

"What happened to the mother?" he asked.

"She's been a resident at Oak Haven Hospital, twenty miles north of Houston, for the last twenty years. In case you hadn't figured it out," Leanne said, "Oak Haven is a mental institution for the criminally insane."

ANDREA HADN'T SEEN her mother since that awful night twenty years ago when Andrea's whole world had been shattered into a million pieces. Pieces that wouldn't be put back together for years and years to come.

But last night, after she and Troy had made love, after she'd given him her heart and her soul, she'd remembered. She'd fallen asleep in his arms and dreamed about the keyhole, the one Mayela had told her about. But in her dream, Andrea was the little girl who had been locked away in the dark room. She was the one kneeling at the door, looking through the keyhole, seeing all the blood. She was the one who heard her father's tortured pleas, her mother's demented laughter and her own terrified screams.

Andrea was the one who had looked through that keyhole and now she remembered.

Her mother had killed her father. Stabbed him so many times Andrea had lost count as she'd watched through the keyhole, screaming for her mother to stop, screaming for her father to get up, screaming because she'd been so bad that day, her mother had locked her in the closet and Andrea was powerless to help her father. He'd lain so still and lifeless, his clothes covered in blood.

"I hate you! I want you dead! Dead! Dead! Dead!" her mother had screamed.

Andrea had screamed, too. "You killed my daddy! You killed my daddy!"

Her father had been the only person in the world who had ever loved her. He never locked her in the dark room. He never told her she was bad.

When he died, Andrea had been all alone.

She closed her eyes briefly as the years of loneliness swept over her now. Tears stung behind her lids, and all she could think as she stood in the hallway at Oak Haven Hospital and gazed at her mother through the thick glass panel in the door was *Why? Why did you do it?*

Memories, long suppressed, rushed through Andrea. For twenty years, she had blocked the image of her mother's face. She wouldn't even let herself remember her father. All she knew was what her aunt had told her.

Something terrible had happened to Andrea's parents. Her aunt hadn't wanted to be burdened with an orphaned niece, and so she had looked at Andrea accusingly whenever she'd spoken vaguely of the tragedy. Because of that, Andrea had assumed that whatever had happened to her parents was her fault. The feeling of guilt had been overwhelming at times.

A tear trickled down Andrea's cheek, and she hastily wiped it away with the back of her hand. She hadn't even known until recently that her mother was still alive. Andrea had assumed her dead all these years, even though her aunt had always referred to her as "away." Why else would her mother never have called or written? Now Andrea knew the truth.

"Would you like to go in and see her?" Dr. Albrecht, the physician who ran Oak Haven, asked softly.

Andrea hesitated. "I'm not sure."

"It's perfectly safe, you know. She won't harm you."

"It's not that…I'm not frightened for my safety."

"I understand." He gazed at her kindly through his wire-rimmed glasses. "It's been a long time, hasn't it?"

Andrea's throat tightened. "I didn't even remember her until recently. I didn't remember…what had happened." *What she'd done.*

"I've often wondered about her family." Dr. Albrecht stroked his chin thoughtfully. "In the twenty years she's been here, she's only had one visitor. Her sister came shortly after Julia was admitted."

"Aunt Clarice came here?"

"She explained to me that she had taken in her sister's child, and she wanted to make sure Julia's illness wasn't hereditary."

Andrea swallowed. "What did you tell her?"

The kindly eyes gazed down at her. "I told her it

wasn't. Julia's illness is rare, one in a million. A brain malfunction that causes violent behavior during seizures. Her condition is treatable but not curable. I'm afraid she'll never be able to leave Oak Haven.'' He paused for a moment, letting Andrea digest everything he'd told her. ''Would you like to go in now?''

Andrea nodded. Her heart pounded as Dr. Albrecht opened the door and she followed him inside. Her mother was sitting in a chair by the window, gazing out. She turned and her blue eyes—eyes so like Andrea's— lit with pleasure when she saw the doctor.

''I've been waiting and waiting,'' she said in a breathless voice.

''Sorry I'm late,'' Dr. Albrecht said cheerfully. ''But I've brought you a visitor. This is Andrea.''

Reluctantly Andrea stepped forward, and Julia clapped her hands excitedly. ''She's come to see *me?* Just *me?*''

''Just you,'' Dr. Albrecht said. ''I'm going to leave you two alone now, okay?''

Julia nodded eagerly and got up from her chair. She came toward Andrea, and Andrea had to resist the urge to retreat, to turn and follow Dr. Albrecht outside. Her heart beat so painfully against her chest, she felt dizzy.

''How long can you play?'' Julia asked anxiously.

''I...beg your pardon?''

''Would you like to have a tea party? Everything's ready. See?'' She pointed to a corner of the room where a small wooden table had been set with a toy tea service. ''Come on,'' she urged, reaching for Andrea's hand.

In spite of herself, Andrea drew back. She wasn't yet ready for physical contact with her mother. She wasn't sure she ever would be.

"What's the matter?" Julia pouted. "You don't like tea?"

"I—I love tea," Andrea stammered. "Why don't you pour me a cup?"

While Julia went off to pour the imaginary tea, Andrea gazed around the room. She'd been too nervous to notice before, but now she took in the stuffed animals on the single bed, the collection of dolls on the wooden dresser, the stack of board games in the corner. By all indications, Julia Evans had reverted back to her childhood.

She crossed the room and carefully handed Andrea the plastic cup and saucer, then waited impatiently until Andrea lifted the cup and tasted the "tea."

"It's very good," Andrea said, and Julia beamed. In spite of her illness and her confinement, the years had actually been kind to Andrea's mother. She was still quite lovely, with short, silky blond hair, wide blue eyes and a smooth, ivory complexion. She wore jeans and a bright blue T-shirt that made her seem young and innocent. To look at her, one would never guess what she had done. She was so happy and cheerful, so eager to please. She wasn't at all like the woman Andrea remembered.

This time, when Julia reached for her hand, Andrea let her take it and lead her across the room to the table.

OAK HAVEN HOSPITAL was located north of the city in a little bedroom community that had sprung up around a handful of high-tech firms opting out of the city. Troy had driven up right after he'd spoken with Leanne, and then with Lieutenant Lucas. After he'd met with the lieutenant, Troy knew it was imperative that he talk to Julia Evans's doctor. The similarities between the murder of

Andrea's father and Richard Malone's death couldn't be ignored, no matter how much he might wish to.

Julia Evans had viciously murdered her husband in a fit of uncontrollable rage. But at the time of her arrest, she claimed she could remember nothing of the attack. She went completely off the deep end and had to be confined to a private psychiatric hospital rather than be sent to prison or to the electric chair.

Twenty years later, Andrea's husband had been brutally murdered, and Andrea had been found with blood all over her clothing. Troy had learned this morning that the preliminary DNA testing proved conclusively the blood was Richard's. Yet like her mother, Andrea could remember nothing.

Or could she?

Troy had long suspected that Andrea remembered more than she'd told him. Question was, what was she hiding? And why?

As he pulled into the tree-shaded driveway of the hospital and showed his ID to the guard at the gatehouse, a chill of unease descended over him. Could Andrea be completely faking her amnesia? Had she followed her mother's example to keep from going to prison?

Was she capable of murder?

He thought about the woman he'd held in his arms last night. The woman who had enthralled him with her beauty. Her passion. Her mystery. He'd fallen in love with that woman, but he really didn't know her. He didn't know what she was capable of.

His unease continued to mount as he entered the hospital and spoke with a nurse at the front desk. He told her who he was, what he wanted, and she got on the phone to summon a Dr. Thomas Albrecht. A few moments later, Troy was ushered into Dr. Albrecht's office by a young woman who offered him coffee, which he declined.

Dr. Albrecht stood when Troy entered his office and reached across his desk to shake hands. "How may I help you, Sergeant Stoner?"

"I'm investigating a homicide which, in a roundabout way, involves one of your patients. Julia Evans."

Dr. Albrecht's brows lifted in surprise. "Julia Evans hasn't left these premises in twenty years, Sergeant."

"I realize that. It's her daughter, Andrea Evans Malone, I'm interested in."

"I see," was Dr. Albrecht's only comment, but something indefinable glimmered in his eyes.

"I've studied Julia Evans's file," Troy said. "According to the records, you were appointed by the court to give her a psychiatric evaluation. You testified at the trial that extensive testing had revealed an abnormality in Julia's brain which caused seizures, and that her violent behavior the night she murdered her husband was due to one of those seizures."

"That's correct," Dr. Albrecht said. "Her condition is rare. I've only heard of one other case similar to hers in all the years I've been a doctor." He steepled his fingers under his chin and regarded Troy thoughtfully. "The homicide you spoke of involving Julia's daughter. Can you tell me about it?"

"Her husband, Richard Malone, was murdered a week ago last Sunday night. Andrea was found wandering down a busy street that same night with blood all over her clothing. She didn't know who the blood belonged to or how it had gotten on her dress. She remembered nothing about her life, her past. She couldn't even remember her own name."

Dr. Albrecht's brows rose again. "Fascinating."

"At the time of her arrest, Julia Evans claimed she had amnesia," Troy said.

"Not amnesia," Dr. Albrecht clarified quickly. "Hers was not the normal repression of a traumatic event. Not even hypnosis or sodium Pentothal could help her remember, because the memories simply weren't there. Her brain had stored nothing of the savage attack on her husband."

"Which brings me to the reason why I'm here," Troy said. "Is there a chance Julia Evans's daughter could have inherited her...condition?"

"There is not."

"You sound pretty sure of that."

"I'm absolutely positive. Julia's illness is not hereditary. In fact, I suspect she sustained a severe brain trauma, perhaps as a child, that caused the abnormality, and hence the seizures."

Relief flooded through Troy, though he tried his damnedest not to show it. He was just a cop investigating a homicide. The fact that Andrea was the chief suspect couldn't be allowed to matter.

But, of course, it did. He was only human, after all.

"I think you can see why the similarities in the two cases would concern me," Troy said. "The violent nature of the murders and the loss of memory in both mother and daughter."

"You say Andrea claims to remember nothing of her life?" Dr. Albrecht picked up a pen from his desk and examined the tip, a casual movement, but something in his tone alerted Troy.

"That's what she claims, yes. Do you have reason to believe otherwise?"

Dr. Albrecht hesitated. He set the pen aside and glanced up at Troy. "It might interest you to know, Sergeant Stoner, that I saw Andrea not more than fifteen minutes ago. She came here to see Julia.''

The implication was not lost on Troy. If Andrea was suffering from amnesia, how did she know where to find her mother?

ANDREA LOOKED UP from Julia's tea party and saw Troy watching her through the glass panel in the door. Her heart bumped against her chest, then settled back into its normal rhythm. She supposed she shouldn't be surprised that he had found her here. He was a cop, after all.

She got up from the table, and Julia looked up at her in alarm. ''You aren't leaving, are you? We're having so much fun.''

''I know, but it's time for me to go home.''

''Okay, but will you come back to see me?'' her mother asked hopefully.

Andrea didn't quite know how to respond. She wasn't at all sure she'd be able to come back for another visit. She didn't know what would happen to her when her memory came back in full.

''I'll try,'' she promised.

Dr. Albrecht opened the door, and Andrea stepped out into the hallway. He went inside Julia's room, and Andrea and Troy stood silently for a moment. Then he took her arm and said, ''Let's go outside where we can talk. Dr. Albrecht said there's a garden somewhere around here.''

They found the garden near the rear of the hospital, enclosed in a wrought-iron fence shrouded with wisteria. They entered through the gate and sat down on a stone bench. The shaded garden was like a cool oasis, but the quiet was in direct contrast to the turmoil inside Andrea. Everything had happened so quickly. The memories had come so fast and furious, she'd hardly had time to think about what they all meant.

And now Troy was staring at her with dark, accusing eyes. Eyes that demanded an explanation.

Andrea couldn't look at him. "I guess you know about my mother. About what happened...back then."

"I saw the file this morning."

She closed her eyes as the memories washed over her again. "After...it happened, I was sent to live with my aunt. I couldn't remember anything about my mother and father except that something bad had happened to them. My aunt made it very clear that she didn't want me, and I assumed it was because whatever had happened was my fault. So I didn't try to remember. I found it much easier to forget." Her emotions were still so near the surface, she had to guard against tears. But she wouldn't let herself cry, no matter what. The last thing she wanted from Troy was his pity.

"Your aunt didn't talk to you about it?"

Andrea shook her head. "Aunt Clarice avoided the subject. If I asked her questions, she would always tell me I was better off not knowing, that I was lucky I couldn't remember. All I knew was that...I was different from the other kids. I never fit in because of something that had happened to me. And because I couldn't remember."

A breeze drifted through the garden, chilling Andrea. She wrapped her arms around herself as she gazed at the trickle of water from the fountain. "Last year, after Aunt Clarice died, I decided to move back to Houston. I'm not sure why. It was just something I was...compelled to do. I got a job teaching in a private school, and then a mutual friend introduced me to Christina Malone. She hired me as Mayela's nanny. The pay was excellent, and

I thought it would be nice to live in a real home. I'd never had one...." Andrea trailed off, realizing that maybe she was trying to play on Troy's sympathy after all. A little comfort might not be so bad right now.

She wished he'd put his arms around her and hold her close while she told him the rest of her story. But unfortunately he seemed to have formed an opinion about her already. She hadn't told him the complete truth, and now he didn't trust her. Andrea couldn't blame him, but the distance between them hurt just the same. Especially after last night.

"Go on," Troy prompted

She took a deep breath and released it. "By the time I came to live with the Malones, Christina was already suffering from depression, and Richard was wrapped up in his business. He was rarely home. I knew Mayela needed me, and that made me feel good. Made me feel needed. I was happy for a while, but after Christina's death, I started having dreams...these flashes of memory that were just enough to make me start wondering about my past. I think Christina's death and my bond with Mayela somehow triggered the memories. Mayela was the same age I was when...I lost my father."

"Is that why you started seeing Dr. Bennett?"

Andrea nodded. "She used hypnosis to unleash the memories. I remembered more and more with each session. She's the one who found out where my mother was. That Sunday evening Richard was killed, I remembered something...important. Something I had to see Dr. Bennett about."

"You went to see Dr. Bennett that night?"

Andrea frowned. She'd been going to see Dr. Bennett when she'd left the Perelli home. It had been a matter of urgency. But...why? She couldn't remember. She couldn't even remember if she'd seen Dr. Bennett or not.

"What is it?" Troy asked.

"I don't remember now what I was going to see her about."

"But you do remember seeing her that night?"

Andrea shook her head. "I remember the storm. I remember leaving the house. I remember seeing Mayela. But then...nothing. It's as if everything stopped for me then."

"You remember everything else about your life except for what happened to you that night after you left the Perelli home?"

His tone sounded skeptical. Andrea supposed she could hardly blame him, but it hurt just the same that he didn't believe her.

He paused, then said, "How much of what you've just told me did you remember before you came to my apartment last night?"

"I remembered quite a bit," she admitted softly. "I'd been having these terrible visions...flashes of memory, I guess, but I didn't put it all together until later, until after we...made love."

"That's why you ran out on me?"

She nodded.

He ran a hand through his dark hair. "Damn it, I asked you point-blank last night if there was anything you hadn't told me. I asked you if you were holding out on me. Do you remember?"

Andrea moistened her lips. "I remember."

"You lied to me. You deliberately deceived me."

He turned to her then, his gaze unfathomable. But Andrea knew there were suspicions lurking in those dark depths. She knew there was distrust. She remembered the woman Madison had told her about, the murder suspect who had duped Troy into believing her. He'd been hurt badly by that woman, and now Andrea had done the same thing to him. She wished she could go back and start all over, tell him from the very first about the awful visions and dreams she'd had, and her fears and suspicions about herself. She wished she hadn't been so self-protective.

But it was too late now.

"I didn't tell you because I didn't remember everything," she said desperately. "I was getting all those memories from my past mixed up with what happened to Richard. Everything I remembered…made me look guilty."

"I see." There was an edge to his words that made Andrea flinch. "You used me."

"*No!* At least, not intentionally," she said softly.

He turned to stare at her, and Andrea's heart plummeted at the expression on his face. "Then what would you call it? You knew how I felt about you. You knew if we became involved, if we became lovers, I'd do anything in my power to help you. Are you telling me you didn't count on that all along?"

She shook her head, tears smarting behind her lids. "It wasn't like that."

"But how can I believe you, Andrea? First you tell me you remember nothing, then I find you here with a mother you haven't seen in twenty years. Now you tell me you don't remember what happened the night Richard died, but you remember everything else. Tell me, Andrea. Just what in hell am I suppose to believe?"

She bowed her head. "I wanted to confide in you from the first. You don't know how badly. But I couldn't. It wasn't just me I had to worry about. I had to think of

Mayela. If I'd been arrested, who would have taken care of her?''

"That's another thing," he said grimly. "You were worried about Mayela even before I told you about Richard. You already knew he was dead, didn't you?"

She wanted to deny it, but couldn't. Somehow she *had* known.

"Tell me something, Andrea."

She looked up at him.

"Were you in love with Richard, or is that one of the things you can't remember?"

"I didn't love him," she said quietly. "I hardly knew him. I agreed to marry him so I would stand a better chance of retaining custody of Mayela when he died."

"You're saying your marriage was a business arrangement?"

"More or less. Richard was worried that Dorian might challenge my guardianship after he was gone. He thought if we were married, the courts would look more favorably on me."

"Did he offer you money?"

Andrea wished with all her heart he hadn't had to ask her that question. She wished he would have known her so well, trusted her enough by this time that the answer would have been apparent to him. She closed her eyes against the keen disappointment. "No," she said. "He didn't offer me money, and I wouldn't have taken it if he had. Mayela was my only concern, and she still is. I love her like a daughter. The ten million dollars Richard left me was a complete surprise. I didn't want anything."

"What about Paul Bellamy?"

"What about him?"

"Were you in love with him?"

The breeze picked up, drawing another shiver from Andrea as she thought about Paul Bellamy. "I came to hate him," she said. "When I first went to work for Christina and Richard, Paul became...interested in me. I went out with him a couple of times, but when I tried to break it off, he wouldn't leave me alone. His behavior became...obsessive."

"You have that effect," Troy said, gazing at her.

Something in his eyes made Andrea's heart beat even harder. "You don't believe me. You don't believe anything I've told you. You think I'm lying, don't you?"

"I think your instinct for survival runs pretty damn deep." He scrubbed his face with his hands. "I don't know what to believe anymore."

"Then what are you going to do?" Andrea asked fearfully.

"What I have to do. I'm going to take you back to Houston." He turned to her, his expression grim. "As of this morning, there's a warrant out for your arrest."

"What?" Andrea stared at him in shock. "But I'm innocent!"

He gazed at her as if she were a stranger. "Are you? How can you be so sure of your innocence? I didn't think you could remember what happened the night Richard was killed."

Andrea tried to swallow past the panic that had risen to her throat. "I can't. Not specifics. But I know I'm not a murderer. I couldn't kill anyone. You have to know that, too, Troy. After last night, you have to know I'm not capable of murder."

He shook his head. "After last night, I'm not sure of anything. I've risked everything for you, and you're still not even willing to tell me the truth."

"I have told you the truth," Andrea cried. "Please,

Troy. You have to believe me. I don't remember what happened that night, but I know I didn't kill Richard. If you take me in, what will happen to Mayela?''

There was no warmth in his expression when he looked at her. Nothing that Andrea could hang on to for comfort when he said, ''If I don't take you in, I'm finished. My career is over. But maybe that's what you've wanted all along. A botched investigation. Police misconduct. After last night, you could say I took advantage of you. Seduced you. There's not a jury in the world that would convict you.''

She looked at him in despair. ''You don't believe that of me. You can't believe it.''

''It really doesn't matter what I believe anymore. I'm still a cop. There's a warrant for your arrest, and I have to take you in. I don't have a choice.''

Andrea took a deep, shaky breath. A sudden calmness came over her. She knew what she had to do. ''All right,'' she said, standing. ''I'll go with you. But first, if it's okay...I'd like to say goodbye to my mother. I may not be able to see her again for a very long time.''

TROY STATIONED HIMSELF by the front desk, waiting for Andrea to return. When ten minutes went by, he began to get a little uneasy. He walked down the hall to Julia Evans's room and found Dr. Albrecht coming out.

''Is Andrea still inside with her mother?''

Dr. Albrecht looked at him, perplexed. ''Andrea? She left with you half an hour ago.''

''But she came back in,'' Troy said. ''She wanted to say goodbye to her mother.''

''I've been with Julia ever since the two of you left,'' Dr. Albrecht told him. ''Andrea never came back.''

Chapter Sixteen

Andrea was back in Houston before she realized her escape had been just a little too easy. Troy was a seasoned cop. No way she could have gotten away from him unless he'd allowed her to. He'd deliberately given her enough rope to hang herself, and she'd fallen for it. Why would she run if she wasn't guilty?

Andrea groaned inwardly. If Troy hadn't been convinced of her guilt before, he surely was now. Maybe the best thing to do was just to keep going, she thought. She could go somewhere far away, where her past wouldn't matter. She could pretend the memories hadn't come back, that she was just a normal woman, leading a normal life, and maybe someday she might even meet someone else she could fall in love with.

But there would never be anyone like Troy.

She had hurt him deeply by not being honest with him, by not trusting him enough to confide in him, and the only thing she could do now was to honor what little trust he might still have in her by going to the police and turning herself in.

But first there was something she had to do. Someone she had to see. No matter what anyone else thought, Andrea knew deep down she wasn't a murderer. She hadn't killed Richard, and there was only one way to prove it.

She had to remember.

By the time Andrea pulled up in front of Dr. Bennett's house, dusk had fallen. There was a light on upstairs, but the downstairs was completely dark. Andrea wondered if Dr. Bennett had retired for the evening, but it was only a little after seven. Surely she wouldn't mind being disturbed. Not for something this important.

Andrea climbed the porch steps and rang the bell. Several minutes went by before she finally heard footsteps inside, and then Dr. Bennett opened the door and stared at Andrea in surprise.

"I'm sorry to bother you like this," Andrea said. "But I really need to see you, Dr. Bennett. Something's happened."

Dr. Bennett didn't say a word. She drew back the door, and Andrea stepped inside. The foyer was dark, except for a brief trail of light on the stairs. Andrea shivered, suddenly feeling apprehensive. Had she done the right thing by coming here?

As Dr. Bennett led the way to her office, Andrea tried to get her bearings, remembering the other times she'd been in this house. Dr. Bennett's office was at the end of a long hallway. Several rooms opened off the hallway, but the doors were always kept closed. Andrea had no idea what was behind any of them.

Toward the end of the hallway, her steps slowed. A memory tugged at her. Something about this hallway...

"Andrea?"

Dr. Bennett's voice snapped her out of her reverie. Andrea gazed down the hall, where the doctor stood in the doorway of her office, waiting. "Are you all right?"

Andrea nodded. "Yes, I'm fine."

Dr. Bennett motioned her inside the office. "Shall we get started, then?"

Andrea stepped inside the office and looked around. Something was different. "You've changed it," she said. The walls had been painted, and the hardwood floor was covered with carpet.

Dr. Bennett took a seat behind her desk. "I had to. A water pipe broke and flooded this end of the house. Everything had to be replaced."

Andrea glanced around at the pristine surroundings. She could smell the lingering scent of paint, and for some reason, the scent seemed ominous.

"Why are you here, Andrea?" Dr. Bennett asked softly. She picked up a pencil, ready to take notes.

"I've got my memory back."

The pencil snapped in her fingers. "All of it?"

"Most of it," Andrea said. "I remember about…my mother…what she did to my father. I remember seeing…everything through the keyhole in the dark room. You helped me remember."

"The hypnosis helped you to remember," Dr. Bennett said. "When the police told me you were suffering from amnesia again, I was afraid it would be a severe setback. All of our hard work undone. But you say now that you remember…everything?"

Andrea drew a deep breath. "Everything except the night Richard was murdered."

Something flickered in Dr. Bennett's eyes, and she looked down quickly, as if afraid of alarming her patient. "You came here to be hypnotized. Is that it?"

"Yes." Andrea sat forward in her chair. "It's the only way I can prove I didn't do it."

"Are you sure you want to take that risk?"

"What do you mean?"

Dr. Bennett hesitated. "What if the hypnosis doesn't prove your innocence?"

Andrea swallowed. "You think I'm guilty, too, don't you?"

"I didn't say that."

"You didn't have to. But you're wrong, Dr. Bennett. All of you are wrong. I know I'm not capable of murder."

"Your mother was."

"I'm not my mother."

Dr. Bennett smiled faintly. "All right," she said. "We'll try the hypnosis. Do you remember the trigger?"

Andrea nodded. After several sessions, when she had become adept at going under, Dr. Bennett had given Andrea a posthypnotic suggestion that when spoken, automatically triggered a hypnotic trance.

"Why don't you make yourself comfortable on the sofa?"

Andrea did as she was told. Dr. Bennett pulled up a chair and sat down beside her. "Are you feeling relaxed, Andrea?" Her voice was very soothing.

"Starting to."

"Good. Think about the garden outside your bedroom when you were a child. Feel the sunshine on your face? Can you smell the roses?"

"Yes."

"There's a swing in the garden, isn't there, Andrea?"

"Yes."

"It's blowing in the breeze. Back and forth. Back and forth. A gentle motion. So soothing. Back and forth. Back and forth. Do you see it?"

"Yes."

"Is your kitten in the garden with you, Andrea?"

"Yes." She could see him. A white fur ball that had been a present from her father. Andrea cherished him.

"Do you remember his name?"

"Snowflake."

"Pet him, Andrea. Stroke his soft fur."

Andrea grew very still. She slipped into the trance easily. She wasn't asleep. She wasn't dreaming. She was very much aware of Dr. Bennett's benign voice, but everything else drifted away.

"Andrea," Dr. Bennett said, "I want you to go back to Sunday night, two weeks ago. Do you remember?"

"Yes. I'm alone in the house. Dorian and Robert are both out, thank goodness. Mayela's spending the night with a friend, and Richard's already left for the airport. He said there was something he had to do before he caught his plane."

Andrea frowned as she walked through the huge house in her mind. She was all alone, and a storm was brewing outside. She grew frightened, not for herself but for Mayela.

"What are you doing now, Andrea?"

"I'm driving to the Perelli house," Andrea said. "It's raining so hard, I can hardly see, but Mayela will be frightened by the storm. I have to see her."

"You're at the Perelli home. Is Mayela okay?"

"She's fine," Andrea said, skipping ahead in her mind. She was standing in Lauren Perelli's bedroom, and Mayela was hugging Andrea goodbye, clinging a bit when a clap of thunder sounded outside.

"There's somewhere you have to go, isn't there?" Dr. Bennett said softly.

"I have to see you," Andrea said, as, in her mind, she dashed back out into the rain. Earlier, when she was home alone, she'd remembered something her aunt had once said, something about Andrea's mother. Julia had fallen out of a tree as a child and had suffered a severe head injury. They hadn't expected her to live, but somehow she'd pulled through, and it looked as though she'd made a full recovery until some months later when she had a terrible seizure.

The memory was important because, after her sessions with Dr. Bennett, when Andrea had begun remembering her past, she'd been worried that she might have inherited her mother's insanity. Dr. Bennett had even hinted that the predisposition toward violence was often hereditary. But if her mother's problem was caused by an accident, Andrea had nothing to worry about. Still, she'd wanted to talk to Dr. Bennett about this revelation.

"Where are you now, Andrea?"

"At your front door. I'm wondering why you don't answer my ring. The door is ajar, and I can hear voices inside. Loud voices. I think at first that you must be with a patient, and I start to leave, but then, someone starts shouting. A man. I recognize his voice."

The voices were coming from Dr. Bennett's office. Andrea heard Richard shout her name, and thought at first he was calling to her. Then she realized, as she entered the house, that he was shouting to someone about her.

Andrea started down the hallway toward Dr. Bennett's office. She'd never heard Richard so upset. What in the world was he doing here?

Andrea paused outside the door, wondering if she should go in.

"Christina wasn't sick until she came to see you," Richard said in rage. *"You gave her those pills to make her depressed, and then you gave her an overdose of amphetamines, so that with her history of depression,*

the police wouldn't look twice at the cause of death. You killed her!"

"That's a lie," Dr. Bennett said. "You'll never be able to prove it."

"Won't I?" There was silence, then he said, "I found these in your room, Dorian. I've had the contents analyzed. They're depressants. What were you doing—slipping them into Christina's food every time you came to visit her? She was always so much worse after you left. I've always known you were a cold, greedy bitch, but I never thought you capable of murder. I hope you rot in prison."

Andrea's hand was on the knob. She started to open the door, but before she could, three shots rang out in rapid succession. Bang! Bang! Bang!

Andrea jerked open the door, startled to find Richard facing her. He was clutching his chest. Blood oozed between his fingers, and for a moment, their eyes met and clung. Then he fell forward into her arms.

His weight drove them back against the wall. Andrea fell hard, trapped for a moment by Richard's inert body. She struggled from under him just as Dorian appeared in the doorway. She stared down at Andrea and lifted the gun.

"Don't kill her," Dr. Bennett said behind her. "She's our scapegoat."

Andrea tried to scramble away from them. Her hands and clothes were covered in blood. Richard's blood.

Dr. Bennett grabbed her arm. Andrea fought her, but the woman was stronger than she looked. She said to Dorian, "Help me hold her down."

Dorian did as she was told, taking pleasure in twisting Andrea's arm painfully behind her. Dr. Bennett reached

*for her medical bag. She extracted a syringe, Andrea
screamed and struggled harder.*

"What is that?" Dorian asked.

*"Just a mild sedative. Something to make her more
susceptible to hypnotic suggestion. I'll inject it between
her fingers, so the needle mark can't be detected. In a
few hours, the drug won't even show up in her bloodstream and she won't remember a thing."*

*Andrea felt the jab of the needle between her fingers,
and almost immediately, her body grew limp. She fought
the effects of the drug, but to no avail. Dr. Bennett's
soothing voice was taking her deeper and deeper into
the trance.*

IT WAS NEARLY eight o'clock, and Andrea was nowhere
to be found. Troy sat at his desk at the station, brooding
about the day's events. Should he have brought Andrea
in himself? Had he been wrong in giving her one last
chance to do the right thing?

Whether he'd been wrong or not was beside the point
now. He had to figure out what to do next. If Andrea
had decided to run—and it looked more and more as if
she had—he'd have to go after her. When a person ran,
it was usually because he or she was guilty, and Troy
would be damned before he'd let a murderer go free.

Even one he'd fallen in love with.

He rubbed his eyes wearily, wishing to hell he'd decided to become anything but a cop.

His phone rang and he picked it up, hoping it was
Andrea. "Stoner."

"Troy? It's Leanne. Listen. I just got something in I
think you need to see." She paused, then said, "It could
blow your case wide open."

"I'm on my way down." Troy hung up the phone and took off at a run.

Leanne was waiting for him. "Take a look at this."

"What is it?"

"It's a photocopy of Dr. Claudia Bennett's yearbook picture."

Troy stared down at the image on the paper. The woman, though years younger, looked nothing like the Claudia Bennett he knew. The discrepancies were so pronounced that not even age could have wrought such a change.

"That's not the woman who came in here claiming to be Dr. Bennett," Leanne said. "I got a good look at her that day. There's no way. And something else. You know that story you told me about Dr. Bennett's agoraphobia and about the housekeeper who died in the fire?"

"She called her Marlena."

Leanne nodded. "I had the police report on the fire faxed to me. The woman's name was Marlena Andersen, except...there's one small problem. Marlena Andersen died five years *before* the fire."

Troy stared at her. "Wait a minute. Are you saying Bennett's housekeeper was using a fake identity?"

"Looks that way. You know who I'm betting that housekeeper was, don't you?"

"The woman we know as Claudia Bennett."

"Exactly. She took Marlena Andersen's identity, and then when Claudia Bennett died, she took her identity."

"And her profession," Troy said. "She's been practicing psychiatry all these years."

"The inmates are in charge of the asylum," Leanne said dryly. "How would you like to be relying on her for your mental well-being?"

Troy remembered Andrea's words earlier. *She used hypnosis to unleash the memories. I remembered more and more with each session. She's the one who found out where my mother was.*

Suddenly he knew why Andrea hadn't turned herself in yet. He knew where she would have gone to for help in restoring the rest of her memory.

He jumped up and headed for the door.

"SHE'S REMEMBERED everything," Dorian said in disgust. "I thought you said you could take care of her memory. You said that the night you went to see her in the hospital. You didn't do it then," Dorian complained.

"I didn't expect Stoner to come back to her room. But I'll take care of it now," Dr. Bennett promised.

Andrea had come out of her trance just seconds ago to find her wrists bound behind her and Dorian holding a gun on her.

"Who are you?" Andrea said to Dr. Bennett.

Dr. Bennett was busy filling a syringe, so Dorian answered for her. "Her name is Helena Kouriakis. She's my sister."

Sister! Of course! Andrea couldn't understand why she hadn't seen the resemblance before. Maybe because Dr. Bennett, who was really Helena Kouriakis, tried so hard to disguise her appearance. The blue contacts, which were gone now, and the unnatural white makeup that covered her olive complexion.

Andrea glared up at Dorian in disgust. "You killed your own daughter," she said.

"Stepdaughter," Dorian clarified, as if the distinction made all the difference in the world. But Andrea knew that even if Christina had been Dorian's own flesh and blood, she would have stopped at nothing to get what she wanted. The money. Always the money.

"I've never known anyone so evil."

"Try your own mother," Dorian said slyly. "She stabbed your father right in front of you. That's why you're so crazy."

"I'm not crazy." Andrea tried to keep her voice even as she struggled furiously with the bindings at her wrists.

"Sure, you are. Everyone thinks so. Even the police. Even your Sergeant Stoner," Dorian added maliciously.

Andrea flinched inwardly. Dorian's words struck home. Troy might not think her crazy, but he certainly had his doubts about her. By now, he probably thought she'd skipped town.

"You brought this on yourself," Dorian said hatefully. "Richard was mine. I waited so long for him. After Christina died, he should have married me. And he would have, too, if you hadn't gone to him with your lies about me."

"They weren't lies," Andrea said. "I knew you didn't love Mayela. You only wanted the money."

"And so you convinced Richard to marry you and give *you* custody of Mayela. You're very clever," Dorian said with grudging admiration. "I'll give you that."

"He would have thrown you out a long time ago," Andrea said. The bindings had loosened, and she worked to free one of her hands. "Only, he suspected you were conspiring with Paul Bellamy. He didn't want to tip his hand before he had the proof he needed to go to the police."

"Bellamy's a fool," Dorian said. "Why would I waste my time with the likes of him?"

"The broken skylight," Andrea said. "Was that meant for me or Mayela?"

Dorian shrugged. "I knew the storm would terrify her. I knew she would call out for you as she always did. I just wasn't sure which of you would come running across the bridge first. Either scenario had possibilities. With Mayela out of the way and you in prison for murder, who else would have inherited Richard's estate? Robert? I don't think so. He would have gambled the fortune away in a matter of months. And if you had died under all that glass, an unfortunate accident as it were, I would have become Mayela's guardian, controlling all her money. Just as I once did Christina's."

They'd thought of everything, Andrea thought. Even going so far as to plant seeds of doubt in her own mind.

"You were up on the roof when the glass fell," Andrea said. "I saw you."

"Not me," Dorian said. "You saw my sister. She's always been very adept at creating...accidents."

Helena turned with the syringe. The needle gleamed in the light.

"What are you going to do?" Andrea asked weakly. Her hands were almost free. A surge of adrenaline shot through her, but she had to remain calm. She had to wait for her chance because Dorian still held a gun on her.

"I'm going to do the same thing I tried to do that night Sergeant Stoner caught me outside your hospital room," Helena said. "I'm going to make sure it's a long, long time before you get your memory back this time. And when you do, Dorian and I will have fixed it so that no one will believe you. They'll think you're insane, just like your dear mother. Maybe they'll even give you a room next to hers."

Andrea pretended to be so frightened she could hardly move. But as Helena bent down to administer the drug,

Andrea's hand shot out and grabbed her. She twisted Helena's wrist until the needle fell from her fingers.

Andrea rolled from the sofa, still clutching Helena's arm. The two of them struggled for what seemed like an eternity. The woman was older than Andrea by at least twenty years, but she also outweighed Andrea by that much and she was strong. She shoved Andrea away from her, and Andrea stumbled, falling heavily against the desk.

Helena was on her before Andrea could catch her balance. The older woman bent Andrea back against the desk as her hands encircled Andrea's throat. Stars exploded behind Andrea's lids. She flailed her arms, trying to find a weapon. Her lungs threatening to explode, Andrea wrapped her hand around the base of a lamp and brought it up as hard as she could against the side of Helena's skull.

For a split second, the woman's hands remained around Andrea's throat. Then she slid to the floor without a sound. Blood gushed from the gash in her temple as she lay motionless at Andrea's feet.

Andrea struggled for breath. Dorian stared down at her sister in disbelief. Then she raised the gun and leveled it at Andrea.

"You really lost it this time, Andrea. You attacked your own psychiatrist. Imagine how the headlines will read in the morning."

Andrea was still clutching the lamp, but Dorian didn't seem to notice. "She's your sister," Andrea said. "Don't you even care whether she's alive or dead?"

"Of course I care," Dorian said. "My sister has always been the one person in my life I could count on. Ever since we were little girls, she always wanted to please me. Take care of me. She'd do anything for me.

But I have to think of myself now. And Mayela, of course. The poor child needs me. With you in prison, or in a psychiatric hospital, there's no one standing in my way. I'll finally have what I've worked so hard for all these years.''

"Richard's money," Andrea said, and with that, she hurled the lamp across the room as hard as she could. It missed Dorian by inches, but it was enough to catch her off guard. Andrea flung herself across the room toward her. The gun went off, and Andrea felt the dull punch of the bullet in her shoulder. The force flung her backward. Andrea stumbled, tried to catch her balance, but couldn't. The room spun around her. She dropped to her knees, clutching her shoulder.

Dorian lifted the gun again. This time she aimed for Andrea's face. Andrea squeezed her eyes closed, wondering fleetingly if the next bullet would hurt more or less than the first.

Then, as if in a dream, she heard Troy's voice order Dorian to drop the gun. A woman's voice began reading Dorian her rights. Andrea didn't remember lying down on the floor, but when she opened her eyes, she was flat on her back and Troy was gazing down at her with so much tenderness, Andrea wanted to cry.

"I didn't kill Richard," she said.

"I know. You can tell me the whole story later. Right now you need to save your strength. We've got an ambulance on the way."

"I'm not crazy," she said.

"I am," he said. "Crazy about you."

Her heart fluttered with hope. "Then…you forgive me for not telling you about my memories? For running away from you?"

He cleared his throat gruffly. "Right now I'd forgive you just about anything. Only..."

"What?"

He squeezed her hand. "Hang in there, okay?"

She squeezed his hand back. "I'm crazy about you, too."

Epilogue

Six months later...

She wore white, a dress so pristine it dazzled her eyes as she gazed at her reflection in the mirror. Andrea couldn't believe this day had finally arrived, that in just a few moments, she would be married, truly married, to the man she loved more than life itself. Soon she and Troy and Mayela would be starting a whole new life together. A wonderful life, in spite of the darkness.

It hadn't been easy, coping with the memories of her past, or thinking about the mind control Dr. Bennett had practiced on her. The evil plot she and Dorian had concocted had very nearly destroyed them all. Both Richard and Christina had been the victims of the sisters' greed, but thank God Mayela had been spared. Thank God, as well, that she seemed to be suffering no long-term effects, as Andrea had.

Andrea would always be grateful to Madison for the way she'd taken care of the little girl while Andrea had been in the hospital, recovering from the bullet wound. Because of Madison, Mayela had a chance to resume a normal childhood, and because of Troy, they both had a chance to love again.

Someone knocked on the door of the changing room, and Andrea turned from the mirror. "Come in."

Madison opened the door and stuck her head in. She wore a long flowing dress in dark red velvet, befitting the Christmas season. "It's time," she said. "Are you ready?"

Andrea smiled. "You have no idea how ready I am."

"Then let's go."

Troy's father, Earl, who would be giving her away, waited outside for her. The church took Andrea's breath away, decorated with hundreds of white and red roses and tiny white lights that glittered like diamonds in the candlelight. Everything was perfect, almost too beautiful to be real. Andrea thought for a moment she must be dreaming, but if she was, it was a dream like no other, and she didn't ever want to wake up.

She took Earl's arm, and together they paused while Mayela, looking adorable in a red velvet dress trimmed with white lace, scattered rose petals in her wake. She was followed by Madison, and then, almost too quickly, it was time for Andrea to walk down the aisle.

She grew nervous and almost stumbled, but Troy's father held her steady. And then she saw Troy, looking so handsome in his black tuxedo, waiting for her at the altar. He smiled, and everything calmed inside Andrea.

With strong, steady steps, she started down the aisle toward him. Toward their future. And she knew if she lived to be a hundred, she would never forget a moment of this perfect, perfect day.

Coming in August...

UNBREAKABLE BONDS

by

Judy Christenberry

Identical twin brothers separated at birth. One had every opportunity imaginable. One had nothing, except the ties of blood. Now fate brings them back together as part of the Randall family, where they are thrown into a maelstrom of divided loyalties, unexpected revelations and the knowledge that some bonds are simply unbreakable.

Dive into a new chapter of the bestselling series *Brides for Brothers* with this unforgettable story.

Available August 2002 wherever paperbacks are sold.

HARLEQUIN®
Makes any time special ®

PHUB-R

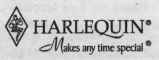

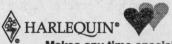